BURNING ROSES

BURNING ROSES

Barbara Bernard

with Scott Michael Long

Fiction

Published by Serenity Corporation, J. Neilson Books
306 Walter Road, New Orleans, LA 70123
Phone: 504-738-3224 Fax: 504-738-9991

Book Cover Design by Lightbourne Images
Illustration by Jesse Bilyeu

Library of Congress Catalog Card Number: 95-071395

ISBN 0-9648592-3-8

Printed in the United States of America
April 1996

First Edition

*This book is dedicated to the memory
of my dear mother, Ruth,
who is the real author of this story.*

Acknowledgements

I would like to thank my wonderful husband, Neil, who had faith in my ability to finish this project; who inspired me to go on even when the demands were so grueling that it seemed impossible to write another word. Thank you, Neil, for your endless love and devotion, your expert critiques, and ultimately, after eight years, the words I most wanted to hear. "I will be proud to tell everyone my wife wrote this book." I also wish to thank my children who are the miracles and the joys of my life; Kim, Shane, Sean, Neille Anne, and my new son-in-law, Todd.

One of the special treats of writing BURNING ROSES was the opportunity to work with my gifted and talented co-writers—Scott Michael Long, Jennifer Grant and my beloved friend and neighbor, Evelyn Anderson. I am grateful to my friends, Charles and Patches Lancaster; to my sisters, Cathy and Ruth, for reading the manuscript, and to all those who share our family lore. Each has contributed to this book, and I thank them from the bottom of my heart.

❧ One ❧

It matters not how straight the gate,
How charged with punishments the scroll,
I am the master of my fate:
I am the Captain of my soul.
  —*INVICTUS: William Ernest Henley*

Caldwell Parish Jail
Columbia, Louisiana
January, 1894

JANE FISHER had never experienced anything as primitive as this jail cell. She had been poor, dirt poor, with Dennis. Yet even then she had had a decent bed to sleep on. Here her bed was a rusted iron frame attached to a moldy wall. The mattress was filled with lumpy Spanish moss, and covered with a tattered blanket that made her skin itch. The ancient cell, lit only during her meals by a lantern, smelled of coal oil and mildew, and the damp cypress floor was dirty. The only piece of furniture was a small table holding a chipped pitcher and a cracked porcelain bowl.

But today, even these dismal surroundings could not dampen Jane's happy spirits. Charles was coming! He had somehow managed to get the circuit judge to grant him a visit. She didn't know how he did it; she was just grateful he was coming, and bringing

Georgia Ann, too. They would be the first family she had seen since her arrest two weeks ago.

She wasn't sure how she would look to her loved ones, but at least she was clean. Earlier she'd taken a hot bath in the cast iron bathtub just outside her cell, and the scent of lavender soap still lingered on her skin. The jailer had slipped her the sweet soap to wash her hair, and she had combed and fussed with her raven locks until they were dry and twisted into a bun at the nape of her neck.

Standing barefoot on the cold floor, she pulled a drab, brown wool dress carefully over her head. The sleeves were long and the collar was stiff and tight, but Charles had delivered it with other things to the jail and told Sheriff Meredith the garments would help to keep her warm. However, she knew the simple dress had been designed to make her appear more ladylike, and she thought, *If that's what Charles Fisher wants, that's what he'll get.* She adjusted her woolen stockings, thinking how desperate she was to see the man she loved and how happy she'd be when he got here.

With the arraignment scheduled for tomorrow, she had been agonizing about what she was going to do. She could not believe she had been arrested for arson with intent to kill, along with her son, Ander; her brother, John Augustus, and his son, George. She hadn't even been there when the fire started. She had first seen the flames from her kitchen window, and it was then she realized that the fire meant bad family trouble. Her papa, Hanan, had been enraged when she told him that one of his sharecroppers had raped her eight year old daughter, Georgia Ann.

She stood up, pacing around the cell in her bare feet, thinking about how it had happened, remembering how she had fled out of the back door that night and sprinted as fast as she could across the cotton field. When she approached the burning cabin, she had put her hand over her nose trying to breathe into her palm. Smoke was billowing towards the sky in giant black puffs and flames had already engulfed the log cabin of the sharecropper, J.T. Benton. She looked about frantically, trying to penetrate the haze of smoke, and spotted Ander, her fourteen year old son. She ran to the horse trough where he was standing with his shot-gun pointed at the only spot that wasn't consumed by blistering flames—the spot where a fallen body lay. She just froze in her tracks and stood staring at her son. Ander's face was streaked with smoke. He turned to look at her. His hair was hanging over his eyes and his mouth was wide open. His body was trembling. Jane couldn't say a word. She reached out and touched Ander's arm as he threw his gun onto the frozen ground and dropped to his knees, clutching her legs. She heard a loud noise, and twisted her body around. She saw her nephew George latch a two by four across the barn door, trapping the baying animals inside. Then everything happened fast. Her mother's wagon came roaring up the dirt road. Her brother, John, rushed over to where she stood, just as the house collapsed in an avalanche of burning timbers. Out of the darkness came the soot covered body of the sharecropper J.T., pointing his twenty-guage at them. He had a smirk on his face as he looked down at Ander. "You just killed your grandpappy, boy," he blurted out. "Shot old Hanan but good. Now you gonna hang. All you sons of bitches gonna hang for what you did!" Then a sound that seemed to come from the very bottom of hell came from Ander's mouth. J.T. poked the barrel of his gun under Ander's chin, roaring out, "You came here to kill me, sneaking around in the middle of the night, nailing up my house like a coffin. Well . . . you can believe I intend to see everyone of you hang for this." J.T. laughed and waved his gun in the air like a mad man, backing slowly away until he disappeared into the dense underbrush of the dark woods.

John and George dashed toward the smoldering house. Jane pulled Ander up from the ground and they ran over to where her mother, Betsy, stood staring at the charred body in the doorway. Betsy was motionless as John took a rope from his saddle, tied it around his papa's charred arms and dragged Hanan's body out of the popping embers. Jane was shivering, watching her mother cry for her papa. She put her arms around Betsy and hugged her. Betsy looked up at Jane. Tears were streaming down her wrinkled cheeks. "Your papa's body is all burned up, Sister," she said.

But there was no time for tears. Betsy wiped her eyes with the hem of her apron and told Ander and George, "Go out there and see if there's a shovel and a wheelbarrow that ain't burned up. J.T.'s on the loose and the law will never believe this was an accident. The only thing to do is bury Hanan where no one will ever find him. As long as they can't find his body, J.T. can say whatever his lying mouth pleases. Nobody'll ever believe him."

Jane tugged on her mother's arm, pulling her away from the dreadful scene. She helped her climb up into the wagon. Betsy closed her eyes and began quoting the words of a long dead preacher who lamented about the suffering of Job. "If I'd believed in God like they say we're supposed to in the Bible, he wouldn't be testing my faith now, testing me so harsh I don't want to live anymore."

"Oh, Mama," Jane said, reaching over to comfort her. "Don't say that. You don't mean it. You're just upset."

Betsy let out a shrieking, bone-chilling cry. She pulled away from Jane's embrace and quickly climbed down out of the wagon. She walked over to the smoking rose bushes that were still clinging to the brick chimney and furiously began pulling the blackened roses off the vines. "Burning Roses," she cried. "These will be the only flowers for Hanan. After a lifetime with him, all I have left to put on his grave is burned roses."

JANE SHOOK HER HEAD as she looked around this depressing jail cell, trying to get the memory of that awful night out of her mind. Her mother's grief was more than she could bear, worse than her worries about Ander and her own predicament. She sighed and took a deep breath, leaned over and pulled on the soft slippers that Charles had carefully wrapped inside the package. She decided not to worry. She had faith Charles would know what she should do. She trusted him.

Jane looked up as the jailer flung open the steel door outside her cell. The old black man slid his feet slowly across the rough planks in the walkaround and slipped a covered tin plate of fried chicken and turnip greens under the bars. The sun had gone down and the cell had begun to grow dark. She didn't feel much like eating—she was too excited for that—but she asked if the jailer would leave the lantern for her visitors. Then she heard footsteps echoing on the heavy steel stairs. They were here! She quickly smoothed the top of her hair, gave her cheeks a pinch, and braced herself for the door to open again. *Don't do anything so stupid as to cry,* she thought, smiling, her heart racing, when the sheriff walked in with Charles, and Georgia Ann trailing behind. The jailer set the dimly lit lantern on the floor and melted back through the doorway.

Georgia Ann clung to Charles' legs as they appeared in the walka-round. Jane could see her child's frightened face, and for the thousandth time the terrifying morning of January third flashed again through Jane's mind. Finally seeing her little girl after all these weeks was a blessing. Georgia Ann's fragile little body, violated by that deranged sharecropper, J.T. Benton, was mostly what had occupied Jane's thoughts these weeks she had been in jail. Now, as she stood behind the bars that separated her from her loved ones, she held her breath trying to hold back her tears. Georgia Ann's crying finally made her call out, "I'm over here Sugar . . . Baby Girl . . . Georgia Ann. . . . "

The near darkness and ghost-like shadows cast upon the jail wall seemed to terrify Georgia Ann and Jane stretched her hands through the bars encouragingly. Georgia Ann pulled slowly away from Charles, releasing her firm grip on one of his legs and then the other, and ran toward Jane, crying out, "I'm so scared, Mama!"

Jane pulled her daughter as close to her as she could. Georgia Ann jumped back from the bars. "They're cold, Mama; your cage is cold. The bars hurt me." Jane tugged on her hands again, pulling Georgia Ann back into her arms. "Get close to me, I'll keep you warm," she whispered, pulling the floppy collar of Georgia Ann's bright red coat around her throat.

Charles adjusted the kerosene lantern in the walkaround until the musty cell was bright. He walked over to the pot-bellied stove that stood in the corner just outside the cell and added another piece of firewood, stoking the log until a flame erupted. The smell of pine, like a fresh cut Christmas tree, filled the cell. Immediately the dismal surroundings took on a more cheery atmosphere. She watched Charles brush away cobwebs, then drag an old rickety chair up to the bars.

"You always bring comfort to my life, Charles," she said. With one hand still around her daughter, Jane reached out and took his hand in the other. He was her strength. She needed to feel him near and touch his warm body.

Georgia Ann climbed up on his lap. Jane didn't worry about her daughter when Charles was around. He'd always been so protective of her.

"Grandma Betsy's cat had kittens," Georgia Ann told Jane. "She let me pick one out and said I could bring it home with me when you came home. We made gingerbread men and she didn't scold me when I ate most of 'em."

Jane marveled that Georgia Ann could still talk about little girl things after all she'd been through. "Thank God she's strong like me," she whispered to Charles. "My baby's going to need every ounce of strength she has these next few days."

There came a gentle knock on the door and Sheriff Meredith appeared in the walkaround. "Georgia Ann," he said, "Miz Meredith is downstairs. She brought some cookies. Why don't you come down and help me eat 'em?"

Georgia Ann clutched at Charles. She glanced up at his face and then at Jane. Getting a nod of approval, she slid out of Charles' lap and skipped through the doorway after the sheriff.

As the sheriff slammed the door shut, Charles stood up, reached his hands through the bars and pulled Jane close to him. "I've missed you so much, Liebchen," he said, his shaky voice hardly above a whisper.

In his arms she felt safe, but her mind would not let her rest. Slowly, she pulled out of his embrace, stood back and gazed into his face. *My mama was right,* she thought. *I am lucky to have a man like you love me.* Looking at him standing outside her cell, she could smell his musky shaving soap and his sweet tobacco. It made her long to melt against him, feel his warm chest against her own, but the cold bars made it impossible. She took a deep breath. Then all her doubts spewed forth, "I want you to tell me the truth, Charles. What's happening with Ander? Is he all right?" When he hesitated to answer, she continued, "what about John Augustus and George? Are they still in jail, too? And what about my brother, Thomas Jefferson—the angry words he said about my son the day after the fire—how he's going to see Ander hang for killing Papa if it's the last thing he ever does."

Finally Charles spoke. "I'm not telling you this to get you upset, but I saw your brother Thomas the other night. I'm afraid he's cooking up a scheme against you and Ander in order to get John and his boy out of this mess. Thomas said it was your own fault Georgia Ann was raped. He said if you'd kept your eye on her, it never would've happened and your papa and brothers wouldn't have gone after J.T. for it. They blame you for everything."

A sudden gust of wind blew the blankets from the window, dimming the lantern and causing the light to flicker. Goosebumps covered her body and she stepped back from his reach. "Dear God, my own brothers are turning against me. Is that what you're saying?" Her head was spinning. She felt faint.

Charles reached into the cell again, trying to touch her, but she backed farther away. "I knew Thomas was up to something," she finally said, sitting carefully on the edge of the mattress in the darkest corner of the cold cell. "I saw him go into the courthouse the day after they locked me up. Well, when I tell the judge the whole story about J.T. raping Georgia Ann, and my menfolk going after him for that, the judge will let us all go."

Charles shook his head. "I don't think he'll listen to anything you say—not now—not with what they're planning. You see, when Thomas spoke with Judge Bear, he knew the judge was having a hard time trying to impose a tax to pay for the new courthouse. Thomas figured that he could work out a deal. If the judge would let him put the blame on you and Ander, and look the other way with John and George, then Thomas would get the *klan* to rough up some of the farmers and make them afraid to oppose the tax."

"How do you know all this?" Jane asked.

He took his handkerchief from his top pocket and wiped his brow. "Part of it I overheard from Thomas himself, the rest from Judge Bear's clerk. He walked in on them the other day and overheard the plan. He said he didn't want to see any more crooked deals from Judge Bear if he could help it, but he's too scared to tell anyone else, afraid he'll lose his job."

Jane stood up quickly and flew back across the cell to Charles. Everything seemed to be closing in on her and she couldn't figure a way out. Charles again took her in his arms through the bars and held her until she stopped sobbing.

"Good God in Heaven," he said, stepping back, running his fingers through his hair. "It's all my fault. I never should have come to Caldwell Parish when Dennis died . . . should have taken you and the children and gone home to Germany when we got married. There's been nothing but trouble with your family since the day I met them, and now this. I've never seen such a mess—brothers scheming against their sister to save their own necks."

"You know they're lying, Charles."

"Yes, I know, and the judge knows it, too. Jane, listen to me. Thomas is going to swear it was you and your son who nailed the boards onto J.T.'s house and tried to burn him up, and Judge Bear is going to accept every word they say as the truth. If you tell the whole story and accuse J.T. of rape, J.T.'s going to swear he saw Ander kill your papa. He even says he knows where the body is. Don't you see it's all fixed up against you and Ander!"

Jane paced around the cell. She was in despair but she couldn't fall to pieces now. "So in other words you're saying there's nothing we can do—nothing we can say about J.T.?"

He shook his head, sadly, and then she whispered, almost to herself. "What's going to happen to us?" Her chest tightened. She tugged at her tight collar, and losing her balance, toppled to the floor. When she came to, Charles and the sheriff were inside the cell and Charles was holding her close to him, cradling her like a baby. Closing her eyes, she lay in the safety of his arms, trying to shut out everything except the caress of his gentle hands. The sheriff told Charles he could stay in the cell with her, when he saw she was recovering. He locked the door and vanished.

Charles carried her over to the old wooden chair that he'd dragged inside the cell. Her new dress was wrinkled; her bun had come loose, and her hair was hanging down her back. "I'm all right," she said as she stood up, raising her hand to smooth her hair. "It's just that I was so happy about seeing you tonight, I couldn't eat. I got overexcited."

She wrapped her arms tightly around Charles, hugging him for a moment. Then they sat together on the edge of the mattress, clinging to each other. She began to bite her nails. He took her hand away from her mouth and stroked her face and hair until she calmed down.

"If only I could have gotten there before the fire started," she mumbled. "Maybe I could have stopped them. I didn't know they were going over there to hurt J.T."

Charles shook his head and just stared at her. "Well, they did and somebody is going to the *Big House* for it. Thomas is hell bent Ander's to hang for killing your papa if you don't protect John and George. I know how you feel about your son, but he killed a man. He fired the shot. That's all there is to it. Don't you understand? He did it. He went out to kill somebody that night, just like your papa and the others did. He's a killer."

"No. It was an accident."

"The only accident was the bullet found the wrong man! Jane, you have to listen to me," Charles pleaded. He reached out and firmly gripped her arm. "Get this through your head. When you go into that courtroom tomorrow, Ander is going to be charged with murder if you say anything about J.T. raping Georgia Ann."

"But no judge would let J.T. get off scot-free for what he did."

"The judge doesn't give a damn about J.T., or you and Georgia Ann. You're just a woman and she's a little child. Thomas roughed up the farmers for him and now he owes Thomas. He'll do what Thomas wants, and Thomas wants John and his boy to go free."

"I know Thomas can be harsh, but I will never believe my own brother would connive against me and my son. I don't care what you say."

"Well, you had better believe it. And its time you open your eyes to what Ander has become. You know as well as I do that ever since we brought Ander here, he and George have been terrorizing the farmers with their foolish pranks. Half that courtroom is going to be filled with those very farmers. If there's a trial, the jury will be full of them and they'll convict Ander."

Her hands were shaking almost uncontrollably. She knew how Thomas felt about their papa dying. She felt the same loss as the rest of her family. But for Thomas to be so vindictive was unbelievable. "They're trying to manipulate me," she said. "Thomas thinks if J.T.

testifies and Ander hangs, I'll leave here and they can have all of papa's land. I know them. I know the way they think. And they're crazy if they think I'm going to let Ander take the blame for what was an accident. Ander's a good boy, Charles. He's not a murderer."

"Jane. I know how much you love Ander, but you are so blinded by your devotion you just can't see him for what he really is."

She looked him in the eyes. These were fighting words. "Just what are you saying, Charles? Do you want me to say that I love Ander more than I love anything? All right, then . . . Yes, I love him, but you're wrong. I'm not blind. I know what he is. He's just as bad as his scheming cousin, George, but you don't understand why I feel about Ander the way I do. Nobody does. You talk about me not ever being a child. I was only a child when I had Ander and I grew up while he was growing up. We were more like brother and sister than mother and child."

She smoothed her wrinkled dress, nervously, tilting her head up to face Charles again. "Maybe I always felt like I had to protect him. Don't you see? He didn't have anybody else but me. Dennis seemed to hate him from the day he was born; said Ander wasn't his and never made any bones about it. Ander never even saw his grand-parents until you brought us back here to live."

She had the feeling that her heart was shattering into a thousand pieces. He couldn't understand how painful this was for her. She knew everything there was to know about Ander, but, right or wrong, he was her child. No matter what Ander did, she would love him. She did not want to stand there and listen to the man she loved saying these terrible things about her son. She didn't love Ander any more than Georgia Ann, but she did feel he needed her more. If she didn't take care of him, what in God's name would become of him?

Charles just shook his head again. "I understand the all consum-ing love of a mother, but this is going too far," he said, "this is madness."

Jane wasn't listening. Her mind was busy as she untangled her arms from his. "It seems all my life I've had to have a plan for get-ting away from people who were trying to hurt me," she said, know-ing once again she'd have to form a plan. "If what you're saying is true, and if I don't say anything about J.T. then he won't say anything about Ander shooting Papa. And if I protect John and George then Ander won't hang."

She thought for a moment and then pleaded, "Go see Thomas and tell him he and John Augustus can have all the land if they will keep J.T. from saying anything about Ander shooting Papa."

"Listen, Jane," Charles said, taking hold of her shoulders. "Haven't you heard a word I've said? The deal is already worked out with Judge Bear. The only thing you can do is try to convince the judge that you weren't there yourself."

"I can't do that to my child. Let him take all the responsibility for this."

"Jane, despite everything you've done for Ander, there's nothing you can do for him now. I know he's had a hard life on account of Dennis, but something's made him mean and twisted. It's turned him into something wild, and nothing you do will ever change that."

His voice was deadly serious, and she felt as if he'd slapped her in the face. She began to beat on his chest, screaming, "Don't say that! Don't call my boy mean and twisted! Don't you ever say that about my boy again!"

Charles grabbed her small fists and held them in his hands until she stopped shaking. "I'm not here to hurt you. I'm here to help," he said. "Oh Liebchen, please believe me, if I could help your boy, I would, but nothing is going to help him now. I'm begging you, think of our marriage. Think of yourself. Think of me. For God's sake think about Georgia Ann. I'm pleading with you for all our lives, begging you, Jane, don't destroy all of us for Ander!"

Her anger subsided as she stood in the middle of the cold cell, facing the man she loved, and saw only his desperate resignation to a hopeless situation. "Are you asking me to choose between you and my son?"

"I would never ask you to make that choice," he said, and she saw a sad and defeated look cross his face. "But I am asking you to think about our marriage and the life we have. If I asked you to make a choice, in time you would hate me. I would despise myself for having put you through that much pain, and I would be afraid of losing you forever. You know I love you too much to even think of a life without you."

She could feel his body strain as he held her close, his lips quivering against her cheek. They clung to each other for a long time before he left the cell. After he was gone she stood with her head pressed against the bars, staring outside her cell at the frayed remnants of an old hanging noose, tears rolling down her face. When she looked down, she saw a small package wrapped in brown paper. She bent over and picked it up. A flutter of dried rose petals fell onto her slippers like soft feathers. *Even when my spirit is as dead as winter blossoms, he's thinking of me. Charles found a way to bring me roses.*

⁑ Two ⁑

THE NEXT MORNING Jane stood looking out the window, slowly running a wooden comb through her hair, remembering her harsh words to Charles the previous night. *He wasn't asking me to choose. He was asking me to make a decision and that's different.* Why had she hit him? It was fear, fear for Ander's life, and her fear had made her turn on the only man she had ever loved, the only person she could trust.

She moved away from the window. She sat down on the edge of the hard mattress and pretended for a moment that she was in her room at home, the room she had shared with Charles Fisher for over three years since her first husband, Dennis Moody, had died.

She trembled inwardly as she remembered her life with Dennis. It had certainly been anything but easy. She had been like most girls in northern Louisiana after the Civil War, trying to find an available husband who was under fifty years old, and in desperation to get away from her family, she had run away to Natchitoches and married Dennis when she was just a baby. He was more than three times her age and the truth was, it had turned out to be more like a war than a marriage. In the beginning Dennis had been loving and affectionate but then he began to beat her and treat her like a slave even when she was bearing his children.

After years of such misery Charles came into her life. She remembered it as though it were yesterday.

She had been alone in the house that day. It was one of those muggy northern Louisiana summer mornings when the humidity made the air so still and heavy that breathing was virtually impossible. *By noon it will be unbearable,* she thought, as she opened the windows in an effort to get some sort of air circulating. Glancing out the kitchen window, she saw a man riding up the dirt road on a bay stallion. She was startled, and her first thought was, *From the way he is dressed, he's not a farmer—more likely a bank president.* She walked out on the porch when he rode up into her yard.

"Morning, Mrs. Moody," he said, touching his hand to the brim of his white straw hat.

Keeping her eye on the stranger as he slid off his horse, she stayed timidly in the shade of her rose trellis as he walked up to her.

"Name's Charles Fisher," he said. "I thought I might have a hard time finding your house way out here, but people in town said I couldn't miss it. Said you had the only one with pretty red roses about it." His voice was lilting, almost like singing, not like the rough country voices of her in-laws or her own kin, whose nasal twang wasn't the least bit melodic.

"What brings you way out here on a day like this, Mr. Fisher?" she finally asked.

"Railroad sent me. I understand you have a son of school age."

"Why yes, I do. Is he in some sort of trouble?"

"It's nothing like that. I came out here to tell you we have a new school in Milltown, and the railroad named me headmaster. It's a fine school, Mrs. Moody. Your son would be most welcome to take part."

"That's mighty nice of you, Mr. Fisher, and I'd like to see my boy get some learning, but Mr. Moody doesn't believe in reading and writing—says schooling's a waste of time. Besides, I'm sure we couldn't afford it."

"It's all free," he said. "The railroad is building the sawmill town. They're starting the school and supplying the books. It doesn't cost the people anything."

She liked the way he looked and the sound of his voice. She even liked the way his lips parted when he spoke, and she couldn't help but smile when she thought what a good looking man he was and so pleasant.

Heat waves were shimmering in the yard and the broiling sun was beating down on him. Jane was concerned he might be overcome with the heat so she asked him, "Would you like to come up on the porch?"

The heat had already taken its toll on her. Her dark hair, which she'd curled early this morning, now hung straight around her shoulders and fell into her eyes every time she moved. Pushing it behind her ears was the only way she could keep it out of her face. And she couldn't help but wonder how she looked to this man. She also thought what in the world would happen if Dennis came home from the fields and found her talking to Mr. Fisher, but she hungered for company. Anyway, it wasn't neighborly to let him stand there suffering in the sun.

He tied the reins of his horse around the newel post and slowly walked up the steps onto the porch. He stood for a moment, then leaned his tall frame against the decaying rails. Jane offered him a glass of cool tea, and when she came back out and handed it to him, she shivered when his fingers touched hers.

A handsome man all right, she thought. By his looks she could tell he wasn't from northern Louisiana. His accent suggested one of the big cities or maybe even a foreign country. *He smells nice, probably wears powder or something like that,* she thought. *And he's not an old man, certainly not as old as Dennis, but not as young as I am either, maybe in his late thirties or early forties.*

"Mmmm, these are the sweetest smelling roses," he said. He reached over and pulled a branch of scarlet blossoms to his nose and smelled the velvety petals. "So soft and silky. Feels almost like a kiss."

His words took her by surprise and she found herself beginning to blush. She had never felt so utterly stupid in all her life, and she really didn't know how to act in front of this man. Then as if he realized he'd embarrassed her, Charles stammered as he handed her his empty tea glass. "I'm so sorry, Mrs. Moody, if I've disturbed you."

"Oh, don't worry about me," she said, hesitatingly. "I wasn't doing anything special this morning anyway." *Nothing but the wash, tending the farm animals and working about an acre of the fields Dennis expects me to plow!* she thought.

"Mr. Fisher," she said, when he put on his hat and began to back off of the porch. "My husband would never, never allow Ander to go to your school."

He pulled his gold watch out of his vest pocket and held it up to the light. "I understand, Mrs. Moody, and I mustn't take up anymore of your time. Perhaps I can come by from time to time and help your son learn the alphabet. Later he can learn to read and write on his own with your help."

Jane sighed. She was too embarrassed to tell him she could neither read nor write herself. "Well, I guess. . . . " she said, before she even gave a thought to what Dennis might say. "I mean . . . if it don't keep him from doing his chores."

"That won't be a problem. I could come when school lets out or perhaps on Sunday after church."

"I wouldn't want Ander to be a bother to you. I'm sure you already have enough worries."

"Mrs. Moody, children getting an education is very important to me. In Germany my parents did without so I could go to the University of Heidelberg and study metallurgy. If spending a few hours a week out here at your farm can help yours to learn, then it's little enough I can do. Whenever I help a child learn to read or write, I always think it's a way of thanking my parents for the sacrifices they made. I can tell you're willing to do the same for your children. Besides, the railroad tells me to educate; they don't tell me how or where I should do it."

Jane didn't say anymore. Charles put on his hat, apologized again for taking up so much of her time, then slowly walked down the steps into the dusty yard. She stood in the shadows of her roses and waited until he got up on his horse. The yard chickens were fussing around the steps. She bent over and opened a bin on the porch where she kept their feed. Throwing corn to the hungry hens, she watched Charles ride slowly out of her yard, thinking, *It's fine to dream, but I'll probably never see him again.* She felt sad when he stopped his horse near a stand of tall pine trees, turned around and waved to her. This was a gentle man, so compassionate to the needs of her son. There seemed to be magic in his voice.

JANE WAS STARTLED out of her reverie by a loud voice outside her cell. She flopped back on the dirty mattress, squeezing her fists tightly, pounding them against the small bed. "Oh, Charles what is going to happen to all of us," she cried out. Then she lay quietly, staring up at the ceiling, thinking about all that had happened, blaming herself. Was Thomas right? Could she have prevented the rape? Was it her fault? For the last four years since she'd lived in the little cottage on her papa's farm she had tried to be everything a mother could be. She doted on Georgia Ann and Ander, and most of her time was spent with them. How could Thomas be so cruel and think such terrible things about his own sister? How could he try to hurt one sibling to protect the other?

EACH MINUTE seemed to drag by until Jane felt she couldn't bear this cell any longer. The damp moldy smell made her sick to her stomach and the twice boiled coffee the jailer had brought up with her breakfast was cold, and so bitter she had to force herself to swallow it. Walking back to the window, she pulled aside the tattered curtain. She scanned the dirt street below and from a distance she could hear the whistle of a nearby sawmill. An early morning delivery wagon was headed toward the river landing and Jane could see a small boy standing on Front Street waving to the driver. The boy held a stack of newspapers in one arm and for a moment reminded her of Ander as a small boy running in from the fields for his lessons.

Four years ago when Charles promised to come to her house and teach Ander, and even Georgia Ann, in spite of Dennis's attitude about education, he had done so. He came out to the farm week after week. As soon as the children heard the galloping of his stallion on the dirt road, they would scamper to their rooms in search of their school books. By the time Charles made it to the door, Ander and Georgia Ann both would be seated quietly, eager to begin. She remembered how they gathered around the kitchen table, looking more like a family than teacher and pupils, laughing and joking with one another. Charles had patience. Never once did he raise his voice or scold one of them for a wrong answer. Jane would sit watching as he leaned back in his chair with a pencil behind his ear and smile as the children tried to decipher the text books. It didn't take them long to learn to sound out the words, and, before Jane knew it, they were making crude marks resembling the alphabet. Charles did have a way with her children. He communicated with them much better than their own father.

Charles didn't work only with the children. He opened the door of knowledge for her, too. At first, when he came for lessons, he'd bring along a copy of the *Daily-Picayune* so Jane could see what was going on in the world, at least in pictures. Later— wonder of wonders—she eventually learned to read along with her children.

It was only a matter of time, though, before Dennis realized what was happening. It was evident to everyone. She had taken on a sunny disposition since Charles came into her family's lives, and when Dennis figured out that she had defied him, letting Charles teach the children behind his back, he gave her a beating she'd never forgotten.

Yes, those were difficult times, but she had fond memories of when she and Charles had fallen in love. And now that they were married and living their lives together as a happy family, this had to happen. It just wasn't fair.

SHE TURNED AWAY from the window and tried to shake off the feeling of impending doom and then pressed both thumbs against her temples, trying to relieve the pounding in her head. She heard heavy footsteps and the jingling of keys. The steel door opened, then slammed shut. It was Sheriff Meredith.

"I hate to do this, Miz Fisher," the Sheriff said. He entered the cell. He put her hands and legs into heavy shackles, locking the irons so tightly they cut off the circulation in her limbs. "If it was anybody else but Judge Bear I'd make an exception, but he's a real stickler for procedure. You understand that, don't you?"

Jane thought about the judge and she stared in awe at her chained wrists. She had enough iron around her small arms to drag her almost to the floor. She wanted to say something, but couldn't. She only thought, *The judge must feel mighty proud of himself to protect the town from me, an eighty-pound woman.*

"Let's just get this over with," she said, wearily.

The sheriff gently cupped her elbow. Walking in front of her, he held her steady, descending the narrow stairs, but before they went outside, he walked back to his office. "Miz Meredith thought you might need this," he said, placing a red wool shawl around her shivering body. "I mean, with your fainting spell, and it being so cold."

"That's very kind of her," Jane said, squinting her eyes, trying to look outside. It took her a moment to focus. Her cell had been like a dark cave and the sudden bright sunlight hurt her eyes. When the sheriff opened the door, she could see the deteriorating Caldwell Parish Courthouse that had once housed the community hall and a church. She'd never been inside the old building or near it for that matter. It really did look dilapidated. Weathered boards crumbled against a rotting porch and only three posts held up the sagging roof where four once stood. Even in its decaying condition the local people and certain members of the police jury were protesting its being torn down.

A crowd had gathered outside the courthouse. *These nosy people must have been there earlier when the sheriff brought Ander out,* she thought. She lowered her eyes, biting hard on her lip, thinking of how they'd probably taunted Ander. This was all a nightmare. Was it ever going to end?

Struggling to put the shawl over her shoulders, Jane became frustrated, unable to move her shackled arms. The shawl fell to the floor but the sheriff swiftly reached down to pick it up, and, sympathetically, once again held it up trying to drape it around her. "Please don't bother," she said, rattling the chains. "I'm not cold. Just cover my hands so my children won't see these things. I don't want them to see me this way." She stepped out into the sunlight, nearly tripping as she struggled to get through the doorway. She tilted her head upward and arched her back, looking straight ahead. "I won't let them see me cry," she mumbled.

Suddenly a hand touched her arm. She turned around. It was Charles. He was trying to give her courage, but she knew he was worried. Whenever Charles was concerned about something his forehead wrinkled up and his emerald green eyes darkened like turbulent seas. She forced a smile. Charles protectively held on to her arm and led her through the crowd. For the first time in weeks she felt safe.

As they walked down the narrow wooden walkway toward the courthouse, Jane looked across the square where wagons were hitched in front of Cicero Bridger's Dry Goods Emporium and saw her mother sitting in a wagon with Georgia Ann. Over the noise of the crowd she heard Georgia Ann's high-pitched screams. Jane forced her lips to part in a smile, pretending for her daughter's sake that everything was going to be all right, while Charles held her steady, making sure the shawl covered the shackles. Then they passed J.T. Benton, standing in the dirt courtyard, grinning as if he enjoyed seeing her suffer. He gave a little bow and with a sweep of his arm toward the door of the courthouse, mocked her. "After you, Miz Fisher."

Jane walked past J.T. without so much as blinking an eye. She wanted to claw his face but just stared ahead while Charles urged her forward. As they entered the old building, she saw her brother Thomas standing just inside. Her first instinct was to run to him for comfort as she had when she was a little girl, but he barely looked at her. He pulled back, trying to melt into the crowd when she attempted to make eye contact. *The coward,* she thought. *Charles is right, Thomas will lie about Ander as long as it saves his precious John Augustus and that little heathen, George.*

She passed by Thomas the same way she had J.T. Then she looked up at Charles, pleading for support. "Please lay your coat around me," she said. He placed the coat over her shoulders, staring into her frightened face as he tenderly brushed fallen strands of hair behind her ear. *He's as scared as I am,* she thought.

The courtroom was packed with men leaning along the walls smoking pipes and cigars. An old wood stove in the center of the room belched thin blue smoke and women in heavy wool wraps were sitting close together, filling every inch of the backless sawhorse benches. The dimly lit room was quiet. Her gaze fixed firmly on the rough pine floor, Jane inched her way down the aisle toward the judge's bench. Loud gasps broke the silence when the shawl suddenly slipped and exposed her shackled hands and feet.

Charles made a mad grab for the shawl while Jane stared at John Augustus and his son, George, sitting at a wooden table on the left in front of the judge's bench. When Jane saw Ander sitting next to the defense attorney, S.H. Gilbert, her stomach quivered. Her throat tightened. She took a deep breath, "Oh, Charles," she said. "Look at Ander all chained up. He can barely move."

Charles said nothing. He just held her arm steady and helped her to a seat beside the attorney. Before melting back into the crowded courtroom, he kissed Jane on the cheek and gently patted Ander's shoulder.

Judge Bear fluttered into the courtroom dressed in flowing black robes resembling a huge buck-moth butterfly, and landed behind a wide table not more than five feet in front of Jane.

"All rise," the bailiff said, and the judge settled into his high backed, cowhide chair looking out over the people in his courtroom. His eyes locked on her face. He gave her a scrutinizing stare. She knew at that moment he could pass judgment without the least bit of remorse. His sagging cheeks emanated meanness. He looked like the grim reaper.

"The Fourth Judicial District of Louisiana is now in session, the Honorable George Bear presiding. Be seated."

Wasting no time in getting down to business, the judge cleared his throat and said to the counselors, "Let me make a couple of things perfectly clear. I know emotions are running high about this case. I hear what's being said, the rumors of things that people say they have seen, of things they say people have done. Rumors have absolutely no business in my court. Do I make myself clear?"

The crowd muttered and became restless. Jane clenched her fists and tried to hold them steady against the rough pine table. She was repelled by him. She could see he felt he had complete control over the court. He opened with the confidence of a successful train robber and she knew he would do and say anything that would keep him in power. Judge Bear wrinkled his forehead looking directly at her, his dark eyes malevolent, then gaveled the court to order. The crowd hushed. The only audible sounds came from the hammers of workmen driving iron nails into the new hanging scaffold. The pounding of the hammers echoed through the courtroom until Jane thought she would go mad. She leaned over and nudged Ander with her head, fighting to hold back the sobs that were overtaking her chilled body. Her face flushed and her heart began to pound rapidly as the foreman of the Grand Jury coldly read the indictment.

The Grand Jurors of the State of Louisiana and of this Parish, duly impaneled, sworn and charged to enquire for the body of the people of the Parish, acting in the name of the State of Louisiana, on their oath do present:

That Jane Moody Fisher, John Andrew Moody, John Augustus Hendrix and George W. Hendrix, late of the parish aforesaid in the Fourth Judicial District of the State of Louisiana on the third day of the month of January in the year of our Lord, one thousand eight hundred and ninety four, in the Parish, District and State aforesaid, did then and there, unlawfully, feloniously, willfully, and maliciously, set fire to and burn in the night-time a certain dwelling house, in which there was at the time some human being usually staying, lodging and residing at night. The said dwelling house being in possession of Hendrix, but occupied by Benton, with the intent thereby to injure the said Benton. And about the hour of ten o'clock at night the same day, they did feloniously and burglarously break and enter with the intent to steal the goods and chattel of Hendrix total value of said goods, thirty one dollars and fifty cents being found at said dwelling of Jane Moody Fisher, then feloniously and burglarously did then and there take, steal and carry away.

Jane lowered her chin to her chest. She wondered how she could be accused of breaking into a burning house and stealing burned possessions of her own papa. Who could have said such a thing? *Thomas!* She tilted her head and twisted around where she saw him staring down at the floor. *My own brother. Now look at him. He can't even look me in the eye.*

The attorney for the defense abruptly stood up interrupting her thoughts. Gilbert was an imposing man, an aging criminal lawyer, president of the Police Jury and one of the many parish residents who opposed the new ten mill tax Judge Bear had been trying without success to force on the impoverished farmers.

"Your Honor," he said, approaching the bench, trying sincerely if ineffectually, to show the court that Jane, who was of such a small stature, and Ander, a young boy, could not physically have boarded up the sharecropper J.T. Benton's cottage and set it on fire; that the fire appeared accidental; that the supposed stolen goods found at her house actually belonged to her family and not to J.T.; and that witnesses had been prejudiced and suspected of perjury.

He asked that the judge not allow the case to go to trial, saying the penalties could be extreme if the accused parties were convicted.

Charles reached over the oak rail separating the spectators from the prisoners, put his hand on Jane's shoulder and gently squeezed it. She broke out in a cold sweat. What if Gilbert failed and they went to trial? If the murder of her father became known, Ander would be hanged. Something had to be done to protect him, and Jane knew she'd have to be the one to do it.

"You can stop. Stop right there," she yelled, and struggled to pull herself up from the table. "Don't say anything else. I know what's going on here. There's no need for it!"

The spectators were in an uproar. Judge Bear gaveled them to order. Jane dragged herself toward the bench. Sheriff Meredith moved toward her. She caught his eye and shook her head. The shackles had cut her wrists and blood was staining the cuffs of her white cotton blouse. The crowd saw the blood. Suddenly the courtroom was deadly quiet.

Jane turned around to look at Charles. She wanted to cry out to him. "I love you," she whispered, moving her lips so he could understand. Then she stood rigid, her eyes fixed on Charles' face. *I couldn't love you any more if you were the father of my children. Though you'll hate me for what I have to do, know I love you. Please always believe that.*

She turned to face the judge, held her head high and looking him in the eye, she announced, "I plead guilty!"

The courtroom roared with excitement like the sound of a steam locomotive bearing down in the middle of the night. The judge banged the gavel again and again trying to bring back some semblance of order.

Jane waited until the crowd hushed, and continued in a crystal clear voice. "I was the only person at J.T. Benton's that night. I set the fire that burned his house and barn and killed his livestock."

The defense attorney quickly walked up to the bench, "Just a moment, Your Honor," he began, and Jane raised her shackled arms to protest.

"Why are you doing this?" the attorney asked her.

Tears streamed down her cheeks. She looked over her shoulder toward Ander. *I had no choice,* she thought as she watched him weaving his body back and forth like a small child. *Everyone has as much as told me that. There was never any real choice. All of them were going to swear that you set the fire, that you killed Papa. Charles is right. These people don't care about the truth. They'll drag you out of this room and throw a rope around your neck—hang you without even thinking about it. They're going to take your life. Hand me a lifeless body to cry over until they snatch you away. Put you in a hole so deep I can't claw my way to the bottom—cover you with dirt while they hold me back as you disappear from me forever. . . . No! I love you too much to let them do it. I can't live without you—I'll do anything for you, Ander—anything!*

"Mrs. Fisher," the judge said, interrupting her thoughts, "do you know what you're saying?"

"Yes, Sir," she said.

Ander then wailed out. He rose from the table, "I did it judge. It was me, not Mama."

The judge raised his eyebrows at Ander. "Come up here," he demanded. "Come up here and tell me what you just said."

"I plead guilty," Ander said, his voice quivering as he stared at the judge.

"Did someone put you up to this, Ander? Did someone tell you to do this?" the judge asked, giving Ander a scathing look. "If you did it thinking it's somehow going to get your mama off, then you've made a grave and grievous mistake son."

Ander moved closer to Jane. What was he doing? She had to find a way to make him shut up. She knew he didn't understand what he was saying. In all this confusion she was afraid he might even blurt out he shot his grandpa. She shook her head frantically.

"Ander Moody," the judge called out loudly, "so that we can be perfectly clear, you're telling this court that it was both you and your mama who burned up J.T. Benton's house? That you both are guilty of killing his livestock?"

Ander stared into his mother's eyes. She could see he was at a loss for words. She watched him look back toward John Augustus and George Hendrix who were staring contemptuously at him. He turned to face Judge Bear before she could get his attention again. He said, "Yes, I was with my mama that night."

"While this is highly unusual," the judge said, pounding his gavel to quiet the room once again, "it is absolutely impossible that a woman the size of the defendant could have acted alone in the crime she is accused of. It is therefore reasonable that the defendant, Ander Moody, was aided by his mama in this tragic crime. I am going to accept both guilty pleas, and this court finds both Jane Moody Fisher and John Andrew Moody guilty of arson with intent to kill."

Then he directed his attention to the defense attorney. "Would you like a recess?"

The attorney nodded, but Jane declined.

"No, Your Honor," he said, shaking his head in defeat.

The judge cleared his throat again, pointing an accusatory finger at Jane. "This court believes that it was you who put this child up to this heinous crime. You stand before me now a woman unrepentant who shows no signs of remorse for the things you've done to J.T. Benton, or to your own son for that matter. In the light of both confessions there is no need for a trial. I therefore sentence you, Mrs. Fisher, to fourteen years at hard labor, and you, Ander Moody, to seven years hard labor, at the Louisiana State Penitentiary."

Charles stood up and yelled out, "Nooooo!" as he dashed up the aisle toward Jane. The sheriff's deputy stepped in front of him as he approached the bench, grabbed both of his arms, twisted Charles around and marched him through the crowd of yelling men and women. Banging his gavel, the judge, seemingly oblivious of the chaos, said, "This court is now adjourned. John Augustus, you and your boy are free to leave. Sheriff Meredith, take the prisoners back to jail and arrange for them to be transported to the State Penitentiary."

Jane stood stock-still, completely stunned. She knew before she even pleaded guilty that she would have to serve some jail time, but not in a thousand years had she thought the judge would sentence them both to the state penitentiary. *Angola is a bloody prison,* she thought, reaching out to touch Ander's hand. *The worst prison in the whole south.* "Now both our lives are lost, Ander," she whimpered, staring at her son in a daze. "Why did you do it? . . .Why?"

⸸ Three ⸸

THE MORNING she was to be transported to prison Jane woke with a start to the hubbub of many voices. She'd slept but little the night before, tossing and turning on the rough mattress until her body was sore. But, in spite of her hard night, all she could think about was the noisy crowd gathered outside, watching the jail-wagon pull up. A lump rose in her throat. She began to dress—then stopped and paced back and forth, wringing her hands, praying that this was all a nightmare and she'd wake up soon. But it wasn't. *There will be no solace this morning,* she thought grimly. It would have been better for them to hang her. At least then her pain would have been quick and she would not have to suffer this humiliation.

The gentle breeze that had flickered rays of sunlight through the ragged curtain suddenly turned angry. Dark clouds filled the sky like furious waves against the seashore and her silent cell darkened. She heard the rush of rain as it struck against the window panes. The agonizing grief in her heart was almost unbearable.

Then suddenly a loud bang startled her. The steel door swung open. There stood a man she'd never seen before wearing a dirty wrinkled uniform that clung to his skin. His pants barely contained his pot-belly. As he pushed himself close against the bars, she could see milk-white skin where buttons had popped off his shirt. The hair on the back of her neck stood up. She cringed at his gaping eyes and jagged stubs of rotten teeth.

"This man is from the prison," said jailer Riley, holding a lantern near the stranger's face so Jane could see him. "He come to git you."

Jane hurriedly finished dressing, trying desperately to preserve some modesty in the process. The stranger's gawking was more than she could endure.

"It ain't gonna do you no good to stand there whimpering, Missy," he said, with a smirk, while the jailer fumbled with the keys to unlock the door to her cell. "Huh! Gals like you git sent to the penitentiary and you think you can cry your way out of it. Well, you can just stand there praying and crying for a week. It ain't gonna do you one bit of good."

Then it hit her. This man must have been outside her cell watching her sleep, watching her in her torment, listening to her weep. She hated him, despised him for gaping at her and violating her privacy.

He pulled a plug of tobacco from his shirt pocket and bit off a chaw. "You ain't going nowhere 'cept to prison," he said, "and from the looks of these here papers it's gonna be a long, long time, gal. You gonna be lucky if you git back here a'tall."

Jane heard this putrid little man saying the same thing she was feeling. *I'll never see my home again. Never see my children or Charles. I'll die in that prison.*

"Do what you will," she suddenly found the strength to say. "I have nothing to fear from you. Go ahead. There's nothing more that you can do to me. They've taken away everything in this world that I love and care about. If death is waiting for me, then so be it. Nothing could be worse than the life I've been living in this jail!"

She thrust her hands together and put them in the convict captain's face. "Go ahead, chain me up like a trapped animal just because they gave you the power to do it. Put me on the boat and take me away—take my life. Do it, but you'll never take away my spirit!"

As she spoke she was overcome with a sudden and total sense of relief. He dragged her out of the cell.

How simple, she thought as she was pushed into the wooden jail-wagon with Ander and another prisoner. *How very easy it is to make the pain go away when you know there is nothing more they can do to you.*

Main Street, muddy from the rain, was furrowed with deep ruts. Water covered the wooden sidewalks and curious people stood everywhere. Women wrapped in heavy wool shawls of various colors, parasols dripping water over frilly rims as they stretched and strained their necks to get a glimpse of this distraught mother who was on her way to prison with her young son. She could see them all clearly from two small barred windows in the jail-wagon. Hoping to shield Ander from their stares, Jane put her hand into her son's and moved close to him as they bounced and swayed toward the river. *Why, this ride is like a funeral procession,* she thought. She felt as if she and Ander were dead bodies in a hearse, whom everybody wanted to see before the burial.

The wagon came to a stop and Sheriff Meredith pulled open the heavy oak door. The hinges squealed. "I'm sorry, Ma'am," he said, "but you'll have to walk from here. We can't get any closer. The wagon's just too heavy in all of this mud. The team can't pull it."

Jane looked out where a circle of people stood around the landing. Faces of men from her childhood who rode with the *Knights of the White Camelias* with her papa and brothers stared at her, all armed, holding the crowd back. *These spineless cowards call themselves a Klan,* she thought as she glanced over at Ander and the short, skinny black prisoner, both shivering, she knew, from fear as well as from the cold. "It'll be fine," she said to them. "It's not far and the rain won't hurt us."

The convict captain shouted, "Get 'em outta there, sheriff. This boat's not gonna wait all day. Cooley's leaving on time whether we're on board or not and I'll be damned if I'm gonna wait any longer. Now git those prisoners out of that wagon."

The shrieks of women chilled her to the bone as the convict captain pulled her from the wooden cage. He fixed a chain between the loops on their leg irons, attaching the prisoners together like an umbilical cord.

"Just take it easy and walk to the boat, Miz Fisher," the sheriff said, turning round to face the crowd. "I'd help you, but I've got my hands full with all these crazy people and that convict captain. That's it, just walk slow. It'll be all right."

The convict captain moved in a circle around the prisoners with the sheriff and his deputy on either side. Jane led the way slowly toward the boat, whose steam engines were fired up and billowing smoke. A steady stream of raindrops beat like small, cold bullets into the red mud. She almost lost her balance and began swaying backwards. She caught herself. Her feet were sunk deep into the mud. Jane tried with all her might to lift her slippers but they would not budge.

"Don't just stand there," the convict captain bellowed, turning his gun toward her. "Leave those ragged shoes and keep going."

Jane stepped out of one and then the other, walking barefoot on the cold ground toward the steamer. The rain beat against her face, soaking her. From a distance she could hear Georgia Ann screaming. Suddenly her child came into view, running through the legs of the tight circle of men toward Jane.

"Please don't shoot!" Jane pleaded when she saw the convict captain turn his shotgun toward her daughter. "She's only a little girl! Please don't shoot her!"

She bent down to pull Georgia Ann close, but stopped when the shackles bit into her wrists. She tried to hide her hands in the folds of her wet skirt as Georgia Ann threw her arms around her crying, "Mama, Mama, don't let them take you away." The child pleaded with the convict captain who had jerked her roughly out of the prisoners' path. "Please don't take my mama away from me."

Jane winced. "Do something, Sheriff. Don't let him hurt my baby."

The sheriff stalked toward the convict captain. "Get your sorry carcass on the boat," he said, waving his gun in the man's face. "You could have hurt that little girl. And believe me, mister, you can mark my words, there'd be hell to pay if you did. I'm still sheriff here unless you've got some orders from the governor saying otherwise. As long as I am, we'll do things my way until the boat leaves."

"Whatever you say, Sheriff," the man said, glaring so coldly at Jane it made her tremble. "Whatever way you want to have it. You do it your way now but when they git on the boat they're my prisoners. I'll do it my way then. You can count on that."

The sheriff looked over toward her mother's wagon, raised his arm and waved to her. "It's all right, Miz Hendrix," he called out. "Come get this little girl. Get her out of this rain."

Betsy slowly climbed out of the wagon. Her back was stooped and her soggy house dress hung limply over her feet, tripping her old and frail body as she stumbled through the crowd. When she reached them she took Georgia Ann by one hand and with her other brushed the rain off of Jane's face. "Don't cry, Honey," she said. "Don't let them see you cry."

Betsy knelt down on the muddy ground. For an instant she seemed confused, then she took off her worn shoes and tried to put them on Jane's feet. "No, Mama, don't do that," Jane said, looking down on her mother. "I can't take your shoes."

Betsy stood up and wrapped her arms around her daughter, squeezing her tightly, "I want you to have them," she murmured.

Tears poured out of Betsy's sad gray eyes, and as she turned to walk away, she reached into her apron pocket and pulled out what looked like a bundle of small charred sticks. "The fire burned all my rose bushes. This is all I have left," she said, placing it in Jane's wet hand. "I want you to plant it wherever you go, and always, I want you to always think of me when you see the blooms. . . . I'll be thinking of you."

Looking back over her shoulder as her mother and child disappeared into the crowd, Jane and the others trudged once again through the mud toward the dock where the captain of the steamboat was waiting. The convict captain yelled at Captain Cooley when Cooley reached out to pull Jane aboard the steamer. "Don't you touch her. They're my prisoners. I give the orders now."

"They may be your prisoners," Cooley said disdainfully. "But long as they're on this vessel, they're my passengers. I saw you out there. I saw how harsh you were with that little girl. I have half a mind to lock you up. Now put that gun away. I don't allow that kind of behavior on *The Ouachita.*"

The paddle wheel began to turn. Deck hands scrambled about, tugging and pulling in the heavy hemp ropes and the boat began to drift slowly down the river.

Jane looked around the busy picturesque landing filled with stately passenger boats and paddle wheelers laden with cotton and other cargo. Steam whistles from a dozen ships filled the air. She looked frantically for Charles, but she could not see him anywhere. "He's left me too," she whispered to herself. "Charles has left me. He didn't even say goodbye."

Captain Cooley suddenly took off his dark blue wool uniform jacket and put it around Jane's trembling shoulders just as the convict captain roughly clutched her arm.

"Mama," Ander said, pointing at a grove of trees above the landing. "Somebody's out there calling for you."

Jane strained against the man's grip, looking back through the driving rain. She saw Charles' stallion galloping down the steep hill toward the river bank. Tree limbs slashed at Charles' face as he stood up in the stirrups, urging the horse forward. "Jane . . . I love you!" she heard him call out. She watched him spur the stallion and guide him into the river. The horse floundered at first, struggling in the icy water moving slowly toward the steamboat. Then both the horse and Charles disappeared.

"Oh God, no, he's going to drown!" Jane cried out.

The convict captain began to drag her up the steps and for what seemed like an eternity the surface of the river was flat. Then, like a tidal wave, the big bay horse resurfaced next to the boat with Charles holding on to the horn of his saddle. The dark water was white with froth as the horse churned his powerful legs against the current. Charles let go and began to swim as the boat gained speed. Suddenly he was caught in an undertow and the water became like a giant monster, sucking him under.

Jane screamed! The convict captain pushed all three prisoners inside a dark cabin.

Four

Out of the night that covers me,
Black as the Pit from pole to pole,
I thank whatever gods may be
For my unconquerable soul."

—Henley

Angola Plantation, headquarters for
The Louisiana State Penitentiary

JANE FELT THE STEAMER slowing down. Its deep throated whistle signaling her approach to Angola Plantation. She had overheard the convict captain telling Captain Cooley she would be getting off there. Angola was now the headquarters for the state Prison farms. It also was the private home of the Browne family. Everybody in Louisiana knew that. Sheriff Meredith had told her that Major Browne, the prison master, ever since the end of the war had held the contract from the state of Louisiana to lease out convicts. He had said that the Major was considered about the most corrupt man in the state. He operated a brutal penal system, working convicts like slaves.

Usually, most of the boy convicts were kept at the plantation with the women prisoners. The men were scattered in penal camps, building levees around the state. She had assumed that Ander would stay with her at Angola, but at breakfast the convict captain said Ander was headed to Hope Plantation, near New Iberia.

As the whistle sounded again, Jane tried to embrace Ander for the last time, in the cabin. He turned his back on her.

"Don't be this way to Mama," she pleaded with him.

He was sullen, refusing to listen to her. She touched him gently on his chin to coax him around to face her.

"Don't be this way, Ander, not today," she said, again, trying to reason with him. Still he would not answer. She realized it was hard for him to understand what was happening to them. He didn't want to hear any lessons on behavior in a prison camp. He was frightened at being told they would be separated, and was taking it out on her. She understood his anger, but continued to try and find a way to reach him; to make him understand he had to be strong enough to survive in prison on his own; and she had to do it before they took her off the boat. "I know I've always told you I'd take care of you and do everything in my power to make things all right. God knows if I could change things I would, but I can't. Don't you see? I have no control over where we're going and what's going to happen to us."

He stood there, defiant. "Ander, listen to me, please. You can't act like this, Son," she pleaded, in a last desperate attempt, reaching out for him. "You have to be a man. Those guards will kill you in that levee camp if you don't straighten up and change your attitude."

"Get out! Get out of here!" he screamed. "I never want to see you again." He was still shouting as the convict captain opened the door. Jane tried to pretend she didn't feel the viciousness of his anger. *Is he so afraid of being alone,* she wondered, *so afraid that he's lashing out at the one person who understands him like no one else; understands how frightened he is of being taken away from me? I am the one person who would do anything, cower over him in a herd of stampeding cattle, put the rope around my own neck to keep him from harm.*

Tears flowed down her cheeks. She found herself thinking back to when her children were young—how close they all were. Sure, Dennis had made it impossible for them to be happy as a family, but she and the children had had their special times. She remembered

Ander as a child, dark brown curly hair that always hung down in his eyes; his favorite ragged shirt, beyond mending, tucked inside beltless pants that he tied tightly with a rope. After Georgia Ann's birth, Ander took charge of the family like a little man, cooking and cleaning. He would carefully stack wood under the wash-pot to boil clothes when Dennis complained of Jane's long recuperation from "something so simple" as childbirth. Her heart fluttered. She almost lost her breath thinking about the sweet little boy who always thought of his mama first; the same little boy who would struggle with his drunken papa to protect her. *Whatever happened to that little boy? Where did he go?*

She stood rigid, looking into the grim face of her son. He was acting like a stranger. For the first time since the night of the fire, she wondered, *when he shot Papa, was it an accident or did he let his temper get the best of him?*

The convict captain clutched her arms tightly and closed the cabin door. She could still hear Ander screaming. "I hate you! I hate you and I hope you die in that place!" Then all she could hear was his sobbing. It was all Jane could do to keep from crumbling to the floor. To her he was still only a child, even though he swaggered around like a man and said words to tear at her heart, words that cut her to the quick and brought burning tears to her eyes. She wanted to rush back to him, try again to find some way to make him understand why she had to leave him. She hated the convict captain for dragging her away. She would never have left him of her own accord. She would have just stood there, letting her child abuse her.

WITH A HEAVY HEART Jane was on deck as *The Ouachita* pulled into the landing. She watched the deck hands cast over the hemp ropes as waves of muddy water sloshed against the cypress filled bank. She looked out over the view before her but couldn't appreciate the beautiful scene from the waterways. Behind her the U.S. Mail steamboat, *City of Monroe,* was going down the river at full steam, and the riverboat, *Natchez,* was coming up the river. The traffic was heavy, but then it would be, considering Angola Plantation was situated on the east bank of the Mississippi at the Red River

Pass where the river was more than a mile wide. It was so wide that it was virtually impossible to see the other side.

Just beyond the boat house, up a small levee, Jane saw a tall paunchy man, smoking a cigar, standing next to a flatbed railway cart. She knew from the steward on the boat, this had to be William Jones, the convict captain of the plantation. She was told he had a shifty look about him, that she'd be able to recognize him even from a distance. His head sat atop a long neck with an Adam's apple that seemed to have a life of its own, and he had a pair of shackles dangling from a loop on his belt. He was waiting to take charge of her.

As soon as the gang plank was lowered, the convict captain quickly herded her off of the boat to deliver her to the Angola convict captain. The closer she got to the man the more distressed she became. He looked surly and when she finally stood face to face with him, she could see that his pale blue eyes were too small for his long face. They were cold eyes, and they, more than anything else, made Jane fear him right off. He just grimaced at her with his cigar stuck between his teeth as he locked the chains around her wrist. He never uttered a word.

The bumpy ride in the mule-drawn railway cart was completed in silence. Then she saw people in the distance, and her fear of Captain Jones subsided. The sound of the ship's steam whistle was drowned out by the chattering and singing of a large group of young black women. When the cart stopped in front of a beautiful two-story white framed mansion that Jones called the 'Big House', Jane heard one clear, alluring voice singing above the others.

> "Oh! Dem Golden Slippers.
> Oh! Dem Gold-en slippers
> Gold-en slip-pers I'm gon-na wear."

It looked to Jane as if it was washing day at Angola Plantation. The group of women presided over a dozen cast iron kettles. Steam rose from the bubbling cauldrons and there was a steady clanging of wood against metal as the women stirred the pots of household linens with long hardwood sticks.

Row after row of luxurious white linen sheets fluttered in the cool breeze, and the yard looked as though a small armada of sailing ships had docked there. The familiar sharp smell of lye soap tickled Jane's nose as she noticed several small black boys of ragtag appearance laughing and running around the enormous fenced-in yard, playing with their sling-shots.

The black women, most of whom Jane thought couldn't have been over twenty years old, stopped their singing and rushed toward her and the convict captain.

"It's a white woman," Jane heard one say as Jones unlocked the chains and pulled her off the cart onto a small wooden platform.

The prisoners, all dressed in identical white dresses with black aprons, crowded around Jane. They laughed and giggled as black hands stretched out to help her down. "You jest go on Mr. Jones," one of them said. "We gonna takes care of her now. You git cleaned up and when you gits back we'll have a nice supper fixed up for you."

Jane stood still, not knowing where to go or what to do. She was paralyzed with fear and afraid the convict captain would accuse her of trying to escape if she moved even an inch.

"Don't just stand there like some cow waitin' for milking time," Jones shouted to her as he headed toward a small group of cabins clustered beside what looked like a stable. "There's work to be done around here, and you best see how you can help."

When Jones disappeared, she realized that the women weren't laughing any longer. In respectful silence they made a path between them. Walking toward her was one of the most beautiful black women Jane had ever seen. The steam from the boiling kettles, whipped by the wind from the river, made it look as though she were stepping out of a white cloud. The woman was tall, close to six feet, with the shape of a goddess. She held her head high and carried herself regally. She was dressed the same as the others, but somehow she looked different. There was an air of authority and quiet dignity about her. She didn't wear a white bandanna around her head as the other young women did. Hers was loosely tied around her neck and black, almost straight, hair formed a crown around her head. Her dark skin had the sheen of ebony in moonlight. She had a beautiful smile worthy of a queen.

She extended her hands. "Welcome to Angola Plantation." Her voice reminded Jane of the lilting, poetic way Charles spoke. Jane realized she had been the one singing about the golden slippers.

Nervously, Jane took her hand, but she was unable to speak.

The woman spoke to her again but this time in some foreign language. "*Bienvenu a' Angola Plantation. La rein a etre de terreur de avec moi.*"

Jane stared blankly at the woman.

The woman smiled and said, "*Yo se que sea una experiencia mas horrible, especialmente si es la primera vez encarcelearse aqui. Pero hay muchos remidios pera sobrevivir aqui en Angola.*"

When Jane still didn't speak the woman said softly in English, "Are you deaf and dumb, child? Do you speak a language that I am not familiar with?"

Jane could only stutter until finally she could make the words come out. "I'm . . . just so . . . tired. They're taking my boy . . . taking him to the penal farm in New Iberia. I don't know what's going to happen to him. I'm so upset I think I'm going mad."

The tall woman took her in her arms. "My name is Laura, though people in New Orleans sometimes call me 'The Countess'. I know what a frightful time you must have had. I think they make the trials awful so you'll be grateful when you're sent to prison and not to the gallows."

Then she smiled consolingly at Jane. "If you want me to, I will be your friend."

"Oh yes, I do," Jane said and collapsed into the warmth of the woman's bosom.

The Countess shooed the other women back to work. She took Jane by the hand, leading her toward the back of the Big House. As they neared the door of the kitchen, which was separate from the main house and connected by a covered walk, Jane hesitated. "Should we be going in there? Do they allow convicts to go near the house where they live? I don't want to get into trouble with Captain Jones."

"Oh, Cherie, you have so much to learn," The Countess said, as she held the door open for her. "If we didn't go into the kitchen the whole family would starve to death. If we didn't tend to the wash pots they'd have nothing to wear and no sheets to sleep on. If we didn't go into the main house there would be no one to scrub, polish, sew, clean, do and fetch. Without us, without the convicts, I fear the Browne family would just wither away to nothing. As you will see when they return from New Orleans, the family is not accustomed to caring for themselves."

As they entered the room Jane was awestruck. Rows and rows of heavy copper pots and pans hung from the walls. Woven willow baskets filled with spices, and dried peppers of a dozen varieties hung in long bunches from the smoke-darkened rafters, along with cured hams and sides of bacon.

Then she turned to the Countess and said, "This room's as big as my whole house. How many do you have to cook for? How many convicts are here?"

"With you, there are now thirty one of us," the Countess said, pulling out a chair for Jane. "You see, the Browne family is quite large, ten in all. They always have house guests, and then there is the plantation physician and several retainers we have to feed. Only a handful of convicts do the cooking, the rest of us are housemaids."

"It takes that many to keep this house clean? They must be a pretty messy family."

"Messy is hardly the word, I'd say," the Countess replied, chuckling.

"Big as it is, it still shouldn't take more than a half dozen good workers to keep it up."

"Even so," the Countess said, "we still work all day and half the night to keep them happy. It's hard work, my dear, but it's not so bad. Not when you think about what happens at the levee camps."

At the mention of the levee camps Jane's heart dropped, thinking about Ander. She couldn't help herself. She began to cry.

"Go ahead and cry it out. Get rid of all of the tears before the family comes back," the Countess said, reaching out to pat Jane's hand. "They don't like tears. They like to see us happy and laughing, as though we somehow enjoy being here. Now tell me, what would you like to drink while I fix something to eat? Tea, coffee? We have anything that you could possibly want. What we don't have, Mrs. Browne orders from New Orleans or New York."

Jane began to relax. She sipped the bitter, dark French coffee with chicory which the Countess poured into a mug, and rested both elbows on the long pine work table while the Countess fixed a supper of southern fried chicken and, Jane's favorite, slender lengths of potatoes and onions fried crispy brown in ham drippings. "Mmmm," Jane murmured as she leaned over to smell the food the Countess set in front of her, "I never thought I would eat food like this in prison."

"What were you expecting?" the Countess laughed as she took a seat opposite Jane and began to eat. "Did you think that we would be shackled together in tattered clothing, hanging from the walls in a dark, damp dungeon with nothing to eat and drink but corn-pone and river water?"

Jane could not answer. Her mouth was stuffed. But never in her wildest dreams would she have thought she'd be sitting in this fancy kitchen with this elegant black woman cooking for her like she was a house guest. And she'd never tasted food with such flavor. Not even her mother could fry chicken this good. As she looked up from her Blue Willow plate she saw the Countess smiling at her and realized that she'd been greedily eating with her fingers. Embarrassed, she started to wipe her greasy fingers on the sleeve of her dress.

"No, no, don't do that. Your dress is not a rag. Use this napkin," the Countess said, thrusting a starched linen cloth in her hands.

Jane lowered her eyes. How could she have done such a crude thing in front of this elegant woman?

"Don't be embarrassed," the Countess said. "There was a time after the war when not only didn't I know what a napkin was, but my family didn't know where our next meal was coming from. You see, my mama and papa had been slaves, as were their folks. When you are a slave, if your white masters have food you have something to eat, even if it is only scraps from their table that their dogs wouldn't eat. Then we were set free, and while the carpetbaggers promised every former slave forty acres and a mule, they didn't care if we starved or not. There were lots of times my mama said she wished they'd kept their promises and given us a mule. At least we could have eaten it."

Jane did not say anything, she just let her talk. The only thing Jane knew about slaves was what her mama used to tell her about the darkies that had traveled with them overland from South Carolina, and how when the war was over they scattered up into the woods of Arkansas somewhere.

"I was young and pretty," the Countess continued as she poured another cup of steaming hot coffee, "and a white man from one of the established New Orleans families that still had money wanted me. I let him take my virginity in exchange for food for my family. Does it shock you that I have sold my body?"

"No, no," Jane said, unhesitatingly, afraid that the expression on her face had offended this woman who had been so kind to her. "It's just that I've never seen a person like you before."

The Countess laughed. She reached into her apron and pulled out a thin black cigar. "You mean you've never seen a black woman, a woman of color, a negress or nigger, as I think they call us in certain circles, speak and act like an educated white person?"

Jane nodded. She wished she could disappear she was so embarrassed. What was wrong with her today? Couldn't she do or say anything right?

"You see, little one, I had a choice. I will always be black. There's nothing I can do about that, and as you know there are people who hate me because of the color of my skin. I had to stay black, but I didn't have to stay poor and I certainly did not have to stay ignorant. I have eyes and I can see. I have a mind and I can think. Most importantly," she said, as she began to clear the table, "I have a soul and I can feel and dream just like the white folks. I learned from them, Jane. I begged the white missionary women at Charity Hospital to teach me how to read and write. They did, and I emptied their slop buckets in exchange for the opportunity to learn. I scrubbed floors in those big mansions in the Garden District, and while I did it, I listened. I heard how the wives and the mistresses of the rich men spoke, and when I would lie in my bed at night, I'd try to speak just like them. I saved their old copies of the *Daily-Picayune* and that's how I learned to read so well, even though at first I could only look at the pictures."

"I wanted to do that," Jane said, interrupting her. "I wanted to order the paper so I could look at the pictures, but my first husband said only foolish women did that. Later Charles taught both me and my children how to read."

"There, you see?" the Countess said. "We aren't so different after all, are we? The color of our skin is different, but we are both convicts. I can read, write and speak foreign languages, and you want to learn more than you know now. Yes, little one, you have a choice. Even in a dreadful place like this where a convict is lower than anything you can think of, you have a choice. You can stay ignorant like the other women prisoners, or you can educate yourself. You can let Jones and the others take and use your body, or you can be like me and learn to use them instead."

Jane pushed her chair back abruptly from the table. She began to pace around the room, wringing the cloth napkin until it was twisted tightly around one hand. "I knew prison was going to be difficult but the thought of any man other than Charles Fisher taking me to bed is enough to make me sick," she said, then wearily she sat down again, letting the tight cloth unwind, thinking about Charles and how much she loved him. She remembered the intimate times with Charles and how much she wanted his child and . . . now . . . if he had drowned? . . . if he was really dead? Charles Fisher dead . . . and she was a convict in a place where any man, black or white, could take her, and there was nothing she could do about it.

"You must have loved this man very much," the Countess said, snapping Jane out of her daydream. "It must have been a very great love."

"Great love? It was. You'll never know nor understand the bond of love between me and Charles Fisher, how much he did for me and my children. Charles was always there!"

SHE REMEMBERED the night Dennis beat her and Ander so badly she had to run away. Dennis's drunken voice still echoed in her mind. She could still see it as vividly as if it had just happened.

"I'm going to kill you, Sarah Jane!" his shrill voice had rang out in the small kitchen of their farm house, "then I'm going to kill these young'uns and find a way to make your fancy school teacher watch me do it."

"You're not going to kill anybody," she sobbed, screaming at him, "what is wrong with you, Dennis?"

Dennis reared back his hand and thrust his fist into her stomach. She doubled over, gasping for breath, then she slumped to the rough pine floor. He stood over her, thrashing his fist about, "You wanna know what's wrong with me? I hate liars," he roared. "You lied to me when you said that teacher wouldn't be coming around here messing with my young'uns!"

She remembered how her head had been spinning, how she had fought to keep from vomiting, and how she had struggled to scramble up off the floor. Through a blur she saw his hands coming toward her lifting her up and slamming her against the wall. Ander had run into the kitchen and jumped onto his papa's back, crushing him to the floor. She had stood up and stumbled to the table. She remembered thinking she had to do something to stop his madness before he killed them all. Then he had overpowered their small son, knocking Ander across the room into the cookstove, gashing his head. And once again, like an angry, wounded animal, he had struck Jane across the face until she landed in a pile next to Ander. She had reached over and grabbed a piece of firewood and came up swinging at Dennis' head. She had struck him—hit him again and again, fighting like a tigress protecting her young, until he staggered back into the cupboard that crashed around him. He kept bellowing he was going to kill her.

It was then Jane had clutched Ander's arms, dragging him to the door. "We have to get out of here, now!" she had screamed. She told him she'd go fetch Georgia Ann, for him to run and wait for her in the woods. But it was too late to get to Georgia Ann. Dennis was on his feet, rushing at them. She pushed her son out the back door and they ran into the dark night finding their way through the briars of the pine forest until they reached the small house where Charles taught school.

Jane shuddered as she sat up in her chair, wiping the tears from her face. The Countess was staring at her, thoughtfully, but she did not pry. She allowed Jane her private thoughts and crossed over to the gigantic slate fireplace and threw several large logs into the fire. Jane watched as she poked the embers, coughing as smoke escaped into the kitchen.

Yes, we were so happy for a while, Charles and I, she thought. *And my family had to ruin the only real happiness I ever had. Now I've destroyed the only man I ever loved.* She lay her head in her arms upon the table, sobbing silently, *I just don't know how I will ever live without him.*

⁑ Five ⁑

JANE WAS GIVEN a small room in the attic of the Big House. Over the next few weeks she worked harder than she ever had in her life. It seemed that she would barely close her eyes when the big bell down by the servants' cabins would ring. But even though they worked like slaves, the Countess always found time to spend a few moments alone with Jane. She'd show her words in a book, and how to sound them out, just as Charles Fisher had done.

"If you're going to learn how to read and write you might as well learn how to speak like a lady, not like a sharecropper. Listen to me and listen to Mrs. Browne when she returns," the Countess told her. As they went about their duties the Countess would point to an object. "This is Limoges china, L-i-m-o-g-e-s. Say it, then spell it," she'd tell Jane. "Before I'm finished with you, Cherie, I'll have you speaking French and Spanish too. And once you learn, I'll ask Mrs. Browne if you can accompany her to New Orleans to the Opera on occasion."

IT WAS the last Monday in February when the convicts were told that *The Sparks*, a privately owned steamboat of the Browne family, would be docking at the landing just after sunrise the following Thursday. The family would be at the Big House for breakfast.

On Wednesday night, after all the work was done, Jane was more than grateful for the chance to relax. The Countess said she wanted every one of the women to be rested and ready to receive the family the next morning. She said once Mrs. Browne was back, the hard work would not stop until the family left for their summer holiday.

When the Countess came to Jane's room that night, she encouraged Jane to go over and over the names of all the china, crystal, and other objects the Countess thought to be important. She told Jane this could help to assure a high position in the Big House for her. They studied recipes from cook books that Jane had learned to read, and simple passages from one of Major Browne's favorite novels. "I want Mrs. Browne to have a good impression of you," the Countess said, giving her a new white uniform and starched black apron to wear the next day. "It is very important, perhaps more important than you know, that she likes you. But one thing, Cherie, don't ever let her think you know more than she does. And don't ever let her get the impression you envy all her pretty things. If you do, she'll distrust you. She hates thieves and I shudder about what happens around here when one of the convicts gets accused of stealing."

"I'll do anything. Just tell me what to do and I'll do it," Jane said. She realized that if Mrs. Browne didn't like her or did not think she was good enough to wait upon her, she could be sent to a levee camp, or worse, to Major Browne's house of prostitution in New Orleans where most female convicts were sent straight from the courthouses. Jane did not really understand everything the Countess told her about the female convicts who were never brought to prison, just that it had something to do with *white slavery*. This confused Jane. Charles had told her white slavery had been abolished in Louisiana back in the eighties.

"Cherie, there is something else we must discuss, something that's perhaps more important than what Mrs. Browne thinks of you, and that is, which one of the men you are going to give yourself to? Have you not found it strange that none of the men has bothered you since you arrived here? Not Jones, who can't let a day pass without at least one woman? Not the other retainers who use most of the young girls at will? The Major overlooks sexual pleasures the men take, Cherie. 'It is expected', he always says. It is the way of plantation life. Always has been and always will be, is the way he feels about it. Have you seen the two octoroon convicts, Annie Barret and Julia White, who stay in their cabins all day primping?"

"Yes, and I've wondered about them. Why don't they do housework like the rest of us?" Jane asked.

"Simple. Primping and keeping themselves groomed is their job. The Major keeps them handy for his overnight guests. You know, the men I told you about who are friends of the Major from Baton Rouge?"

Jane just shrugged and sat there shivering. The thought of it made her skin crawl. *Someone other than Charles . . . touching me . . . loving me! Oh God, I'd rather die first,* she thought. Then she protested, "Countess! Do I really have to submit to one of these men? Isn't there a law against that? Can't we get word to the Governor and tell him what's going on here?" By the look in the Countess's eyes, Jane knew that would be impossible, and she finally understood what the Countess was trying to say. She knew someone would take her, and whether she liked it or not, use her.

"Don't you understand, Cherie," the Countess snapped. "The retainers are waiting to see if Major Browne or his son, Master Lawrence, or Mrs. Browne's brother, Mr. Henry Smith, or the son-in-law, Mr. George Ivan, wants you. They won't touch you until the family members have had first choice."

"Oh Countess, that can't be!" she said, burying her face in her hands. When she finally stopped crying she looked up at the Countess, "Did one of the family take you?"

"Yes," the Countess answered, holding her head slightly up where the lamplight cast her profile on the wall. "The Major."

The Major? Jane was frightened. She felt a sudden surge of distrust and wondered if she was talking too much, if she could really put her faith in the Countess. She could tell that the Countess sensed her anxiety. The Countess sat beside her on the bed and put her arms around Jane. "Don't let that frighten you, Cherie," she said. "I will have no secrets from you. Do you know why I am in this place?"

Jane, who had heard the other women talk about the crimes that had gotten them sent to Angola, had never heard anyone mention anything about the Countess. She shook her head.

"It was murder, Jane—murder that I was accused of, and it was a murder that I committed. I was being kept by a man from New

York, one of the carpetbaggers who came here after the war and got rich, while people like me and my family starved. He treated me well. I had a carriage and driver, beautiful clothes and my own house. I didn't love him, but he wasn't very demanding of my time and I didn't mind the arrangement.

"Then he told me he had a wife who was coming from New York to live with him and I'd have to leave his house. That would've been fine with me; those arrangements are never permanent, you know. There wouldn't have been any difficulty if only he'd given me a satisfactory allowance, as is the custom, to tide me over. But he didn't. He became drunk and abusive and threw me on the street with nothing but the clothes on my back. I pleaded with him, trying to reason with him. Then, when he began to beat me, I killed him with a knife."

Jane pulled away in horror and stood up. She had had all she could take, talking about murder. Every convict except her in the Big House was a murderer. It was all Jane could do to keep her sanity and her mind off of it.

She interrupted the Countess, "When my first husband Dennis Moody beat me and my son, we ran away in the middle of the night. I could have probably killed him, but I didn't. I guess I was just grateful I had someone to run to. If it hadn't been for Charles Fisher, I don't know what would have happened to us."

"Ahh, this Mr. Fisher," the Countess purred. "The man you love so much?"

Jane nodded and her eyes got misty at the thought of Charles. She began to wonder if somehow he could have survived the river. *Oh Charles, that was so foolish to give up your life for me,* she thought. *I'll always feel guilty now. I'll never forgive myself.*

"You see," the Countess said, disturbing Jane's thoughts, "as I have told you before, we are very much alike. I, too, had a great love, the man who took my virginity. And who knows, perhaps one day if I ever get out of here, he will love me again. But for now, we have to forget about the past, think of the future."

The Countess stood up to leave, and Jane crawled into her small iron bed, wishing that she could turn back the clock and somehow prevent all that had happened. She thought about Charles and wondered what he would think of her letting another man put his hands on her. Their love had been so tender and pure; full of emotion. How could she bear it? Wasn't the humiliation of going to prison enough? It just wasn't fair to suffer such degradation.

She spent a sleepless night, worrying that Mrs. Browne would not find her suitable for service in the Big House. As dawn began to break, she finally drifted off to sleep. Her last memory was the night before the trial when Charles told her, "Think of yourself, Jane, think of yourself." And she knew she had to do whatever she could to survive.

Thursday morning dawned cold and clear. She heard Jacob, the rail cart driver yell out, "Steamboat comin', Marse Browne home." Jane, along with the other neatly dressed servants, hurried to the side yard outside the Big House. All of them stood in silent rows at the request of the Countess, to welcome home the Browne family.

This place is peculiar, Jane thought. *The Countess was right; it's not a dungeon; it's not even even a real prison. It's a stage and all the convicts are the actors; just like now, prisoners standing at attention, dressed up in finery like the King of England's staff awaiting the arrival of royalty. Yes, at Angola Plantation everything on the outside is pretend; on the inside a living nightmare; a nightmare no one fully understands.*

Jane looked up to the skies, remembering the terrifying screams that had awakened her on several occasions these past weeks—screams that seemed to echo through the quiet of the plantation, and she would hear the whispered conversations about convicts who were mangled and brutally murdered, some supposedly buried in the levees, some tortured to death and sunk in the Mississippi. She had overheard tales of physical and sexual abuse, but when she quizzed the young convict girls, no one actually admitted to having been beaten or whipped. "We all gonna die in heah," the convicts confided to one another, their heads pressed closely together in whispers when Jane was near. "George Ivan's the devil sent to persecute us," they all agreed and each had her own story to tell of George Ivan's black-leather whip. Virginia Reed, as old a convict as she was, carried the mark of it. Virginia bore a big scar across the right side of her blue-black face. She didn't mind telling all she knew about the man who mistreated the convicts. But most of the girls were afraid to discuss the torture they suffered at the hands of George Ivan, the son-in-law of the Major and Mrs. Browne. They just endured.

She sighed and lowered her head as Jacob pulled the first of the carriages that carried the Browne family into the side yard and stopped. Mrs. Emma Browne extended a green silk slipper out of the elegant carriage, stepping onto Angola soil for the first time in several weeks. She was followed by her daughter, Ella Marie Ivan and the man Jane most dreaded to lay her eyes on, George Ivan. The Major wasn't with them. He was said to have taken the horse at the landing and gone directly to the fields.

"Welcome home, Mrs. Browne," the Countess said. "We missed you and hope your stay in New Orleans was a pleasant one."

Emma Browne ignored the Countess and glanced at the line of convicts. In a loud nasal voice she asked, "Where's the new girl?" The Countess motioned for Jane to come forward.

Jane walked nervously down the long path toward the strangers. She held her breath, barely able to put one foot in front of the other until she stood face to face with the prison master's heavy-set wife.

"This is Jane, Mrs. Browne," the Countess said, her eyes still lowered. "I'm happy to tell you she's a very good worker. She can read and write. With your permission, I'd like to have her assist me in taking care of your needs."

"What's she in here for?" Mrs. Browne asked. "What did you do to get sent down here, girl?"

Jane was so afraid it was impossible for her to speak. She waited for the Countess to say something. The Countess looked at her with pleading eyes, then spoke. "She was sentenced for arson, Mrs. Browne."

Jane's heart sank when Emma Browne turned swiftly and walked away without a second glance at her, much less her approval. About half way to the house Mrs. Browne stopped and spun around. "You know I prefer murderers," she said. "They're much more trustworthy. But if you think she can be helpful, Laura, then let her try. We'll see how she works out. You had better tell her that I'm going to be watching her to see if I can trust her, though."

Before Jane could move back to her place with the other women, Jones opened the door of the second carriage and a man stepped out. She knew it had to be the son, Lawrence, just by the way he carried himself. His dark blue suit was smart and even with the wind mussing up his locks of dark brown hair, he was handsome. All Jane could see as he grinned at the Countess were sparkling teeth on a flawless young looking face. He was flirting with all the convict girls.

"So this is the new one, is it, Countess?" he said, as he surveyed Jane from the tips of her black high buttoned shoes to her face. "Keep her in the Big House. I wouldn't want that pretty white skin to get all burned working in the fields or those soft little hands to get all rough and red."

Lawrence Browne winked at Jane and strode toward the Big House. Jane watched his dowdy wife, Sara Rose, who looked several years older than he, struggle to get their two children out of the carriage. Jane felt sorry for this woman. It was obvious to Jane the kind of life she must lead with Lawrence. She reminded Jane a great deal of herself when she was married to Dennis although this woman was rich where she had been poor. Then Jane heaved a heavy sigh. *I can't think about her,* she thought. *I have to get through this somehow and Lawrence Browne may have to be my ticket out of here.*

⚓ Six ⚓

S THE GRANDFATHER clock in the foyer resounded three times, Jane hurried up the stairs to the second floor balcony to serve afternoon tea, as she had done every day since the Brownes returned to the plantation. If she was even a second late there would be hell to pay. The Madam expected tea to be served precisely at the stroke of three. This was the sacred hour the Madam spent with Lawrence, the time of day she boasted that they both looked forward to—an hour of mother and son chatting.

Balancing a tray of delicate china and a plate filled with small biscuits, Jane turned the polished gold door knob of one of the balcony doors, and pushed the door open with her foot. The afternoon breeze caught hold of it and whipped it open with a thud against the wall. As Jane was about to apologize to the Madam for her clumsiness she noticed only Lawrence Browne seated at the wrought iron table. Although he had his back to her, Jane could see he was lost in his own thoughts. He didn't even notice her presence.

She set the tray down on the table and placed a napkin beside Lawrence's plate. When she looked up, Lawrence locked eyes with her. She quickly looked away and without a word continued setting the table, but before she knew it, he'd reached out and grabbed her hand. "You know I could make you go to bed with me, don't you?" He brushed his full lips against her hand. Jane was so startled, she jerked back and tipped the cup of tea she was pouring. As the liquid overflowed onto the cup's saucer, Lawrence grinned with satisfaction. He seemed to love toying with her. "But I won't," he chuckled. "I would much prefer you to fall in love with me first."

Still flustered, Jane didn't answer. She stared at the floor. Fall in love with him? How utterly impossible! He was a married man with children. Jane couldn't even imagine it, although it occurred to her she was married when she'd met Charles Fisher, and they'd fallen in love.

That was different, though. Charles wasn't married, and Lawrence was totally different from Charles. She could see he took what he wanted and was fickle with his affections. Then she thought about what Charles had said the night before the trial. *Think about yourself, Jane. Think about yourself.* And she realized at that moment, if she planned on doing what the Countess told her it would take to get out of this place, she'd have to find some way to become the object of those affections. If the sorry fact was that one of the plantation men was going to take her, at least Lawrence Browne was a sight better than anyone else. He was good looking and clean and wouldn't be as repulsive as the others.

Jane broke away from her thoughts. Looking up she noticed Lawrence's boyishly handsome face still staring intently at her. Suddenly she heard Mrs. Browne's footsteps headed out onto the porch. Jane nervously waited for her to sit down. Lawrence stood up and kissed his mother on the cheek as she reached the table, and the two began talking as if Jane were invisible.

"I don't want you carrying on with a convict servant, Lawrence," Mrs. Browne told him, obviously having noticed his behavior. "Not here at Angola. Not under my very nose. You know how servants are. Convicts always try and take advantage of us. Making that girl think you have some interest in her will be nothing but trouble. Jane," she barked, "are you going to stand there all day or are you going to pour my tea?"

"I'm sorry, Mrs. Browne," Jane said, picking up the tea pot, angrily thinking the old harridan should have to serve herself.

Lawrence chuckled. "Why don't you just call her, 'Madam', like everybody else around here does?"

Jane repressed a smile as she glanced at Lawrence, thinking she'd like to call her a few other choice words as well.

"Stay out of this, Lawrence," Mrs. Browne said.

"I'm just trying to help you out, Mama. You know how formal you like the servants to be."

Jane curtsied to the two of them and walked back inside but could still hear them bickering. How Lawrence could be Mrs. Browne's son was beyond her. He seemed to be a more realistic person, down to earth. Not at all like the Major or Mrs. Browne who could sip afternoon tea with higher-ups in state government as if they were born to aristocracy, and at the same time send a load of convicts to a levee camp, knowing most of them would die.

Curious about what his mother had to say about her, Jane stood behind the drapery listening.

"I mean what I say, Lawrence, I will not have people gossiping about our family. If you commit adultery with this girl I will have her sent to one of the levee camps."

"There's no need for that," he said.

Lawrence hastily finished his tea, stood up and kissed his mother on the cheek. "Forgive me, Mama. You're right as always. I was indiscreet and should've known better." Like a bolt of lightning he left the porch and passed Jane in the hallway without even noticing her.

Full of surprises that man is, she thought later as she hurried down the stairs with the dirty tea dishes on a tray. She knew if anything was to happen between her and Lawrence it would have to be kept very quiet. Mrs. Browne might pretend she didn't know what was going on between the men on the plantation and the convicts, but one thing Jane knew for sure, Mrs. Browne was not about to tolerate it from Lawrence. She placed him high on a pedestal and would just as soon die as have him get into a relationship with a convict.

"If I'm to get out of here I have to plan carefully," she mumbled to herself as she swung open the kitchen door, walked over to the work table and set the dishtray down.

"Good God almighty! What happened to your face?" she asked Nellie, the thirteen year old convict servant who stood next to the table peeling potatoes.

Nellie turned her face away from Jane but Jane persisted. "I asked you what happened? Who did this to you?" she demanded.

Nellie's eye was bruised and swollen so badly it was oozing pink liquid. "Nobody did nothing to me," she said. "I run into the fence post coming out the garden. Don't ask me no more questions. If you do I won't answer nohow."

"Sugar," Jane said, placing her arm around the skinny little black girl. Nellie must have had a hundred plaits in her wiry hair and she looked an awful fright. But Jane's heart went out to her. Jane picked up a clean rag and dipped it in the boiling pot on the cookstove, carefully wiping the child's eye. "Oh, Sugar, why won't you tell me who did this to you? You can trust me. I wouldn't betray you for the world."

"Miz Jane," Nellie whimpered. "If I tells you who did this, by morning I'd be in a six foot hole in that levee out there. Don't ask me no more questions!"

Jane took the frightened child by the hand and stormed into the Big House, dragging Nellie behind her.

"What are you doing bringing her into this house?" the Countess snapped, rushing the two of them inside the front parlor. "You know she's kitchen help. They're not allowed to come inside. Go on, gal. Scoot! Get on out of here!"

Jane held Nellie's hand firmly. "No! We have to do something for this child, Countess. Look at her face. She's scared to death. We have to protect her—find out what happened to her—turn in whoever did this."

"Jane you have a lot to learn about the goings on in this place. I told you the first day you arrived here to mind your own business. If you think for one moment you can do anything about this little girl, you're wrong. Now let go of her. Don't give me cause to worry about you. I already overheard Miss Sara Rose telling Madam Browne you're going to be needing a lashing soon for dallying around. You know that's just the way these people are, and the Madam likes nothing better than a good lashing. She says it keeps convicts from getting uppity."

"Laura!" the Madam called out. "What's keeping you? Who's that in this house?"

"Now, you see what you've done!" the Countess scolded, waving them out.

But as soon as the Countess disappeared, Jane clutched the girl's elbow and sneaked her up the back stairs to her room in the attic. "Take this off," Jane said, unbuttoning the child's uniform top. "I'm going to doctor you up."

Nellie flinched and withdrew from Jane's touch.

"Don't fret child. I'm trying to help you."

"That's what he said," Nellie whimpered.

"Who?"

"Miz Ella Marie's husband," she said, and slipped her blouse off of her shoulders.

"BeJesus! You've been whipped!"

"I begged him, Missy Jane. I told him I is a good girl. Really I did. I told Mr. Ivan if'n I did the things he wanted me to do, I is going to hell. But he didn't care."

"It's all right, Nellie," Jane said, trying to soothe her. "Calm down. I'll try to help you."

Nellie raised her sad little face. There was fear, the likes of which Jane had never witnessed before, in her bulging black eyes. "What you think you can do? We is their prisoners!" the girl said.

"Lay down. I'm going to put some ointment on these cuts. And when I get finished I want you to get on back to the kitchen— listen to what I'm telling you. If you stay close to someone else at all times, it'll be hard for anyone to do these things to you. I'll see if I can't get the Madam to let you work the dining room—pull the punkah or something. Maybe she'll let you stay in the attic with me. In the meantime, you do as I say. You hear?"

Jane knew Nellie was right. Convicts were nothing but slaves to the Browne family, and she knew that whatever pain and suffering the prison masters gave out, the convicts must endure it. It was the only way to survive in this cesspool of sin.

She pulled Nellie off of the bed and held her for a moment. She thought about her own child—Ander, was he suffering the same abuse in the levee camp? It terrified Jane. She knew that she could be next, and maybe she wouldn't be as lucky as Nellie. No, she knew she would not be. She would fight these monsters before she would endure their sadistic demands. She knew in her heart she would die first.

SINCE THE MADAM HAD AGREED for Jane to work with the Countess, Jane had tried to prove herself worthy of her position, but she realized after a while none of these people were interested in worth. Lawrence's wife was so cold-hearted that she could, on a whim, command a servant to be whipped just because she felt bad. What is the use? And Lawrence, what kind of man was he? *Didn't Mama always say that birds of a feather flock together?* Jane reminded herself.

In the following months Jane watched the members of the household grow meaner and more cruel to the servants. Even when the Madam was entertaining the major's "friends in high places" from Baton Rouge, a convict wasn't safe from the Browne family's wrath. A few of the girls tried to run away, but they were caught and by the time Jane would see them again, they were nursing open, infected wounds from dog bites. She often thought she'd be better off if she flung herself off the balcony or better yet, drowned herself in the Mississippi River. But with the Countess's encouragement she tried to make the best of daily life at the plantation, even when she would get a glimpse of ghostly figures like Sara Rose or Ella Marie stalking around doorways, slipping up on her just to see if they could get her into trouble. Ella Marie was a strange woman. She seemed to be emotionally ill at times, but Sara Rose? Jane couldn't figure out Sara Rose's role in all of this. She had heard the woman had come from a respectable New York family, but she didn't act like it. At times Sara Rose acted as though she were trying to be another Mrs. Browne.

Each day became a trial in itself. Then one night, when Jane had completed her work for the day and had left Madam Browne's room, crystal lamp holder in hand, stealing down the front staircase, Lawrence was on the landing.

"Mighty nice evening, Miz Fisher," he said, brushing up next to the railing.

"Yes it sure is a nice evening, Master Lawrence," she said, almost whispering. "It looks as though we might have a full moon out tonight."

Lawrence looked at her quizzically. She guessed it was because he had caught her off guard or maybe because she'd barely spoken to him since that day on the balcony. "Well, indeed I believe you're right," he answered, "the sky is as bright as day." He stretched out his hand and gently brushed her hair away from her neck. "And if I might ask, is that magnolia blossom I smell on you?"

"Right . . . right out of this very yard," she stuttered.

Lawrence flashed a big smile and clipped her chin with the tip of his finger. "Don't you know my mama will have your hide for cutting her favorite flowers off the tree?"

"Don't you know your mama would have my hide for anything I do, Master Lawrence?"

He laughed. "Yeah, I suppose she would."

Jane stood stiff, wondering if she was moving too fast. Finally she smiled when she realized he was playing a game with her. She knew she had to play along, but he wasn't letting her off the hook yet. The bold look in his eyes told her that.

"And to what do I owe the pleasure of such a beautiful smile this evening?" he asked, sounding almost sincere.

Her mind drew a blank. She didn't know what to say to him now. She'd have much preferred to push him down the stairs, but this was the second time he had made a play for her. *May as well do it now and get it over with*, she thought. "Oh, Master Lawrence, it's just that I've been thinking, that's all," she quickly said.

"Is it possible I've been one of the things you've been thinking about?"

"Yes, that's possible," she said, "that's very possible."

"Good," he said, walking up the stairs toward his mother's room without looking back at her. "You just keep thinking that way. You never know what will happen. And you're right, it is a beautiful night." As she turned to walk down the stairs, he added in a low voice, "I've always loved the smell of magnolia blossoms on warm skin."

Her face flushed and she thought about Charles. *Oh Charles, what am I going to do?*

She could have flung herself down the stairs, she was so humiliated. Why was she so nervous? He was just a man, but it was more than that and she knew it. Lawrence was playing hard to get. And what for? He could take her at will. He didn't have to play games. It just gave her one more reason to dislike him. It seemed he wanted to insult her, *actually enjoyed it,* she thought. The more she thought about it the angrier she got.

She was still shaking when she walked into the kitchen. She made up her mind to forget what had happened with Lawrence and picked up the straw broom and began to sweep when Virginia Reed came through the door. Virginia, a wooly haired, obese woman, was one of the oldest convicts at the plantation and a notorious gossip. Actually Jane found her amusing at times when she'd entertain the convicts with her mockery of certain members of the Browne family, Ella Marie in particular. But tonight Virginia seemed a little reserved, not at all her usual jovial self.

"Is there anything bothering you, Virginia?"

"Yes, this whole godless place bothers me," she answered.

"Other than that, I mean?"

"Jane, let me tells you something. I watched your little act on the stairs just now."

"And what is it you think you saw, may I ask?"

"You can act stupid if you wants to. But I can see what you have on your mind. If I was you girl, I'd watch myself. I can tell you, same as the Countess done said it, he wants you all right. You is a white gal and a mighty pretty one at that. I'm just saying, don't let that snake fool you. He's as slick as they come."

"What makes you say that? You talk as if you know plenty about Master Lawrence."

"Plenty enough I'd say. I been in this prison since he was a boy. I've seen him do things to convicts that would make yo' skin crawl. What I'm trying to tells you is, you'd better get your romantic thoughts straight about him. You is the same as the rest of us, a convict. And convicts is convicts no matter if Marse Lawrence is picky about who he beds up with. I'm telling you, gal, he's as ruthless as Jones and that George Ivan—only he don't use whips and chains; he uses his smarts."

Jane laughed even though her stomach was quaking so hard she could barely stand it. "I think you give him too much credit, Virginia. It seems to me, he just lets his manly needs rule his life."

"Don't be such a fool, child . . . he'll ruin you, same as them others—maybe worse if he really takes a liking to you, makes you falls in love with him."

You don't have to worry about me loving Lawrence Browne, she thought as she began to sweep. *Love is one thing he will never get from me.*

THE COUNTESS LOOKED UP from her writing table when Jane walked into her room later that night. Jane told her what had happened with Lawrence and what Virginia said about him.

"You listen to Virginia Reed and you'll be leaving this place in a pine box," the Countess said. "As I told you, he wants you in the worst way, but you're going to have to make the first move."

"Make the first move! You mean just pull up my skirt and show myself to him? Just fall back on one of the feather beds, open my legs and tell him to take what he wants? Is that what I'm supposed to do for Master Lawrence?"

"No, Cherie," the Countess laughed. "That's what Jones or one of those others would like, but not Master Lawrence. He wants you to want him. That's why he likes women like me and other older women who'll make the first move. He doesn't care why we do it. He just wants us to do it. It makes him feel less guilty."

The Countess got up from her chair and sat beside Jane on the bed. "Now listen to me, child. He wants you now, but he's not going to want you forever. He won't take you like Jones and the others just because he's attracted to you. He'll do something worse. He'll just forget about you, amuse himself with one of the other convicts and then where will you be? You'll wind up with one of those old retainers or worse yet, George Ivan, Ella Marie's rotten husband."

When she got in her bed that night all she could think about was what the Countess had said. The thought of it sickened her. She just couldn't end up like Nellie or some of the other women—abused and feeling worthless. *I felt that way enough with Dennis,* she thought. *This time I'm going to be stronger. This time I'm going to do it Charles' way. I'm going to think of myself. That's what I'm going to do. And Lawrence? In spite of what Virginia says about him, I think I can stand his company.* Or could she? Prostituting herself? Would God forgive her? Would she ever forgive herself? She was so full of fear and doubt and struggling with her conscience between right and wrong, tossing from one side of the bed to the other, she didn't hear her door open.

"Make one sound and I'll slit your throat from ear to ear," said a man's voice, crushing his calloused hand over her mouth. Jane opened her eyes and saw Jones standing over her. Her heart pounded. *Oh my God, he's going to kill me,* she thought, thrashing about trying to get out of his firm grip. "You been trying to get friendly with Miss Sara Rose's husband, haven't you, you little harlot?" he smirked, leaning close to her face. "If it's a man you after, you'd best stick to your own kind, somebody like me who understands you convicts." He grinned as he loosened his fingers just enough for her to sink her teeth into one. She bit down so hard she could hear his bone crunch. He yelped, pulled back, and ran out of the room. She sprang out of the bed and latched the door behind her, leaning against the hardwood, crying. "Oh God. Please help me!" *It must have been Sara Rose that sent him up here,* she thought. *God I'm not even safe in my own room. I'm doomed either way I go. I'll just have to think of another way of getting out of here. . . . Yes, that's what I'll do. I'll have to find another way besides Lawrence.*

Jane cried herself to sleep that night. She awoke to someone tapping on her door. *Oh God he's come back,* was her first thought, and her heart leaped up in her throat.

"Open the door," the Countess called out. "Nellie's gone. I can't find her anywhere. Is she in there with you?"

"No," Jane said, removing the chair from under the knob and unlatching the door.

"Well, she's gone. Dead I imagine," the Countess said coldly, craning her neck to look inside the room. "You didn't put any of your ideas into her head, did you?"

The bell rang down in the servant's quarters and Jane hurried to put on her uniform. "No, by God I did not!" Jane said. "But I can tell you this! Jones came into my room last night threatening me. I bit his hand and he ran out. You think he did something to Nellie when he left me? I smelled moonshine on his breath."

The Countess put a finger to her lips, "Shh. Don't ever mention that again," she whispered. "You be careful, Cherie. I don't want anything to happen to you."

As they stole quietly down the stairs Jane realized the Countess knew best. If she was going to survive, have any sort of life at all, she would follow her advice. If it took running after Lawrence Browne, then so be it. And she didn't have long to wait. As they walked through the back door, he was coming in from the fields. She noticed how different he acted this morning, how cheerful his mood was when he made eye contact.

Maybe he's not such a bad man, she thought. *Survival, that's what this is all about.* She saddened at the thought of it, turning her face away from Lawrence. *I'll never love anyone but Charles Fisher,* she silently cried.

⚓ Seven ⚓

"**T**HE CISTERN NEEDS cleaning badly, the water's full of larvae," Major Browne barked to the Countess before she even had a chance to pour his cup of hot chicory coffee. Jane stood behind the Countess holding a breakfast tray, hoping the Major would not have some new job for her today. Taking care of the Madam and Ella Marie's whims was already more than she could keep up with.

"Tell the stable boy he needs to clean the dirt-daubers out of the horse shed and the fence needs whitewashing. Now, see you get on it right away, Laura. Angola's party season is coming up soon. I don't want any of those legislators coming to my home and looking down their noses at me."

"I'll take care of it first thing this morning, Major," the Countess said to the master of Angola, who sat at the head of his massive rosewood dining table, knife and fork in hand, looking for all the world like a much older Grover Cleveland.

"See that you do, and get hold of the overseer Taylor and have him check out the warehouse by the landing. I found some washout next to the levee," he said, stuffing his mouth with a forkful of eggs.

The Major turned his attention to Lawrence who had just sat down for his breakfast. "There's some mending needed on the rails down by the brick yard. You might get some of the croppers to check out the levee in the bend. I was riding yesterday and saw some leakage. River water's coming fast from up north. Could bust the levee. If it does we're going to be in one hell of a mess."

"I'll talk to Taylor. Also I'll take a ride this morning and check it out, Papa," Lawrence said. He winked at Jane as she served him a plate of fried eggs, bacon and grits. "Might be it's just weak in that one spot."

"Yeah, well it won't hurt to see how solid it is all the way to the lake, maybe as far as the Pass. And while you're down there, look in on the hog pens. Make sure the rafts are good and sturdy just in case we flood out this year.

"Jane you get one of the little nigger girls in here. Have this furniture stripped and repolished. I want this house cleaned from top to bottom before you hang up those new curtains you sewed. My feather bed smells bad. Have Virginia Reed cut it open and empty the feathers. She can wash them in a tub of cold suds. Get the two octoroons up here to help. A little soap and water ain't gonna hurt them. Show them how to lay the feathers out in the garret to dry. You can't expect Laura to do everything. Dust must be an inch thick on that punkah," he said, waving his hand at the wooden fan above the table. If one speck of it falls on my plate I'll have the whole bunch of you whipped till you can't walk."

"Yes sir," Jane said. She hurried out to the kitchen before Lawrence and his father had a chance to dish out any more chores. "Annie May, Sugar, fetch that can of turpentine. Grab some clean rags and a bucket. I need you to help me in the Big House this morning."

As she and Annie May followed the Major's instructions white curtains fluttered in the open windows of the dining room. The heavy smell of the cleaning liquid burned Jane's nostrils as she thought about what Jones had done the night before. She wondered if she should keep quiet about it like the Countess had said or should she take a chance and say something to Lawrence or the Major. She didn't know what to do. She finished scrubbing the table legs, rubbed her hand over the clean surface, and tossed the smelly rag in a pan. "Take that out to the trash pile," she waved to Annie May, "it's choking me to death."

She began to spread the beeswax on the massive table that could seat twenty four. This was the great ancestral room the Madam liked to brag about. Her eyes wandered up toward the wall over the fireplace where a painting of the Major's father hung. Displayed proudly underneath, on the mantle, lay a saber. The sword was from some ancient battle the Madam had told Jane her father-in-law had fought in. The portrait of the man gave Jane an eerie feeling she was being watched even though she was alone in the room. His beady eyes reminded her of the Major. She looked away.

She thought about Nellie. No one dared to mention that the child was missing, since the guards hadn't said anything about a runaway, and Jane hadn't heard the dogs barking in the swamps. In her heart, she just knew Jones and Ivan had killed Nellie. Then a scratching noise came from inside the breakfront near the window.

"Miz Jane," came a soft whisper from inside the beautiful piece of furniture.

"For heaven's sake," Jane said. She yanked open the door with great relief. "What are you doing hiding in there, Nellie? You nearly frightened me to death! You know the Madam would skin you alive if she caught you in here."

"I is scared out of my wits—scared to go to sleep—scared they gonna bury me in that levee," Nellie said, as Jane pulled her out of the small opening.

"Well, I don't care how scared you are," Jane fussed. "Don't you do anything like this again. I told you I was going to speak to the Madam about you. Now don't make trouble for us or I won't do it."

"Yessum, Nellie will be real good if you does that."

That same night Jane sneaked Nellie up to her room and tucked her snugly into a quilt beside her bed. She secured a chair under the doorknob and bolted the lock. Then she lay awake listening to rain drops beat harder and harder against the dormer windows. Lightning lit up the room continuously. The rain had settled in late in the afternoon, but everyone thought it would be gone by nightfall. Storms, even heavy ones, never lasted very long in Louisiana. But when they did, if more than a foot of rain fell within a few hours, the Mississippi would swell to full bank.

Jane remembered one spring when she was a young girl. The river waters overflowed and swept away whole houses, even an entire community along the Black River. And she could never forget the death and devastation. Yellow fever had killed several in her papa's family. It made everyone afraid of flood waters and the diseases it brought.

The whinnying of horses and mules struggling to get out of the mud awakened Jane out of a deep sleep. It was barely daylight.

"You don't have time for breakfast, Master Lawrence!" she heard the frightened voice of the overseer shouting from down below. She swung her legs out of bed and dashed to the window that overlooked the Mississippi. The muddy river water was raging at full speed. Logs as big as trees were floating past steamboats struggling to tie up to the larger Cypress trees along the banks. *One more inch of water and that levee will be gone.* She shuddered at the thought as she stepped into her uniform skirt, pulling it up to her waist as quickly as she could.

"Nellie. Get up, Sugar," she said. "We've got to get downstairs."

As they ran into the dark hallway, Jane heard the Countess bustling about in her room and the Madam banging her cane on the hardwood floor for some assistance. "You scoot on down to the kitchen. Start a fire in the cook stove," she told Nellie. "Then go wake up Virginia Reed and the other women. I'll go see what the Madam wants."

"Jane, what's all the commotion going on downstairs?" the Madam demanded as soon as Jane opened her bedroom door. She motioned for Jane to lift the lid of her chamber pot.

"Looks like we might be sandbagging the levee this morning. River's awfully high," Jane said, pushing the chair up close to the bed.

"Well, scat," the Madam said. "Get on downstairs and ask the Major if we should be packing. I don't want to be caught up here in this dreadful place if it floods. The last time it took six weeks before the water went down and no boats could get near the landing for nearly a month—we could die up here—tell the Major I want to go to New Orleans."

"Jane," the Major yelled as she came out onto the porch. "You and the Countess get some gals in the kitchen. Pack up everything that ain't nailed down. If it floods we don't want to lose any food. Tell Virginia Reed to have the women pack all the bedding and their clothing. They may have to sleep on the balcony for a while. Send the stable boys to fetch a couple of the croppers. Have them haul all the furniture upstairs."

"Master Lawrence," the overseer Taylor said, as he walked off the back porch, "you need to have somebody move the cows to high ground—gotta get them hogs on the rafts—send somebody to move the sheep and let the horses loose. They'll find their own way."

"Jane," Lawrence said, as he got up on his horse, "make sure my children stay close to this house—on the porch if you can keep them on it."

"Jane," the Countess said, waving to her from the kitchen door.

"Wait! Wait! Wait!" Jane said, pounding her hand firmly on the wrought iron table beside the back door. "I can't do everything all at one time. I only have two hands and feet. We need to calm down. Everybody's in a frenzy."

"You gonna think frenzy if that river water comes pouring over that levee," Virginia Reed said, as she passed Jane with a rolled up mattress sagging over her head. "Way I sees it, ain't got more'n an hour before that levee breaks. This porch you lollygagging on will be ten feet under water."

"No . . . you don't," Jane screeched. She reached out to grab Lawrence's five year old son, Lawrence Jr. who sprinted out the back door with a red toy shovel under his arm. "Your Papa said he'd get the hair brush to you if you dare to get off this porch." The little boy took off back into the house, screaming for his mother. Sara Rose came out fussing, dodging the workers who were busily rushing in and out of the house with armloads of household goods. She shouted at Jane to leave her child alone.

Jane looked out toward the levee and could see Mary Ann, Lawrence's twelve year old daughter, running toward the river. *Good God in heaven, that child is going to drown if the levee breaks.* And Jane knew her own life hung in the balance if that happened.

"Pray for me," she said to the Countess, as she ran off the porch, heading for the side yard. She hopped up on the railway cart, grabbed the reins and nudged the old mule forward, moving slowly toward the levee. She heard the overseer calling out, "Head for the hills! Crevasse broke . . . levee's caving in!"

Before Jane could swing around, water came rushing up and sloshed over the cart knocking her off. She fell backward, struggling to keep afloat. She heard Mary Ann scream and looked out over the raging water. The child was clinging to a board jutting out from the warehouse. "Hang on, Mary Ann," Jane called out. She could hear Sara Rose screaming from the house.

"If my child dies, you can believe your days will be numbered!"

Probably so, Jane thought, as she thrashed about trying to swim toward the little girl. *And I suppose it's all my fault her child left the house? Can't Sara Rose take any responsibility for keeping her children safe?*

Jane reached the spot where Mary Ann was hanging on to the board and the two of them clung together for their lives. Screams coming from the Big House were drowned out by loud hollering from men who had been swept into the river. Animal carcasses floated by. Mary Ann was so frightened, Jane fiercely held her closer to her own body to hold down her fear and keep her warm. Then Lawrence came into view, paddling a small flat boat up to where they were holding on. He grabbed Mary Ann and jerked her into the boat, then reached out for Jane, pulling her in also.

The boat, flimsy against the wild waters, rolled side to side while Lawrence rowed close enough to the Big house for the Countess to throw them a rope and pull them in.

"I'll have you whipped for letting my child get out in that water," Sara Rose hissed at Jane. Hanging over the rails, she took Mary Ann out of Lawrence's arms and into the Big House.

"Don't worry about her," Lawrence said, as he lifted Jane's wet, shivering body out of the boat and up onto the second floor porch. "She's just talking out of her head like she always does. It's something about the wilderness out here that gets to her, just like the croppers when they eat Polk-salad that's not cooked right. Makes her crazy sometimes." He pulled himself out of the boat and stood looking down at Jane. He dropped his hand on hers and squeezed it, "Thank you for helping Mary Ann," he said. "She would have drowned without your help."

She shared a warm smile with him and thought that no matter what kind of man he was to others, he stood before her a concerned and loving father. Then, piercing screams rang out across the balcony. Lawrence Jr. had fallen in the water on the back side of the house. She saw Sara Rose run out of the back door, climb over the rails and jump in. Jane took off running into the wide hall, up to the rear balcony, with Lawrence fast behind her. They both dove into the water searching for his son. Her foot touched the struggling little body and when she reached down and grabbed the child, he went limp. Pushing up through the water with all her might, her hand clutching his leg, Jane surfaced, and saw the Countess waiting to haul the child out of the water.

Jane and Lawrence were pulled onto the balcony by George Ivan and the plantation physician, Dr. Taylor. Lawrence quickly swept his child out of the Countess' arms. He began to beat on his back, holding him head down while everyone stood around moaning, praying Lawrence, Jr. would make it. Finally the boy began to spit up the muddy water. His body wiggled out of his papa's arms on to the floor. Lawrence picked him up and carried him into the parlor where Ella Marie threw a blanket over his wet body. A dozen cheers rang out for Lawrence, Jr. Then Virginia Reed burst through the door, her arms flapping above her head, crying loudly as she ran into the room. "It's Miz Sara Rose! She done drowned! I seen her floating in the water on the other side of the pecan orchard."

The Madam fainted onto the rattan sofa and Jane collapsed in a chair. *Dear God in Heaven,* Jane prayed, too exhausted to move even a muscle. *How could she drown with over forty people standing around on the porches?* "What will happen to those little children?" she whispered. "God, why did you take Sara Rose away from them?"

Jane thought about Georgia Ann. She could still hear her own child crying after her that day at the landing, begging them not to take away her mama. She dropped her face in her hands. The sobs coming from deep within almost took her breath away. From where she sat, Jane could see Ella Marie crushed up against Virginia Reed's big bosom. *A convict giving Ella comfort,* she thought as she watched Sara Rose's children crying and clinging to their mama who lay dead on the porch after she was pulled from the water. Lawrence was trying to coax them away from the dreadful scene. Jane had to close her eyes. Georgia Ann's little face kept creeping into her thoughts until Jane shook her head so hard she thought she might have sprung her neck. *Little children need their mama,* she kept saying over and over to herself.

She took a deep breath and pulled out her wet handkerchief to wipe the tears from her face. She had to try and help these children. Somehow if she could ease the pain in their hearts, it would relieve the guilt she was feeling. She thought about her plan of committing adultery with Lawrence for her own gain and she felt ashamed. Maybe after this tragic accident she could persuade Lawrence to allow Ander a transfer to Angola. Maybe Lawrence would be more understanding now that his own children were motherless. Just maybe Lawrence would help to get her and Ander out of their troubles without her having to sell her soul to the devil.

⁑ Eight ⁑

TENSION WAS HIGH at the plantation following the flood and Sara Rose's death and burial. Jane and the other convicts worked around the clock to please the Major and Mrs. Browne, but it was three weeks before the water receded, before she could see some semblance of normal life returning.

The warm weather dried up the ground quickly and male convicts from the camps were sent to help the sharecroppers clear and plow the fields. Some were sent to the Big House to clean the first floor and basement, and haul all the furniture back downstairs. In spite of all the activity, though, a terrible gloom pervaded the Big House. Ella Marie sank deeper into her depressed state. She clung to Lawrence's children. With Lawrence's permission, as soon as the steamers could dock safely at the landing, the Major sent the children with Ella and George Ivan down to New Orleans for a change of atmosphere. The convict women moved back to their quarters and the Big House began to settle down. Jane thought it a pity that only the Madam and the convicts ever mentioned Sara Rose. To the men of this household it was as if she had never been here in the first place.

"Laura! Jane! One of you get up here this minute!" Jane heard the Madam shout, and she sprinted up the stairs, two steps at a time.

"Hand me that invitation from Governor Foster over there in my mail basket," the Madam barked from her bedside, pointing to her Chippendale claw-foot writing table.

Oh, there's going to be a big fight over this, Jane thought as she picked up the small envelope and placed it in the Madam's hand while the Major looked on.

"What good is reading that letter again?" the Major shouted at his wife. "You're going with me to Baton Rouge even if I have to haul you there in a cotton wagon. This is one party we are not going to miss. We can't afford to." He lowered his voice and sat beside the Madam on the four poster tester bed. "You know Foster's clipped the wings of Norris and his state lottery, and now he's threatening to take away my leasing contract."

"But darling. We just lost our beloved Sara Rose. They'll understand. Besides, I don't feel like going to their party," the Madam said and snapped her fingers for Jane to hand her her spectacles. "You know how I feel about your cronies and the parties those men have down in Baton Rouge. I just don't want to go."

"Well, I don't give a damn! You're going!" he bellowed.

"But why?"

"Because it's important to me, Emma. You know all the talk about abolishing convict leasing. Baton Rouge says they're going to reform the penal system if they have to throw me out of Louisiana to do it. Foster's behind it. I sure don't want to do anything to offend him now. If I can't buy him off like I did the others, maybe I can flatter the do-gooder and stop him that way."

"Jane, pour me a glass of water and get my medicine out of the cabinet," the Madam whined. "My head's about to split wide open."

Jane jumped at the chance to get out of the line of fire of these two. When the major pushed the Madam to anger, you never knew what she'd do. Once Jane had seen her pick up the nearest object and hurl it at his head and several times Jane noticed the convicts with cuts and bruises from the Madam's flying glass.

"Major, you know I can't ride on bumpy country roads. I'd just as soon walk first," the Madam said after swallowing two spoons of the cloudy liquid.

"Don't worry about how we're going to get there, Precious," he said, as he pecked a wet kiss on her sagging jowl, then walked out.

After the Major shut the door, the Madam threw the envelope on the floor. "Jane, you go down to the landing and tell Captain

Williams that unless he wants to find himself another job, he'd better see to it *The Sparks* is at my disposal for this trip."

"Yes Ma'am," Jane answered and waited a moment for the laudanum to soothe the Madam. She knew if she was going to ask a favor she needed the Madam as calm as possible. "The Major seems a little disturbed about the lack of help the Countess and I have had for the downstairs parlors," she said. Jane waited for a reaction but only got a blank stare. "Madam, do you think it's possible for the girl Nellie to be trained for house work? She's strong and I can teach her to give you back rubs. It will give the Countess and me more time to spend on your personal grooming."

"Well, I don't see any harm in it," she slurred, lying back on her pile of feather pillows, admiring her hands. "I could use more care on my fingernails. God knows I need more attention for my poor aching feet, and my jewels haven't been cleaned in over a week."

Jane was grateful. That was one less worry for her and now she could keep an eye on Nellie.

The following Monday Jane and the Countess hauled valise after valise down the stairs while Nellie dragged as many as she could out on the front porch for Jacob to load onto the railcart.

"Going to be some peace and quiet around here for the next four days," Jacob said as Jane walked to the cart and handed him the Madam's two hat boxes.

"It will be nice to have a breather, Jacob," Jane said. "And even nicer that George Ivan is in New Orleans."

"Yessum, you is right about that. That's one man I believe is touched by the devil. When Marse Browne gone away from the plantation that Marse George shore is bad. Just as bad as that man Jones, and us convicts don't know what to expect from Jones this time, since he's been left in charge all by hisself."

"I don't think we have anything to worry about with Jones. Master Lawrence will be staying. I heard him tell his papa he wouldn't be going to Baton Rouge. He has a lot of work to do."

"Yessum, if you says so," Jacob said, and held the reins on the old mule tight, as the Major and his wife came out of the house.

WITH THE FAMILY GONE, Jane decided now was the time to try and talk to Lawrence about Ander. She knew Lawrence's routine as well as she did the Major and Mrs. Browne's. He always made sure he was back at the Big House to join the major for breakfast at nine o'clock every morning, and was usually at the table for dinner, but Jane wasn't so sure what his routine would be now that the family had gone to Baton Rouge.

That morning, when nine o'clock had come and gone and there was no sign of Lawrence, Jane was disappointed. She had planned on serving Lawrence breakfast at the big dining table, and even got up earlier than usual to sprinkle sugar on fresh strawberries because she knew how much he liked them. There was no sign of Lawrence at noon either. Jane figured he would skip the afternoon tea since the Madam was gone. That evening she set the elegant table for dinner and lit every candelabra Mrs. Browne had in the house, waiting for him to come until long past suppertime. When he didn't show up, she sadly blew out the last of the candles. She sat in the kitchen until Virginia Reed had finished cleaning up and had gone back to the quarters.

The night was humid, typical for Louisiana late spring evenings, and Jane felt a restlessness envelop her. She walked into the warm night air, and began thinking about Charles and how nice it had been at the end of the day when they would spend the evening on the front porch swing until time to go to bed; how he had held her in his arms and how much she'd loved the old German songs he sang; how much she'd missed the way she melted against his body when he kissed her.

Wandering through the warm night, sounds from the river enticed her past the pecan orchard. The moon slipped out from behind the clouds and the dark night became almost as light as early morning. Nearing the landing she could smell the wild onions that were blooming in profusion near the little lake behind the Big House.

This was the first time in a while she could remember not being dog tired. She wanted to savor every moment of it. When she reached the levee she sat down on the grassy slope watching the steamers that slowly passed, churning the murky waters of the Mississippi River. The torches encircling the steamboats lighted up the river like a giant stage as the sounds of, "Hel-lo My Ba-by, Hel-lo

My Hon-ey, Hel-lo My Ragtime Gal", drifted from one of the paddle wheelers, piercing Jane's lonely heart.

Then she heard a soft voice behind her. "Beautiful night, isn't it?" It was Lawrence. He rode up next to her and slid off of his horse.

"Yes, it is," she said, looking straight ahead into the river pretending not to notice as he sat on the slope beside her.

"It's a shame the onion fields are the only crop to survive the flood. They sure have a nauseating smell, don't they?"

"Oh, I don't know about that. I kind of like the aroma."

He chuckled as he always did. "Wild onions smelling good? You're the only one I have ever heard say that."

Watching out the corner of her eye she noticed Lawrence take off his riding gloves, lay them on the slope, and fall back in the cool willowy grass. She didn't know what to say to him. She wanted to ask him about Ander, if maybe he could help her get out of Angola, but this was not the time for that kind of conversation, she realized.

They sat silently, listening to the night sounds as thousands of crickets clicked their heels trying to drown out the music and laughter of the river traffic. She took a deep breath and slowly let it out. Still after all they had been through this past month, she couldn't bring herself to feel a spark or even a twinge of emotion for Lawrence. She was confused by her lack of feeling. The day they had buried his wife, she had cried, and if the circumstances had been different she would have put her arms around him at the gravesite to comfort him. Now she felt dead inside. All along she'd been hoping for such a moment as this, only to dread that the time had come.

"I was hoping that you would come out for a walk tonight, Jane," he finally said, then gently clutched her hand, pulling her down beside him. He rolled over in the grass until he was staring into her eyes. "You know you're a beautiful woman. I've been thinking about you all day. I wanted you to come to me. Did you know that? Did you feel me wanting you?"

She cringed. *Let go of my hand,* she thought, but before she could stop him, he was tugging at the buttons on her bodice. She could see his face clearly in the moonlight and for a moment the look in his eyes reminded her of Charles.

"Damn these things," he swore and pulled so hard the buttons popped off.

Warm tears slid out the corner of her eyes. She bit the inside of her mouth to keep from crying out. She really didn't want it to happen. Not tonight. Not when Charles was so much in her thoughts. *How could he do this so soon after his wife died?* she wondered and wriggled away from him. She sat up, but she knew she had to let him do it no matter how immoral or distasteful it was. He was going to take her and nothing she did was going to stop him. He clutched her arm and pulled her back down, crushing his full lips against hers. He pinned her beneath him and pulled her bodice apart, staring at her naked breasts. Tugging on her underdrawers, he pulled them down her legs and over her feet. He stood up. Unbuttoning his shirt, he slipped both arms out, and dropped it. He pushed his pants below his knees and lowered himself on her, gliding his fingers slowly up her leg. Her insides quivered. Moist lips nibbled her neck. Her nipples hardened against him. Sliding down her stomach, his warm mouth suckled her breast. He groaned. She could feel his perspiration, his broad chest, slick with sweat. The moon drowned behind a large cloud, a gentle breeze whipped around them. He whispered, "Do you want me, little one?"

She swallowed hard and placed her arms around his neck.

He began to kiss her roughly. "Try to love me just a little," he murmured passionately.

I'll try Lawrence, but I can't promise you anything, she thought. She closed her eyes and the memories of a hundred nights in Charles Fisher's arms overcame her. Lawrence's body became Charles' body. His manly smell mingling with the smell of tobacco, and his skin, so soft, yet firm and so warm, awakened her senses. Charles had come back to her and her mind was firmly focused on his smiling lips. She was looking at Lawrence, but when she reached out to touch his face, it was Charles' face she felt, Charles' hot kisses on her mouth. It was Charles moving around on top of her, and she silently called his name, *Charles, Charles,* as Lawrence crushed himself hard against her.

⚓ Nine ⚓

JANE STOOD behind the balcony doors on the second floor listening to Lawrence and his mother arguing as they sipped their afternoon tea. Once again she was eavesdropping when she should have been working, but the heated discussion involved her—her and Lawrence. She had feared it would come to this. Now all she could do was stand by and listen to the insults, and the Madam's harsh words struck her to the heart.

"I told you if you became intimate with that damnable convict, I'd send her to a levee camp, and by God I'm going to do just that."

"What are you talking about, Mama?"

"Don't you pull one of your papa's stunts on me, Lawrence Browne, lying like a dog trotting. You know as well as I do everybody on this plantation is talking about you and that convict. You think they don't see you sneaking her down to the boathouse? Jones told me he's seen you twice riding with her, riding in your papa's carriage down by the gin, and George Ivan said you opened an account for her at the store."

In a rage, the Madam picked up her Limoges tea cup and hurled it at the floor. Jane winced, realizing she would have to clean up the shattered pieces later. But she stood frozen, almost afraid to breathe when she heard Lawrence shout. "If you try to do anything to her, Mama, I promise, you'll never see me again."

"Don't you threaten me, Lawrence Browne. This isn't your papa who backs down every time you have a temper tantrum. This is me, your mama, and I won't have it."

Jane peeked through the crack of the open door. The Madam was flushed and her hands were shaking. But Lawrence looked calm. His voice softened. "This isn't a threat, Mama. This is a promise," he said. "You do anything to hurt her and the last thing you'll ever see of me is my back as I leave this God-forsaken place, and I'll take her with me."

The only answer Lawrence got was a hysterical scream that echoed through the whole house, but Lawrence did not back down. He stared at his mama as if she were a lunatic. Jane watched as he handed the Madam his handkerchief.

"You just don't understand," his mama said, shaking her head and blowing her nose. "Don't you realize how very embarrassing this is to me? Don't you realize you're sending your own soul to hell, all for a convict? I regret now I felt sorry for her and took her under my wing."

Under your wing? Jane thought. *Why if it wasn't for your need of house slaves at your beck and call, the Countess and me and that poor simple child Nellie would all be pushing wheelbarrows in a levee camp.*

"Oh, Mama, you don't feel sorry for anyone," he quickly answered.

"Well, I did for her."

"Mama. . . . "

Lawrence had told Jane many times since the night he first took her how much he loved her, and that he would fight anyone on the penal farm who tried to do her harm. At first she didn't believe him. She thought it was only his conquest of her, and her giving in to him without a fight—or the fact that she was the only white woman he could have on the plantation. But more and more lately, he had become a different person; a gentle man, almost proud when he was with her. And now with the things he was saying to his mother; even Jane had to believe he might love her.

"Lawrence, don't do this," the Madam said, getting up from her chair and moving behind him, placing her arms around his neck. "My little Punkin' Pie," she cooed in his hair. "Don't you realize what this girl is trying to do to you? She'll ruin you if she can. Hasn't Mama always told you what convicts will do to the men here if given half a chance? She's just using you, Lawrence, thinking somehow you have the power to get her out of here."

"Mama, you don't know what you're talking about. Jane's not the using kind. You took her under your wing, as you so eloquently put it. Don't you know her by now?"

"Very well, if you don't care about yourself, have you at least thought about what you're doing to your family? Your children will be home soon. Mary Ann's old enough to see what's going on; and what about your young son? Are you going to tell him a convict is taking his mama's place? Do you realize what your papa will do if you get this woman with child?"

Jane hadn't thought about Lawrence's children. They had never discussed them. The Madam was right about one thing, they would hate her when they found out. And sooner or later Lawrence would think about what his mama was saying. Jane twisted her body out of the folds of the heavy drapery, but she couldn't bring herself to walk away. She stood still listening to every word.

"Papa doesn't care what I do with her," Jane heard him say.

"Oh, my boy, you're wrong about that," the Madam scoffed. "You do anything to embarrass your papa the way you're doing me, you know what he'll do? He'll make you rue the day you met that convict. He's got enough to worry about now with Governor Foster and those penal reformers. He's like a stick of dynamite and I don't think I have to remind you, it won't take much to set him off. Is that what you want for this woman, Lawrence? Do you want your papa to take care of her?"

Lawrence fidgeted with his teacup. Standing up, he hesitated, then kissed his mother and Jane heard him tell her he'd think about what she had said.

"Don't go yet, Lawrence," the Madam said, almost pleading. "While I can never condone your behavior with this woman, perhaps if you'll be more private about it, your papa won't have to know. Let this just be a warning. We'll keep it between us. You watch yourself, though. Don't let her use you."

Jane stood silent, waiting to hear the rest of the Madam's pleas to Lawrence. The woman infuriated Jane. What nerve she had saying Jane was using Lawrence. Mrs. Browne used everyone in sight.

When she had no more use for them, she cast them aside like one of her old dresses.

"I asked you kindly, Mama. Don't say she's using me. Don't say it again, please," he said, his jaws clenched as he walked away from the table.

"For pity's sake, Lawrence, don't you know who you are? You're a Browne and she's nothing," the Madam said, reaching out to grab his arm. She raised her voice. "She's used her body to trick you. Don't you see that? Don't you see what she's trying to do? Convicts will try anything to gain their freedom!"

Lawrence pulled his arm away from his mother's grasp and gave her a burning look. "She may be a convict, but you're wrong. She hasn't used me. Have you forgotten she's the one who jumped into the flood water to save your grandchildren? You know the reason why she's in this place. She's not a criminal. I've fallen in love with her, Mama. Can't you understand that? For the first time in my life I am really in love."

Jane watched as the Madam's face grew stark white. "Love?" she yelled. "You don't know the first thing about love, Son. Do you remember telling me how much you loved Sara Rose when you wanted to marry her? She was from a fine family and yet you remember how your papa reacted and how much trouble it caused. This woman is a common criminal. Your papa is liable to kill her!"

Jane slipped and fell back into the curtain. But instead of waiting for Lawrence to answer his mother, she struggled up, tiptoed to the stairs and hastily walked down. She was surprised at what Lawrence had said to his mother. The thought of his feelings gave her a warmness toward him, but she knew in her heart the Madam was speaking the truth about the Major. He was capable of anything. The only one who had influence over him was his wife, and that worried Jane. If the Madam told the Major to get rid of her, he would do it. And Jane didn't think even Lawrence could stop him.

AFTER THAT DAY on the balcony, Jane worried incessantly about her situation. It was never far from her mind.

"I know that you say you love me, and I don't doubt that you mean it," she told Lawrence that night as they lay together by the

river. "But there's no future for us. I am a convict. You can have pleasure with a prisoner, but you can't be in love with one. Your world
doesn't allow you to fall in love with just anyone that you take a
fancy to, especially someone like me."

"I'll make it work," he told her, sounding more sincere than she'd
ever heard him. "I assure you I can do it. I know what people think
about me, what they say about me: that I'm a rich dilettante who
cares more for gambling and horses than anything else; that I never
loved my wife when she was alive; that I keep women in New
Orleans; and that I've never done an honest day's work in my life.
Well, it's true. All of it. At least it was until I fell in love with you.
Everything's changed now. I've changed. I don't want to drift along
anymore accepting things the way they are. I don't want to continue
to be the son of a rich man who has to ask for money to gamble,
like a little boy asking for money for penny candy."

Jane stared into his face intently as he spoke. She wanted to believe in him. "Lawrence, if what you're saying is true, do something
about it. Don't just talk about it. Take me out of here. Send for my
little girl and have Ander taken out of the levee camp. Take us
some place where we can be safe, some place where we can be a
family. I'm afraid of what your mama will do to me if I stay now.
You know the business your family's in; the way they feel about
convicts."

"I know. But I just have to think about it," he said. "Where could
we go that you would be safe?"

"Any place would be better than in here."

"Don't start worrying about your safety. Nobody is going to harm
you as long as I'm around."

"What about your papa? He doesn't think twice about killing
convicts if they step in his way."

"Jane. Papa only kills niggers and lazy Irishmen."

"What do you think I am, Lawrence?"

"I know you're Irish, but you're being foolish. I don't know of a
white convict that's died yet except from a disease or being eaten up
by the dogs as he was trying to escape. I know my father's not what
he'd like for people to believe, but he would not murder a white
woman."

"Your mama seems to think he would and I think you need to wake up to what he is, Lawrence. He could cut my throat and eat an apple at the same time. I've heard your mama say those very words to her brother, Henry. You told me yourself you question where any of your family would be if your papa hadn't gotten in with the Ring Bosses after the war. Everybody in Louisiana knows what those men are capable of doing. They don't care what color a man is. If they came here tomorrow and said cut off the white girl's head, your papa would do it. If he takes a hankering to get rid of me, there's not one thing you can do about it, and from the looks of it, I don't think you want to."

"Jane don't say things like that. I hate all of this scheming and skulduggery as much as you do, but I can't take you out of here. There's no place we could hide from him. Papa would track us down and kill you for sure."

"Then you're saying I'll never get out of here?"

"I'm not saying never."

"You're just like your mama and papa," she said, and stood up. "You'll use me until I can no longer be useful; the way your mama accused me of using you. If all you wanted was to bed me, why didn't you just do it and let it go at that? You didn't have to pretend to love me." She brushed the tears from her cheeks and dusted the back of her uniform skirt, turned away from him and stalked off.

"I didn't mean to say anything to hurt you. Don't judge me by them, Precious," he pleaded, running along beside her. "I'd be the happiest man in the world if I never again had to see Angola and all the misery it stands for. I promise as long as we stay here, I won't let them harm you. I've told you that a thousand times. I'll find a way for us; and I'll find a way to get you and your boy out of prison."

THE NEXT MORNING the Countess accosted her. "Cherie, there is hell to pay. The Madam has locked herself up in her boudoir, pouting. She has requested that you work in the kitchen," she said, as she filled a tray with the Madam's boiled egg and toasted biscuit, her voice full of concern. "She said you are not to show your face in her room if you know what's good for you."

"Did she give you a reason why?"

"Did she have to?" the Countess said, coldly, staring at Jane with scornful eyes.

"No."

"You wait for me right here until I get through with her this morning," the Countess said, and carried the tray out the door.

Jane was in the kitchen mopping the blue stone floors when the Countess came back a while later. "Let's you and me sit down and have a talk," she said and shooed Nellie out of the door. Pouring two cups of hot coffee, Jane placed one in front of the Countess and sat opposite her at the work table.

"If you are to be with Master Lawrence," the Countess said, taking a sip, "then you must learn to be discreet. The Madam is in such a rage, she's ordered a small pistol to be brought to her room."

"I told Lawrence something like this would happen," Jane said, picking up her spoon, stirring it around and around in her cup.

"Well, you obviously didn't make him understand. I've never seen his mama so angry."

"I've tried. God knows I have. I told Lawrence he would get us in trouble. I really did try," she cried, terrified she would be sent to a levee camp in spite of Lawrence's promises to take care of her.

"Oh no, you didn't, Cherie," the Countess said in an icy voice that Jane had never heard before. "You didn't try hard enough. You gave in. You let Lawrence have the upper hand."

"But I. . . . "

"There's nothing wrong in letting Lawrence have you, even for a price," the Countess interrupted, placing her fingertips on the table in front of Jane's cup. "There is nothing wrong in enjoying the pleasure of it, but you wanted more. You wanted him to love you." She leaned back in her chair, lifting her cup to her lips, glaring at Jane over the rim. She sighed, "Don't you know that women in our situation can never have love? Not the kind of love that I had from my friend in New Orleans. Not the kind of love that Charles Fisher gave you. Don't you realize that's past for us now."

"Just because we're convicts doesn't mean we're not supposed to feel anything any more, does it?" Jane asked, tearfully. "Did we lose that privilege too when we were sent to this wretched place?"

"Don't be foolish, Cherie. You wanted more from him than he was free to give you. You used your body to get it, and Mrs. Browne knows it."

"Are you calling me a whore?" Jane blurted out without thinking. "Is that what you're saying? Are you saying that I'm just like you, that I only let him have me because I wanted something from him? Did you forget you're the one who threw me at him."

As soon as she said the harsh words, Jane regretted them. This was the woman who'd been her friend, the woman who'd taught her how to survive in this dreadful place and get through those first terrible months. "I'm sorry. I didn't mean that. I didn't mean any of it," Jane said, reaching across the table, trying to grab the Countess' arm.

The Countess pulled back. "Yes, you are just like me, Jane," she said, slamming the palm of her hand on the table. "You are a whore as surely as I am. Whether men pay you with money or with kindness and favors or with the promise of love, most women are. Women are considered not much better than slaves. Convict women, free white and black women, even rich women like the Madam use their bodies. We have to. We have no choice."

"I don't understand what you're talking about," Jane said, flatly.

"Well, let me see if I can explain it better. The law treats us no better than chattel. It's men who have the power. They control our lives. If women are not clever enough, they could all find themselves locked up the way we are, or walking the streets begging for food, or scratching for money to buy clothes. That's why we have to be clever, and like all women who are, we use our bodies to get ahead in this world."

"Are you trying to say that I'm clever, Countess?"

The Countess relented and chuckled out loud. "Jane, it's women like you who give women like me a bad name. Of course you're clever. Too clever by far. He fell in love with you, didn't he?"

"I still don't know what you're getting at," Jane said.

"No, Cherie, I don't believe you do."

Despite being a bit annoyed with her friend Jane could tell the Countess was exhausted and seemed to have an awful lot on her mind. "Countess, you have black circles under your eyes. Are you all right? Are you sick?"

The Countess stared blankly at Jane. "I am going to have a child, Cherie, and I haven't told the Major yet."

Jane's eyes popped wide open.

"Don't look at me like that," the Countess said. "It will be all right. Nobody else knows about it. And don't worry, I have great hopes that he will take me out of here, maybe to his house in New Orleans and maybe Lawrence can have you brought with me."

"Do you really think so? I don't," Jane said. "If we left, who would take care of the Madam? She will never let both of us go."

"Perhaps you are right, Cherie. Perhaps so," she said. Both palms down on the table, the Countess pushed herself up out of the chair. There was something she wasn't revealing. Jane could see it in her eyes, the way she seemed to suddenly become listless. The look of fear, that's what it was, and Jane knew the Countess wasn't at all sure of how the Major would react, but she did not confront the Countess with any more questions.

"I'll talk to Lawrence if you think I should, Countess, and I'll tell you this much, I am going to stop seeing him if he doesn't take me out of here. I intend to tell him so tonight. My safety is more important to me than he is. Besides, he's already said he couldn't help me. I can't see any reason to continue with him, especially if it causes so much anguish to everyone."

"Well even if you continue seeing him, make sure it's in the dead of night so no one will see you. The Major has already made the remark to the Madam he only tolerates you because you amuse Lawrence."

Jane took a deep breath through her nose. Her nostrils flared out. *Amuse his son!* she thought. *That hateful old man.*

That night Jane was careful when she sneaked out to meet Lawrence at the boathouse. She crept silently along the rail track instead of going the short way through the pecan orchard.

"Lawrence," she said, pulling out of his embrace in the doorway and quickly closing the door behind her. "Put out the lantern. I don't want anyone to know I'm down here."

"What are you so afraid of, Precious?"

"Lawrence, be serious. I am not in the mood for your silly jokes. You know good and well I'm afraid of your mama and papa!"

"That's nothing new, so's everyone else in this place," he chuckled, pulling her into his arms and pressing his lips hard against hers.

"You're not funny, Lawrence," she said, wriggling free of his arms. "Your mama has locked herself up in her room. She won't let me near her. The Countess is very worried about it."

"Well, don't you worry about Mama, I'll talk to her. And Papa, he'll be in Baton Rouge until the session is over. He's got his hands full. Papa's about to lose the convict leases, girl. You're the least of his worries."

"Well, I have other things to say to you and you're going to have to take me seriously this time. I trusted that you could keep me safe from your parent's wrath, but now, the way your mama's acting, I just don't think so. You're not standing in my shoes, Lawrence. You could never understand my fear. I have a small daughter waiting for me to come home and I want to get back to her in one piece if I can, even if I have to serve out my whole sentence. But that will never happen unless I can get your mama's trust again. She's upset with me enough to send me to a levee camp. I believe she means what she says, Lawrence."

"I've never known Mama to mean anything she says. You're being ridiculous. You're just trying to hurt me because I won't take you and your son out of here," he said, clutching her arm tightly.

"You're wrong, Lawrence," she whispered, and for a moment he frightened her. "You're going to have to accept it, too. Our relationship can never be any more than it is—an affair."

"Do you love me?" he asked, tightening his grip on her arm.

"I care very much for your feelings," she answered. Instantly she was more than afraid of him. Perhaps it was the way he was staring into her eyes; something about the intense look on his face as his jaws tightened; or it was the way he clamped his teeth tightly together that made her heart suddenly start to throb rapidly.

"I asked you, do you love me?" He pulled her into his arms and slid his fingers slowly around her neck, brushing his lips across her eyes and then to her ear. "Do you love me?" he demanded.

"Yes, I love you, Lawrence," she lied.

⫴ Ten ⫴

THE AFTERNOON was so hot and humid, Jane thought she'd die before night came and cooled down the house. The Madam had relented and was using Jane as before, but she had been in a terrible mood all morning despite Jane's eagerness to please her. She had just received a letter from the Major, delivered earlier by steamer from Baton Rouge. Jane knew it had something to do with the business of the convict lease the Major was fighting the state government so hard to retain. She realized that the Madam was scared of losing her posh life at Angola.

"Well, I guess he'll be coming back from Baton Rouge with his tail tucked between his legs," the Madam told Jane as Jane bathed down her sweating body with a damp cloth she had dipped in cool spring water. "He lost the contract."

"You mean there will be no more leasing convicts out to levee camps?"

"Yes, dearie, that's exactly what I mean," the Madam said, rolling her gross body over on her stomach pointing to the back of her head. "There, wet my neck down."

Lawrence knocked gently on his mother's bedroom door. "Can I come in, Mama?"

The Madam tried to sit up. "Here, pull me up, girl. My Lawrence is here to see me," she said, both of her heavy arms clutching to Jane's smaller one. "Get on out of here and bring us some cool lemonade. Scat," she said, waving Jane out.

"Whoa . . . Where are you going in such a hurry?" Lawrence asked, reaching out to slow Jane down as he came through the door.

"She's going to get us some lemonade, Punkin'," the Madam answered.

"She's staying. I don't want any lemonade," he said. "I just ran up for a minute to see what Papa had to say. I heard you received a letter from him this morning."

"Yes," she began, then shot a look at Jane. "Lawrence, let her go to the kitchen. I don't feel comfortable talking with her in here."

"For God's sake, Mama. What did Papa have to say? Don't worry about Jane. She's not going to spread our business around."

"Well, if you're going to stay and listen to my conversation you may as well continue wetting me down," she said to Jane, easing back on her pillow.

"And yes, Lawrence, your papa lost the contract. Seems all his friends in high places have abandoned him. Didn't do him one bit of good, spending all his money trying to buy off those do-gooders. The letter said that after the contract runs out, in five years, the state intends to take back all the criminals and house them in the old prison at Baton Rouge."

"Did Papa say when he was coming home?"

"Said he was taking the train to St. Francisville to see his lawyer. Then he'd be on home sometime this afternoon."

"It's awfully hot out there for him to be riding that distance," Lawrence said. He put on his hat and walked to the door. "Jane if you have the time, you think you can fix me a bite to eat?"

"Let that Virginia Reed do it," the Madam piped in. "I need Jane up here."

"I want her to cook me some chicken and dumplings and fry some potatoes," Lawrence insisted. "Virginia Reed doesn't know the first thing about dumplings. I like the way Jane cooks them. They're creamy and taste good."

"Mrs. Browne, I won't be long," Jane said, giving her one last wet rub. "I'll go put the chicken on and get back to you as soon as I can."

"Never mind," the Madam grumbled, swatting her hand away. "Send Nellie up here. She can do it."

The kitchen was even hotter than the Madam's bedroom. The July wind which stirred the leaves of the pecan trees seemed to penetrate mercilessly through the twelve inch brick walls. Jane opened the window above the worktable for a little ventilation and asked Virginia Reed to cut up the hen. She mixed up the flour and water for the dumplings, kneaded the mixture until it was stiff and then set it aside. She began to sprinkle flour on the table to roll out the dough when she heard a buggy come into the side yard. She looked out the window and noticed the Major motioning one of the stable boys to unhitch the horse. The Countess, who'd been picking herbs in the kitchen garden, approached him. Jane gave them no more than a curious glance, until she realized that the Countess was crying. Jane stood silently watching. She could see they were arguing about something, and guessed immediately what it might be.

Suddenly the Major pulled back from the Countess's reach. He stumbled and fell back against his horse and tried to grab hold of the buggy. His sudden movement frightened the animal and the horse whinnied and danced away, trying to break free from the young black stable boy. The Countess leaped toward the Major and grabbed him with both hands to keep him from falling. For a moment the white master and his black concubine looked as though they were about to dance. Then the Major regained his footing, used his weight to throw the Countess to the ground and without saying a word began to beat her with his whip. Each time the Countess screamed, begging him to stop, he slashed her body again with the black leather whip. The Countess covered her face with both hands to ward off the savage blows and as she did, the Major kicked her repeatedly in the stomach with his boot.

Jane couldn't believe her eyes. She had to help the Countess or the Major would kill her. She dropped everything and dashed out the door, sprinting toward the Major.

"Don't you touch her!" he bellowed, still holding his whip. "Do you hear me? Let her be. I don't want a God-damn one of you convicts helping her."

Brushing the dust off his clothes, the stout little man waddled up the steps and disappeared into the Big House as though nothing had happened.

Jane grabbed one of the little black boys and had him run out in the fields to get Lawrence. For more than half an hour the Countess lay in the dusty yard with the sun beating down on her, her skirt soaked in blood. Jane was on her knees, cradling the Countess's head in her lap, when Lawrence rode into the yard. Without a word he jumped off his horse, picked up the Countess and carried her up the back steps and into the house.

"Put that God-damn nigger down, Boy," the Major said, intercepting Lawrence as he and Jane tried to make their way up the narrow stairs to get the Countess back to the safety of her room.

"Get your hands off me, Papa!" Lawrence yelled. "Have you lost your mind? Get out of my way." Then he pushed the Major to one side.

Convicts stood inside the large hall, wide-eyed, as Lawrence and Jane ascended the back stairs. Jane called out for Nellie to run and fetch Dr. Taylor.

Lawrence gently laid the Countess down on her bed and Jane grabbed the bed covers and stuffed them between the Countess's legs. Blood was gushing from her and Jane held the quilt firmly, trying to slow down the bleeding.

The Countess murmured, "Did he kill my baby?" Jane shuddered at the thought, and Lawrence jerked back from the bed, shocked at what he'd just heard. The Countess passed out as Dr. Taylor came rushing into the room.

He took one look at the Countess, realizing immediately what he had on his hands. "Jane," he said, tearing at the bloody quilt, "I'm going to need plenty hot water and rags. Get Virginia Reed to tear up some old sheets. If we don't stop this bleeding, we're going to lose both her and her baby."

Jane ran from the attic, calling out for Virginia. Nellie was close on her heels. "Nellie, Sugar, you go find one of the Madam's palmetto fans," Jane told her as she went down the stairs, "and fan the flies off the Countess. It's awful hot up there."

"But Marse Browne done said for none of us convicts to touch the 'God-damn convict'," Nellie said, tagging behind Jane.

"Hush your mouth, Sugar," Jane said, placing a finger over Nellie's lips, as they stopped at the bottom of the stairs. "Don't repeat words like that. Do as I say. Go find a fan and get back upstairs, fast as you can."

Jane and Virginia ripped the faded cloth into large pads and the two of them applied one after another when Dr. Taylor said the baby had been born dead. All through the night they bathed her sticky body and prayed she would live. Finally toward dawn Doctor Taylor washed his hands and began to pack his instruments and medicine in his black bag. "She'll live. The Countess is a strong woman in more ways than one," he said, "but I'll tell you one thing, Lawrence. If you let the Major send her away to one of those levee camps, she'll die."

Jane put her hands over her face and let out a deep breath. What was going to happen to the Countess now?

"No one is going to send her away, Doctor. I promise you that," he said, and Jane looked up through her tears and gave Lawrence a grateful smile.

THE NEXT MORNING Jane was awakened by the Madam pulling on the bellcord. She jumped up off the floor beside the Countess's bed and ran immediately down to the Madam's boudoir.

"How in God's name do you expect me to be ready to leave for Saratoga with only an ignorant girl like you to help?" The Madam glared at Jane who stood before her in a white uniform still flecked with the Countess's blood.

She'd tried to fix her hair and realized only when she saw the Madam staring at her that she'd forgotten to change her clothes.

"It was so stupid and inconvenient of Laura to fall down those stairs like she was nothing but a drunkard. I've warned the Major about not punishing you servants when you steal our liquor, and now you see what happens. I've no one to help me," the Madam whined, curling back into her bed.

Jane felt like hitting her, but clenched her teeth and said to the stern-faced woman, "Don't worry, Mrs. Browne. I'll work twice as hard. I'll do my work and Laura's as well. I won't let you down."

"I doubt that," the Madam said.

Jane bristled at the tone in Madam's voice. How could she be so utterly uncaring? Her husband had almost beaten a woman to death and all the Madam could do was whine about being inconvenienced. Jane kept her anger to herself, though. "Mrs. Browne, I've learned a lot since I first came here. The Countess has taught me well. Taking care of this household and seeing to you and the Major's needs won't be a problem for me. I know how to work."

"Well, we'll see. My sisters are arriving soon with Ella Marie and the children. I'm taking Ella Marie and one of my sisters with me this year and we're leaving on the twenty-seventh for Saratoga. I want everything perfect. Everyone who's anyone in New Orleans will be there and I want everything I own packed to perfection. Do you understand me?"

Jane nodded, knowing full well she'd better please the Madam. The Countess's life depended on it.

TRYING TO BE as efficient as the Countess was harder than Jane imagined, but she did her best to organize the house and the other servants to prepare the Madam and her daughter for their annual journey north. Every gown, handkerchief and piece of lingerie that they owned had to be washed, hung in the sun to dry and pressed until each looked as though it had never been worn. Trunks and valises were brought down from the attic and taken outside to air in the sun. When the Madam pronounced them fresh enough, they were lined with thin, sachet-scented tissue paper, packed and repacked.

The Madam sat nearby in a chair next to her bed, leisurely passing the time with Ella Marie as Jane slaved over the trunks. The Madam did everything in her power to belittle Jane, second guessing her every move. "Even if they get it right the first time, have them do it over again," she told her daughter. "You never want a convict to get uppity with you, and they will if you let them start thinking they can do something as well as you."

Jane shrugged off the comments and continued her work as best she could, but she was exhausted. Getting up before dawn and tending to the Countess, and then being ready to bring the Madam her coffee at precisely eight o'clock, took almost every ounce of energy she had. Whenever she could, though, she'd slip away to the kitchen, take a slice of crusty bread and cup of soup up to the Countess and be back to attend the Madam before she was missed.

Finally, when she finished rubbing Madam's feet before she retired for the evening, Jane would rush back to the attic where she'd bathe her friend, feed her soft porridge and hold her until she went to sleep. The only time Jane saw Lawrence during those grueling days was when he'd slip up to her room for a few hours, equally exhausted from a long day's work.

"Isn't it amazing," Lawrence said to Jane one day when they'd managed to steal a moment alone in the pecan orchard. "Mama was right. As long as you pretend, life can go on as though nothing is wrong. Just look at what's happened, yet Mama is planning to receive her sisters and brother-in-law, Dr. Langtree, in her usual grand style and then leave for Saratoga to escape the heat.

"Papa goes about his business as though his only concerns were cotton and boll weevils, and even you and I have to pretend. If we didn't act like nothing had happened, Papa'd have the Countess thrown into the back of a cotton wagon and hauled to a levee camp."

Jane certainly did not want that. Lately she'd been scared for the sanity of the Countess as well as her safety. The Countess had told her what the Major had said about the baby the day he beat her. He'd said, "No nigger convict will bear any child of mine and if you don't know how to get rid of it, I do." Jane wanted to tell Lawrence about it, but she knew he had enough on his mind. What good would it do anyway?

The Countess was a strong woman and within a few days of the beating she was able to sit up and even move slowly around the room. She continually thanked Jane for the things Jane did for her, but never spoke about what happened. If she had any fear she was in jeopardy of being sent away, she did not say anything. But Jane would see her sitting for hours in a small straight-backed chair by the window, looking out, but never uttering a sound.

The Countess insisted on taking the night watch in the kitchen to keep the fires burning even though her pain must have been excruciating. After Mrs. Browne dismissed her for the evening, Jane helped the Countess down the three flights of steep stairs to the kitchen, then back up again each morning. After what seemed like weeks of this ritual, Jane awoke one night to the sound of singing from outside. She ran to the window and there she saw the

Countess picking herbs from the kitchen garden. In the bright summer moonlight, dressed in her white uniform and black apron, the Countess looked like the apparition of a dead convict who was rumored to haunt the Big House. *What in the world is she doing?* Jane wondered.

Without bothering to put on her clothes, Jane hurried down the stairs and out into the yard in her cotton night-dress. A question kept racing through Jane's mind—*had her friend gone completely insane?* Afraid that the singing would wake Mrs. Browne or the Major, Jane put her arms around her beloved friend and tried to coerce her inside. "You can't do this, Countess. If they see you out here singing in the middle of the night, there's no telling what they're liable to do."

The Countess just smiled. "Don't worry, Cherie, there are things that I must do. Things that are best done at night. Now you go on back to bed. You need your rest. You don't have to be concerned about me." Jane hated to leave the Countess alone in the dark, but she was exhausted and too tired to argue.

The next morning when Jane awoke, she felt overwhelmingly worried and anxious. She sensed a heaviness in the air, even though the sky was bright and the sun shining. The scent of the summer flowers, both sweet and sour, made her think of a sick room or even a coffin. It wasn't what had happened the night before with the Countess or even her apprehension over the Madam's departure for Saratoga that caused her to worry. Her intuition just told her something bad was about to happen. Every time she thought about it, she got a sinking feeling in the pit of her stomach.

Even the hard work of packing and re-packing for the Madam couldn't dispel the sense of foreboding that Jane felt. Several times during the morning she ran to the attic to see about the Countess, but each time her friend lay fast asleep with no sign that she had ever left the room.

Maybe my worries are unwarranted, she thought as the morning passed into afternoon. Then she thought about Lawrence. She had not seen him in days. *He might have had an accident,* she worried, but her cares about him were soon cut short. When she went out to the garden to cut fresh roses for the dinner table, he rode up.

"What's wrong?" he asked. "It must be a hundred degrees out here, but you're shivering. Did Mama say something to upset you?"

"No, no, nothing like that," she said. "Your mama's fine. She's so caught up with getting away tomorrow, I don't think she even realizes I'm around. I've had such a terrible feeling all day, that's all. I thought maybe something bad had happened to you."

"Well, there's nothing wrong with me that a hug and a kiss from you won't cure."

"If you'll help me cut some of these roses, I'll give you a kiss," she said, handing Lawrence a pair of shears, admiring the Cherokee rose vines she had planted when she first arrived at Angola. Hundreds of red blooms were cascading all the way down from the top of the stable wall. It gave her comfort to see her mama's roses until something suddenly crossed her mind. *Ander!* "That's it, Lawrence! Maybe it's Ander. Maybe he's been hurt. Yes, that could be why I'm feeling so anxious today. Ander must be hurt."

"That I seriously doubt, Jane," he said, placing the cut flowers inside the brown paper she was holding.

"But how would you know? Are you keeping something from me?"

"No silly. I talked to J.L. Row, the man who runs the levee camp at New Iberia. He says Ander's doing fine. They have him living on the plantation like the women convicts do here. He's working in the sugar house now. I paid Row to get him out of the camp," he said, as they walked toward the kitchen. "Just like I told you before, you know nothing bad is going to happen to your son as long as I'm around. I made you that promise, didn't I?"

Jane felt a little better after talking to Lawrence and went back to her work. She found Ella Marie with her mother and the two of them were giggling as they tried on new gowns, barely noticing Jane.

The rest of that day seemed endless. Jane, busy as ever, ran up and down the stairs, fetching items and running last minute errands for the Madam. But even with all the activity around her, she could not shake off the sense of impending doom.

The Madam came out of her room late in the afternoon, dressed in white from her high buttoned top to her silk slippers. She went out to the balcony where the Major, her sisters, Dr. Langtree, and her brother were waiting for her. Like a gosling following a white goose, Ella Marie trailed after her. Jane, still apprehensive, went back to the attic where she sat by the sleeping Countess, but when she heard a terrified scream she ran back downstairs.

When she reached the balcony she stood silently in the doorway watching the Major who was leaning forward in a chair, gasping for breath. She could see he was trying to speak, but only gurgling sounds came out. He clutched his throat, then stood up. His face had turned completely white, as though all the blood had drained from his head. He staggered toward the porch railing and Jane watched helplessly as Dr. Langtree rushed over to loosen his string tie and open the collar of his shirt.

The Major's hands clutched the railing. Henry Smith and Dr. Langtree took his arms. He pushed them away and leaned further over the railing, then began to vomit. Madam rushed to his side. When bright red blood spewed out of his mouth, turning the white flowers on the oleander bushes below to crimson, Jane gasped but did not move from the doorway. Madam screamed, letting go of her husband's arms, and moved back. The Major tossed his head from side to side, with the blood pouring from his mouth like a waterfall.

The Madam just stood against the wall like a stone statue. Dr. Langtree held the Major until the vomiting subsided. The Major collapsed on the floor, his eyes closed, his breathing shallow. The doctor took the Major's pulse and slowly shook his head. "There's nothing I can do, Emma," Dr. Langtree said. "There's nothing anyone can do. I've never seen a hemorrhage this massive."

The Madam seemed to be glued against the wall, her face horror stricken. Jane knew she couldn't just leave the Major like this without making an effort to comfort him. She knelt beside him and blood seeped onto her uniform, but she did not move. *You're nothing but an old devil,* she thought, as she stared into his bulging eyes, *but you're still a human being, and I pray for your soul.* She took the Major's limp hand and leaned down. Blood was still trickling from his mouth. "Can you hear me, Major Browne?" she asked. He moved his eyes to answer. "I pray God have mercy on you," she whispered to him.

In a voice that sounded as if it were coming through the water of a deep well he managed to speak, "I knew this would be my fate. I'm ready."

Jane glanced up at the Madam and motioned for her to come to her husband. If there was a time that the Major ever really needed his wife it was now, but the Madam did not move. "Mrs. Browne, he's trying to speak and I think it's you he wants to speak with," Jane pleaded.

The Madam nodded and shook out a white lace handkerchief she had pulled out of her pocket. She inched her way across the porch where her husband lay. She was too slow, though. The Major took one last breath and murmured, "Tell the Countess I'm sorry."

The Madam leaned down and grabbed for his hand, but the Major was dead. She stood up and backed away as Jane tried to touch her in a gesture of condolence. "Jane, you just go tell Jacob to have Captain Williams get *The Sparks* ready," she said, coldly. "The Major will rot in this heat. We have to get him to New Orleans so we can embalm him and give him a proper funeral. That's the least I deserve."

Horrified, Jane ran off the porch.

⚔ Eleven ⚔

THROUGHOUT THE NIGHT, after the Major's body was thoroughly washed and laid out on the rattan sofa in the front parlor, Jane heard a thunder of horses' hooves as hundreds of croppers and nearby neighbors rode up to the house to find out what had happened.

She walked over to the window and watched as torches were lit up in the front and side yards. It looked like one of those *Klan* rallies she remembered as a child. Buggies and men on horseback made their way into the already crowded yard. Black men and women held small children by the hand and sang some Negro gospel song Jane had never heard before. Some of them moaned and groaned as if actually grieving for the man who'd tormented them practically every day since they'd come to Angola. It crossed her mind for a moment that some of the convicts might have thoughts of running away.

"Damnation!" she swore softly to herself, closing the curtain and moving back into the parlor. She felt exhausted. A few of the servants, especially the younger girls were complaining because they had to scrub the blood off the porch. *I can't really blame them,* she thought. The entire convict staff was worried. Their future was uncertain, and that fact made everyone edgy.

Jane and Virginia Reed dressed out the dead body and Jane decided it was something she wished never to do again. She had tried to persuade some of the other convicts to help her, to no avail. They were superstitious and afraid. As distraught as Lawrence was, he and

Dr. Taylor had to pitch in. When the moment finally came to take the body away, Lawrence had to beg the Negro sharecroppers to help. They were all scared of the dead. After several pleas from Lawrence, a few of the older men nailed together a wooden box, helped to load the Major's body onto the railway cart and followed it to the landing.

No sooner had the family departed when the Countess showed up out of nowhere and started to pull the household back together. Although surprised at how fast the Countess had recovered, Jane was relieved to see her up and about, taking charge of the Big House as always. Calling all of the convict servants into the dining room, the Countess told them what had to be done while the family was away in New Orleans for the funeral.

"The Major's room must be closed off immediately," she said, ignoring remarks from the convicts about how glad they all were that the Major was dead. "Nothing must be touched until Master Lawrence gets back and has a chance to go through the Major's things and take inventory. If I catch one of you taking anything that belonged to the Major, you won't have to worry about what will happen to you. I'll send you to the levee camps myself." Then she asked Jane and several other girls to go up to the storeroom in the attic and bring down all of the black crepe they could find.

"I want the upstairs gallery as well as every window and door heavily draped. Cover the mantels as well as the chandeliers. If there isn't enough crepe, gather the old sheets and you, Virginia Reed, make up some black dye to boil them. Crinkle them up to look like crepe. I want it done right. Remember this isn't a sharecropper's house. This is the home of the Browne family.

"Every room, with the exception of the Major's, is to be cleaned. I want fresh flowers in the house. Go down behind the stables and cut Jane's red roses. When the family returns from New Orleans, I want this house filled with them. If they wilt replace them ten times a day if you have to. Make sure you use only red roses. I don't want any of those pathetic pale pink things from the cutting garden. The only color appropriate for this house now is the color of blood." The Countess had returned.

Later that day when Jones rode up to the Big House, Jane
watched from the doorway. He looked over the long line of convict
women walking back from the stables, each carrying dozens of red
roses in their black aprons. "Jest what in the hell is going on?" he
shouted at them. "The funeral is in New Orleans, not here at Angola."

"The Countess said to do it, and that's what we're doing," one of
the women said in passing.

"Well, we'll just see about that," he said, bombastically. "If the
Countess thinks she's in charge and can strut her high and mighty
self around here like always, then she might as well haul her black
ass to a levee camp. Don't she know the Major's dead? Things are
going to change around here. You mark my words. When Mrs.
Browne's brother, Henry, gets up here, it's gonna be him and me
in charge. The Brownes won't have nothing to say about this place
anymore."

Just the thought of this wicked man having any say in the day to
day operations of the plantation made Jane's blood curdle. But she
was comforted by the fact that Jones might shoot his mouth off
about the Countess, but never to her face. She was the only one on
the plantation he seemed to be afraid of.

By the middle of the week, life at Angola settled down once again
to a lonely, isolated plantation existence. With all the cooking,
cleaning, polishing and scrubbing, Jane didn't have time to worry.
The yard was filled with a dozen iron wash pots stuffed with sheets
being dyed to make ersatz crepe, and throughout the days and well
into the nights the servants worked under the direction of the
Countess.

From the Daily-Picayune, Jane read about the clamor for penal
reform and the end to the leasing of convicts. Headlines every day
spoke of Governor Foster's anti-convict-leasing-campaign. Jane
could not understand all of the words in the newspaper concerning
prison reform and asked the Countess if the articles meant that
some of the convicts would be allowed to go free. She thought of
being able to take Ander and go home to Georgia Ann. She would
see her mama again, but her heart ached when she remembered that
Charles would not be waiting for her.

"No, no, Cherie," the Countess said, laughing at the absurdity of such an idea. "Nothing has changed. The good men from Baton Rouge, the ones we go to so much trouble to entertain so lavishly, say that they have stopped all the abuses in the levee camps, that they will no longer allow convicts to be treated like slaves. The good people of Louisiana, especially the ones who like to sit in the front row of their churches each Sunday, can go to sleep at night believing convicts will no longer be beaten or worked to death, or die from hunger or disease. They will pretend that convicts can no longer simply disappear from the official records—but nothing has really changed. Our lives, the life of your son, won't change, because no one in power wants changes to take place, at least not for the next five years. That is exactly the time remaining on the present contract to lease out convicts.

"Imagine how much money the Browne family can make off of a thousand convicts in five years, Cherie, and if the convicts die while they are building the levees, cutting the cane or picking the cotton, no one will care because on paper it says that such things no longer happen."

Lawrence had sent word that the family planned to return in early August after his father's will was probated. He also sent a note to Jane: "Please take care of yourself. I've heard many disturbing rumors here in New Orleans, about the future of the plantation. I pray they are only the grumbles of desperate men wanting to keep their power."

When she read the note aloud to the Countess, she asked what it meant. The Countess just shook her head, "You must understand this has been a family driven by greed for power and money. There has never been enough for them, but neither has there been enough for the people they do business with. The men Master Lawrence is involved with, "The Ring Bosses," are masters of political corruption, and I don't know if he can stand up to them."

"Lawrence and I have talked a little about these men. He didn't call them by name, just said they were powerful business men, mostly from New Orleans."

"Well, the only thing I can really tell you about those men is that the Major was able to do business with them in the leasing of convicts, but Lawrence is another story. They don't have the same respect for, or fear of, Master Lawrence that they had for the Major. They remember that Master Lawrence gave up his levee camp when he could have just sat back and spent the money it brought him. He has no taste for this life, which requires convicts to become objects, not people—a life that says if a man falls dead while he's working, his body should be left as a reminder for the other men to work harder. I overheard conversations the Major had with these men. They called Master Lawrence a weakling, saying he could be a danger to the business."

A chill went through Jane. She remembered what Charles had told her about her own brothers and Judge Bear. *Money and power,* she thought, *rich or poor, when you get right down to it, it's all about money and power.*

❦ Twelve ❦

WHY WAS the Countess so calm? Had she forgotten all the pain she'd been through recently? It made Jane livid, just thinking about it. "I don't understand any of this, Countess. You pretend nothing is different. We're working ourselves to death getting this place fixed up for mourning. Why in God's name are you doing it? After all the Major did to you—after he killed your unborn child—why are you working yourself and everyone else like this?" They were harsh words, but Jane needed answers.

The Countess patted the bottom step, motioning for Jane to sit beside her. She put a match to a small thin black cigar and considered her words deliberately. "It's very simple, Cherie," she said. "This is my job. My family, poor as they were, brought me up to believe if people pay you two bits, you give them six bits worth of work in return. They expect it. The rich white people are like that. They always want more than they're willing to pay for.

"When they sent me here, I vowed to work even harder than they expected. That's just the way that I am. As for the Major, I told you that's all over."

The Countess exhaled a cloud of smoke. She was silent for a moment. Jane could see pain in her deep, dark eyes, but she revealed nothing further. "You have seen the eraser the schoolmarm uses to clean the blackboard the children do their sums on?" the Countess asked. "When they finish, she simply wipes off their marks and they can begin again. Death is the same. The Major is gone and I can begin again. Why be angry at something that's no longer there? He can't hurt me and I only hurt myself by thinking about it."

"I guess that makes sense," Jane said, but she really did not understand.

The Countess stood up. "Now we must get back to work. The family will be home any day and, I believe now more than ever, we must all watch every step we take. There is no certainty for any of us."

She went about her work, but Jane couldn't help but wonder about the Countess and the sudden death of the Major. There had been some mutterings from the Negro population, and she remembered the night she found the Countess singing in the herb garden and how the Countess had said, "There are some things that are best done at night." While Jane vowed she'd never ask, the thought that the Countess was somehow responsible for the Major's death was never far from her. "What does it matter?" she said to herself, sighing. *The Countess is right. Men have all the power. They can do anything to a woman they want. The law always looks the other way. It doesn't matter if you're black or white, a convict or free, rich or poor. A woman's life isn't worth a damn if a man decides it isn't.*

The next day Jane walked into the kitchen just as Jones handed the *Daily-Picayune* to the Countess. "Read it to me," he barked. "Read me all about the funeral and be sure to read me anything about Henry Smith. I want to be sure I understand it all."

Jones ordered one of the women to get him a bottle of whiskey and sat down at the kitchen table as the Countess began to read. All work stopped. Even the small kitchen boys gathered near them to hear about the Major's New Orleans funeral.

MANY FRIENDS ATTEND IMPRESSIVE FUNERAL SERVICES

The funeral of Major Browne took place last evening at the Penn Flats No. 2 South Street, the temporary residence of the family when in New Orleans. The throng of citizens that attended the obsequies represented the best element of this community.

Rev. A. J. Cardy, a personal friend of the deceased, officiated at the house and at the grave. A profusion of floral emblems were heaped around the casket, evidence of the kind remembrance of sorrowing friends.

Crowns and symbols wrought with choicest flowers were sent.

Rev. Cardy paused in the midst of the service to say a few words of eulogy for the deceased, who was one of his best friends. He bore witness to the sterling character of Major Browne. He extolled his kindness of heart, his nobility of soul, and his virtues in the domestic circle. He was a true and affectionate husband, the kindest and most indulgent of parents.

He was happiest when making others happy.

To his deeply afflicted family and friends the reverend speaker addressed words of consolation, telling them of the infinite mercy and goodness of God, and assuring them that to such a true and noble Christian as the deceased 'Death had no terrors and the grave achieved no victory, for there is a life beyond the grave and an eternity of joy for the righteous and the just'.

The departure of a man of strong character, of public spirit, leaves a void in all circles that he has adorned and beautified, but such a good man never dies.

'A good name is never erased from the record of time'.

Everyone listened in silence. Finally, Jones, disappointed that the Countess hadn't read anything about Henry Smith, grabbed one of the women by the arm and headed for his cabin.

"Well, well," the Countess told Jane when they were alone. "It appears that the Madam managed to get the only kind of funeral that would matter to her: the best money can buy."

ON THE MORNING the family returned from New Orleans the Countess assembled the entire convict staff in front of the house to welcome them. The beautiful white mansion wore a somber air as the hot wind blew against the hundreds of yards of black crepe that draped the house. The windows were open and still the overwhelming scent of roses filled every room.

Jane's fears about her future escalated when Lawrence returned that day looking tired and broken. She overheard him say to his mother, "It's started. Papa's not even cold in his grave and already your beloved brother Henry Smith and Papa's old cronies have taken over. They made sure I was cut out of the will knowing full well it'll take years of legal battles to get my rightful share."

The Madam did not say anything to her son. She just gazed around the room as Lawrence left her standing in the front parlor of the Big House and went outside to shake hands with Dr. Taylor who had ridden up with a few of the other retainers. Lawrence smiled and nodded at the servants. He thanked them for their sympathy. Standing on the steps of the porch, he addressed the group gathered around. "The next few days, weeks and months are going to be difficult. As all of you know, this year has not been good for Angola Plantation. I'm going to ask everyone who is here at Angola, whether they be convicts, sharecroppers or members of my family, to work harder, but I promise you'll be treated fairly. No one will be driven off as long as they carry their load of work. No one, not even me, is going anywhere until we're ready."

Lawrence's sincerity made Jane feel a little better until she heard a noise behind a clump of oleander bushes. She turned around and saw Jones, watching and listening. She heard Jones mumble, "That dandy's gonna be singing a different tune just as soon as Mr. Henry Smith gits up here. Yes sir, all them Brownes gonna be singing a mighty different tune."

I'll have to warn Lawrence about that wretched man, she thought, when the Countess shooed everyone back to work and organized the wagons to go to the landing to pick up the mountain of valises and trunks. Lawrence took Jane's hand. They walked into his father's library.

Selecting one of the array of Waterford decanters, Lawrence poured himself a large brandy and raised his goblet to a portrait of the Major in his Confederate uniform hanging above the fireplace. "You took care of everything, didn't you, Papa?" he said, taking a gulp of the brandy. He then hurled the glass at the portrait. His crystal glass shattered into pieces and the dark amber liquid ran down the Major's face onto the mantel. Jane had never seen Lawrence so angry.

The Countess raced into the room with a startled look on her face. Lawrence picked up another goblet and shakily filled it with brandy. "It's a shame to waste good liquor," he said, and took a deep breath, "but I could hardly drink alone, not this early in the day. Seeing as how Papa's lying dead in Metairie Cemetery, it was the only way I could get him to join me. Do you think he enjoyed it?" he asked the Countess sarcastically as Jane stood silent. "Do you think he enjoyed that circus show Mama put on for him? The funeral was practically a replica of old Jeff Davis's. Mama wouldn't have it any other way. Now tell me," he said, turning to face the Countess, "you knew him probably better than anybody else, certainly better than my dear devoted mama. What do you think?"

"I think," the Countess said, quietly, taking the glass from his hand, "you are exhausted and confused. There are many things you don't understand."

"Oh, I understand all right, Countess," he said. "I finally understand everything. All of Papa's cronies were like vultures at the funeral, just waiting to see who was going to take over the convicts." Then he glanced up at the portrait once again. "Well, I don't care about the convict lease. I just want my share of the estate so I can get the hell out of this place."

"I don't think you really understand, Master Lawrence. You of all people should know that nothing at Angola is as it appears. What you see on the surface is merely a reflection of something else. Living here is like being in a hall of mirrors. No one is who or what you think he is, and what appears to be real is nothing more than pretend."

"The Countess speaks the truth, Lawrence," Jane spoke up. "Your papa was a very strange and strong man indeed, but his successors are lurking around the plantation at this very moment, making changes right under your very nose. The ones you might think you can trust are the very ones you should not turn your back to."

"Perhaps you are both right," he said, seemingly crestfallen. "I've already had my first taste of Papa's successors. And I can guess who you are referring to. But, if you will excuse me, Countess, I'm tired, just plain exhausted. Dealing with all those lawyers is worse than trying to stop the Mississippi when it's in full flood. The river's like the lawyers; the water keeps coming and they keep talking in circles. There isn't a thing you can do to stop either one of them."

Lawrence glanced at Jane standing by the rattan settee. He looked so browbeaten she wanted to take him in her arms and tell him everything would turn out all right, but then she wasn't so sure about that. She wasn't sure about anything anymore.

Hitting his fist on the door, Lawrence grimaced. He glanced up at his father's portrait once more. Then he said, "Have some of the women move Ella Marie and George's things out of their single rooms. Put the two of them in a double room. They don't need separate bedrooms. It'll give George Ivan a chance to see what his own wife looks like in bed. Have Jane's things moved out of the attic into George's old room. She'll be more comfortable in there. Clean the Major's things out of his room. I'll be moving into it. Have all of my clothes brought from my cottage up here to the Big House, but leave the furniture. I have plans for the cottage."

The Countess started to protest, as Jane wondered what those plans were.

"Just see to it," he said. "If anybody complains, tell them I told you that's the way things are going to be. Maybe Uncle Henry will change everything around when he gets here, but for now I'm running this place."

Lawrence then took the Countess's hands in his. "You're a good woman, Countess. You were good to my father when God knows he didn't deserve anyone's goodness. You somehow managed not only to get along with my mama, but made her admire and respect you as much as she can anyone. Wouldn't you like to be free to leave this place and go back to New Orleans? You've earned it and I can make it happen. Maybe not exactly legally, but who knows what's legal and what isn't when it comes to convicts?"

Jane's heart leaped for a moment. Freedom—what a sweet sounding word. She watched as the Countess looked from her to Lawrence. The Countess replied, "Yes, I want my freedom. I believe I've earned it. You and I both know, Master Lawrence, if I killed a man starting today and one a day until the day I die, I'd never catch up to the bunch that wants to take over the running of this plantation."

Pouring another brandy, Lawrence stared at the Countess for a moment. Without saying another word he led Jane silently out into the hall and up the stairs to his father's room.

⁜ Thirteen ⁜

THE NEXT NIGHT Jane and Lawrence spent most of the early hours of darkness snuggling together on the four-poster bed in Lawrence's small cottage. The furniture had been left, as Lawrence had instructed. Lawrence had said it would be a place where he and Jane could spend time in private. And although he seemed to be happy while lying next to her, his mood shifted to gloom.

He began to tell her about what had happened at the Major's funeral. "There is nothing left here for me except you, Jane," he said, sitting on the side of the bed with his arms stretched behind him.

"What are you saying?" she asked, getting out of bed and throwing on her clothes. She lit the oil lamp and took a pot, filled it with water and some salt and placed it on the cook stove. "Just a minute, Lawrence. Let me fix us some supper and then we'll talk."

Lawrence stood up and pulled on his clothes. He struggled with his boots while she cracked eggs in the iron skillet, swishing them around until they were firm. Then she poured bubbling grits on a plate, spooning the scrambled eggs on top. She set the plate in front of Lawrence who sat at the small rosewood table in the middle of the kitchen, filled her plate and sat across from him.

"Now you were saying something about nothing being left for you. What did you mean?"

"Papa left me nothing, absolutely nothing in the will. Mama and Ella Marie got everything. You know that speech I made yesterday morning about how everyone had to work together to keep the plantation going and how I would work with them to be able to pay the bankers? I let them believe I'd be in charge. I'm not. According to the will the executors of the estate are Uncle Henry and Edward White, a crony of the Ring Bosses. They're the ones who call the shots now."

"Well, you said you didn't want anything to do with the convicts anyway, didn't you?"

"Yes. But certain members of the Ring Bosses made it perfectly clear to me at the funeral that they'll be running everything. And that means the plantation as well. They said they intend to crack the whip and turn Angola Plantation into a money maker, as well as the levee camps Papa owned. You know what that means?"

"No, I can't say that I do know what that means."

"They're desperate, Jane. There's only five years left on the convict lease agreement with the state. The only way the Ring Bosses can continue to get their cut from the leases is to take control of Angola. If they control Angola, they control the convict lease. And the bankers have to be paid. The funeral was barely over when they started pestering me about the money Papa owed—money the plantation doesn't have."

"Lawrence, I'm sure your papa has plenty of money stashed, at least enough to pay his debts."

"Obviously not. I've got to go to court with an inventory of all the personal belongings of the plantation in a few weeks."

"You think it's going to do them any good, selling everything on the plantation, I mean."

"They're not selling anything if I can help it. I'm going to fight them. I don't know how far I'll get, but I can't let them take away everything that I have without a fight. I am Papa's only son and I know he couldn't have written such a will. We were never close, but we were learning to work with each other. You've seen how I've worked the plantation since the flood."

"You want another cup of coffee?" she asked, sympathetically. He nodded, pushing his empty plate back. "Why are you so sure your papa didn't cut you out of his will?"

"Back in May when he and Mama went to Baton Rouge, he told me as soon as he returned that he'd beaten Governor Foster and those so called friends of his in the legislature and had made certain that when he was gone, none of the Ring Bosses could get their hands on Angola. He told me he wanted me to take care of Mama and Ella Marie and make Angola a fine place to raise my family. He said everything would go to me. He wanted Angola to stay in the Browne family forever. He never mentioned Uncle Henry or Edward White. Hell, he never trusted Uncle Henry. All my life I've heard him say Uncle Henry wouldn't have amounted to anything if he hadn't grabbed on to Papa's coat-tails. And as for White and the rest of the Ring Bosses, he always said he wouldn't trust them as far as he could throw 'em."

"What did the will say? Was it typewritten or handwritten?" she asked.

"Handwritten."

"Was it your papa's handwriting?"

"It looked to me like it was, best I could tell. I even had to sign a document stating it was Papa's handwriting."

"What did you do that for?"

"At the time I wasn't thinking straight. I don't suppose I really understood it all. I guess I was thinking since he left the plantation to the women, he must have left the convict lease to me in another will. It just happened so fast and Mama wasn't there for me to get her opinion."

"What does your lawyer say? Does he think you have a chance to reverse the will? Contest it maybe?"

"Jane the estate is being raped. He says we will have to work it out one step at a time."

"And your first step is to do an inventory?"

"Yes."

"In the mean time what do you do for money?"

"I never before bothered about money. We always had it. I just don't know what I'm going to do."

Jane stood up and crossed the kitchen to a table where a coal oil lamp sat. She swung the globe up and struck a sulphur match, lighting the wick. She picked it up and walked toward the front door.

"Where are you going?" he asked.

"I'm going to the Big House to get the Countess. I think you need to talk to her. I think she knows more than she's telling about the will."

As she moved quickly through the dark yard she could see lights shining from every room as she approached the Big House. Some of the convicts were standing around the side yard with lanterns as a never ending procession of carriages began to arrive. *My God,* she thought, *surely the Madam isn't having a party this soon after burying her husband!*

Jane stalked into the kitchen where Virginia Reed and most all of the other servants were bustling around, preparing trays of party foods. She could hear piano music coming from the main salon as the servants went back and forth with the trays, one going out the door as another came in. She bumped into Nellie. "Where's the Countess?"

"She's busy in the Big House. The Madam's been hollering at her all this afternoon about you not being here."

She sprinted out of the kitchen, up the back steps to the porch and through the back door. The Countess was nowhere in sight and Jane went up the back stairs to the second floor gallery where she could peek over the railing and not be seen.

Down below, the long hall was filled with men in dark blue suits and women in gowns of subdued colors. Her eyes trailed off to the huge rosewood table in the dining room that was covered with silver dishes and platters of hot and cold foods. Two of the young convict girls were standing behind the table ready to serve. Farther into the front parlor the Madam was sitting stiff as a ramrod on a red velvet settee, dressed from head to toe in black silk, dabbing her eyes with a little black handkerchief. Jane realized, when she saw the long line of men and women waiting to speak to the Madam, that this was not a party. Only a reception for people wishing to pay their respects to the bereaved widow of the Major and his family. Sitting beside her was Ella Marie and standing behind her was the Madam's brother, Henry. Edward White, the man Jane supposed was Henry's Ring Boss partner, stood next to George Ivan.

She could see the convict captain Jones lounging against the mantle holding a crystal goblet in one hand and scratching his neck with the other. She wondered for a moment who might have loaned him the heavy black suit and starched white shirt that seemed to be causing him so much discomfort in the August heat.

Why isn't Lawrence here? she thought. *He doesn't even know this is going on. Surely the Major's only son has a right to be here. Don't these people respect anything? Don't they care for anybody?*

Above the quiet murmur of the crowd she could hear the people, many of whom she recognized from dinners at the mansion, pay their respects to the Madam. "Your husband was so kind," she heard one of them say. "The Major was the best friend that anyone could have. We were fortunate to have him render such great service to the state," said another.

To each mourner Jane watched the Madam give a small sad smile and extend her hand for a moment. When each passed on to speak with her daughter the Madam would wipe tears from her eyes. Jane noticed Henry's hand never left his sister's shoulder, and occasionally he would lean down and whisper in her ear when someone Jane recognized of particular importance approached. Then Jane spotted the Countess, with her eyes appropriately downcast as befitted a convict servant, moving between the main salon and the dining room issuing orders to the other servants who were waiting to serve food or drinks. As the Countess passed through the main hall, she looked up at Jane and motioned with her head for Jane to go up to her room in the attic.

Jane stood at the Countess's door, waiting. She heard footsteps and she whispered. "What's going on here? Why doesn't Lawrence know about this?"

The countess leaned up against the wall, took a small black cigar out of her pocket and struck a match to light it. She dragged a deep puff into her lungs and blew the smoke out all at one time. "Because I was told not to tell him. I was told to tell anyone who might ask, that Lawrence was too distraught over the death of his papa to make an appearance.

"The truth is they don't want him around. They don't want anyone asking questions about anything until they get everything settled in court. Surely Master Lawrence told you the contents of the will."

"Yes, he told me his uncle is trying to take charge and that everything at the plantation has been left to his mama and sister. He's terribly upset about it. Said he doesn't believe his papa could do that to him."

"His papa didn't do it," the Countess said, mashing out her cigar in a small plate she'd been holding. "It was the Madam and her brother Henry who cut him out. The Major died thinking Master Lawrence would take over the plantation. The Madam and her brother forged the will."

"I knew there was more to it than you were saying yesterday," Jane said. "How did you find out?"

"Since I am one of the few people around here who can read and write, I witnessed the will that gave everything to Master Lawrence."

"I don't understand about wills and all these legal things, but why would the Madam go to so much trouble to hurt her son—a son whom she adores?"

"Oh, Cherie, there is so much you have to learn. Everyone was frightened, especially the Major's business associates, the Ring Bosses. They were afraid if Master Lawrence took over, the state would give the convict lease contract to someone else. They would be out in the cold."

"Are you saying the Madam and her brothers are now associated with the Ring Bosses?"

"I am. And I am saying I saw with my own eyes the Madam and her brother open the door to the Major's room while the Major was still lying in his own blood on the porch. I saw the Madam pull out of his top drawer a large envelope and put it into her handbag. I saw them tearing through the drawers of his desk, ripping up papers. She and her brother carried what she took out of the top drawer into her boudoir."

"Why didn't you come down and say something to Lawrence about it then?"

"Cherie, I am a convict. If I'd said anything about the Madam and her brother, I'd be dead by the next morning. You know that. But that's why I had the Major's room sealed. I had hoped that when Master Lawrence returned from the funeral there might be some papers left that could help him prove his case. I may be a prostitute and a murderer, but you know how much I despise lying and deception."

She reached out for Jane's hand. "There's no time to explain everything to you now. You run on and get Master Lawrence. Tell him what's going on over here. Tell him what I've told you and he'll know what to do. I have to get back downstairs. Despite Master Lawrence's good intentions, he has no power; there's no one to protect any of us any more."

Jane slipped down the back stairs and ran out of the kitchen all the way to the little vine covered cottage. She burst through the door. Lawrence was pacing back and forth. "Where have you been? I was worried sick that something had happened. I thought you were going to get the Countess. Where is she?"

As Jane began to explain what she had seen at the Big House and what the Countess had told her, she could see the anger and rage rising inside of him. "My own mama?" He clutched her arms roughly. "Are you trying to say my own mama did this to me?"

Jane nodded.

"I wouldn't put it past that brother of hers. If it hadn't been for Papa he'd still be picking up mule dung from the barn on Nayades Street or driving one of the mules that pulled the Omnibus like Papa once did. . . . Well . . . damn them all to hell! They stripped me of my inheritance and now they're humiliating me in front of everyone. I won't have it!"

He jerked open the front door and jumped off the porch. Wearing only a white silk shirt, tan cord breeches and high brown riding boots he walked fast toward the Big House with Jane trailing behind.

"Please Lawrence, don't do anything foolish," she pleaded. "You know what they can do. I don't want to see you get hurt." She knew that if Lawrence was thrown off the plantation the convicts would not have a chance. He was their only salvation.

Lawrence did not stop. He kept a steady pace, twisting his chin around to talk to her, "Don't you worry about me. Remember, I grew up in this family. They would rather die than lose face, cause anyone to talk. You know how Mama likes to pretend. Well, at least for tonight the whole family can pretend that I am Master of Angola Plantation just like Papa intended."

He pulled open the back door with such force Jane thought it would come off it's hinges. He grabbed her hand and stalked up the stairs. She could see the last of the mourners had paid their respects to the Madam and had scattered throughout the first floor of the house eating the feast the servants had prepared for them.

"Look at her," Lawrence mocked, clenching his jaws. "Mama for all her pretensions and airs has never gotten over her Irish upbringing. A fancy funeral in New Orleans was one thing, but in her family a soul doesn't get a proper send off until the mourners have gorged themselves on enough food to feed an army and enough liquor to drink themselves into a stupor."

You forget Lawrence, I am Irish. I've seen a lot of these funeral receptions, she thought, afraid to say anything out loud for fear he might turn on her.

"May I have your attention," he called out in a loud clear voice from the landing overlooking the main hall. "I am so sorry I could not be here to welcome you into my home along with my mama and my devoted family. However, while the shock of my papa's passing has taken its toll on all of us, life does go on and I have had to attend to the many pressing matters that involve Angola Plantation and the future I envision for it."

Lawrence left Jane's side and began to walk down the massive staircase. Jane saw Henry move from behind the Madam and motion for Jones to come to him. Jane saw it was only the Madam's sudden gasp and hand on her brother's arm that stopped him from rushing toward Lawrence.

Lawrence reached the bottom of the stairs, walked over to the Madam, leaned down and kissed her on the cheek and tugged on her arm until she was standing on her feet beside him. He walked her into the hallway. "On behalf of my family I want you to know how much we appreciate your coming tonight to express the respect and admiration that you felt for my papa. However, I know that you will understand that his sudden death, his funeral and the long trip back have exhausted all of us," he said, turning to face the Madam as he reached the front door. "Again, may I thank all of you for coming, but now I am afraid we must bid you all a good evening."

From where Jane was standing she could see that not many of the mourners, who had probably anticipated an all-night send-off for the Major, knew quite what to do. She watched as they quickly downed their glasses, gave a parting glance to the barely touched feast on the tables, nodded to the family, murmured further words of condolence and filed out the door to their waiting carriages. As the last person fled through the door, she saw Lawrence turn to the Countess. He said, "Please have all of this food taken out to the yard and set up on the washing tables. Have someone go and get the sharecroppers. I'm sure the Major would be delighted that they, as well as the servants, have the opportunity to partake of such a feast on his behalf."

As the Countess hurried the servants out of the room, Jane heard Henry shout. "Damn you, Lawrence! I don't know what in the hell you think you're doing, putting on this little performance. But it won't work. I'm in charge here now. Nothing you do can stop me either. I've got the law on my side."

Lawrence picked up a goblet full of red wine. He put it to his lips and sipped as he stared with contempt at Henry. "I have no doubt about that, Uncle Henry, but even in Louisiana we still have courts and that's exactly where you can expect to see me. Now take your brother and that thing you call a partner and get the hell out of here. It may not be my house any longer, but it is my mama's."

Jane stood watching. Henry glared at his sister and then back at Lawrence. Jane could see that the Madam was unsure of herself and it seemed for a moment to Jane, that she might actually be afraid of her son. "You know, Mama," he said, "I bet you didn't think when you helped your brother forge the will, you'd be giving him power you might one day live to regret, did you?"

"But Lawrence," the Madam protested, reaching out for his hand. "You don't understand. Henry said it was just to make it look better for the probate court. Just to help me get what's rightfully mine."

Lawrence stared at Henry and Edward White. Neither of them said a word. Finally the silence was broken when the Madam said to her brother, "Henry, as my son said, this has been a very trying time for all of us. Perhaps it would be best if you and Eddie and the others left so I can speak privately with my son."

Henry just stared at Lawrence before he said, "You can be foolish and fight me. But if you do that, you take on all of the establishment in both Baton Rouge and New Orleans. Don't be a foolish boy, Lawrence. Listen to your mama. She knows how the Ring Bosses operate."

The two men walked out and Lawrence slammed the great mahogany door shut. He stood in the high-ceilinged main hall right beneath a massive seven tier gasolier with the Madam, Ella Marie and George Ivan. Jane could hear the clatter of horses' hooves as the carriages pulled away from the house. She looked on as Lawrence walked into the parlor and poured himself another glass of red wine. He turned to his brother-in-law. "George," he said, lifting his glass, "I have no need of you now. What has to be said is between Mama and me. Perhaps you should take your wife to your new quarters, and consider yourself the luckiest man in the world tonight. Yes indeed; lucky I didn't throw your mooching self out with the rest of the trash."

George stood still for a moment. "How dare you move us out of our rooms, touch our personal things," he said, and Jane thought George had an unaccustomed boldness when he sneered at Lawrence. "My wife is one of the heirs to Angola, not you. She will decide where we live."

"How dare I?" Lawrence yelled as he threw the goblet of red wine in George's face. "It's quite simple. If you don't get out of my sight right now I will beat you within an inch of your sorry life even though I would hate to embarrass you in front of my sister. Besides, George, you might find sharing a bed with your own wife can be a novel and interesting experience, something quite different from what you do with the convicts."

George grabbed Ella's hand and Jane watched as he dragged Ella up the stairs. Jane could see his lips quivering. Red wine dripped down his chin. Then Lawrence called out to him, "The only reason Papa let you into this family was to keep Ella Marie from the cold lonely sheets of spinsterhood. I suggest you get about the work you were hired to do."

Jane spun around and went out the back door where the other servants were. She had no desire to hear the argument that would begin between Lawrence and the Madam.

Fourteen

THERE WAS NO LONGER ANY PEACE at Angola Plantation. No one, not even the Madam pretended that life was normal. There was uncertainty about everything. The Madam's brother Henry and Edward White were legally in charge of the prison operations. They showed no compassion for the prisoners and Jane saw that the convicts at Angola Plantation were well aware of it. You could no longer hear singing as they did the washing on Mondays or at other times as they went about their chores. Not one of the convicts wanted to be noticed, especially Jane. Where she had been afraid of the Major, she was now terrified of Lawrence's uncle Henry and Edward White. While the Major was alive there had always been the possibility the Countess could say something on her behalf if she did something to cause the Major or the Madam displeasure. With Henry and Edward White, there were no appeals. She had overheard it said many times that these two men constantly complained about the plantation convicts—saying they should be leased to the levee camps where they could bring in money instead of living in luxury and being pampered. And what Lawrence had predicted to Jane after his papa died came true. The prisoners at the levee camps were more brutally mistreated. So much so that it was published in every newspaper from New Orleans to New York. The Madam stopped the *Daily-Picayune* from reaching any of the convicts' hands. She told Jane if she ever caught her or the Countess talking about the cruelty of levee camp convicts to the ones who could not read, she would have the two of them whipped.

When word reached the plantation about a special meeting between Henry, Edward White and the prison Board of Control, Lawrence went to Baton Rouge and sat in on the meeting. He told Jane about it in great detail when he returned.

"You should have seen White showing off his power now that he's the manager over the convicts in the levee camps."

"I can imagine the discussion," she said, and a vision of the meeting of the prison Board of Control flashed across her mind. She could see Henry and Edward White denying any wrongdoing—denying that the death rate in the camps was climbing faster than the Board of Control could keep up with. She sat still for a moment, staring into space, until Lawrence said.

"All White did was shoot off his mouth after the Board of Control came down on him. They told him in no uncertain terms to slack up on the work hours in the camps or the governor's suffrage committee was going to have his ass. And White knows the only way the camps can make a profit is pushing the prisoners from daylight to dark. He got mighty irritated when they told him to ease up or else. When they pressed him about the penal reformers, he began to shout, cursing the suffrage committee, saying they didn't know one thing about lazy nigger criminals and white trash. And you should have heard him going on and on about how hard work is good for 'em. 'Helps to cleanse their soul', he said. Then one of the board members accused him of treating the convicts worse than animals. He really got mad then. Went to shouting that the only way the state could collect fifty thousand dollars rental fee a year for the convicts, would be for the lessees to work the prisoners twice as hard. And what he's saying is the truth. I heard Papa say many times if he had to feed 'em, the work hours would be from daylight to dark. That was the only way he figured he could keep his head above water."

Jane sighed. "Oh God," she said. "You think they'll take the convict management away from White?"

"Take away White's managerial position? Not in this world. When they threatened to hire a warden to oversee the convicts, he told them flatly he didn't want any do-gooders hanging over his head."

"Can't the Board of Control arrest him if he doesn't stop mistreating the convicts?"

"Jane, the lessees have a valid contract that doesn't run out for another five years. It doesn't say anything about how the camps are to be run. So long as the convicts are fed once a day and are given a blanket to sleep with, the suffrage committee can holler all they want. Getting the work done is Uncle Henry and Edward White's business. There is not one thing the Board of Control or anybody else can do about the mistreatment of convicts. The way the laws are written, none of the reforms will take place until the contract expires. As long as Uncle Henry and Edward White don't start shooting convicts on Canal Street, they can do pretty much what they want. You see Jane, the only result of the suffrage committee and the penal reformers' uproar is that the food in the camps will be cut back and the men will work until they drop. Trust me. The Ring Bosses will milk the convict lease dry, and it doesn't matter how many they have to bury to accomplish it."

"Please, Lawrence," she said. "Please find a way to help Ander before it's too late. Can't you have him brought here?"

"I'll do my best," he said.

But there was something about the tone of his voice that failed to ease her concern.

⚓ Fifteen ⚓

WHEN JANE OPENED HER EYES one morning a few months later, Lawrence was sitting next to her on the bed, moodily staring at nothing. Without even saying good morning, he said, "Uncle Henry is really mean and vengeful. Mama says that being spiteful to me is Uncle Henry's way to pay Papa back. He thinks Papa mistreated him all those years they worked together."

"Lawrence," she said, pushing him out of the way as she got out of the bed, "what's happened now?"

"Mama told me last night Uncle Henry is selling everything that belongs to the estate. He even tried to take away her railroad stock. Claimed the money she used to buy it rightfully belonged to the estate."

"Well, you warned her not to trust him."

"I know that, Precious. But he duped her."

Jane did not comment, only gave him a suspicious glance. Sometimes she thought Lawrence to be awfully naive, especially when it came to his mother. But either he didn't notice her attitude or pretended not to notice as she threw a few logs in the dying embers, stoking until a flame caught the wood on fire.

"I know Mama can be just as spiteful and hateful as her brother," he said, as Jane turned to face him. "But I feel sorry for her. I overheard her telling Ella Marie this morning she was going to have a good Christmas around here even if she has to sell what jewelry she has left to do it."

"Yes, I know she doesn't have any money, Lawrence. She tells everyone in this house about it enough. And while we are on the subject of your mama, I think you need to know she's been acting very strange lately."

"Yeah. How's that?"

"She rides off in the farm wagon so often that it's beginning to worry even the Countess. Where do you suppose she goes?"

Lawrence did not answer, but Jane could tell he was withholding some secret information and wondered if what the Countess suspected was right. She had told Jane she suspected the Madam was operating a levee camp not far from Angola. As far fetched as it seemed at the time, something told Jane it might be the truth. The Madam was desperate. All of her income had been taken away when the Major died and, as desperate as the Madam was to continue her lifestyle, Jane felt she was capable of anything. The Madam had learned from the Major, hadn't she? As she stared at Lawrence the saying crossed her mind, "Like Papa like Son."

Lawrence stood up. He scratched his head nervously. "I'm going to New Orleans today," he said, and Jane noticed how he ignored answering her question about his mother's strange behavior. If it had been Charles Fisher she was talking to, he would have quizzed her and tried to get to the bottom of what was troubling his mother. But Lawrence? He was a strange lot, all right. Jane felt he and the Madam must be up to something.

"I need to find Uncle Henry," he said, breaking her train of thought. "He's petitioned the courts to put *The Sparks* up for sale. I saw the advertisement in the *True-Democrat* this morning. I thought maybe I could get him to change his mind. Maybe he'd do it for Mama. We need the steamboat. I don't see how we can survive here at the plantation without it."

"When do you think you'll be back?" she asked.

"I don't have any idea. I was told the payment on the lease contract that's due in January can't be paid. The current income from the camps is not enough. Supposedly the state is coming after the plantation to make up the difference. Looks like I've got to go back to court and begin another round of legal maneuvers."

"You know, Lawrence, when all of this first started you told me you would fight for what was rightfully yours. I want to tell you, I'm proud of you for trying as hard as you have. At the time I didn't realize what you meant by what was rightfully yours. Now I think I'm beginning to understand better. A lot of men would have given up a long time ago. I'm glad to see you're going back to court with that bunch. Somebody needs to stand up to them."

Lawrence took a deep breath and said, "I'm broke, Jane. The lawyers took what little money I had. Uncle Henry has even cut off the pay Papa used to give me for managing the plantation. Even in New Orleans, all those bookies who used to give me as much credit as I wanted have turned their backs on me. I just don't know what I am going to do. I've got to get some money. Somehow, some way, I've got to figure out a way to get some money."

It was difficult for Jane to fully comprehend the pain Lawrence seemed to be in. While she was sorry for him and all his troubles, her life had always been one of hard work. No one had ever given her anything. The only way she knew how to get what she needed was to work for it. She looked around the room as he continued complaining about how hard his life was. What she saw was the fine Chippendale furniture and Currier and Ives prints, the knick knacks and other frivolous items that must have cost the Major a fortune. Cost probably more money than she and her entire family had seen in a lifetime. She could think only of the men whose lives had been ruined and the others who had died dreadful deaths so this family could live a life of luxury. Yes, it was difficult for Jane to understand or forgive this family.

⚜ Sixteen ⚜

FTER JANE SETTLED into the enormous bedroom where George Ivan had spent several years carrying out his sexual fantasies with a few of the young convict servants, she started having a recurring dream. She was alone on a beach—alone and frightened. Then Charles Fisher appeared to her. Without speaking, he kissed her and in his gentle way, took her hand. They walked along the water until they came to a dark tunnel, but she was afraid to go on with him. *Take my hand,* he kept encouraging her. *There's nothing to be afraid of.* They entered the tunnel. She could feel his arms around her as they walked through the dark. He kissed her tenderly and then a bright light appeared. A feeling of serenity overcame her as they floated toward the light. He pulled her body close to him. Her eyes were closed, yet she could see everything perfectly. She felt the pleasure of his body against her. Then suddenly she awoke crying. Although she never wanted to lose that feeling of happy fulfillment, the touch of the man she loved, she prayed silently, *Dear God, please, help me to forget my Charles.*

She lay quietly listening to the ticking of the English grandfather clock just outside her door in the hall. It was shortly after daybreak when she heard the plantation bell ringing. Through the window she could see a heavy fog creeping out of the wintry December sky and she knew heavy frost was probably everywhere. She wondered and worried about Ander. Sure Lawrence had told her Ander lived on another plantation similar to Angola, but sometimes she wondered if Lawrence was telling the truth. In the distance she heard the voice of Jacob calling out, "Steamboat coming." The whistle from the steamer signaled the beginning of another busy day as Lawrence walked into her bedroom. She knew he had been out making rounds before daylight with the sharecroppers, as he usually did. She shivered as he lay down next to her.

"Pull your clothes off, Lawrence," she said. "Your body is ice cold."

Without a moment's hesitation he stripped off his damp winter coat, his clothes and boots and climbed under the warm quilts next to her. He caressed her warm foot with his cold one and buried his head against her.

"I have to go off today," he said.

"Where?"

"Back to St. Francisville. The judge is going to hear my appeal again to set aside Papa's will and make me executor of the estate. I don't know what to expect."

"Well, maybe it'll all be over today and you can finally get your inheritance," she said, getting up to start a fire in the fireplace.

"I wouldn't be too sure. I turned in the new inventory for the plantation, but Uncle Henry sent word he intends to dispute it."

"You put everything on it, didn't you?"

"No. I didn't put Mama's jewelry or the furniture."

"Lawrence, the judge said to list everything on the plantation so the courts could decide the value of the estate. He told you not to come back until you did. This is the fourth time you've been to court fighting your uncle Henry. Why don't you do what you've been asked to do?"

"Nobody but God knows what Mama owns, and they'd never find anything if they came here looking for it," he said. "And besides, Uncle Henry is a liar and the judge knows it. This is just another way for him to stall, a way for him and Papa's old Ring Boss cronies to rape the estate of everything before the judge grants me my rightful inheritance. They don't give a damn about my inventory. They know practically everything Papa and Mama ever bought. They're not worried about cheap jewelry or a few wheelbarrows. They're stalling to get as much out of the lease contract as they can. Hundreds of thousands of dollars are being made off prison labor. Don't you understand that? Anyway, that's not what I came here to talk to you about. I don't feel good about going off and leaving you today. I want you to be careful. You've seen how Jones and George have been playing up to Uncle Henry and Edward White. Mama says they've been stealing everything they can get their hands on, trying to get in the good graces of Uncle Henry by infuriating me. There's no telling what they might try and do."

"Well, I'm not afraid of those two scoundrels," she said, crossing her arms in front of her, leaning against the mantel.

"I know that, but you know whose side they're on. I got a little rough with George last night; embarrassed him again in front of Ella Marie about spending too much of his time in the convict quarters. He resented the hell out of it, but it's the truth. He doesn't have any business treating those young girls the way he does. The sharecroppers are all starting to talk about it, and it could mean real trouble for all of us if he doesn't stop. He can go into St. Francisville or Baton Rouge and get him a whore for that." Then Lawrence chuckled, "Actually, it was pretty funny at the time, watching old George squirm, but he'll be looking to pay me back."

"Oh God," she said, pacing back and forth in front of the hearth. Lawrence's words had made her apprehensive. "You know, Lawrence, every time you go away from the plantation, George makes it his business to watch every move I make, especially since Peter Baulfield came here."

"Yeah, that's another one I want you to watch out for. That Baulfield's a sneak. I've known him since I was a child and he's never been anything but trouble."

"I can't understand your mama. Why did she put Baulfield up in a bedroom in this house when he was sent to the plantation as a convict?"

"Because he was a good friend of Papa's. Always looking out for Papa's best interests in New Orleans, and always with his hand out, I might add."

"Yeah, well that's what got him and that other city councilman two years in the penitentiary. Weren't they taking bribes from the railroad when Governor Foster did that major shake up in New Orleans city government?"

"Yes. How did you know about that? Nobody said anything about Baulfield being a convict."

"I read it in the *Daily-Picayune.*"

"Well, I don't have time this morning to be going over the list of convicts from New Orleans city council members or from the rest of the council members in this state for that matter," he said. Jane thought she detected a hint of hesitancy in his voice.

"The only reason I'm telling you about George is that the Countess has been after me constantly. She said you needed to know so you could put a stop to it."

"Jane, there is not a thing I can do to George for looking at you. Just be very careful. Take the Countess with you if you go anywhere, or have Jacob ride you on the rail cart. If George bothers you in the house, threaten to tell Ella Marie. That should stop him for awhile or tell him if I catch him hiding behind doors waiting to touch you when you pass through, I'll throw him out the window. Tell him anything. He's not hard to scare off."

Huh! she thought. *And what am I supposed to do when he sneaks up to the sewing room again and locks the door with only the two of us in there? What am I supposed to do then, chase him out with my scissors?,* but she didn't say any more. She had decided long ago it wasn't good to burden Lawrence with more problems.

The sun was trying to creep through the winter clouds, she noticed, as she pulled on her boots and told Lawrence she'd hurry downstairs to get his breakfast ready.

"Mama and Ella Marie are taking the children and leaving for New Orleans today," he said. "They're going Christmas shopping and won't be back for two weeks. I don't know when I'll get back from St. Francisville. Meantime, you keep this room locked up when you're alone in here."

Lawrence ate as quickly as he could, buttoned his thick wool coat and wrapped the red scarf Jane had made for him tightly around his neck. She watched him walk across the frozen yard to the small stable where he saddled his stallion. She stood in the doorway until he was only a blur up the road. *How bleak the future seems,* she thought. *Lawrence's case is hopeless. Even with Governor Foster hot on their tails, the Ring Bosses are still powerful men. Other than determination,*

Lawrence has little to fight them with. He can keep his uncle at bay with legal maneuvers, but that won't last forever. The truth is on his side, though being right means precious little when the stakes are this high. Lawrence could fight these powerful men, but in her heart, Jane was afraid he would lose.

The Madam banging on her floor startled Jane. The banging was getting louder and the Madam was beginning to yell. *Something must be wrong,* she thought. Jane had seen the Countess go out behind the stables to the little wooden shack. She became concerned the Madam might be in distress. She left the back door and went straight up the stairs to the second floor. The pleasant smell of burning pecan wood filtered through the hall from the fireplaces in every room. The grandfather clock struck nine as she approached the Madam's bedroom and heard loud voices coming from it. She peeked inside, and saw the Madam and Nellie on their hands and knees, clawing through the Madam's jewel box, scattering pieces of diamond, ruby and emerald jewelry around. "Where are they?" the Madam shouted at Nellie. "Where are my pearls? Someone has stolen my double strand of matched pearls."

Nellie scrambled up off of the floor when she saw Jane come into the room. Jane could see Nellie was frightened, as the girl came and stood behind her. "Madam," Jane said. "Here, let me help you. Come on, get up off the floor."

Together they emptied every chiffonier, drawer and box in the room. Jane looked under the bed and the Madam tore off the bed clothes and searched under the mattress. They searched every nook and cranny, every dresser drawer; rummaged through every piece of lingerie and every pair of shoes the Madam had. There were no pearls to be found. Jane knew that anyone in the house could have taken them.

"Go, wake up that good for nothing George Ivan," the Madam told Nellie. "Tell him I want to see him this very instant. I want to see him right now. Then go bring me that little black whip he likes so much."

Jane sat at the Madam's writing table. She pulled out every drawer in it, stacking each one on top of the other, going through each one very carefully. Within minutes there was the sound of feet in the hallway and George Ivan, wearing only his gray flannel night-shirt, stood in the Madam's doorway.

"What's going on in here?" he asked as Nellie handed the Madam the whip.

Jane heard the click of the lock. She looked up again just as the small black whip in the Madam's hand bit hard into Ivan's face. The Madam began to scream at him. Jane sat frozen.

"Steal from me, will you? I think not, George."

George was screaming and wiping his bloody mouth. The Madam raised the whip to strike him again when Jane heard Ella Marie banging on the door. Jane stood up, ran to the door, opened it and let Ella into the room.

"Mama! Stop! Why are you doing this to George?" Ella cried.

"Every since your papa died," the Madam said, "Your husband has been stealing me blind. Whatever he gets his hands on he sells to those roustabouts on the river boats. Now he's stolen the precious pearls that your papa gave me on our wedding day. You know how much they mean to me, Ella Marie. Either your husband gets back my pearls or I'll have your uncle Henry after him. They are not only a token of your papa's love, they're priceless. I want them back."

Jane watched as Ella Marie nodded and left the room holding George by the arm. The Madam called after Ella in a changed voice, as if nothing had happened. "You'd better get your valises out in the hall. Someone will be up for the trunks before eleven. The boat leaves at noon."

"I'll be ready, Mama," Ella called back to the Madam.

"Scat," she said to Jane and Nellie who stood speechless, staring at the disarray of the Madam's bedroom. "See that the children are ready. You can clean this up after I leave."

THE REST OF THAT MORNING and on into the afternoon Jane went about her sewing. She was trying to finish a dress she was making for Nellie before she started the new dresses the Madam and Ella Marie wanted in time for Christmas. But her mind was never far from what Lawrence had said about being care-ful. She got up and walked around the silent room. The clock downstairs struck three. Jane wished she could be with her children and her mama for Christmas—or forever for that matter. She longed to hold her little girl again and tuck her into bed at night. For a moment she wondered if John Augustus's wife might bake Christmas cookies with her—or maybe her mama would. *What are they doing? Why doesn't one of them try to contact me—write me a letter or something?* Then Ander flashed across her mind again. *I wonder if Lawrence would bring him to Angola while the Madam is away?* All kinds of thoughts kept going through her mind. She had to fight with herself to keep from thinking about Charles Fisher. She couldn't allow her pleasant memories of Charles to occupy her thoughts anymore, the way they did when he was alive. *No, when your man is dead you can't allow yourself to think about him. If you do, you'll just go mad,* she thought, trying to shake the vision of Charles from her mind.

A few minutes later there was a soft knock on the door. Jane put a log on the dying fire before she went to answer it.

"The Madam and her troop finally left, so I thought I would spend the rest of my day sewing with you," the Countess said, setting the tray with a pot of coffee and two cups on the table near the fireplace.

"I hope Lawrence doesn't have any trouble on the road," the Countess said, worriedly, walking over to look out of the window. "Weather sure is bad out. Paper says a blizzard is expected to come through here any day now."

"Lawrence didn't think it would snow today," Jane said, "but even if he did I doubt if it would've stopped him."

The Countess didn't comment. From the look on her face, Jane figured she wasn't here to talk about Lawrence's journey to the courthouse.

"What's on your mind, Countess?" she asked.

"I want to talk about the fight Lawrence had with George last night. Did Lawrence tell you about it?"

"A little," she said, pouring coffee into the cups. "Why? Was there more to it than Lawrence might have told me?"

"Well, Cherie, it's not so much about the fight. I was passing their door when I overheard George saying to Ella he should be in charge of the plantation since Ella had been left part of the estate.

He also said he was going to kill Master Lawrence the next time he humiliated him—or at least run him off the plantation."

"George Ivan can't do that," Jane said.

"Can't do what? Run Lawrence off the plantation? Where is your brain? You know as well as I do, Master Lawrence has no legal rights to this plantation any longer. They can do anything they please and it doesn't matter how many times Master Lawrence takes them to court."

"Countess, you worry too much. The Madam would kill that shifty eyed weasel before she'd allow him to hurt Lawrence. You know how she feels about George Ivan. Look what she did to him this morning."

"Maybe so, but it's you I'm worried about. The Madam isn't awake twenty-four hours a day. You just be careful. Keep your guard up. Don't let anybody near you but me and Lawrence. You can't trust anybody."

That night, Jane waited and worried. It had snowed all day and when Lawrence hadn't returned by eight o'clock she figured he'd stayed in St. Francisville. She put away supper and went into the Big House and on up to her room after she checked on Nellie. She had just settled into her warm bed at nine o'clock when she heard someone tapping on her door. Shivering as her feet touched the cold floor, she put on the heavy velvet robe Lawrence had brought her from New Orleans. She struck a match and lit her oil lamp and hurried to the door thinking it was Lawrence or the Countess.

"Is that you, Countess?" she called out before opening the door. "Is that you?"

No answer.

"If that's you, say something."

There was still no answer and Jane backed away from the door. Then a deep muffled voice answered, "There's been an accident. You'd better come real quick. The Countess is hurt."

She began to tremble and without thinking, set the lamp on the table and opened the door. George Ivan was standing there with Jones just a step behind him. She tried with all her might, struggling against the man's weight, to close the door, but George shoved it open with his boot and pushed her back into the dim room. Her feet flew out from under her as she stumbled backward. Her robe and nightgown flew above her knees.

George straddled her. Put his face so close to hers the stench of whiskey almost knocked her out.

"You were right, Jones," George spat. "This is a hell of a lot better than that nigger pussy. And this is one little girl who needs a lot of lessons about how a convict's supposed to act, don't you think?"

"Yeah. This one's got a lot to learn," Jones said, as he looked around the room. "Hell, since Lawrence took up with her, she don't act like a convict any more. She don't work, just sits here in your old room like a queen or something. Ain't that right, gal?" Jones smirked and walked up to Jane, rubbing his cold boot on the skin between her knees.

Jane was terrified. There was no way out of this. She doubted if anyone could hear her from where her room was located. What in this world was going to happen to her now? She knew right then she had a good chance of being killed. These two men were drunk—and out to pay Lawrence back. Oh God, how could Lawrence even let this man stay in the house after what happened last night? Or the Madam? She should have run him off before she left this morning.

"When I finish with her," George said, taking off his belt, "I'll bet she'll forget all about pretty boy Lawrence."

"Yeah, George. She'll be singing a different tune," Jones burst out laughing.

George reached down and grabbed her foot and began to twist it. "How do you like this, little convict gal? Don't you like your man to give you a little pain once in a while?"

George cackled loudly and twisted her foot back and forth. Jane screamed. She'd never felt such pain. She beat her fist on the floor, kicking out with her other foot, trying to free her leg from his grip. She thrashed about on the floor and her robe came open. George and Jones leered at her. Jones grabbed her other leg. They began to drag her toward the bed. In an effort to stop them, she locked her hands around the leg of a heavy oak library table until George twisted her foot so hard she could barely stand it.

"You'd better let go," George shouted at her. "Let go or I'll break it."

"Break it, you red-eyed devil!" she screamed. "That's the only way you'll get me into that bed."

Jones was grunting lustfully as he leered at her, and just as Jane felt the hard snap of her bone breaking, a twenty-gauge blast shattered the crystal lamp on the table. George dropped her leg and howled like a wounded animal, his face cut and bleeding in a dozen places from the shards of flying glass. Jones took off, running out of the bedroom, but George couldn't do anything but sink to his knees, groaning.

The Countess stood over him with the shotgun pointed at his head. "I'll kill you if you don't get out of here," she said, with a deadly calmness. "If I ever catch you around her again or causing her or me any trouble, I suggest you think about what happened to the Major!"

George struggled to his feet. Covering his face with his coat, he staggered off into the dark hall. The Countess called after him, "I'm certain one of the women in the quarters will be more than happy to tend your wounds. After all you've done for them, I think they'd love to get their hands on your stinking face."

Jane passed out. When she awoke, Dr. Taylor stood at the foot of her bed. The Countess stood right beside him but Jane had to strain to understand what the two were saying.

"That idiot shattered her ankle. If she were one of the family, I'd put her on *The Sparks* and take her to Charity Hospital in New Orleans," he told the Countess. "But she's not family and you know the policy on convicts who get hurt."

Jane heard the Countess ask. "Can't we send for Dr. Buffington, that old prison doctor in Baton Rouge?"

"The Ring Bosses would have a fit if I called in Doctor Buffington. Besides, he claims he already has his hands full. Convicts are dropping dead by the dozens in the levee camps—so many the old doctor can't keep up with 'em. And that's just the ones he knows about. Don't you see, Laura, there is not much any of us can do to help you convicts."

Jane struggled to sit up. "Dr. Taylor, I've always wanted to ask you. . . ." She winced. "Why do you work for these people? You're a physician, you could practice anywhere—why here?"

"Lie still Jane. You will only cause yourself more agony if you move. It started many years ago with the Major. You see I don't have a medical degree. Never had one. And just like over half the physicians in Louisiana now, didn't need it. Anyway, most of us who were under the Major's employ can never leave. Once you are involved with these people, there is only one way out. That's in a pine box. Jane, you convicts are not the only prisoners in this system. We all are."

"It didn't change with the Major's death?"

"Indeed not. It only worsened. Up until his death, most of us were treated pretty good. Now, things have changed for the worse."

Jane again struggled to sit up. "Dr. Taylor," she whispered, "how is the situation at Hope Plantation?"

"Be careful, Jane."

"Please, Dr. Taylor, I need to know about my boy."

"There is nothing I could tell you about your child that Lawrence hasn't already told you. From what I understand, the situation at the sugar house is not critical. They still use hired help there. Only in the levee camps is it out of control."

"What do you mean out of control?" Jane asked.

Doctor Taylor threw the instruments into his black bag and snapped it shut. "Listen to me, women," he said. "You don't realize how lucky you are. Look at the both of you. You're living better than you ever did in your own homes. Those poor devils in the levee camps are struggling daily to stay alive. Every day is a challenge for them just to see if they can make it till nightfall. It's freezing cold outside right now, but you don't feel it, do you? No! But the poor devils in those camps do. Most are in makeshift housing and drafty canvas tents. They're freezing to death, the ones not dying from dysentery and malaria or the pox. When is the last time either of you drank a cup of water full of wigglies or had a steady diet of corn-pone and fat-back?"

The Countess sat down in a chair beside Jane's bed, shaking her head and Jane noticed she had tears in her eyes. "You are right, Dr. Taylor," the Countess said. "We convicts at Angola do have a lot to be thankful for. Most of the other convicts are treated no better than the slaves were before the war. The only difference in slavery now is the color of the skin." She chuckled and Jane knew it was only to keep from crying. "You know if you think about it, the powerful men in the south won the war anyway."

"The War?" Jane said, "Countess, what are you talking about?"

"I mean, all the prisons in the south are operated basically the same. Most all of them are operated by private companies who make a profit off of slave labor. What I'm trying to say is, the south fought a devastating battle to retain slavery. It was the only way they knew and when the war was over the men in the south had to find a way to replace the slave labor they had lost or they were all doomed. They would never regain financial stability again without it."

Dr. Taylor stared the Countess squarely in the eye. "Laura, you are very perceptive for a woman," he said, "and you hit the nail right on the head. Been many a poor devil incarcerated for his strong back. And I've seen many a good man not live to tell about it."

"Dr. Taylor, I've seen what you are talking about myself," Jane said. "The Negro man who came to prison with me and my son was sentenced for stealing three school books."

Dr. Taylor just shook his head and walked to the door. He turned and looked at Jane as he twisted the doorknob. "And God only knows if he lived to get out," he said. He opened the door and quietly closed it behind him.

The Countess stayed by Jane's bed until late the next evening when Lawrence came home. "No sense in you trying to get even with him, Master Lawrence," she told him, after explaining the incident about George in detail. "He's not worth it. There's something mighty wrong with Mister George's mind but if you kill him, they'll just put you in jail."

"If they don't ever find his body, they won't," Lawrence said, pounding his fist into the wall.

"Go on down to the landing and tell Captain Williams I want a full head of steam on *The Sparks* in an hour," he told the Countess. "Then get your belongings and Jane's packed; I'm taking her out of here."

Jane raised her head and looked at Lawrence. "Did I hear you say you're taking us out of here?" she asked.

"Yes, ma'am," the Countess said, stifling her enthusiasm. Lawrence just nodded.

"Go get Nellie. I'm not leaving her here," Jane told the Countess.

"Master Lawrence, can we bring Virginia Reed?" the Countess asked, when he nodded it would be all right to take Nellie.

"Whoa," he said. "We can't take 'em all. The Ring Bosses will track us down for sure if we do that." He called out to the Countess as she fled down the hall. "Tell Jacob to bring the flatbed. Have him put a mattress on it so we can move Jane without hurting her foot."

Lawrence sat down beside Jane on the bed. They looked at each other silently for a moment. "Don't do anything foolish, Lawrence. If it takes a broken foot to get me out of this damnable place, it's nothing compared to the broken heart I had when I got in here. And, Lawrence," Jane said as Lawrence tugged on her, lifting her to the side of the bed. "Can't we take Ander with us? Please, can't you send for him?"

⚔ Seventeen ⚔

Under the bludgeonings of chance
My head is bloody but unbowed.

—Henley

New Orleans, Louisiana
Four years later

JANE TIED BACK the lace curtains of her bedroom window and stood staring down at busy Royal Street lined with delivery wagons, drays and buggies making their way toward the vegetable markets. Looking out across the cobblestone street she could see the tower of Saint Louis Cathedral. She loved her cozy home in the French Quarter. It was a far cry from the Big House at Angola, but it was hers—hers and Lawrence's.

Now just thinking of her husband distressed her. How different her life had been when she and Lawrence first came to New Orleans four years ago. They were married right away by one of his uncles who preached at the First Presbyterian Church at Lafayette Square. She remembered back to all the good times; the fun they had at the Fair Grounds Racetrack; the wonderful restaurants, *de la Louisiane* and *Antoines;* the beautiful clothes and jewelry Lawrence had brought her from New York and Saratoga. And who could forget the Opera and all the plays at the *Varieties Grand Opera House.* But more wonderful than anything, she had given birth to Mildred

Louise and also now had her other two children with her. Lawrence had sent for both Georgia Ann and Ander when they arrived in New Orleans, and they were all free. She could walk to Canal Street without a care in the world. No one, not even Lawrence's uncle Henry would dare to question her. Lawrence would not allow it.

But that was then.

She shook her head, breathing deeply, as tears slid down her cheeks. *How could everything have gone so wrong in four years?* she thought. She should have paid more attention to the way Lawrence had treated his first wife when she was living—as if she was a nothing, a nobody—how quickly he had forgotten her after she drowned—how quickly he had taken Jane's body.

His complete disregard for her had started, she remembered, the day Deep Pockets Malone came into their lives. Malone, a high stakes gambler from New York's underworld, had moved into New Orleans shortly after Storyville became a legal red light District and set up in a saloon on Customhouse Street in what is known as the Restricted District. He became a *District Boss*, competing with the unofficial mayor of Storyville, Tom Anderson.

She remembered that Lawrence had become acquainted with Malone through his involvement with the Countess. As the prostitutes moved into Storyville, Basin Street became world renowned as the "Street of the Mansions." Jane first met Deep Pockets Malone the day she went with Lawrence to the Countess's to see the new house on Basin Street between Bienville and Conti Streets. "Oh Lawrence this house is so magnificent," Jane had exclaimed as their carriage pulled up and stopped in front of a huge two-story white house that sat amid two entire blocks of such places, most of them with imposing entrances.

"Jane, this is a whorehouse. Don't carry on so. Everybody on the street is looking at us."

"When did it ever make any difference to you if people stared at you? Don't try to be so high-falutin'. It doesn't become you, reminds me too much of your mama," she had said.

"Lawrence Browne," a voice called out. Jane turned around and noticed a sandy haired man with a blonde handlebar mustache coming down Basin Street. His hair was parted in the middle and

Jane could see a large scar going down his neck into his shirt. She cringed at the sight of him.

"Precious, this is Tom Malone, more commonly known as Deep Pockets Malone," Lawrence chuckled, slapping the man on the back. "Luckiest man in the whole world. Yes siree, 'Deep Pockets'," he winked at Jane and said. "Tom, I want you to meet my little lady, Jane."

She remembered how the man had parted his lips and smiled a wide toothy grin, "Pleasure's all mine, Miss Jane," he had said and motioned Lawrence away from the carriage.

Jane sat quietly looking out toward the row of imposing houses. The street was filled with mule drawn wagons full of the Countess's new furniture which Lawrence had bought. Maids hurried in and out the front door of the gingerbread decorated house with their hands full of brooms, buckets and feather dusters. A Hook-and-Ladder-Shop was not more than a hundred feet from the Countess's house and at the corner of Conti Street was the St. Louis Cemetery. *God, I don't know why the Countess would want to live so close to a graveyard,* she remembered thinking. *Virginia Reed is scared of the dead. I know I wouldn't enjoy them as such close neighbors.*

When the Countess stuck her head out the front door and saw Jane, she came running out to the street. "Cherie, come in. I want you to see how Lawrence has set me up. It's so beautiful. I'll never be able to thank Lawrence enough for being so generous and having so much faith in me."

"Well, he's happy to do it for you, Countess. We owe you everything. You saved my life," Jane had said, climbing out of the carriage, reaching out and hugging the Countess and Virginia Reed who had run up to greet her. They walked toward the house and were about to enter when Lawrence called out to her, "Let's go. I've got to get you home. Malone and I are going out to the Fair Grounds Racetrack. The whole bunch from Saratoga will be out there today and I want to meet with them." Jane had nodded and waved to Lawrence that she'd be only a minute.

"Miz Jane, you shore is looking mighty fine since you got out of Angola. I shore does miss you," Virginia said before the Countess shooed her back inside the house ahead of them. And the house was gorgeous—a combination of imported European furniture with a touch of local New Orleans flavor that was even more appealing with the gold colored drapery Jane had completed for all the tall windows.

And she'd never forget the serious look in the Countess's eyes when she told her that day, "You tell Lawrence to watch himself with that bunch of Saratoga cut-throats. I heard Mary Deubler, a Madam who has a house in the next block, saying those men are a dangerous lot. Tom Anderson won't even let them enter the District. And you know those men have to be bad sports for Tom not to want their money."

And Jane said, "I don't think we have to worry about Lawrence, do you, Countess?"

"It's not Lawrence I'm worried about. It's you."

"Why me? What are you talking about?" Jane asked.

"When a man gets involved with the underworld, his life is never the same, Cherie. His family comes last. Do you understand what I'm talking about? If you don't, then let me explain how characters of that sort operate."

That won't be necessary, she remembered thinking and wished the Countess would not talk to her as if she were a child, or someone brainless who couldn't think for herself. "I think I understand what you're saying perfectly," she snapped as they walked back to the carriage. And then Jane asked her, "Are these men friendly with the Ring Bosses?"

"For now, but from what I've heard, it won't be long before they'll be trying to cut in on the Ring's territory. That's when the war will start, you'll see. You just watch out for yourself, and if you can, keep Lawrence away from them. All right?"

IN THE THREE YEARS that followed, Jane would many times remember the Countess's words. *All the happiness we knew, gone, just like that,* she snapped her fingers. *He acts as if our baby and I don't even exist anymore. It's his gambling, that's what it is. I should have known better than to think he could associate with these men and not change. I should have left him when he first met them way back then.*

Yes, that's what I should have done and this is exactly what I deserve for staying with Lawrence—God is punishing me.

Mildred Louise's cries snapped Jane out of her thoughts of the past. The baby needed to be fed. Jane sadly lowered the curtain, crossed the room and picked up her child. She was such a tiny baby, so delicate. Jane had worried constantly about her ever since her birth three months before. She cradled Mildred Louise in her arms as she sat down on the bed and opened her bodice for the baby to nurse. Suddenly Jane heard the front door downstairs open and slam shut.

"It's about time he got home, she thought. "Lawrence!" she said coldly, "where have you been?"

Lawrence walked over to the mahogany half tester bed and angrily threw the *Daily-Picayune* at her. "Don't they raise anything up in Caldwell Parish except cotton, corn and thieves, Jane?" he slurred.

"What are you talking about? Are you drunk?"

"Drunk! Not nearly as drunk as I would like to be," he said loudly, stumbling to the foot of the bed.

"Please don't yell at me, Lawrence," she said, putting her hand over the baby's face, trying to protect her daughter from Lawrence's wrath. "It's not fair the way you're treating me. I don't like it."

His eyes were puffy and bloodshot, and the stubble on his face made him look much older than his thirty-two years. His clothes, so handsome when he left the house yesterday, were wrinkled and soiled, and the anger in his voice was unsettling.

"You don't like it?" he shouted at her, picking up the crumpled newspaper, slamming it again and again against his open hand near her face. "Well let me tell you what it is I don't like. It's that criminal no good son of yours that's put us in jeopardy, getting himself involved with train robbers. That's what I don't like. When he comes back to New Orleans, you might as well hang a sign out front that says 'escaped convicts live here'."

She snatched the paper out of his hand and read the article about a train robbery near Columbia. *Ander didn't have anything to do with this, I don't care what you're saying,* she thought. She stood up and laid the baby in her crib, thanking God Georgia Ann had left earlier to go to work at the Charity Hospital. Her anger became outrage. "What is wrong with you lately, Lawrence?" she demanded, rummaging through the bureau to find something to wear. "I'm tired of the way you treat my children and I'm tired of the way you treat me. Coming home anytime you feel like it, lying to me about where you go. I'm tired of it! Do you hear me? I'm tired of it! I don't need a man just to say I have one. If you can't be a better husband and father than this, you may as well just move out."

She threw the newspaper back at him, "And you're mad to think Ander had anything to do with this. He's no thief. He left New Orleans to get away from you and all of your high-toned racetrack cronies. He didn't leave here to go and rob trains in northern Louisiana. Besides, what makes you an authority on this train robbery? The paper said it was an unidentified man."

Lawrence sighed. "You forget who I am. If there's anything criminal going on in this state, I know about it and I know who did it. Uncle Henry may have thrown me off the plantation, but he didn't cut off my connections. You can believe what you want, but I know for a fact Ander didn't do anything but steal for the captains while he was in prison at Hope Plantation. As for the train robbery, even a simpleton like you should be able to figure that one out. That is, if you could ever stop thinking of your son as St. Andrew The Good."

Jane wanted to claw Lawrence's eyes out. Nothing was right any more. All the happiness she first knew with Lawrence in New Orleans had vanished. He had changed so much. They never went out together any more and every bit of the money he made lately was spent on gambling. Sometimes when he would win, he'd be generous and give her a stack of bills to cover expenses. She learned to stash money aside for the hard times when he'd be on a losing streak, so he wouldn't take her jewelry and sell it. She planned on giving the emerald bracelet to Georgia Ann for a dowry when the time came, and the pearl necklace she was saving for the baby.

Jane scooped up Mildred Louise without saying another word to Lawrence and carried her downstairs into the kitchen where Nellie was cooking. Nellie immediately took the child into her arms. The smell of turnip greens and fresh pork diverted Jane to the cook stove.

Lifting the lid, she scooped out a spoonful of the pot-liquor and sipped it. "Mmmm. Nellie, Sugar, you sure are getting to be a great cook."

"Everything I learnt you taught me," Nellie replied, "and I gots a surprise for your supper, Miz Jane. Them sweet potatoes I grew by the back fence, I gonna fry 'em for you tonight. Georgia Ann showed me how to cut 'em up so they fries thin. I gonna sprinkle sugar on 'em for you."

"You're a sweet girl, Nellie. Don't you ever change."

"No mam, I don't plans too."

Jane slowly walked back upstairs into her room and stared down at Lawrence who had passed out. Shaking her head, she pondered on why she stayed with this man who had become so cruel and unreasonable. Was it for Georgia Ann and the baby? Was she afraid to break up the home she'd made for them, take away the security she had tried to give Georgia Ann since she got out of prison? Was it Lawrence's endless threats of sending her and Ander back to prison if she left him? *What really is my reason for staying with you?* she wondered, then turned away from him, grabbed her handbag and went back downstairs again.

"Nellie, Sugar, I promised the Countess I'd go out to the racetrack with her this morning. If Georgia Ann gets back before I do, tell her I'll be back sometime this afternoon. But don't tell her I went off with the Countess. You know how Georgia Ann feels about me going anywhere with her. She doesn't want me seen with the Countess. She just can't understand the bond we have, can she?"

"No mam, I don't guess she does."

When she heard the sounds of carriage wheels in the back alleyway, Jane took a quick glance at herself in the mirror and straightened her hair. She kissed the baby and went out through the back door.

JANE LOVED being with the Countess, in spite of the fact the Countess filled her carriages with the beautiful young girls from her sporting house and took them out to the Fair Grounds Racetrack. It bothered Jane the way the crowd murmured as the drivers helped the women out of the elegant black carriages drawn by high step-

ping horses crowned with purple plumes, but she tried to overlook
it. The Countess was still very dear to her even though she had become the talk of the town, operating one of the most elegant sporting houses in Storyville.

"Smile, Cherie," the Countess said, leading the way as they
walked toward their seats in the club house. "Everyone is looking
at us."

The Uptown men and women stared and whispered as Jane, the
Countess and the Countess's girls passed. Jane knew these people
weren't talking about the Countess's ivory and gold, diamond-
studded cigar holder or the diamond choker that had become her
trademark. But if people wanted to whisper about the Countess,
there was nothing Jane could do. Even though the Countess liked
to flaunt herself, Jane was always reminded that they had come a
long way together. She refused to snub the woman who had saved
her life.

Tuxedo clad black waiters brought champagne to their seats. Jane
confined her conversation to the Countess. The people staring at
them began to irritate her and she said, "Perhaps we shouldn't be in
the Club House, Countess. Maybe that's why they're being so rude,
staring at us."

The Countess grinned, "Shouldn't be here? Why not? I own
this box."

"Then why don't you speak to them?" Jane asked, motioning to
the fashionable crowd. "I can see they're looking at you. I know
they're talking about you."

"Of course they're looking," the Countess said, smiling. "Other
than the fact I like to bet money on the horses, why do you think I
come here? It's good for business. I get a chance to show off my
creamy skinned octoroon girls. The men tell me they love it. It gives
them a chance to see what the girls look like in the daylight."

"I see," Jane said, and cringed that the Countess would make
such a spectacle of them all on a day that should have been an out-
ing among friends. But she didn't say how she felt about it. She
slumped down in her seat and the Countess kept on talking.

"And I know they're whispering about me. But Cherie, it
wouldn't be good for business if I acknowledged I have the

acquaintance of any of these men, even though more than a few found pleasure and comfort in my house last evening. Yes, let them talk. Let the women look at our gowns and have the illusion that their husbands find them more attractive than they do my girls."

Jane looked toward the track waiting for the beginning of the first race. *Sometimes the Countess says things that just don't make any sense,* she thought. *Since we got out of prison, she's a totally different person. And she acts like she doesn't care who recognizes her.*

"Look," the Countess said, tapping Jane on the shoulder, "it's that woman from Antoine's Restaurant, the one we saw when we first came to New Orleans. Who did you say she is?"

"Mrs. Stanley, the wife of the bank president," Jane reminded her.

The woman was talking to someone down by the rails, then she began to walk gracefully up the steps. She was holding the full skirt of her dark green silk dress as she passed through the crowded seats, making her way up to the Club House. Occasionally she reached up to straighten the wide brim green hat with yellow flowers that the wind kept blowing to the side of her head. She swept through the open door and her smile seemed friendly enough as she brushed past them. Jane faintly smiled back. The well dressed society woman took a seat next to an older white haired woman sitting in a box directly behind Jane and the Countess.

"Did you see those whores smiling at me?" Jane heard Mrs. Stanley whisper to the white haired woman.

"From the moment I saw them step out of their gaudy carriage, I knew what they were," the other woman whispered. Jane's eyebrows lifted instantly, her forehead wrinkled up and her heart began to palpitate rapidly. *Whores?* She looked over at the Countess to see if the Countess had heard what Mrs. Stanley had said.

"I heard her, Cherie," the Countess whispered, placing her finger to her lips. "Shh. Don't pay any attention to them."

"The black one. Isn't that the darky Emma Browne used to bring with her from the prison?" The other woman asked Mrs. Stanley.

"Yes, I believe you are right, Gladys. Emma always said she was real royalty. From Haiti, wasn't it?"

"Yes, yes. Of course my dear, but I never believed a word of it," Gladys replied.

"I wonder how she got out of prison?" Mrs. Stanley said. "I guess when the state took over they probably sent all the women home. At least, I believe, that's what I heard Mr. Stanley say."

"Have you seen Emma Browne since the state took the plantation away from her?" Gladys asked.

"Heavens no! That was pitiful. My husband said she left New Orleans owing a lot of money to his bank. Her brother Henry had to see that all her debts were paid."

Jane and the Countess exchanged a curious glance. They sipped their drinks, listening to every word the two ladies were saying. Jane was more worried than the Countess about being recognized, but she didn't let on. Finally she relaxed even though people all around them were whispering and some actually stood up in their seats to get a glimpse of the Countess's young girls.

The Countess, as much at ease as if she were entertaining a personal friend at home, put another cigar into her holder and waited for the waiter to light it. Jane leaned as far back in her seat as she could. The two ladies had lowered their voices and she had to strain to hear them.

"I think it's a disgrace what those awful Brownes did to the people who were sent to their prison," Gladys said, stopping a moment to sip her champagne. "Our people have suffered terribly since the war and men like the Major who fed off the distress of his own kind are no better than the Yankees. I am ashamed to say this, but my husband was relieved when that man died. Practically every man I know gave a sigh of relief," she said, with a sound of utter disdain in her aristocratic voice.

"I know exactly what you mean," Jane heard Mrs. Stanley say, her words slurring a little. "When the old man was alive, no one did business in Louisiana without association with the Browne family. There were several occasions, for business reasons, mind you, my husband insisted that I invite them to dinner at our home. Well, all the Major talked about was his lucrative convict business, and Mrs. Browne talked only about how much money she spent on her clothes. A completely objectionable woman. You know, I doubt if she ever had a thought about anyone other than herself. I remember one evening, I took the ladies upstairs after dinner, and, while freshening up, Mrs. Browne asked me why I had so many books in my sitting room. 'Why, to read', I told her. Why else would one have books? Then she thumbed through one and tossed it aside. Do you have any idea what she said?"

Jane heard the woman named Gladys say, "No."

"She said she found her own thoughts much more interesting than anything someone could write in a book! Can you believe the stupidity of that woman?"

"I can well believe it," Gladys answered. "Neither the Major nor Mrs. Browne were God's more enlightened creations, shall we say."

"How correct you are," Mrs. Stanley said. "And have you heard the most recent news about that awful family?" Before Gladys could answer Mrs. Stanley said, "I'm sure you know of Lawrence, the handsome son of the Major and Mrs. Browne."

"Yes, I remember him. Didn't his daughter, Mary Ann, just get married?" Gladys asked.

"And such a young girl," Mrs. Stanley answered. "Quit school and married a foreigner so she could help take care of her younger brother. It is being said that Lawrence won't even buy bread for his children's table. Mr. Stanley says he's supposedly broke again and courting a woman from one of New York's old families for her money."

"Who is she, Mrs. Stanley?"

"I don't want to tell you her name—there's no point in advertising her foolishness, but I can assure you that you know her. She's convinced Lawrence is going to marry her, and Mr. Stanley says she gives him money for one scheme after another. I'm surprised they're not out here today. Why, he's even convinced her he has a way to handicap the horses and never lose a bet.

"I don't know who is the bigger fool, he or she. I guess she is. She's telling everyone who will listen that Lawrence has taken out a license and is marrying her. Can you imagine anything so silly and foolish?"

Jane was stunned, completely speechless as the Countess stared at her. People in town knew more about Lawrence's strange behavior than she did. She sat there shaking her head, unable to move, trying to clear her mind and calm her racing heart.

"I told you not to pay any attention to them," the Countess finally said. "That woman obviously has had too much to drink. She's just a gossipy person who doesn't realize the consequences of foolish tale-bearing. Don't think about what she said."

It's easy for you to say. It doesn't hurt you one bit, but she's talking about my husband; my life, she thought. "And what does she mean?" Jane snapped. "Lawrence courting a society woman?"

The hooves of the race horses against the soft dirt of the track and the roar of the spectators in the grandstand faded into the distance as Jane waited for the Countess's reply. Even though she tried to deny it, Jane already knew the answer to her question.

‡ Eighteen ‡

"**G**ET UP you two-timing scoundrel!" Jane said, tugging Lawrence out of a deep sleep. "I've just heard some interesting gossip about you."

He pushed her hand away. "Get out of here and let me sleep," he said, slurring his words.

"Get up, Lawrence," she said again. "If you don't, I'll find out who this woman is on my own and I'll go over and tell her everything I know about you."

Lawrence finally sat up. Rubbing his eyes and yawning loudly he asked, "What's got you so stirred up?"

"Who is this woman you've promised to marry?" she demanded, standing in front of him with her hands on her hips.

Lawrence got out of bed and put his arms around Jane. She was so mad she felt like striking him. "You know I don't care about anyone but you." He said it with such sincerity Jane began to calm down. For a moment she thought the Countess might have been right when she said Mrs. Stanley was carrying foolish tales. And besides he was married to her; he couldn't marry anyone else; at least not without a divorce. She melted into his arms and let him kiss her, wanting to believe his every word. Then he pulled back a little and held her by the shoulders, staring into her eyes. "I just need a little help right now," he whispered. He had a tense look on his face and his voice was shaky. There was something bothering him, she could tell.

"Who is she Lawrence?" Jane demanded.

"She's nobody for you to worry about." He quickly pushed her down without saying another word and laid her across the bed, pulling up her skirt. Roughly he snatched her underdrawers with one hand and pulled them below her knees. His coarse whiskers stung as he kissed her neck, and without any gentleness, he unbuttoned her blouse, wrestled with her corset until it was half open and nuzzled on her breasts. His breath smelled foul from whiskey. Her body was trembling. She wanted to feel like she was important to him, more important than any other woman. So she lay in his arms without a fight. Afterwards he told her about the woman—how she had loaned him big money to gamble on his handicap system.

"But Lawrence, why won't you let me help you? I promised you at Angola I'd work side by side with you. I can get a job. Mrs. Cambers at the Variety Goods store down the street has already asked me if I would be interested in making curtains for some of her better customers."

"I don't need your help," he said, angrily flinging himself out of bed. "Besides where in the world could you get that kind of money? 'Making curtains'? For God's sake, let me be the man. Let me take care of the money, please. When I want your help, I'll let you know." Then he stormed out of the room, slamming the door shut.

Though he didn't reveal what was really bothering him, she sensed it was serious. She realized that whatever it was that Lawrence had gotten himself involved in had caused a wedge between them. He had become like a complete stranger and she didn't know what to do about it. And while she never again mentioned it, she could not forget the words she had heard at the racetrack that day. Sometimes she thought she noticed a slight change in Lawrence which held out a small hope that things would get better between them, if nothing else for the children's sake. But his frequent association with Deep Pockets Malone only worsened the situation. She knew in her heart the main reason he tolerated her and the children was rooted in the fact she didn't question his activities.

SEVERAL MONTHS passed, and one morning on a cold wintry day while he was getting dressed to go off, out of the blue he said to her, "Only a fool plays the horses. I know that now. Papa was right.

The people who make the money are the ones who own the horses."
Jane nodded, hoping that this was the beginning of a more careful
life for Lawrence. She held the baby to her breast and watched him
as he got dressed. He put on his black frock coat, spun around in
front of the mirror a few times, and then asked her, "You wouldn't
happen to have a few bills put back that I might use today, would
you?"

"Only what I have in a jar in the top drawer." She hated lying to
him about money, but if he knew how much she really had saved
he'd wiggle it out of her somehow.

"Mama," Georgia Ann called out, tapping lightly on the bedroom door, "I'll be going to the hospital in a little while. Do you
need me to stop off at Krauss's Store for anything on the way home?"

"No, Georgia Ann," Lawrence answered before Jane could say a
word. "You just come home from work as quickly as you can this
afternoon. I'm taking your mama out to supper tonight to meet my
new business partner."

Jane's eyes lit up and her heart fluttered a little. "Lawrence, what
do you mean we are going out for supper tonight? Where?"

He certainly seemed in high spirits. "*de la Louisiane.*"

"And who is this business partner? I've never heard you mention
any of this?"

"Well, he's not exactly a partner yet. His name is Cabot Fillmore.
I guess you could call him a potential investor. He's someone from
New York Malone introduced me to the last trip he made to New
Orleans. I received a telegram saying he arrived last week and is
ready to do business."

"What kind of business?"

"Jane, how many times do I have to tell you not to ask me questions about my business deals?"

Jane lowered her head and cooed at her baby. Her eyes were
misty, she did not want Lawrence to see her cry. She didn't know
why she asked him about it in the first place. She knew his only business was the Countess's house and his gambling. The man Cabot
had to have some connection with either one.

And then as if he'd never been curt to her, he said, "I want you
to wear the red silk dinner gown, the one with the big sleeves, and

put your hair up high on your head. I like it best that way. You look younger and prettier. Go over to Solari's and buy some of those little red roses. Put 'em in your hair the way you used to. Wear your pearls. They enhance your neckline."

"You really want me to gussie up, don't you?" she asked, without looking up.

"Yes. Gussie up in all your finery. You're a big asset to me, Jane," he said, while he adjusted his string tie, admiring himself in the mirror. "You're clever and beautiful. You can help this deal go through for us."

Later that evening as they were dressing for dinner, Lawrence seemed fidgety and Jane knew it was only a matter of time before his nerves got the best of him and he'd take it out on her. Finally, after they were dressed, he said, "Be especially nice to Mr. Fillmore tonight. This deal has to go through and it all depends on you."

"What do you mean, it all depends on me?" she asked, cautious with her words so he wouldn't get upset with her. She motioned for him to fasten her necklace. She stretched her neck staring into the mirror as he adjusted the double strand of real pearls that reminded her of the ones the Madam used to have. "I'm always nice to your friends, aren't I? You remember the man from Paris? I even spoke French with him."

"I know that, Precious," he said, reaching up and picking out a few strands of her hair to hang loosely around her face. "But this time it's different. You must be more than charming. I have no doubt that he will want to be intimate with you, and I want you to let him."

He said it so matter-of-factly Jane thought she had misunderstood him. She gave a faint chuckle, "Did you just ask me to go to bed with another man?" she demanded.

Lawrence did not respond, just stared seriously at her in the mirror. She turned to face him. "How dare you!" she said, her eyes full of fire. "If he wants a woman there are more than enough on Basin Street. Take him to Mary Deubler's, or have the Countess send one of her girls for him."

When he still offered no response, she pulled on his sleeve, clawing into his arm. Clenching her teeth, she raised her hand and slapped his face. "You know I'd never do that for you or anyone!" she screamed.

Lawrence pushed her hands away and poured himself a glass of brandy from the decanter which Jane noticed was almost empty. He downed the drink in one swallow. "That's just the point. He doesn't want just any woman. He's from one of those stuffy New York families, one of the so called 'Four Hundred.' He wants a woman but thinks it's beneath him to pay money for one. As I told you before, there's a special way that gentlemen have of doing business with other gentlemen. This is simply business. Nothing else."

"That's very amusing, Lawrence. Your investor is too high in New York society to pay for a woman, but he's willing to take another man's wife to bed."

This was too much! Jane raised her hand and slapped him as hard as she could again and then started to cry. He clutched her arms roughly. "Don't you start that. This is no time for tears. I don't want your eyes red and puffy. No man wants to bed a sniveling idiot! You're going to walk into that restaurant and do exactly as I say!"

"I will not! I will not do it!" she screamed, pulling away, running downstairs and into the kitchen. She picked up a kitchen knife and Nellie reached in the crib for the baby and ran out of the room. "I'll put this through your heart first," she hissed, holding it up to protect herself when he walked into the kitchen.

"Put that knife down, you silly woman. I could take it away from you, but it's not worth the effort," he said. "I am not in the mood to play this little game with you. Did you forget who I am?"

"I haven't forgotten who you are. You've never let me!" she cried, furiously.

"Put the knife down, Jane. We're going to be late."

"I'm not going, Lawrence, and you can't make me!"

"Huh! You have one of two choices, my little one," he said, parting his lips to show clenched teeth. "You either do as I say or I'll take Mildred Louise to my mama in New York and have you and that son of yours picked up and hauled in a jail wagon all the way back to Angola! And your pretty little Georgia Ann will bring me a hefty price on Basin Street!"

She lunged at him, the knife barely missing his arm. He stepped back into the doorway. She stood glaring into his eyes. She felt so helpless. She knew she wasn't strong enough to fight him physically and for the first time since she met him, she realized how depraved he really was. Her chin dropped to her chest. He stepped close, taking the knife out of her trembling hands. She was silent as he dragged her back up to their bedroom, threw her mink wrap around her shoulders and poured a tall glass of brandy. He placed the glass to her lips and she drank until it was empty. Then he tugged on her arm and dragged her downstairs and out the front door.

He pushed her into his buggy and she sat stiffly in her seat as they made their way up Royal to Customhouse Street. Her breath coming from her lungs in gasps, feeling the warmth of the brandy, she wished she had the guts to jump out of the carriage and run away from him.

Unceremoniously Lawrence propelled her out of the buggy and into the foyer of *de la Louisiane.* Jane squinted into the chilly room, trying to penetrate the cigar smoke haze over the tables. She was dazzled by the brilliant chandelier but she followed Lawrence over to a table near a massive stone fireplace. Mr. Fillmore stood up, pulling out a chair for her.

"This is a pleasant surprise, I assure you," he said to Lawrence, giving him a gentleman's handshake and then without as much as a formal introduction, he said to Jane. "I think that Lawrence is fortunate to have a cousin as beautiful as you, Madam. Fortunate indeed."

She sat with a blank expression on her face, swallowing hard, trying not to make eye contact with Lawrence when he removed her wrap and laid it in the empty chair beside him. The waiter brought a carafe of sparkling wine to the table and three wine glasses. Jane fortified herself with several glasses of the clear grape vintage and sat with her eyes glued to a candle flickering in a Waterford crystal candlestick. Lawrence and Mr. Fillmore talked mainly man talk without once including Jane in their conversation. Throughout the entire meal, she went through the motions of eating, picking at her food, stirring it around in her plate and onto her fork. Even taking small bites was an enormous effort.

After the meal was over and after the dishes were cleared away, Lawrence announced he was leaving. He said something about a meeting at the Jockey Club before going on to other important affairs. She noticed Mr. Fillmore reach inside his coat pocket and pull out a leather pouch. Fillmore stood up as Lawrence gathered his top coat and hat, reached out and placed the pouch in Lawrence's hands. Lawrence nodded and said good night to Jane, raising his eyebrows at her as a reminder of his earlier threats.

Jane had several more glasses of wine while Mr. Fillmore had black coffee, and smoked a cigar. To her surprise he seemed a gentle man. He was very kind and considerate, telling her of his adventures abroad this past summer and how pleased he was to become Lawrence's new partner in the Countess's house on Basin Street. Jane was shocked that Lawrence would sell out the Countess.

Although Fillmore touched her hand during the course of the evening several times, for a while she thought this would be the extent of it. He seemed like such a lonely person and just maybe, she thought, all he wanted was a supper companion for the evening. Then he crushed out his cigar. "If it would be pleasing to you, I would like us to leave now," he said. "I've taken a small house in the Garden District while I am in New Orleans. I am sure you will find it far more cozy than this chilly restaurant."

Jane stood up. Fillmore pulled her chair away from the table. She felt slightly tipsy and he held her arm as they made their exit to the cold street.

"Before I left for the evening I instructed my staff to take the night off," he whispered in her ear.

"Were you so confident I would be going home with you that you dismissed your staff in advance?" she asked, wondering how she was going to get through this.

"Not confident but hopeful," he said, taking her arm and lifting her into his waiting carriage. "My experience with a woman as beautiful as you is that a gentleman can always be hopeful but never foolish enough to be sure."

HIS HOUSE was small but elegant, tucked away behind a high iron fence, surrounded by giant live oak trees. Jane smelled roses when he opened the front door. Obviously, the servants had only recently departed. Candles were lit, casting shadows over a tall vase of long stemmed roses. A silver coffee service was set on a mahogany library table beside a decanter of French brandy and two goblets.

"How did you know I love red roses?" she asked and accepted the glass of shimmering amber liquid. "Did Lawrence tell you?"

"No, it was a feeling I had about you. Nothing more than a lucky guess."

They sat in silence for a while, and then he made his way to the small piano at the far end of the room. Softly he tinkled the keys, producing not the popular ragtime songs that were played so loudly you couldn't hear yourself think but a lilting kind of music, the kind Charles Fisher used to hum to her.

She closed her eyes and memories of Charles Fisher flooded her mind. She had done a lot of things since the last time she saw Charles but she never expected to stoop this low. She sadly shook her head to chase his image from her mind. She slowly walked over to Mr. Fillmore. Lawrence's threats echoed in her ears.

"What is this beautiful music?" she asked, reluctantly placing her hand on his shoulder. "I've never heard it before."

"It's Wagner. Do you really like it?"

"I do."

He stopped playing and turned to face her, "Then does there exist a possibility that you may perhaps like me, just a little?" he asked, shyly.

She shivered, biting the inside of her lip and looked around the dim room, and with the sensual strains of Wagner's *Tannhauser* in her ears, she left his side and slowly sank into a chair beside the roaring fireplace. She began to sob, and her emotional outburst disturbed Fillmore. He came to her and gently took her trembling hands into his own. "Jane, why are you crying so? Have you changed your mind about me? Surely not. Lawrence assured me this very afternoon that you had given this evening considerable thought."

"Mr. Fillmore, I found out about you only today," she said, wondering what Lawrence would do to her for betraying him. "I should be at home with my children, not here in your home selling myself to you to help finance one of my husband's schemes."

"I assure you, Madam, your husband has nothing to do with your being with me this evening."

"Mr. Fillmore, Lawrence Browne is my husband," she confessed.

"Husband?" He gasped. She saw his eyes widen, staring at her in disbelief. "Lawrence told me his wife was dead. He said you were a distant cousin."

"Mr. Fillmore, forgive me. I would have never gone along with this charade in the first place if Lawrence had not threatened me with a fate far worse than death. You see, a long time ago I was sent to Angola to serve a fourteen year prison sentence. Lawrence's father was the prison master and after he died and Lawrence's wife died, Lawrence took me away from the prison and we were married."

Fillmore paced in front of the fire, running his fingers through his graying hair, shaking his head. He finally stopped and turned to face Jane. He said, "Madam, did you know your husband has taken out a marriage certificate this very afternoon to marry my sister? They are by now on the train on their way to New York for their honeymoon."

The muscles in Jane's throat constricted, choking her. She stood up. "Married your sister? The woman who loaned Lawrence money a few months back? The woman everybody in New Orleans is talking about? The woman Lawrence said was nothing to him? And . . . and how could he marry her? He's married to me."

Fillmore flashed her a grim look. "I'll see you home now, Mrs. Browne," he said, picking up her mink wrap and placing it around her shoulders. She was in shock, unable to say anymore and Fillmore obviously was seething with rage.

He was silent as he sat next to her, holding her trembling body against him. The rented carriage made its way through the cobblestone streets of the French Quarter, and Jane saw her house in the distance. As they neared it she saw that a small crowd of people had gathered. At first she thought it might be the men from the racetrack looking for Lawrence, but when the driver maneuvered his way around several carriages, she heard someone screaming.

"Oh, my Lord!" she cried. "Something's happened!" The driver stopped and Fillmore was out of the carriage in an instant and turned to lift Jane out. She began to run down the narrow street as the screams grew louder. Nearing her front door, suddenly she tripped. Flying forward, she felt her breath leave her and the rough cobblestone tear at her face. She tasted a mixture of blood and tears. She struggled to get up and Fillmore pulled her to her feet. She saw Nellie come out the door crying, rushing toward her.

"I didn't do anything," Nellie babbled. "I didn't do it. I held her likes you told me to when she gets the colic."

Jane's stomach churned wildly. She saw everything going on around her but couldn't move. The frightened girl stood in front of her, trembling, wringing her hands. A small group of Italian women from the neighborhood held lanterns in their hands, staring at Jane with pity on their faces as the doctor who had delivered Mildred Louise appeared in the doorway of the house and walked toward her. She heard him say, "There was nothing anybody could do. I'm afraid. . . . I'm afraid your baby's dead."

She fainted dead away.

Nineteen

JANE OPENED HER EYES and realized she was in her own bed. She recognized the lace curtains on the tall windows and the familiar smell of lavender on her pillow. Hazily she saw a group of people gathered around her bed and felt her hand being held by Georgia Ann.

What's going on? She felt dizzy, her head pounding.

"Mama, it's me, Georgia Ann. Can you hear me?"

Jane rubbed her eyes and attempted to sit up, but the throbbing of her head kept her from succeeding.

"No, no. You just lie there," Doctor Cochran said. He walked to her bed from across the room. "You gave us quite a scare."

"I don't understand," Jane whispered. "Why is the room so dark? Why are there flowers and candles everywhere? It looks like a funeral room."

"Welcome back, Cherie," said the Countess smiling down at Jane. "We were beginning to think you didn't want to come back to us."

Jane wondered just how long she had been in bed. Then she remembered—"Mildred Louise!" she cried out, clutching hold of Georgia Ann's arm. "My baby . . . where is she?"

"Now don't get yourself worked up, Cherie," the Countess said. "You've had a very difficult week."

Her legs felt numb as she tried to sit up and get out of the bed. "What did you do with my baby?" she demanded, as Georgia Ann and the Countess struggled to hold her down. "I want my baby!"

she kept screaming over and over until the doctor filled a syringe and poked her arm.

"Dr. Cochran," she pleaded, "please don't put me back to sleep."

"Don't worry, child. That little bit won't make you sleep. I gave you just enough to calm you down. But you've got to get a grip on yourself. You're frightening Georgia Ann, she's as distraught as you are. You've got to pull yourself together."

He took out his stethoscope and listened to Jane's heart. "Your breathing sounds less labored and that scrape on your face will heal in no time," he said, sitting on the bed opposite Georgia Ann, patting Jane's hand sympathetically. "I know what you're feeling. Losing any child is the worst nightmare a mother can imagine. And a baby! It's got to be hard on you, but you have to go on. It's one of those crosses in life we must bear, and wishing for your child to be alive is not going to do you one bit of good."

Jane knew what Dr. Cochran was saying was the truth. Her mother had told her many times how empty she had felt when Jane's twin brother had died as an infant, from the fever. "The hurt just never goes away," she'd told Jane. "It haunts you even in your dreams." Now Jane understood the far away look her mother always had in her eyes when someone mentioned her dead baby.

She took a deep breath as Georgia Ann nestled on her chest. She felt Georgia Ann's hot tears on her cotton nightgown and she placed her hand on her child's trembling body, running her fingers over her back—her little Georgia Ann, grieving too for their precious baby. The loss of her baby and Georgia Ann's grief was almost more than Jane could bear. "Georgia Ann, Sugar," she cried. " It's going to be all right. We'll get through this together, I promise." She stroked her daughter's hair, fighting to hold back sobs, trying to fight a grief so deep, a pain so bad that nothing anyone said could ease it. She thought, *I've got to be strong for Georgia Ann. She's taking this hard.*

There wasn't a dry eye in the bedroom. Dr. Cochran took out his handkerchief and wiped away tears as he put his instruments back into his bag. Then Georgia Ann sat up. "I'm so sorry I wasn't home when she died, Mama," she said, sniffing into a handkerchief the Countess put in her hand. "I had to stay at the hospital. There was a tragic accident on the river. . . . "

"Where did you bury my baby?" Jane asked, interrupting Georgia Ann.

It was the doctor who answered. "Somehow Lawrence found out about it. Sent me a telegram saying I was to call the undertaker, Sam Bell. I did, and when Sam came he took the baby with him. He said Lawrence wanted her burial out in the Metairie Cemetery."

Lawrence wanted! Jane cringed.

There was a knock at the front door and after a while Nellie came into Jane's room.

"There's a man here to sees you, Miz Jane. Says he's an old friend but I never seen him before."

Jane motioned for Nellie to come over to the bed as the Countess went downstairs to greet the caller. Giving Nellie's hand a squeeze, Jane saw the tears roll out of Nellie's big black eyes and run down her cheeks. "Don't cry Nellie, Sugar. It wasn't your fault—it wasn't anyone's fault. God was just lonesome. He needed our sweet Mildred Louise to hold in his arms." Nellie sat down on the edge of the bed and put her arms around Georgia Ann. The three of them cried together. Then Nellie sat up, wiped her eyes with the back of her hand, and said, "I gonna go to that church house with the pretty painted windows and burn one of dem candles in the red jar. Then God gonna tells our baby we loves her and we'll always be thinking about her. We's never gonna forget her."

"Oh, Nellie, you're right," Georgia Ann said. "We just have to pray and pray that God will help us get over this. I know he will. Every time I think about Mildred Louise, I think about our blessed mother of Jesus who stood watching those soldiers kill her son. I know it doesn't make it any easier, Mama, but if we pray hard enough, God will make us feel better about it." Jane didn't say anything. She couldn't. She just lowered her eyelids and turned her face to the wall and let the tears slide out of the corner of her eyes.

The Countess returned a few minutes later with a bouquet of hot house roses. "He says his name is Cabot Fillmore and that if you feel up to visitors, he'd be more than pleased to see you," she said, giving Jane a curious glance.

Jane wiped her eyes with the edge of her sheet. "Countess, would you find out if he has news of Lawrence. If he doesn't, please tell him he's very kind to be concerned, but I just can't receive visitors yet. Perhaps in a few weeks would be better," she said, as the Countess walked to the door. "Tell him the roses are beautiful. I can't imagine where he got so many of them this time of the year, but tell him thank you."

"Doctor Cochran shooed the girls up off of Jane. "I need to have a talk with your mama, Georgia Ann," he said, dragging a wooden high-backed chair up to the bed. And would you tell the Countess I'd like to do it in private? Perhaps she could come back another time. I think our patient here needs some time alone."

When the girls closed the door, the doctor whispered, "I don't know how well you're going to take what I have to say, but if my stethoscope tells me the truth, I hear a faint heart beating in there," and he pointed to her stomach. "I believe you must be with child."

"Oh Dr. Cochran, you must be mistaken," she said, shaking her head. Then it flashed in her mind what happened with Lawrence the day she returned from the racetrack. She reached for the headboard and he helped her to sit up.

"I want you to take it easy, young lady," he said, placing the cold scope to her stomach and putting the instrument up to her own ears. *Thump..thump,* she heard a new baby's heart beating inside her. She gently placed her hands over her stomach, "God heard Georgia Ann's prayers," she said. "It's a miracle, Dr. Cochran. I was with Lawrence only once since Mildred Louise was born."

"Well, that's all it takes," he grinned. "Now you've been through a difficult time. I want you to stay in bed for at least another week. Take it easy. I don't want you doing anything that could cause complications later."

"You don't have to worry about me getting up. I'll do anything you say. God couldn't have entrusted this baby to anyone better than me," she said, and a smile crossed her pale face.

SPRING CAME AND WENT and the days of the hot and humid summer arrived. Jane and Georgia Ann spent every evening sewing clothes for the new baby, knitting hats and sweaters and tiny socks, enjoying the peace and contentment that engulfed their quiet lives now that Lawrence was gone.

One day Jane went to Canal Street, shopping for a pair of shoes for Georgia Ann and material for a few new dresses for Nellie. For the latter she had searched the stores until late in the afternoon for a certain button she had seen in the *Picayune* patterns. By the time she arrived home she was exhausted. Her feet and ankles were swollen inside her boots and it took every bit of the energy she had to walk up the steps to her house.

"Will someone tell me what's going on in here?" she asked as she walked into her parlor. In the room opposite a wall of high windows, Georgia Ann and the Countess were huddled together on the gold and green velvet settee, in deep conversation.

The Countess laughed. "Well, she's definitely back to her normal self, needing to know everything that's going on. Hold on to the edge of your seat. Georgia Ann has news about someone very dear to you."

"It's Ander, isn't it?" Jane said, her eyes flashing around the green oriental carpet lying over a brightly polished hardwood floor, and beyond to a tall door that was open. "He's here and he's hiding from me, isn't he? Ander . . . Ander," she called out. She knew he was home. She closed her eyes and breathed in the scent of lingering smoke of his little sweet cigars. He was playing a game with her. It was his way, just like the day he arrived with Lawrence from prison, hiding behind the back door until Lawrence enticed her outside so Ander could surprise her.

She opened her eyes. Before her stood the son she'd been praying to see for nearly two years. Sporting calf-skin shoes, a *Perry* shirt and a corduroy coat, Ander Moody walked toward his mother, grinning a smile that put a sparkle in her eyes.

"Ander," she cried. "My boy."

"Well, I'm not exactly a boy any longer, Mama. I'm a man now."

"You're my baby boy," she teased, stepping up on the tip of her toes to hug him.

A beautiful, young, fair haired girl appeared from the shadows of the wide hall and stood shyly beside Ander. She had the prettiest crystal blue eyes Jane had ever seen and she was almost a head taller than Ander. She stood proudly clutching his hand.

"Mama, this is my wife, Mary Parthenia."

It really didn't surprise Jane. The girl's protruding stomach was almost as big as Jane's. The little gold band on her left finger suggested who she might be.

"Mama, you have to sit down," Georgia Ann said. "Ander has brought us the good news."

"You mean there's more?"

"At first I didn't think they should burden you with it," the Countess broke in. "Then it just seemed to me, you have a right to know."

Georgia Ann squeezed Jane's hand when she sat down next to her. "Mama, all these years that you thought Uncle Charlie was dead, he wasn't."

Jane stared at Georgia Ann, wide-eyed, her eyebrows crunched up nearly into her hairline, then her eyes wandered over to Ander. She was unable to say anything. *If this is supposed to be a joke it is not funny,* she thought. Her heart skipped a beat when she realized no one was laughing and yet she didn't understand because of the grim look on the Countess's face.

"You know I've always been honest with you, Cherie," the Countess said. "And . . . to tell you the truth, all of the news is not so good. Your Mister Fisher did not drown that day as you thought. He's alive . . . but . . . well, he's very much married."

"Charles. Alive?"

She stood up and walked to the window almost afraid to breathe. She reached down and began to pull the tall window slowly up from the floor until it disappeared above her head. Then she floated out onto the balcony. "How do you know?" she asked as her family followed her out.

"Charles Fisher is married to my mama," Mary proudly said.

Dear God, Charles married to Ander's mother-in-law!

Jane prayed silently for a moment, thanking God for saving Charles. "At least that puts an end to one burden I've carried for a long time," she said, almost choking on her words. She sucked in a deep breath, sighed, and took hold of the iron railing to steady herself. Too much was happening too quickly. *All these years I worried that Charles had died because of me,* she said to herself. *I truly believed I was responsible for his death. . . . I punished myself over and over mentally because I thought I'd killed him, and now . . . this.* She bit her bottom lip. Tears slid down her cheeks as she looked out over the skyline beyond Royal Street, over the town's buildings jutting closely together and on to the giant Mississippi River paddlewheelers crowding the Toulouse Street wharf. She stood there silently watching the smoking stacks of the steamers, pondering over her memories of Charles. *Oh God, I loved him so much. How will I ever live now knowing he's alive . . . alive but married to another woman? He's the only man I ever truly let into my heart, the only one who ever loved me and treated me like a human being,* she thought, raising her hands to her temples and pressing hard on both sides of her head as if she could squeeze her loving memories of Charles out of her mind.

She sniffed and wiped her nose. "My Charles is alive. I just can't believe it," she said, turning to Ander. "Did he ask about me? Did he ever mention me to any of your family?" she questioned Mary Parthenia.

Before Mary could answer, Ander pulled his distraught mother into a wrought iron chair against the wall. He sat in a chair in front of her holding both of her hands. The Countess excused herself to go home and Georgia Ann took Mary Parthenia downstairs to the kitchen.

"Uncle Charlie told me that after we went to prison he found a lawyer willing to fight Judge Bear," Ander said, "but by the time the lawyer got around to doing anything, the prison officials told him you had escaped and no one knew if you were alive or dead. They painted an ugly picture of you being eaten up by alligators in the swamp, or being drowned in the Mississippi River.

"He didn't give up but searched for you up in northern Louisiana. Then when Uncle John Augustus died he found out somebody had come up to Columbia and taken Georgia Ann to New Orleans and Uncle Charlie came to New Orleans looking for you. Lawrence Browne found out about him being here and told him you and your children had run away from him, and no one knew where you were."

"Lawrence knew all along that Charles was alive?"

"He knew it while you were still in prison."

Jane sighed. "All those years, Ander! I can't believe it. What kind of people are those Brownes? They knew I didn't deserve to be in prison in the first place. I lived on that plantation with them, working like a slave, grieving over you and Georgia Ann and my beloved Charles. They could have at least eased the pain in my heart about Charles. They could have told me he was alive. Oh . . . the Madam must have really enjoyed seeing me grieve—all those times my tears fell on her bare feet while I rubbed her legs, my heart aching so badly I couldn't even talk, and all along she knew my Charles was alive. When her son took a fancy to me, instead of helping me get out of there and go home to my family, she constantly threatened me with whippings and with being sent to work in a levee camp."

She buried her face in her hands. "If only I had known Charles was alive, somehow I would have tried to escape, tried to get back to him."

"Mama, you've got to try and forget all of that now. Live for today. There's nothing you can do about yesterday. That's what I've been trying to do every since I got out of prison."

"I know, Baby," she sniffed. "I know it was hard for you living in that levee camp, and you were just a child."

"Boys didn't stay children very long in there, Mama. I never really told you what went on in that levee camp in New Iberia. Lawrence told me if I knew what was good for me, I'd better not say anything to you about it."

"Lawrence Browne is a devil," she said, staring into Ander's angry face.

"Mama, you don't know the half of it. Lawrence Browne is worse than the devil. After his papa died he became something of a monster in the camps. The things that went on—all the young boys drilled to go out and rob plantation houses along the river banks from Monroe to New Orleans. And if we didn't do as the captains said, we were taken to the camps in the swamps and forced to work on the chain gangs. We worked in water knee deep, fighting snakes and rats and mosquitoes. We ate boiled beans and corn-pone and drank swamp water.

"I seen with my own eyes one of the guards beating a black man to death while he was still shackled to another convict just because he had dysentery and fell out pushing a wheelbarrow. They made us all work around the man while he lay there dying, and the convict he was chained to had to dig a hole in the levee and bury him while we all watched." Ander stood up and walked to the railing. "Mama, I tell you," he said, clutching the wrought iron, "I could kill Lawrence Browne. I could kill him and never give it a second thought."

"No Ander," she said, strongly. "Don't ever say that again. Don't ever say you could take someone's life. I can't bear to hear those words come out of your mouth. Promise Mama," she said, reaching up to pull his face down to hers. "Promise you'll never think about those days. They're over . . . over . . . Son. We never have to think about it again. And now Lawrence is out of our lives. He's gone. He married a woman without getting a divorce from me. I doubt if he ever shows his face in New Orleans again. We're finally free of him."

"Don't ever be so sure. When I left New Orleans two years ago it was only because of you, Mama. Lawrence said if I didn't get the hell out of here he would send both of us back to prison and neither one of us would ever see Georgia Ann again."

"I know how much you must hate him, Son. I feel the same. He stripped me of everything, Ander, my dignity, my self-esteem. He even had my dead baby buried where I can't find her grave."

"Oh, Mama. I'm so sorry about her. I wish it could have been different for you."

"I do too, Son. But it was meant to be. There was nothing anyone could do for her. She had had something wrong with her ever since the day she was born. Even Dr. Cochran doesn't know what it was."

"You don't think anything will be wrong with the new baby, do you?"

"I certainly hope and pray to God there's nothing wrong with this little baby," she said, rubbing her hand across her protruding belly. "Now, I don't want to talk about Lawrence Browne any more. Tell me about this woman that Charles married. Is she as pretty as Mary Parthenia?"

"She's just a plain woman about your age, Mama. Only she looks a lot older than you. She's not well and something's wrong with her legs. Sometimes her legs get so stiff and sore from arthritis that she can't walk. But she's a nice enough person."

"I don't understand how Charles got a divorce. Did you ask him?"

"No. I never thought about asking him that. I suspect because you went to prison. You know we lost all rights as citizens when we went there," he said as they walked inside to the parlor.

Later that evening as they sat in the dining room, Jane, Ander and the girls exchanged information. Georgia Ann talked of the Sisters of Charity who were praying New Orleans wouldn't have another yellow fever outbreak like the one after the big flood, and Ander told of a beginning of the decline of sawmills in northern Louisiana—how men were scattering down to South Louisiana looking for work and that he was expecting Mary's brother, Gatlin Cauthron, to come to New Orleans soon. They both were going to try and get on with the railroad.

Nellie spooned the cornbread dressing onto Ander's plate beside thick slices of white turkey breast and poured giblet gravy over both until Ander told her to stop. Jane watched as he wolfed down every bite. *It's no wonder he eats the way he does,* she thought, remembering the food he had told her he ate when he was in prison. Jane just smiled to herself as Nellie brought into the dining room Ander's favorite, mincemeat pie, that smelled so good even Jane could not resist a big slice.

"It's just like the old times when we first came to New Orleans, Mama," Georgia Ann said, and Jane and her young family laughed and talked about the new babies she and Mary would give birth to in the fall. Georgia Ann was so happy about the babies she could hardly contain herself. She had already bought a new crib with her own earnings.

Jane sat quietly at the head of the dining table that Lawrence had brought from Angola when the state took the plantation, thinking about Charles, wondering if she had any right to her memories of him now. *If Charles is happy, I'll just have to live with it,* she thought. *I have my children and my new baby coming. Right now, they're the most important beings in my life. Maybe now we can start to live again. Soon as I get up in the morning I intend to go out and get myself a good job, something I'm good at, so my children and I can at last have a life together.*

Twenty

THE FIRST BOLT of red silk arrived shortly before noon. Jane stood just inside her front door in the wide hall waiting to sign the delivery ticket. It had been sent by Anna Cambers who operated a *rabais* shop on the bottom floor of her home, just a few blocks from Jane on Royal Street.

"This is the most beautiful fabric I have ever seen," Mary Parthenia said, running her slim fingers over the intricate weave. "Real expensive, I bet."

"Yes, this is a very expensive material, Mary, but it will hang well and last for years. All the women in town are changing their window coverings to this new fabric. You can see that the green that I used for my parlor turned out beautifully. I talked Mrs. Cambers into doing a dummy window in the red for her shop. I'm hoping I can sell more custom jobs after the baby comes."

"Where did you learn how to sew this beautiful stitch?" Mary asked, picking up the hem of Jane's dark green drape, examining the stitching Jane had made for her own window coverings when she and Lawrence had first moved into this house.

"I learned to use the needle and thread from my mama when I was a young girl, and I learned finer stitching from the Countess."

"Did you make the drapes for the Countess's house?"

"Yes, I did way back when we first came to New Orleans. And quite nice they turned out too, or at least that's what Lawrence always said. He used to brag about them, claiming they were shipped here from Paris. Said they were far superior to any in the other houses on Basin Street. Of course I didn't tell Mrs. Cambers I made them for the Countess. She might not like my sewing for a Madam."

"You enjoy your work don't you, Mama Jane?"

"I'm happier now than I've been in a long time, Sugar. I've got everything I could possibly want." *Everything except my beloved Charles,* she thought, turning to leave the room without making eye contact with Mary. It made her feel guilty sometimes when she thought of Charles, especially if she was around Mary. She didn't know why, but every time she and Mary were alone lately, it seemed Mary was prodding her for information about Charles and the life they once had. She even got the impression sometimes that Mary might be writing her mother and telling her everything Jane ever said about him. However, Jane would shrug it off, telling herself it was just her imagination. Today she didn't feel like talking about Charles. It upset her too much to have to pretend in front of her daughter-in-law that she didn't think about Charles Fisher all the time.

"I'm going up to rest for a while before we have our noonday meal. It wouldn't hurt for you to get off of your feet, Mary. The swelling in your legs seems to be getting worse. You've got several weeks to go before the baby comes. It won't get any better if you don't take care of yourself. You need to stay off salt. Dr. Cochran says salt is the worst thing you can eat right before you give birth," she said, slowly climbing the stairs.

She heard a carriage stop in the alleyway behind her house as she went into her bedroom. Before she could lie down, loud voices drifted up from the hall below.

"Nellie, where is Jane?" she heard the Countess say.

"Up here," Jane called out and the Countess came swiftly up the stairs and into her bedroom. "What's the matter?" she asked the Countess, teasingly. "You see smoke?"

"You're going to wish it was a fire when I tell you what has just happened."

The look on the Countess's face told Jane she was serious. The Countess was always coming over and telling her happenings in

Storyville, harlot stories, or Tom Anderson's opening of another mansion, or some fascinating tale about one of the high-toned landlords, but this was different.

"Countess, you're the best friend a woman could have, but don't stand there with your mouth open. What's so important that you couldn't call before you came?"

"Jane, there's trouble brewing in Storyville. Ander's involved in it."

"What kind of trouble?" Jane asked as Nellie came in with a tray of tea, pouring two cups before she walked out.

"Don't tell me that you didn't know Ander's been working for Mastri all these months?"

"Yes, I know he works for Mastri's furniture store on Rampart Street."

"Jane, Mastri runs low-class houses of prostitution on Customhouse Street. Ander has become one of his prized pimps."

"That's ridiculous, Countess."

"Cherie, I am not here to educate you on your son's employer! I came here as your friend. Deep Pockets caught Ander honing in on his crib girls the other night and he's sent out word on him—they catch him back in their District again, they'll cut his ears off and send both of them to you in a black box."

Jane's heart began racing. The Countess set her tea cup down and said seriously, "You need to get him out of here."

"I don't know about that, Countess. His wife's about to deliver."

The Countess stood up, dug into her handbag and tossed a slip of paper into Jane's hand. "Give this to him. It's an address across Lake Pontchatrain in Abita Springs where he can take his wife. He'll be safe there, at least until Mastri gets back from New York. Now do as I say if you don't want to see your boy hurt." She pecked Jane on the cheek and fled down the stairs and out the back door to her carriage. Jane watched from her window as her carriage went up the alleyway.

This is no joke. Ander could be in real trouble, she thought. "How could he do this to me and Mary?" she grumbled, making her way back down the stairs. "How could he be so stupid as to bring this kind of attention to himself? God, if word gets to New York, and

Lawrence finds out about it, he's liable to have Ander sent back to prison."

"Mary," she whispered when she found the girl lying on a cot in the kitchen where Nellie was cooking. "I need to talk to you, Sugar. Has Ander said anything to you about what kind of work he's been doing?"

"Not much," she yawned. "When I ask him about his job, he just says he's a salesman of sorts; working all day calling on houses, selling furniture."

"Well, he's selling something all right, but it's not furniture. What time did he say he would be home tonight?"

"Oh, he's not coming home tonight. Said he'd be out in the town of Carrollton all day and would be staying over. He won't be home until sometime tomorrow late."

Jane ran into the front parlor and dialed for the Countess. "Number please," a deep throated voice said on the line.

"3-9-4-2," Jane said, hurriedly and heard the operator give a deep sigh. He always did when Jane called the Countess's house. She just assumed the operator hated connecting the sporting houses, but right now Jane was in no mood to worry about that.

"Yes," the Countess said.

"Countess, Ander's not coming home tonight. He told Mary he was going to be out in Carrollton."

"Let me see what I can do, Cherie," she said, and hung up without another word. Jane crossed the hall to the dining room just as Georgia Ann came in the front door, arms loaded with packages and her white uniform pulled up midway to her knees. She had a big grin on her face. "Could somebody please help me?" she called out. Nellie came out of the kitchen and took the brown wrapped bundles.

"Why so solemn, Mama?"

"Georgia Ann, we have to find your brother. He's in trouble."

"What did he do, Mama?"

"He lied to us. He's not working in a furniture store as he claims. He's working in Storyville, selling cheap prostitutes and peddling illegal whiskey. The Countess said the man, Deep Pockets Malone, is after him for trying to make money off of Malone's crib girls."

Georgia Ann flopped down into a nearby chair. "Just when everything was starting to get good for us, he has to go and do something
like this. I don't understand Ander. You'd think he'd be so grateful
for getting out of prison, that he wouldn't ever do anything dis-
honest again. He's got so much, Mama. Mary Parthenia loves him
and treats him wonderfully. Why would he do anything to bring
harm to her?"

"I don't know, Georgia Ann, and there's no use to speculate about
your brother. I have to wait and ask him his version of things."

The phone rang. "I'll get it," Georgia Ann said, and her voice
rose, "Ander, where are you?" She handed the phone to her mother.

"Ander, don't say anything. Just come home right now, I mean
immediately, through the alleyway. Do you hear me, Son?" And
Jane hung up the receiver.

Night came and the three women sat alone in the parlor, waiting. The Countess called once and said as soon as Ander arrived to
ring her. Shortly afterwards, the back door creaked as he slowly
opened it, and Nellie rushed into the dimly lit room to say that
Ander was in the kitchen. Jane told the girls to wait until after she
had talked to him. She followed Nellie out.

"Ander, we have very little time. I don't know what you've gotten
yourself into, Son, but the Countess called several hours ago and
said Malone's men are after you."

"I'm surprised the Countess cared enough to call you. She's the
one that had better watch her back on a dark street."

"Ander, what are you saying? What's come over you? Why did
you lie to us about your job?"

"Mama, don't ask me questions now. I've got to get out of town
and I'm taking Mary with me."

"I know, Son, she's all packed. The Countess is sending her carriage to take you out to the pass on Shell Road. You can catch one
of the flatboats at the New Basin Canal and go across the lake. She
gave me an address where you and Mary will be safe."

Jane watched Ander as they waited for the carriage. She noticed
her son's behavior had changed. He didn't act like the same person
who'd walked out of the house this morning. He was uneasy and
restless. He could hardly sit still. Jane kept her eye on him. "What

were you talking about when you called this afternoon? Have you had words with the Countess?"

"A few."

"About what, Ander?" she asked, and heard the carriage in the alleyway. Ander picked up their valises without answering his mother, and he and Mary rushed out the back door. "Be careful, Ander," Jane called out to him from the doorway. "Take care of Mary and let me hear something soon. I want to know where you'll be staying. Send me a letter."

Jane and Georgia Ann stood in the darkened doorway until the carriage was out of sight. Jane slowly made her way back up the stairs and plopped on her feather mattress, worrying and wondering if Ander and Mary would make it to safety. She tossed and turned for more than half the night, unable to sleep. As she finally began to settle down, a loud crash from below startled her. "What in the world?" she said to herself, getting out of bed, lighting an oil lamp and stealing out to the stairwell. "Someone must have knocked over my pretty vase on the hall table."

"Did you hear that noise?" she asked, thinking she was talking to Georgia Ann coming up the dark stairs toward her.

"Yes, I heard it, Mrs. Browne," came a familiar voice. It was Lawrence. She held the lamp up to his face as he approached the top of the stairs. He stood staring at her. "Where is that no good son of yours?" he asked and grabbed the lamp from her hand, roughly pushing her back into her bedroom.

Jane felt her anger rising as she watched him put the lamp on the table and pace around the bedroom. Moonlight filtered through the sheer lace that covered the window panes and she thought he looked smart in his New York fashions. She wondered how much it had cost his new wife to keep him in this finery. The new diamond on his finger must have set the wife back aplenty. "What are you doing in my house, Lawrence?" she asked, staring at him with contempt. "You think you can come in my home, stalking around in the dark, scaring the daylights out of me? I should think you'd be ashamed to show your face to me again after what you've done."

"Your home? The last time I was here, it was our home!" he said.

"It was our home when we were married, but now, it's my home."

He lowered his voice and his manner softened. "Jane, I'm not here to argue with you over this bunch of sticks and bricks. I came here because I'm worried about you. I want to offer you my help with Ander. I know if anything happens to him, it'll kill you," he said, and walked over to a small table beside the fireplace, poured himself a brandy, sat in the dim corner near the window, and propped his booted feet on a small ottoman. "Didn't your precious boy tell you he ran into me night before last?"

"No, he didn't," she said, moving closer to him. "Why . . . what happened?"

"Ander thinks he is such a dandy; thinks with the ease only the incredibly calculating or extremely insane have, that he can move into Ring Territory. Personally I believe the boy's nuts. We're talking underworld here, Jane! Nobody just comes into Storyville like Ander Moody did and sets himself up in another man's District. Mastri may have given him a job, but he didn't turn his District over to him. Barging in on Ring territory is a death sentence. Now, where is he? Are you hiding him?"

"Ander's not here, Lawrence. I haven't seen him," she lied.

"Well, it's just as well he's not here tonight. I need a place to stay. Go get the other bedroom ready, that is, unless you would like to share your bed with me?" he said, standing up, then, moving behind Jane. He put his hands gently on her bare shoulders. "Don't be unkind to me, Precious," he whispered, passing his lips over her ear. "I need you now, more than I ever have."

"You stay away from me, Lawrence," she said, trying to pull herself away. Once a safe distance from him, she said, "I'll have Nellie fix you a hot tub of water in the kitchen. Go take your bath and get comfortable. I'll move Georgia Ann in here with me."

"I guess that's best. From the looks of your stomach I don't think there would be room in your bed for all of us. By the way, who's the lucky father?"

Open mouthed, Jane glared at him. She was torn between the anger that still seethed within her and the gratitude that she would always have for him. *Why wouldn't I expect you to say something like that?* she thought. *It's no surprise. You abandoned me, dragged me out of the house for your own selfish reasons, caused me to lose the last*

precious moments of our child's life, and left me for another woman!
Why should anything you say surprise me?

He grinned at her the way he had that first day at Angola when
she'd nervously stood by the Countess, waiting to see if she would
pass his mother's approval. She studied his New York fashions—
tails, topped with a black lined cape, Homburg hat and silverheaded
walking stick in hand as he walked to the door and disappeared into
the dark hall.

She wasn't going to let him charm his way back into her life. No
way! It was her turn to take control. *It's time I gave Lawrence a taste*
of his own conniving ways, she thought. When she opened the door
to Lawrence's room he was lying on the black Chesterfield sofa. His
hair was slightly damp. He wore a dark green silk robe from Sulka
that Jane assumed he had acquired in New York. She sank down in
a deeply tufted chair, staring at him.

When Lawrence saw how angry she was, he refilled his glass and
said, "You're angry because I pretended to marry Cabot's sister so I
could get my hands on her money."

"Pretended? Come on, Lawrence," she said, "I know now we
were never legally married. Georgia Ann found out from City Hall
that you never took out a marriage contract for us. Your friend, Ted
Boule, forged the one we have, didn't he? And by the way, I guess
you heard Cabot was found dead a few months ago. But then you
would know about it. You married his sister."

"Precious, I did it all for you. Don't you understand that? It was
nothing more than business, the same as you going to bed with
Cabot. It wasn't about love or sex, just business. Don't you understand anything after all I've tried to teach you?"

She had to stand up to him. If she gave in now, no telling what
scheme he'd pull next. "Lawrence, I didn't go to bed with Cabot that
night. As a matter of fact the last time I saw him, he was ready to
tear your head off."

"That explains a lot," he said. "Why ole Cabot tried to give me
big trouble. Well, it's too bad about his unfortunate death. And I
guess I just can't depend on you in a crisis, can I?" He laughed as if
none of the tragic events that occurred mattered to him or that her
delicate condition was of any importance.

"I want to go to bed with you," he said as she scooted to the edge of the chair and stood up. "I liked it when you were big with Mildred Louise. It's something special loving a woman who's carrying a child."

"You're a mental case, Lawrence," she declared, disgustedly.

His eyes went wild. Jane flinched as his glass tipped, spilling onto the carpet. He took a step toward her, "How dare you insult me in that condescending way of yours," he spat, raising his hand as if he were going to strike her. "Did you forget who I am?"

"Oh how stupid of me to forget how important you are."

"That's right. I am a Browne and you're still obviously nothing but an ignorant convict."

She found the courage to say, "But you have that all wrong, Lawrence. I'm not just a convict, I'm an escaped convict, and one that you helped escape. As for being ignorant, you're right. At one time I was quite ignorant and illiterate as well, but not any more. No, Mister Browne, you'd be surprised at how much I've learned. And as for forgetting who you are . . . never! Not in a thousand years. I doubt that anyone could ever forget the Browne family."

She stood looking at him for a moment longer. "And another thing, I found out Charles is alive and both you and your mama knew it—let me believe he was dead, knowing how I felt about him. I know about your lies to keep Charles away from me when he came to New Orleans looking for me."

"Yes, and your precious Mr. Fisher ran from me like a scalded dog," he laughed, and reached for the decanter, pouring himself another drink.

"I wish I had the guts to kill you!" she said, and spun around on her heel and left him standing speechless.

⚔ Twenty-One ⚔

JANE TOSSED AND TURNED the rest of the night unable to get the image of Lawrence out of her mind. Her nightmare was a familiar one—Lawrence was pressing his fingers around her throat, choking her. She tried to scream. No sound would come out. He tightened his grip, standing there grinning into her face, his fingers squeezing tighter and tighter until suddenly she woke to Georgia Ann's friendly voice. "What's wrong, Mama. You were crying in your sleep, moaning something about Lawrence hurting you. Are you that upset he's back?"

"Yes I am, Sugar," she said. Rolling over to the edge of the bed she sat up. "I'm afraid if Lawrence stays in New Orleans there will be more trouble than I care to think about."

She smelled the aroma of fresh boiled coffee and fried bacon coming from the kitchen. It made her realize how hungry she was. She remembered she hadn't eaten anything since noon yesterday.

"I thought about Lawrence last night when I heard you talking to him," Georgia Ann said, pulling her white uniform over her head. She picked up her nursing shoes she'd dropped beside the door the night before, sat on the bed and pulled them on. "I hate him, Mama. I hate what's he's done to you."

"Georgia Ann, you're too young to have so much hate in your heart. I don't want you to feel that way about anybody." Jane tied her robe the best she could, fumbling with the string ties, then gave up. She and Georgia Ann walked down the stairs into the dining room in silence. When they sat down Georgia Ann started up again.

"Well, I do hate him, Mama. And I hope you're not planning on letting him move back in with us. If you do, I'll leave here. I'll go back up to northern Louisiana. They have good hospitals. I can do nursing up there."

"Sugar, don't you even think about leaving me. I'd just get sick if you did."

"Promise me you won't let him come back here to live then."

"I can't promise you that. If he takes a hankering to move back into the house, what can I do about it? You know how he is. If I anger him too much, he might call the constable and have me sent back to Angola."

Georgia Ann pushed her chair abruptly back from the table. "I am so tired of hearing that," she said. "He's just trying to scare you. If he was going to have you sent back to prison, he'd have done it years ago. Why don't you stop using that as a crutch? The fact is, you don't want to leave him, do you?"

"Georgia Ann, you're a young girl and really don't understand the danger of being involved with a man like Lawrence. Men like him thrive on the power of manipulating women. Lawrence doesn't love me or want me as a woman the way Charles Fisher did. I know that. But as long as I let him think he has control over me, if I'm submissive to his every whim, he's harmless to me. It made me sick last night to even look at him. The way he brags about who he is makes me as angry as a hornet. I don't ever intend on having anything to do with Lawrence again. But I realize one thing—he's a sick man. If he has a mind to be vindictive, he could send me back to prison. He'd do it if for no other reason than to show me how much power the almighty Brownes still have in this state, and I know it. Now don't get into my business with Lawrence. Whatever it is I have to do to keep him happy, I'll do it. Nothing is worse than going back to Angola."

"Men are just mean, self-centered creatures that live to torture us," Georgia Ann said. "I'll never fall for any of their tricks like you did with Papa and that Lawrence Browne!"

"Don't say that, Sugar." Jane wasn't surprised her daughter could have such a view of men. The men she had known were not exactly role models. First there was the sharecropper who raped her. Then

Jane's brothers John and Thomas, and now Lawrence. Georgia Ann had so much hatred for men she could not even remember Charles and his goodness. "There are plenty of gentle men in this world," she said. "I used to be skeptical too, until I met Charles Fisher." And just saying his name spread warmth throughout her body, touching her heart, giving Jane a feeling of contentment she hadn't felt in a long time.

"Mama, would you go back to Uncle Charlie if he wasn't married to Mary's mama?"

The thought of it made her heart flutter. *Would I go back to him?* She poured thick cream into her mug, stirring the hot liquid while her mind wandered back to the night when Dennis had beaten her and Ander so badly that she had run away to Charles.

"Georgia Ann, Sugar, the last weeks I lived with your papa were a nightmare. I thought my life would always be nothing but sheer misery. Charles Fisher helped me get through those tough times. If I had the chance to be with Charles again, I'd thank God for the rest of my life. If it hadn't been for him, I might not have ever gotten away from your papa. I'd be just like you. I would have never known what it's like to have a real man."

"What happened that night, Mama, when you left Papa? I don't recall too much of it. I just remember hearing you screaming and being scared Papa was going to hurt you."

"Well, Georgia Ann, I remember the cotton picking season was finished and what a blessing I thought it was," Jane said, launching into her story. As she spoke, she began to feel as if the huge load of her past was being lifted from her shoulders. It was something she'd never explained to Georgia Ann, but Jane knew it was time her daughter heard the truth about that night. Maybe, just maybe, she could show her that some men like Charles were good and kind human beings.

"Your papa thought I was cheating on him with Charles when Charles would come to the farm for you and Ander's learning lessons. One day he gave me the worst beating of my life. It was the following morning when Charles and I realized we loved each other. Charles rode up to the house and I walked out on the porch to greet him. . . .

"Dennis says you're not to come back on his property any more, and he's right. None of this is worth a beating," I said to Charles that morning, then I walked back inside the house.

"Charles got off his horse. He ran into the house after me, pulling me around to face him. 'I won't let you give up,' he said. He lifted my chin up and looked into my face. When he saw my bruises he went wild with rage. He ask me if Dennis had beat me.

"I told him that he had when Dennis found the learning books he'd left for you and Ander. You were looking at the pictures when he came home, and he went crazy."

Jane remembered every word she and Charles had said that day, she would never forget them. She remembered how Charles stared into her eyes trying to reassure her. . . . "Oh, Charles, what did I do that's so wrong? Is wanting a better life for my children a crime?"

"No, Liebchen, what you want for your children is not a crime. It's normal for a mother to want more for her children than she had. You don't have anything to feel guilty about. No matter what he tells you, you're only his wife. He didn't buy you, he married you. You're not his slave and neither are these children."

Jane remembered feeling the tension in Charles's hands. He had reached out and embraced her, cradling her close while she cried. He clutched her arm and led her out to the porch. She could still see how he snapped off a tiny rosebud, gently poking the stem in her hair. "Now stop crying," he had said. "You've got to pull yourself together. And I'll tell you this much. There comes a time in everyone's life when they have to ask themselves, 'How much punishment am I willing to take?' If you let people like Dennis Moody fill your heart with pain, your life with misery, then after a while it drives out all the love you have for yourself. Liebchen, when you stop loving yourself, you can't love anyone else."

JANE TOOK A DEEP BREATH, moving nervously around in the chair. She looked at Georgia Ann, who sat quiet as a field mouse, waiting to hear every detail she had to say.

"What happened after you and Ander left the house that night?"

"I couldn't find Charles's house, so we stayed on the steps at the school until he came the next morning. He was whistling when he rode up in his buggy and saw us," she recalled. She shut her eyes and could still see Charles clearly, his frock coat tail flapping in the wind as he got out of his red and black buggy, and rushed over to her.

"What in God's name happened to you?"

"I'm sorry, Charles," I told him, as he helped me to my feet. "We had to get away from Dennis."

"Charles asked one of the boys who had arrived early to sweep out the schoolhouse to run and bring Dr. Beall to his house as soon as he could. He bundled me and Ander into his buggy and drove us there.

"He boiled water and washed the dried blood from my face, but I stopped him. "Don't worry about me, Charles," I said. "Please, just see to Ander."

"Why did Dennis do this?" he asked, gently lifting up matted pieces of my bloody hair.

"He must have been around the house yesterday and saw us together," I answered. "He didn't say anything to me when he came in last night. He just picked up a piece of wood and started hitting me with it. When Ander ran into the kitchen to stop him, he began using it on him. He hit him, Charles. He hit my boy over and over again on his head and kept kicking me when I tried to make him stop."

"After the doctor had cleaned up our wounds, and had given us medicine for the pain, Charles carried me up to his room. I remember how he sat on the side of the bed and held my hand until the laudanum made me drowsy, and I fell asleep.

"Over the next few weeks he took care of us as if we were his own, but in spite of the loving care he gave me, I became more and more despondent, fearing for all our lives. Charles told me he realized that something had to be done about Dennis. One morning he rode out to our farm. Later he told me Dennis was drunk and unreasonable. He said he'd even stopped by the sheriff's office and pleaded my case, but the sheriff wasn't interested in 'family troubles.'

"When he returned home that night I knew Charles was deeply troubled. He poured a bourbon whiskey for himself and a glass of pear brandy for me. "No good can come of this," he had said, holding me in his arms as we sat quietly on the settee in his front parlor. "Not if you stay in this town. Even the sheriff said he's afraid Dennis might try to harm you."

Jane closed her eyes and remembered sipping her brandy, staring silently into the single flame of a candle on the mantle. *It's strange, isn't it, Charles? You're the first man who ever treated me like a person, like a friend, and I didn't have to do anything to get you to do it. Do you know how good that makes me feel? You once said you felt sorry for me because I never had time to be a little girl. Now that I think about it, I never had time to be a woman either. Dennis married a little girl and never cared one way or the other if I grew up. He just wanted somebody to have his children, clean his house, get behind a plow, and serve his meals—someone no better than one of those slaves he liked to pretend he owned before the war. Then you came along and tried to help me and my children. You treated me with more respect than I've ever known in my life. Just when I start to feel good about myself, I have to leave. It's not right.*

He took her face in his hands, cupping her chin tenderly. "No, Liebchen, you've got that all wrong," he had whispered. "You don't ever have to leave. Stay with me. I want to take care of you the rest of your life."

"YOU WERE really in love with Uncle Charlie, weren't you, Mama?" Georgia Ann asked, interrupting Jane's thoughts when Jane finally opened her eyes and sat staring at her cup.

Jane sighed. "There's a part of God in Charles," she said, smiling to herself as she remembered Charles's gentleness—the kind way he always treated her. Almost the way a mother loves her newborn. He gave nourishment to her heart as well as to her mind. She could still see his green eyes staring into her own when she was troubled, offering consolation. And she breathed heavily thinking how they would sparkle when he smiled his wide grin just to make her feel better. Every time she took a deep breath she could smell his musky man scent. She thought about how she used to shiver when his fingers would glide across her skin—how she felt just having him near her—how she wanted to commit her life and her heart to him forever.

She was still staring into the cup of coffee, tears falling down her cheeks when she looked up into her daughter's face. She was silently pleading to God for some solace. "I can't talk about Charles any more right now, Georgia Ann. Every time I think about him, I get sick in my heart. I love him so much, sometimes I think I'm going mad," she blurted out. "You don't have any idea what it's been like. All these years of loneliness without him. I think it was easier when I believed he was dead. At least I didn't yearn for him. My heart didn't ache the way it does now. It's been terrible for me since I found out he's alive. Some days it takes all my strength just to keep from sending him word where I am. My dreams are filled with him, night after night. I just can't forget him—I can't. I pray everyday for God to help me get over him."

"For God's sake," Georgia Ann said, "if you love him that much why don't you try to contact him anyway?"

"I can't. He's married to Martha Ellen now. And wouldn't I look foolish running after Charles Fisher carrying another man's baby."

"Well, well, if this is not the most interesting conversation I've ever heard," Lawrence, who suddenly appeared in the dining room, mocked. Jane stood up and turned around so swiftly she lost her balance and tumbled into his arms. Lawrence pushed her away. She fell hard against the table.

"So this is the real reason I got the cold shoulder from you last night," he said, each word getting harsher. "It didn't have anything to do with my going to New York. It's that wonderful Mr. Fisher who occupies your every thought. You really didn't give a damn if I ever came back, did you?"

Jane sat down in her chair at the table. Georgia Ann stood behind her while Lawrence walked out of the room and stalked up the stairs two at a time. Neither Jane nor Georgia Ann said a word while he was gone, but they could hear him throwing things around in the bedroom. When he came back down he stopped and stood in the dining room doorway. "I'll be at the track today," he said, flashing the string of pearls before him. "And I'm taking Mama's little gems with me."

"Well, like I've always said Lawrence, there's nothing cheap about you," she said. Then it hit her. "Mama's pearls? Did he say that?" she asked Georgia Ann.

"Yes."

Jane was flabbergasted. He stalked down the hall and slammed the front door shut. She felt like a lone Confederate general standing in the middle of a battlefield waiting for the entire Union Army to descend upon her as she thought about the morning the Madam whipped George Ivan for stealing her pearls when all along it had been Lawrence.

No longer preoccupied with her thoughts of Charles, she continued to stare blankly. *Lawrence Browne is a devious man and if I don't watch myself, he's going to have me sent me back to prison.*

Twenty-Two

JANE FELT very much alone as she lay in her bed waiting to see if she was in labor or if this was just another false alarm like a few days ago. She was still worried a full week after Lawrence had overheard her and Georgia Ann's conversation at the breakfast table. All day she had lain quietly listening to the sounds coming from outside her window. The bells of St. Louis tolled each hour, mule hooves clopped slowly on the busy street below and from off the river steamboat whistles drowned out the shouts of street vendors selling their wares. In spite of all the noise, though, she felt as if she were all alone in the world with nothing and no one to share in her pain except Georgia Ann. She stiffened her body as the burning cramps increased.

As Jane held her breath waiting for the pain to subside, Georgia Ann came into the room and Jane moaned loudly again. Georgia Ann rushed over to the bed. "What can I do for you, Mama?"

"Nothing, Sugar. The way this is going it might be tomorrow before the baby comes."

"Are you sure?" Georgia Ann asked. "Can I get you something to make you more comfortable?"

Jane lay back and sighed. She thought the soft goose down pillows and her cool clean sheets were a sight better birthing bed than the bare corn shuck mattress she had lain on when her older children were born. She wasn't about to start complaining over a few labor pains. Worrying about Lawrence and Ander and having this baby were enough.

A sharp pain swept through her lower back. Jane closed her eyes, gritted her teeth and writhed in agony until it subsided. The soft strains of Stephen Foster's *Beautiful Dreamer* drifted up from the parlor. Georgia Ann had cranked up the *gramophone* and it made Jane feel better. They hadn't played any music since Lawrence had returned. Nobody even wanted to go near the parlor, fearing they might bump into him if he came home.

The melody began to relax her. Jane loved that music. It was pleasant, the kind of music she and Charles Fisher often listened to. She began to hum along with the song and the words came back to her, "Beau-ti-ful dream-er wake un-to me, star-light and dew-drops are wait-ing for thee."

Another sharp pain. This one lasted several seconds. She cried out and frantically tried to reach the bell beside her bed. Nellie scurried into the room reaching Jane's side in no time, wringing her hands as she looked down on her. "You wants me to send for the doctor, Miz Jane?"

"No, there's no need for him to come now. Just call the Countess and tell her my labor has started. Tell her not to rush. I know she has her hands full. She's giving some big party for the Confederate Home."

"Yessum. I just thought if the doctor was here he could give you something for the pain."

"I have medicine for that. Look over there in that little cabinet and you'll see a dark blue bottle," Jane said, pointing to the corner of the room. "If you will, put a few drops in a glass of water for me, please."

Nellie picked up the pitcher of water and poured it into a glass carefully, allowing only a few drops of the medicine to go in. Jane drank the cloudy liquid and sank back into the soft pillows. "Thank you, Nellie. I'll be fine now. You call the Countess and go on back to bed," Jane said, waving her out of the room.

"Anything else I can do?"

"No, Sugar. You just get some rest until we have to call the doctor. He'll need your help."

"Yessum, I gots everything ready and waiting for this baby. The scissors been burned and they all wrapped up; rags piled knee high.

All I gots to do is put the boiling pot on the fire. You jest try and rest now. Keep that bellcord near you in case you needs me. I'll be listening for you."

Jane lay quietly on her comfortable bed, listening to the soothing music. She was relaxed. The laudanum was a blessing. Her thoughts began to drift and before she knew it she was thinking happy thoughts about Charles Fisher and what it would have been like to have his baby. She pictured him beside her bed, holding her hand, telling her how much he loved her or singing one of his German love songs. He would have anticipated the birth of this baby. She knew he would never have left her alone the way Lawrence was doing. There would have been flowers all over the room, and Charles would have been the first to hold his precious child, thanking Jane for such a treasure. *We could have been so happy,* she thought.

She closed her heavy eyelids and wondered for a moment about Lawrence. Did he still care enough to be with her when the baby was born? Would he be drunk again if he finally did come?

The Countess slipped into the dimly lit room without Jane hearing her. She gently tapped her finger on the bedside table, "I can see you're doing a little day dreaming again," she said. "Where's Lawrence?"

"I don't know."

"Cherie, this is not right. Lawrence knows you're ready to have this baby. He should be here with you."

"Well he's not, so don't worry about it."

"I can't help but worry about it," the Countess said. She sat on the edge of Jane's bed as Georgia Ann walked in.

"What does she need Lawrence for?" Georgia Ann asked the Countess.

"Child, when a woman is giving birth to a baby, she needs all the support she can get, especially consideration from the father."

"How would you know? You've never had a baby."

"Georgia Ann!" Jane said.

"Well, it's true, Mama," and Georgia Ann flashed the Countess an angry look. "She never has."

"You're right, Georgia Ann," the Countess conceded and smiled at Jane. "But I still say damn that man for not being more dependable. You're not some woman who's just his bed partner when he is in need of pleasure or someone to provide him a place to live!"

"But he thinks so, Countess," Georgia Ann said, her lips faintly parted and her eyebrows raised.

Jane could see that Georgia Ann was irritating the Countess. *God I hope they don't get into a fuss tonight,* she thought, but Georgia Ann's motives were clear to her. She'd planned on getting into a confrontation with the Countess about Lawrence. Jane had seen all the signs. First, Georgia Ann didn't lift a finger to tell the Countess Jane was in labor. She made the Countess wait until Nellie had to call her. Secondly, Georgia Ann repeatedly had said since she had come home from the hospital, how she wished "that whore didn't have to be here when the baby is born". And thirdly and most importantly, Georgia Ann was suspicious of the Countess and Lawrence. "They work together," Georgia Ann had said that very afternoon, "how can you trust either of them?"

Jane managed to sit up. Georgia Ann and the Countess moved to the head of the bed, one on one side and one on the other. They propped the pillows behind Jane's lower back. "What Lawrence ought to do and what he does are two entirely different things," Jane said. "But I have to accept Lawrence for what he is. He will never be a devoted companion to any woman."

"But damn it, he makes me so mad," the Countess said. "The least the scoundrel could do is be here when his baby is born. If he didn't spend so much time with that Malone bunch, he'd know what's going on with his family. I hear talk Tom Anderson is getting fed up with Lawrence. Tom may have been in cahoots with the Major, but I seriously doubt he will put up with Lawrence's shenanigans much longer."

"What are you talking about? Is he in some kind of trouble with the Ring Bosses?" Jane asked the Countess.

"Well, I don't know how deep it is, and I don't want to worry you at a time like this, but there's talk of gang trouble brewing between the District bosses. I've told you about that other gang of hoodlums from New York and how the Ring Bosses shut them out of Storyville. Well, they're still operating and from what I hear, trying to move in on Mastri's territory. Up until now, Malone and

Anderson have been working out their territorial problems, and thank God we got Ander out of that, but word is Malone has the money and the backing from New York and Chicago to barge in on the Mansion District. The Ring Bosses are not going to stand for it. You wait and see, there's going to be an awful lot of bloodshed in the District. I hope you can talk some sense into Lawrence. He needs to stay away from it."

"Countess, how do you know about this?" Georgia Ann asked. "Is it street-walker's gossip or did you get this from a reliable source? I work with the Sisters of Charity and you know they know as much about the prostitutes and what's going on in Storyville as you do. I haven't heard the first bit about what you're saying."

"Whether or not you think I know my business, Georgia Ann," the Countess snapped, "is beside the point. What I am trying to tell your mama is hard, cold street talk facts."

Jane rubbed her hard stomach, feeling for any movement. She pushed up a sleeve of her nightgown and gently touched the bruises on her arms. "Well, if it keeps me from going back to prison, I don't care what Tom Anderson does to Lawrence. I worry so much about Ander—and now that Lawrence is back, I'll have to worry constantly about him as well. Sometimes I think I'm going to lose my mind. It's like having two spoiled children, each clutching at my skirt and each one wanting all my love and attention, and when they don't get it, they start hitting at each other."

"Oh, Cherie. How I feel for you," the Countess said, patting Jane's arm.

Jane didn't want anyone feeling sorry for her and she was in no mood for this conversation. "Countess, you look tired," she said, trying not to sound irritated. "It's going to be a while before the baby comes. Why don't you go on home? I'll send for you when it's time. Besides, I need to get some rest."

"You're right. I am weary. I could use some rest. When it gets time, have Georgia Ann or Nellie call me."

Jane had been dreaming about Ander when an excruciating pain woke her up. "Oh, God! Somebody help me!" She could feel the warm water from her womb spreading out under her body, soaking the sheets and her nightclothes. "Please help me," she cried out.

"I'm here, Mama," Ander said, slipping quietly into the room and sitting down on her bed.

Jane grabbed his arm. "Ander, what are you doing here? The Countess said there's gang trouble about to break wide-open. Please, Son, go back across the lake with Mary. She must be ready to have her baby."

"She had a baby boy, yesterday," he said. "That's why I came to town, to tell you all about him."

"Ander, don't lie to me, Son," she said, and at that moment her pains intensified.

Georgia Ann came into the bedroom and lit another oil lamp. "Ander, go call Dr. Cochran and wake up Nellie," she said. "Please, Ander!" Georgia Ann pleaded with him when he sat there looking as if he hadn't heard her. Georgia Ann took the blue bottle out of the cabinet and stirred up another dose of pain medicine for her mother. By the time Doctor Cochran arrived the Countess had come back and, though heavily sedated with laudanum, Jane screamed out as one pain went right into the next.

"Doctor Cochran?" she weakly murmured as the doctor pulled the bed covers down and pushed her legs apart.

"Yes, Jane. I'm here. Now you've got to wake up and push as hard as you possibly can. I can see your baby's head."

She felt her body pushing, straining, doing all the things the doctor told her to do. She heard Nellie's whimpering and the Countess trying to give her comfort. Then she heard a baby cry. The doctor said, "It must be twins—that's the first one, a boy. Now let's get the other one out. Push Jane," he commanded. "It'll be over soon." Then suddenly Doctor Cochran shouted at her, "This one's coming out feet first. Push Jane. Its head is still inside. Push, damn it—If you want this baby to live, you'd better help me out."

Jane dug her chin sharply into her chest. Her hand gripped the side of the bed and she clutched the sheet tightly, her fingers digging deeply into the mattress, and she was grinding her teeth. She groaned, then screamed out and pushed with all her strength. Suddenly the pain ceased. Her body went limp. A cool cloth touched her face. The Countess started to mop the perspiration but Jane pushed her hand away.

"Let me sleep for a minute," she murmured. "Just a little while, then I'll look at my babies."

She was on the verge of falling asleep when she heard Doctor Cochran. "It's better this way. The cord wrapped around his neck—that's why it took so much effort to get him out. It's better to let him die now."

"Doctor, do you know what you're saying?" she heard the Countess ask.

"Yes. Even if he lives there's no telling what shape he'll be in. I've seen it happen before. You have to trust me. When the cord gets wrapped around their throats, it cuts off the oxygen to their brains. It happens all the time with twins. There's nothing anybody can do. Now let's just be thankful she's got one healthy baby. Don't you see that, girl?"

Jane could hear them mumbling and the women crying. *There's nothing anybody can do,* echoed in her mind until she shook herself awake. The words were like sharp arrows in her heart and Jane knew she had to get up and do something. "Someone's trying to kill my baby," she screamed out.

Hands held her down and the Countess and Georgia Ann stood around her bed. "See if you can get her to sip this, Countess," Doctor Cochran said. "The pain's made her delirious. Listen to how she's talking. I want her to sleep. I don't want her waking up now and seeing a dead baby in this room." Jane felt something cool touch her lips. She didn't want to sleep. She closed her mouth tightly when the glass touched her lips. She thrashed her arms about, trying to get up.

"Come on, Cherie," the Countess said. "Don't fight me! Do what the doctor says. Everything will be all right."

Jane tried to push her away. She lifted her head and saw the doctor looking down into a wicker basket shaking his head. Using all the strength she could muster, she sat up and slapped the Countess's hand. The glass of dark liquid sedative flew across the bed.

"No. . . . " she cried out. Grabbing her stomach she rolled over the side of the bed. "You can't let my baby die."

Georgia Ann darted over to the dying baby, picked him up and laid him in her mother's arms. "Hold him, Mama, before he dies!"

Quickly, Jane unwrapped the cord and began blowing in her baby's face. He had turned blue and his little body just sagged in his mother's fingers. She took his tiny legs in her hand and turned him upside down. She beat on his back. "Breathe," she kept saying. She wanted to scream, and scream and never stop screaming.

The Countess grabbed Jane's shoulders. Doctor Cochran reached down trying to take the baby from her. Jane clutched the tiny infant to her chest, defying the doctor to touch him. Dr. Cochran shook her forcefully. "Jane, don't do this. Let the baby die," he said. "He'll never be right. Don't put this burden on yourself. Let him go, and love the healthy one you have."

"Get away from me," she shouted. "You tried to kill my baby."

Again and again she pounded his tiny back. The baby finally coughed, his mouth moved and the bluish color began to disappear. He wailed out as his tiny body wiggled in her arms. She hugged him to her breast as Georgia Ann dropped to her knees, hovering over her mother. "He's alive, Georgia Ann. Our baby is alive," she kept saying over and over. "Doctor Cochran, my baby's going to live."

Doctor Cochran relented and sat on the edge of the bed, shaking his head, both hands hanging between his knees. "Yes, Jane, your baby is alive. And I hope you won't live to regret what you've done, child."

"What happened?" A voice called out from the doorway.

Still holding her baby, Jane looked up and there Ander stood, his face bleeding. Apparently there had been trouble.

"Well, I found your baby's papa," Ander said. "He was in one of the houses on Customhouse Street with a whore, Maureen. He was drunk and acted like a cock-eyed smart ass, so I let him have it."

"What are you talking about?" Georgia Ann asked him.

"What were you doing in the District, Ander?" the Countess demanded, interrupting Georgia Ann. "You think you're indestructible? You don't care anything about the rules, do you? You're lucky Malone's men didn't grab you and cut your throat! Next time they might get you."

"Not if I can get them first," Ander hissed, and then Jane heard him gasp, "Lawrence Browne," he cried out. Jane looked up. Lawrence was standing in the dark hallway. He staggered into the bedroom, reaching out for Ander who fell to the floor beside his mother's bed.

"Get up from there, you no good, worthless coward!" Lawrence yelled.

"Lawrence, don't hurt him," Jane pleaded, reaching out her arm to shield Ander.

Lawrence had a scowl on his bleeding face. He stared into Jane's eyes. She could not see the least bit of compassion. "I'm not going to hurt him, I'm going to kill him!"

"Master Lawrence?" It was the Countess who spoke first and the Countess whom Lawrence responded to. "Jane has just given birth to your children. You are completely out of control and showing the manners of a drunken District pimp. I am surprised and appalled by your behavior."

"The show's over and the fun is about to begin," he slurred to the Countess. "And you Madam, I believe have work to do. Call your carriage at once and go home. I don't want to see you here in this house ever again."

He turned to Georgia Ann and hissed at her. "And you girl, get out of this room! Get out of this house for that matter!"

Georgia Ann rose slowly from Jane's bedside giving her mother a terrified look. She pulled open the drawer next to Jane's bed, pulled out her mother's Derringer and pointed it in Lawrence's direction.

"Put that gun down!" he demanded, stumbling toward her.

Georgia Ann pulled the trigger. Jane screamed. Lawrence fell back against the floor. Jane could feel the blood pounding in her head and feared she would black out.

Dr. Cochran rushed to Lawrence's side. He knelt down and felt his wrist. "His pulse is good. Countess, call the ambulance wagon," he said, tearing at Lawrence's shirt, searching for the bullet hole. "It's only a flesh wound," he finally said. "Just get him to the hospital. I think he's passed out from too much liquor."

"Come on, Ander," he said, standing up and waving his hand motioning for Ander to get up off the floor. "I need to finish up with your mama and get on home."

"Georgia Ann," the Countess said, "child, there won't be a safe inch in this city for you now. You get packed up. Before Lawrence gets out of the hospital, you've got to get out of here."

The Countess and Ander continued to argue. "If you know what is good for you, Ander Moody," she heard the Countess say. "I strongly suggest you high-tail it back across the lake and take your sister with you. I suspect after this, when your mama and the babies are well enough, she'll have to join you."

But Jane became oblivious to what they were saying. She turned her head when the ambulance doctor arrived to haul Lawrence out. All she cared about was that her babies were alive.

After everyone left her room, she lay quietly hugging her tiny twins to her warm breast, praying. *God if you will only give me the strength to get well, I'll do all I can to get my family away from Lawrence and out of this city of sin.*

She looked across the vast expanse of the room out of the window. The pink tinge of the sun was beginning to light up the dark sky and down below the rumble of early morning delivery wagons was busily bringing in the new day. Somewhere nearby she could hear the faint sounds of peddlers and she was getting drowsy—falling, falling asleep, and somewhere in her memory she heard a voice, *Think of yourself Jane, think of yourself.*

Twenty-Three

FOR THE NEXT SIX MONTHS Jane spent almost every morning attaching tasseled swags to a large order of curtains for the Robalard family on Bourbon Street, paying careful attention to detail. It wasn't hard work, just tedious. *At least I have a good job,* she thought, *even if I am lonely.* And she had been lonely since Georgia Ann moved back to northern Louisiana. The babies, at six months old, spent most of the time in their cribs and she missed Georgia Ann so much she almost couldn't bear it. This morning as she walked the two blocks to Anna Cambers' shop, she wondered why she hadn't heard from Georgia Ann and Ander, and she wondered about Lawrence. Where he was, she could only guess. He'd show up again, though, she was sure of that.

Jane pushed open the glass front door and a little bell tinkled, summoning Mrs. Cambers from behind a curtain that separated the display section of her small store from the work shop.

"Jane, I have good news. Two more orders for the red silk have come in," Mrs. Cambers proudly said, as she stood behind the sales counter in front of boxed shelves filled with hats in different shapes and shades and bolts of brightly colored ribbon hanging from the ceiling. She reached out to open a large brown ledger book. She pulled out two slips of order forms filled with window measurements. She handed them to Jane. "With orders like this coming in, you'll soon have enough money for a nice holiday," she said, smiling warmly at Jane.

Jane respected this woman. She and her sister had built the variety goods shop in the front room of Anna's home on a shoestring budget after Anna's husband had died from the fever epidemic. The Cambers' store was highly regarded for the quality of its merchandise and service to its customers. Jane felt proud to be a part of it. It crossed her mind that even though Emma Browne had had her faults, she was the one who had given Jane the opportunity to learn about beautiful things.

As she walked out of the shop, opening her parasol, she heard the familiar sound of chimes from St. Louis Cathedral. They were tolling noon and she knew she had to get home to nurse her babies. Rushing toward her house to try to escape the pervading smell of the horses and mules, she noticed a small black woman who was known to openly practice voodoo, scattering brick dust on doorsteps along Royal Street. Even though Storyville was several blocks from Royal, the talk of gang violence hung over every street nearby. She'd heard that the shops on Royal to Canal Street were burning incense to keep away evil spirits.

Jane hadn't seen much of the Countess since her babies were born. Mostly she'd talked on the phone with her, and when she reached her home she was surprised to see the Countess's purple plumed carriage sitting in her alleyway.

"Cherie," the Countess said, embracing Jane in the parlor as she walked in. There was a frightened tone in the Countess's voice. Laying her parasol and the papers on the table, Jane called out for Nellie to bring to her Alfred, the smallest of her twins. She and the Countess sat down on the settee in the parlor.

"Something's happened hasn't it?" Jane asked.

"Cherie, I'm afraid so. And I have to tell you that your son is involved again."

"Is he back in Storyville, Countess?"

"I'm afraid so."

Jane sighed and took a deep breath, leaning her head against the back of her chair. She looked at the Countess bewildered. "I just don't understand Ander. Why does he keep coming back here?"

"Cherie, please believe me, I don't mean to intrude upon your relationship with Ander. If I offend you by coming here to let you know the danger he is in, then it grieves me. You know I am always direct with you and my only concern is that he do nothing more to cause you trouble with Lawrence, especially after the ordeal you have just come through."

"Countess, I appreciate your concern," she said, taking her baby from Nellie's arms. "If you didn't keep me informed, I'd never know what Ander is up to. Every time I hear from him he denies any dealings in the District."

"I fear for him, Cherie," the Countess said, as she watched Jane begin to feed her hungry baby boy. "And it's not so much because of his association with Mastri, but of the disturbing rumors I'm hearing about a crib girl named Ella Peck with whom he's having a well advertised liaison."

Jane placed a blanket over Alfred as he greedily sucked the milk from her swollen breast. She glanced up at the Countess. "Are you saying Ander's having an affair with a prostitute?"

"Cherie, having an affair would be putting it mildly. Your son is obsessed with this woman. You asked me earlier why he won't stay away from Storyville. It's because of her. She is one of Mastri's prized girls and I suspect a love interest as well, for the old man. And up until now, Mastri has been Ander's life-line in the District. For Malone or the Ring Bosses to harm Ander, they would have had to go through Mastri to do it. That would have been the start of a territorial war and Ander Moody wasn't that big a threat to anyone. But now, I don't know, Cherie. Ander's been bragging in the saloons about how he's taking Ella Peck and starting up his own District."

"Good God! Has he lost all sense of reality?" Jane said. Her heart raced at the image of the District mobs chasing Ander. She pulled the cover away from Alfred's face and laid him against her shoulder, patting his back until he burped. She breathed heavily and motioned for Nellie to take him. "Maybe I should contact Lawrence. He may hate and despise Ander, but I know if I beg him enough, he'll see that Ander leaves New Orleans unhurt."

"Would he?" the Countess asked incredulously. And Jane realized that she must be dreaming to think that Lawrence would help her son.

The Countess stood up quietly and looked down at Jane. "Besides, Lawrence is back in New York," she said. "I heard rumors his new wife begged him to take her back; sold her beautiful home on Prytania Street to one of the Major's old cronies; and they left for New York as soon as she sold all of her furniture." She chuckled, "Heard she got a good price for it too, and, if I know Lawrence Browne he won't be back in New Orleans until he's spent every dime she has.

"Anyway, Cherie, I didn't come over here to discuss Lawrence. Tom Anderson's on his tail about the possibility of him fixing races at the Fair Grounds. The day before Lawrence left for New York, a jockey threw a race. They found him floating in Bayou St. John the next day, and I imagine it'll be a while before Lawrence comes back to town."

The Countess reached into her tiny handbag and pulled out a small slip of paper. "This is the name of the saloon where you can find Ander most of the time. I'd go over there myself and get him for you, but it's in Mastri's District. If Tom Anderson caught me over there, he'd most likely do to me what he did to that vulgar mouthed madam, Mary Duebler. He'd burn my house down and put me to tricking in a room over his saloon." She picked up her parasol and leaned down, pecking Jane on her cheek. Jane watched as the Countess melted through the doorway, then she heard the back door slam shut.

ALL AFTERNOON, on into the early evening, Jane worried about what the Countess had said. She finally gave up trying to figure what Ander was up to. She knew she had to go and find him. All she could think about was getting him out of town—getting him out as fast as she could.

"Nellie, you watch the babies good now, you hear?" she said, after she decided to go find Ander. "Don't pick them up if they cry. Just leave them here like I have them." Jane tucked the blankets around their chubby little faces. She bent over the crib and kissed Alfred first, tasting his sweetness and then she rubbed her cheek over John Joseph's sleeping face. His pink little lips puckered. She stood for a moment, looking down at her babies. Her chest swelled. She loved them so much, and tiny Alfred was finally beginning to pick up weight. He wasn't as alert as John Joseph, not nearly as much as she could wish, but he was alive, and at least for that she was grateful. "Remember, Nellie. You stay right here in this bedroom with them. Don't leave for anything."

She slipped down the stairs and out the back door. Nellie had hitched the carriage for her and before she took off, she lowered the wick on the lanterns until a dim yellow light shown through the smoked glass. Up the alleyway she rode until she came to an opening onto the street. As she approached Customhouse and Royal she turned the carriage to the right and lowered the lantern above her face again. The night was dark, no moon at all, as the mule trudged forward into the blackness of Customhouse, past Rampart, to Basin Street. *All I need is to get caught by the constable going into Storyville and be arrested for looking like a prostitute trying to go out of the District*, she thought. *Then who would take care of my babies?*

Basin Street was so crowded with men she had second thoughts about going forward, but it was too late to turn back. She squinted her eyes as the mule crossed the Southern Railroad track, the carriage swaying roughly over the bumpy rails. She heard the distant echo of a gunshot, then another and another and then saw suspender clad men of all shapes and sizes pouring out of the brilliantly lit Tom Anderson Saloon, some running toward Canal Street but most heading toward the fire coming from up the street near the next corner.

Jane stopped the carriage in front of the *Shooting Gallery Saloon* and climbed out. She quickly tied the reins to a hitching post and walked to the corner of Customhouse Street where she ran along the brick walkway, hugging the wooden buildings. She burst through a crowd of men struggling with fire hoses, stopped and looked up at the burning saloon where she thought Ander might be. The column of smoke seemed to be caused by several structures on fire and puffs of black smoke ringed toward the sky through leaping flames, one after the other. As Jane watched, she saw flames work their way to the row of cribs where scantily clad women were running out of doorways, tripping and then scrambling to their feet, running into the crowd until they were out of view. Burning boards and shingles and other flaming objects were hurled through the air until they crashed to the street. Her first impulse was to run into the burning structure. *Ander, Ander,* she kept screaming over and over in her mind, turning around and around in the stinging cloud of smoke that threatened to choke her if she went even an inch farther. Suddenly a burning wall collapsed. She heard the frightened screams of a firefighter caught under it. Terrifying yells deafened her ears. She twisted away from the flames trying to run when a soft hand with long red fingernails clutched her arm. Jane looked up and a raspy voiced, red haired woman said, "Are you Jane? If you are, Ander's all right. I know where he is. He wasn't involved in this shooting here tonight."

"Where is he?" Jane demanded. The girl clutched her arm, dragging her away from the sickening scene. "Who are you? How are you involved with Ander?"

"Name's Ella Peck. I work with your son. We work in Mastri's District a couple of blocks from here on the other side of Franklin Street."

"Let's get to my carriage," Jane said, and they ran back to Basin Street without stopping.

"I know you don't approve of the kind of work Ander does," Ella said, as Jane untied the reins and climbed up into the carriage. "But it's a job and it puts shoes on that young'un of his."

"Miss Peck! My opinion of my son's employment in Storyville is not important to me at this moment—his life is. I need to get to him if you will be kind enough to take me to where he is. If I don't get him out of New Orleans, he'll be killed. Do you understand? That is my only interest right now," she snapped.

Ella Peck told her to turn right at Krauss' store on Canal Street and go several blocks to Marais Street.

Jane jerked the reins. She began nervously talking and tried to get Ella to tell her more. This young harlot seemed to know Ander better than his own mother did.

"You're the girl that Ander's been living with, aren't you?"

Ella answered surly, "That's me. Why?"

"I want to know what happened to Mary and the baby. Why did he leave them? Where did they go?"

"Oh, he didn't leave them. He still goes home now and then."

Ella reached up and pinned on her head a worn and tattered yellow hat with a pink ostrich feather she'd been holding tightly in her hand. She began to point to a dark alley between two brick and stone high-rises.

"I'll walk from Canal Street. It'll be safer to hide the carriage behind this warehouse," Ella said. "You can stay here while I go get Ander and sneak him back."

Sitting in the alleyway, Jane noticed how different the neighborhood was, how shabby the houses of prostitution were compared to the stately mansions on Basin street. Every dark stable could be a hiding place for criminals, and she yelped as a black cat jumped up on the seat beside her, but she would not be scared away. She was determined to sit here. She was going to personally escort Ander to the New Basin Canal and put him on a flatboat going across the lake. What was he doing here anyway, running around with some prostitute when he had a wife and family? *That boy seems to look for trouble,* she thought. *And when he can't find it, trouble comes looking for him. Well, it's not going to find him tonight if I can help it. His behavior could get himself and even his wife and baby killed. I'm going to see to it he leaves New Orleans once and for all even if it takes me all night.*

⸸ Twenty-Four ⸸

THE HORROR of the territorial gun-battle stayed in Jane's mind. She had succeeded in getting Ander away but the frightening possibility that Ander would resurface in New Orleans was always with her. Even the passing of two years hadn't dimmed the uneasy feeling that had jolted her awake in the middle of this night. She lay in bed until morning thinking about Georgia Ann and Ander, wondering how they were until the harsh rumble of wagon wheels upon the cobblestone below disturbed her thoughts. The loud voices of delivery drivers filtered up through the open windows and she heard the twins giggling in her doorway. She turned over, outstretched her arms and caught the little tykes as they ran to her, struggling hard to climb up on her bed.

"Miz Jane, is you awake?" Nellie asked, poking her head inside the room.

"Yes, Nellie. You go on down and start breakfast. The boys are with me. I'll dress them this morning," she said, hugging each of them to her bosom, showering kisses over their faces.

"Hungry, Mama," John Joseph said, pulling out of her embrace and standing up on the bed. Alfred lay quietly against his mother, sucking his thumb as he watched his brother bouncing around.

They've grown so much, she thought, *and you'd hardly believe they are identical twins.* Alfred was slow where John Joseph was bursting with energy and always eager to learn, but it didn't worry her as much as it once did. Alfred was such a joy to be around she thanked God daily that he could walk as well as John Joseph and sometimes even babble intelligible words. She knew she would always have to take care of him, but she didn't really mind. His eternal good nature gave her solace.

JANE STARTED sewing at eight-fifteen and was finished by noon, tired but happy. She put aside her thimble and thread, calling the boys for their noon-day meal. She felt like she was in a swamp here lately with the humidity so bad. Mold spores growing wildly along the Mississippi and mixed with the dampness from open street gutters kept her with a grievous headache. Today it seemed especially bad and after they ate their noon day meal, she took the boys up to her room for a nap.

She was humming a familiar song and the boys drifted off to sleep. She heard the front door open. *Probably another cloth order,* she thought, sinking into her pillow for a much needed rest. Then heavy footsteps on the stairs startled her. She sat up and got out of the bed, tucking the mosquito netting securely under the mattress. She turned around. Lawrence was standing in her doorway, obviously dead drunk.

He threw his hat onto one of the bedposts and, without as much as a hello, sat down in a deeply cushioned green velvet chair beside the bed. At first he didn't say anything and Jane just stood still, staring at him, wondering what in the world he could want.

Then he rose from the chair, stumbling against the night table. "Doctor Cochran says one of the boys is simple minded. Says he'll be lucky if he ever learns to piss by himself," he said, weaving unsteadily over to the bed.

The loudness of his voice woke the boys and Lawrence bent his head, peeking through the netting to look at them. They both started crying. Jane reached over to the bedside table, pulled open the drawer and took out her Derringer. She had no idea what Lawrence was doing here. She hadn't seen or heard from him for God knows how long. She wasn't about to take any chances in case he had some sort of deranged revenge on his mind after all these years. He turned to face her, hissing when he saw the gun, then dashed over and knocked the gun from her hands before she could think of pulling the trigger. He grabbed both of her wrists, slung her into the netting and pushed her against the pillows. She struggled to get up.

"You're hurting me, Lawrence," she said, wriggling to get out of his firm grip. "Get your hands off of me and get out. I don't want you around here. I don't need you any more."

Lawrence bent down, kissed her hard on the lips and reared back before he let go of her arms. Staring into her face he said, "Oh, I have no doubt you have little need of me. You never did, did you? But I have need of you."

Jane shoved him off of her, got out of the bed and pulled the netting up off of her boys. She stood between him and the twins. "What is it you want, Lawrence? Is it a place to stay again? Has your new wife run out of money?"

He poured himself a brandy from a small table near the foot of the bed. He settled back into the chair, propping his feet on the edge. "I'll have to admit, it was pretty comfortable here. As a matter of fact, you keep a damn fine house. You're almost as good as Mama when it comes to that," he said, taking a gulp of the brandy. "But then why wouldn't you be? She taught you everything you know about gracious living." He belched loudly, tapping his hand on his chest, paused a moment, then said, "However, my dear Jane, there's more to life than what you think you have to offer a man. And you want to know why it is I like being with women like Maureen? It's simple. They're intelligent. They can talk to me about business. They take care of me. They love me for what I am."

"Love you for what you are, Lawrence? I doubt that."

"Think what you might, but the one I have now loves me more than you ever did. You treated me like a whore. You used me when you wanted me—used me to get out of prison just like Mama said you would. Closed your door without a thought about what I needed when your fancy man, Charles Fisher, crept into your mind. And don't try to deny it," he said, staring up into her eyes. "Many was the night I lay next to you, wiping sweat from your brow while you called out his name in your sleep—crying out for that worthless excuse for a man until I wanted to put my fingers around your neck and choke him out of your mind. Well, my other women are different. With them I never have to compete with other men. They know how to treat their man."

Jane bit the side of her lip as she sank down on the edge of the bed. Her body was trembling, but she fought the urge to shout at him. She gathered every bit of the self restraint she had and said, "Lawrence, don't sit there pretending you ever loved me. It's a lie and you know it. If you could ever stop for one minute and think about someone other than yourself you might one day find the kind of special love I have for Charles—the kind of love that makes you a better person. You talk about your women. Lawrence Browne, you are a poor excuse for a man. If you don't change your ways you'll die just like you sit before me—a drunken fool. The next woman you get just might be your last. Wouldn't you like to one day say that you love someone so much it makes your life worthwhile, the way I do Charles, or do you think you can go on with your life, as miserable as you are now, pretending to be a whole man."

Lawrence stood up. He slapped her with such force she fell back across the bed. "What would you know about being a whole person?" he shouted. "I found you in a prison, a lowly convict. You should be thankful to me for the rest of your life."

She flew up off the bed and struck out at his face with both hands. He put his fingers on her forehead and pushed her backward, jumped up on the bed and pinned her arms down on the mattress with both of his knees. He yanked the front of her blouse, ripping it open. She screamed. He stretched his legs out and lay on top of her, breathing heavily. John Joseph and Alfred flung themselves on top of his back. John Joseph bit him on the shoulder, pulling his hair. Lawrence reached his hand up and backhanded the little boy. Jane went wild, thrashing about until she got from under him. "I'll kill you Lawrence Browne if you strike my child again."

He overpowered her, pinning her against the mattress again. "You're getting to be a regular little spitfire, aren't you, Jane?" he hissed. "And a damn pretty one at that. Maybe we can make arrangements with the Countess to rent you one of her rooms, bring a few men into your bed," he said, squeezing her arms as he glared down into her eyes. "I need money, Jane, and I need it bad. You're going to make me some."

She wiggled under him frantically, trying to push him off. She hissed at him. "You're crazy if you think I'd sell my body for you. I'd rather die first!" she said. She screamed out for Nellie when John Joseph began tugging on Lawrence's arm again. "Nellie, come get the boys! Go, John Joseph, get out of the bed—take your brother. Go find Nellie."

Lawrence grinned as he tightened his fingers around her arms. "You'll do exactly what I tell you to do!" he said, ignoring the children. "Unless you want a one way ticket back to Angola." Then he clutched her jaw, squeezing it until she could barely stand it.

"Please . . . The children," she pleaded. "Don't do this in front of the boys, you're scaring them to death."

"Maybe they'd like to see what I'm going to do to their ma."

She went limp. She knew he meant it. There would be no reasoning with Lawrence today and if she fought him, she would only lose. Somehow, she thought if she could only get him to release her now, maybe she could talk to him when he sobered. Maybe she could share her earnings with him. *Yes, that's it,* she thought. *I'll offer him half of my money. I make enough. I can get by.* He held her life and the life of her young boys in his hands. Whatever he wanted, she would have to give to him.

"Lawrence, how much money do you want from me?" she finally asked, and he released her and stumbled over to pour himself another brandy.

"What I want is very simple," he said. "I need enough to get by on every month until I can figure out what's wrong with this system I've devised to beat the horses."

"How much do you think that will be?"

"A couple hundred a month."

"But that's about all I take in."

"That's just the point. I want everything you make. I don't think that's too much for you to keep your freedom, do you?"

Jane slid off the bed. She stood facing Lawrence. "You can have whatever it is you want," she said, lowering her eyes to the floor. "Just leave me and my boys alone. That's all I ask. Leave us alone. And please don't come back here again. I don't want them to ever know you're their father."

"I'll leave you and your boys alone," he snickered, "but not for nickels and dimes from your change purse—don't get any ideas about double crossing me, either."

He sat down for a moment, his eyes scanning the bedroom. Jane stood silent watching him. *Will I ever be free of you? Will God ever give me the strength to walk away from you and your endless threats?* she thought, afraid to say anything more; afraid to move even a muscle; afraid she'd dash and pick the gun up from the floor and shoot him in the heart.

Between the two chairs was a small filigreed table on which rested Jane's jewelry case. Opening the box, he picked up some rings and a bracelet and held them up to the light. "You did learn a lot from my dear mama, didn't you? This collection is almost as good as the one she used to have." He took the jewels and dropped them into his vest pocket. "I'm taking these little baguettes with me," he said. "Call it insurance if you like, just in case you decide not to keep up your end of the bargain."

Twenty-Five

JANE DID NOT SEE LAWRENCE after that day. She only heard disturbing rumors about him from the Countess. And although she made monthly deposits in his bank account, there were many times over the next few years the pressure of not a word seemed worse to her than knowing his whereabouts. This Sunday morning as she stood in the downstairs hall staring into the floor length mirror, she noticed tiny creases were beginning to form around her eyes. Several more strands of gray were showing as she combed back her hair and twisted it into a bun. *More than I want,* she thought, running her fingers over the spot where the coarse hair seemed less shiny to her, reminding her she was getting older. *My whole life is just slipping away from me. I'm no further today than I was three years ago when Lawrence started demanding money from me.*

She twirled around to see how her new dress fit. She glanced at the hall clock, another of the Browne family's heirlooms from Angola that Lawrence had taken against his mother's wishes, thinking she wasn't surprised the Countess was thirty minutes late. It was awfully early to come to a birthday party she knew, especially for someone like the Countess who stayed up almost all night. But Sunday was the only day Jane did not work. She had told the Countess if she didn't feel up to it not to worry about coming. The boys would tell her all about their party when they next saw her.

She watched Nellie put the finishing touches on the chocolate sheet cake. She had whipped up a white butter and sugar icing, and was adding the boys names and little leaves to hold the six candles.

When she finished they followed Nellie to the dining room where everything was so beautiful. The table was full of presents wrapped with green and yellow bows. Two hobby horses of hand carved wood covered in unborn calf-skin were proudly displayed next to the table. Jane noticed Nellie pause. Nellie stood admiring the room like a child standing outside a candy store with her head pressed against the window.

"Six years old today," Jane said, wrapping her arms around both her boys, exchanging nose rubs with each as she heard the Countess's carriage stop in the alleyway. John Joseph grinned and darted for the back door toward the Countess. Jane knew how fond the boys were of the Countess. She was so good to the both of them.

"Tante Laura," John Joseph squealed in delight. Following the Countess came her coachman pushing a blue wooden tricycle. John Joseph rushed to climb up on the seat. Jane knew he was trying to figure out how he would ride it, while Alfred hung back by the newel on the stairs waiting for the other tricycle. Jane sat on the bottom step beside Alfred who was watching the Countess and his brother go over the instructions, laughing as John Joseph's short legs struggled to maneuver it. When Alfred's tricycle was pushed into the hall, Jane stood, picked him up and sat him on the high seat. He clung to her, and she could see he was afraid, so she took him down.

"Get down, John Joseph, and let's see what is in these," the Countess said, walking into the parlor with two yellow boxes in her hands.

"You do too much, Countess. You spoil them."

"That's what little boys are for," the Countess said, as Nellie lit the birthday candles. They watched as two little raven haired boys, both missing their front teeth, struggled to blow out the small flames.

After the birthday cake was cut Jane and the Countess stood back watching as the boys pulled off the pretty ribbons from the boxes. They greedily attacked the goodies inside. John Joseph tried to show his brother how to use the toy Jane had secretly asked the toy maker on N. Dorgenois St. to make especially for Alfred. It was a small red wooden hay wagon, pulled by two mechanical tin horses with printed paper overlays. Alfred sat sucking his thumb, staring at his brother as he went from toy to toy, as if this was the first birthday they had ever had.

"You know, Cherie, I often wonder if God gave you these boys just to share with me," the Countess said as she and Jane settled into the chairs near the fireplace. "There are many times when I dream about the baby I lost and I have to admit I get a little envious of you."

"I think about your baby too, Countess," Jane said, pouring each a cup of coffee. "And I think about Mildred Louise all the time, same as I do Georgia Ann and Ander. You know having children is the most fulfilling thing in life. There's no love like the love you can feel for your child. Oh I know we're capable of loving the men in our lives, but when you get right down to it, the love of your child is more precious than anything. Place your man beside your child on a railroad track and watch as the locomotive bears down on them. See which one you try to rescue first."

The Countess sighed. "I never thought about it that way before," she said. "I guess I'll never get the chance to find out either."

Jane refilled the Countess's cup. *Well, we each must make our own way,* she thought, and she couldn't help but feel this must be the Countess's penance for killing that man she had lived with. Maybe even the Major. Although Jane believed the justice system was completely unfair, she also believed murder was a mortal sin. As many times as she was beaten by Dennis and mistreated by Lawrence, she might have thought of killing them, but that was all it ever was. She would have never gone through with actually harming either one of them. She simply didn't have it in her. And as many times as she thought about the course her life had taken, she knew she could not complain. She had her boys, and although she hadn't heard from her older children, she guessed they were getting along all right. No, she could not complain, not when she compared herself to the Countess.

Stirring in cream, Jane said, "Let's not get melancholy. Not today. I wanted to ask what you think about the monthly deposits I make to Lawrence. I was wondering, do you suppose there is any possibility he would let me stop the payments so I could save for the boys education? Since he hasn't bothered me, I thought he might have finally perfected his handicapping system and be rich by now."

The Countess laughed. "I hardly think Lawrence Browne will ever be rich, Cherie. That's foolish of you to even hope for. And, to answer your question, I suspect if he didn't need your money, he'd tell you. You know, underneath all that meanness is a man capable of kindness. He showed us that when he took us out of Angola."

"I know that, Countess. And I know, as much as I despise him, I can't help recognizing that he has done a lot for us. He's a very confused, unhappy person."

"Yes he is," the Countess said. "I guess he has the Major and Mrs. Browne to thank for that. It's a shame the Madam ever had children. She never tried to raise them right. She always thought that was a nanny's job."

"Wrong. She always thought it was a slave's job," Jane said.

"Well, whoever's job she thought it was, it sure messed up her children. Lawrence is a total mess and I heard Ella Marie is still in a mental hospital up in Virginia."

"That wasn't Emma's fault. She can't be blamed for that."

"Sure she can. She let Ella Marie marry that George Ivan, didn't she?" the Countess snapped.

"Countess, what ever happened to him?"

"That man is up north somewhere. The last time I saw Lawrence he said his mama was with Ella, and they don't know if she'll ever get out of the hospital. Lawrence said he'd heard she got worse after they left the plantation. Of course they don't talk to Lawrence any more since he forced Ella to sign over part of the estate to him."

Jane took a sip of coffee, careful not to spill in her saucer. "Did Lawrence ever get any money out of the estate?"

"No. Lawrence said the state cheated him out of the plantation. They promised to buy it from him, but when the lease contract ran out and the state took all the convicts back, they kept the plantation and made a real prison out of it. Of course Lawrence won't ever admit it. He tells everybody he lost it gambling."

"Lawrence is just like his mama for keeping up pretenses," Jane exclaimed. "I get sick every time I think about that family. When I look at my boys I pray they don't ever turn out like any of those people."

The Countess rubbed her hands together. She was staring at the boys. "You know I've often wondered what the Madam would think if she ever saw these babies. Would she dote on them the way she used to carry on over Lawrence and his older children?"

"If I have anything to do with it, she'll never get the chance," Jane said, chilled at the thought of it.

"I hope not," the Countess replied.

Jane sat up straight in her chair, shifting her body around nervously, crossing one leg over the other. "I don't want to ruin my day talking about the Brownes and all the misery they stand for," she said. "I just want to know, what do you think I should do, Countess? You think Lawrence will find it in his heart to leave me alone? Let me use the money to take care of our children?"

"Ask him, but what are you going to do if he says no?"

"I've thought about taking a chance and leaving New Orleans. Going some place up in northern Louisiana close to the other children where he can't find me."

"You know if you try that, he'll find out about it and force you to come back."

"You are probably right about that and you know, I just can't figure why Lawrence wants me here? It can't be the money. There's not enough of it to justify his behavior toward me."

"I suspect, Cherie, it has something to do with Charles Fisher. That's just the way men like Lawrence are. He doesn't want you, but he can't stand for anybody else to have you either. He figures if he takes what little money you have, he can still control you without even laying his eyes on you." The Countess reached over and laid her hand on top of Jane's and squeezed it. "Anyway, whatever you decide to do, think it over carefully before you do it. Now let's you and I have fun with these little boys. I have to be home by five o'clock. Another big night tonight. It's awfully busy right now. I don't know why but fall is even busier than spring. It seems to fill up the houses better than any other time of the year."

JANE HEARD from the Countess, several days later, that Lawrence was in New Orleans for the *City Park* racing season. One afternoon, having finally gained the courage to talk to him, she headed out to the racetrack at City Park to confront him. She spotted him as soon as her carriage pulled up under a thick grove of oak trees. He was not in his usual box, but standing by the white fence that encircled the dusty track, with the *rail birds*. He was studying what looked to her to be a racing form.

Trudging around the smelly stables and through the crowd of fashionable men and women who were rushing to the grandstand, she approached him cautiously, standing a few steps behind him.

"Lawrence," she whispered, tapping her finger on his arm. He glanced at her and moved over so she could stand next to him. He never uttered a word, just turned his attention back to the paper he was looking at.

"Lawrence," she said, again trying to get his attention. "I want to talk to you about the children."

"What about them?" he replied without looking up.

"Well . . . it's not really about the boys . . . it's just . . . well Lawrence I don't think I should have to share my earnings with you any longer. I need to start thinking about our boys' education. I want them to have the chance to go to college."

The horses were being led onto the track and it seemed to her his every thought was on them. The more she tried to talk to him, the less he seemed to listen. A gunshot rang out. The horses took off in a cloud of dust. Her words were drowned out by the roaring crowd. *He's not listening to a word I say,* she thought, fanning the dust from her face. *He's heartless. I don't even know why I bothered to come out here and ask him in the first place. I should just take the boys and leave. If I hide well enough, he'll never find us.*

The horses were in the home stretch. The one Lawrence was yelling for was coming in second and he began to bang his fist on the fence, cursing. The race was over before she knew it. His horse had dropped to fourth. She knew he'd be in a foul mood now. For a moment she thought of backing away from him and getting out of there. He turned and glared at her. The wrinkles deepened around his eyes. His nostrils flared. "You know Jane, I really don't give a God-damn about you or your problems. What I know is, despite how you feel about the little bit of money you give me, you owe me that. If it weren't for me you'd either be dead or passed around by the men who operate the prison up there now. A deal is a deal. I suggest you find a way to keep up your end of the bargain. Because of me you're still a free woman. Don't jeopardize that. You'll find a way. You always do. Go work for the Countess or invite a few men into your bedroom at home. You would do well as a working whore. You're good in bed. Now get out of here and leave me alone," he said. "And whatever it is you decide to do, do it quickly. It's almost the first of the month and I'm counting on that money." He raised his eyebrows, glaring into her eyes as if to say, or else!

You heartless man, she thought, and stalked off. She left the racetrack trying to keep her mind clear so she could figure out a way to get out of New Orleans without him knowing about it. She had a little nest egg she'd been saving for years. It could last her for a while even after she paid all the expenses to move, but it would be months before the racing season was over and he'd be at the bank or on her doorstep come the first of the month. *Well, this is one month, Mister Browne, you're going to find an empty account. I'm not giving you any more of my money. I don't care what you try to do to me. I'm tired of the way you treat me,* she angrily thought to herself as the driver maneuvered the rented livery buggy away from City Park.

STILL UPSET over the scene at the City Park racetrack and determined she wasn't going to be afraid of Lawrence's wrath, Jane worked long hours into the nights, day after day, trying to finish up the last order of curtains she intended to sew in New Orleans. Her next job would be to set herself up in a shop wherever it was she would be moving. The thought of a new home in a new town close to her other children kept her energy level high and she never gave Lawrence a single thought as one week passed into the next. Each day she was up at dawn, enjoying breakfast with the children, spending a few hours on learning lessons with the boys, then retreating upstairs to her workshop.

Then her life was shattered. It was shortly after three o'clock one day when she heard Nellie screaming in the back yard. She ran to the window overlooking the stable. Nellie was running down the alleyway toward Customhouse Street, waving her arms about frantically, screaming at the top of her lungs. Jane took off, running out of the attic, flying down the stairs, through the dining room and out the back door.

"Nellie!" she screamed as she reached the back ditch. "Nellie! Where are the boys?"

A distraught Nellie came running toward her. "It was him, Master Lawrence. He come up into the yard and grabbed our babies. I seen him pick 'em up, one under each arm and pile 'em into his carriage. He took off fast before I could gets out the door."

"Are you sure it was Lawrence?"

"Yessum. I is sure. I knows that man anywhere."

"You go in the house, Nellie. Call the Countess," Jane said, pushing her toward the door. Jane didn't know what she should do. She couldn't go to the constable. They would want to know who she was, who the boys were, and who their father was. "Oh God, what am I going to do? Who can I turn to?" Then Tom Anderson leaped into her mind. "Yes, I'll go to see Tom. He's probably the only one who can help me. Besides, he'd like to get his hands on Lawrence, from what the Countess has told me."

IT WAS way after dark before Jane heard the Countess's carriage in the alleyway. The back door opened, then slammed shut. The Countess came into the dimly lit parlor. She sat in a chair facing Jane in front of the fireplace.

"That low-life took my babies," Jane said. "He's a despicable human being. He's beaten me, threatened me, extorted money from me, stole everything I had of value and now has kidnapped my boys. What's going to happen to them?"

"Maybe you should have waited until he left New Orleans before you stopped depositing his money."

"The money's not the main reason he did this, and you know it," Jane said. "He did it to show me—show me how much power he still has to make me do his will. I should have known not to expect anything less of him. He has a cruel twisted mind, Countess. He'll do anything to prove he can control me. Anything!"

"What else could you expect from a man who was raised by the Major and Emma Browne?"

"It's time we stopped blaming his parents for the way he is. Nobody makes you what you are. Nobody controls your mind, only you can do that. And I don't know what he thinks he's going to do with two small boys clinging to his legs. And what if they wander away from him, get run over by one of those damn race horses?"

"Cherie, the boys are six-years old. They're used to horses. They know better than to get in their way. Anyway, it's highly unlikely Lawrence would take the children to the racetrack."

"Oh, I don't know, Countess. I saw the way he acted when I went to see him out at City Park. I could tell all he thinks about are those horses." She tried to hold it in, but sobs burst out of her.

"Well, calm down. Shush," she said, patting Jane's hand. "Crying is not going to get the boys back. Nellie told me you went to see Tom Anderson. What did he say?"

"He's just like all men. He told me how sorry he was and that unless I wanted to take Lawrence to court, which he strongly advised against, he could do nothing."

"Cherie, you have every right to go to court. Lawrence kidnapped your children. I'll ask the madam Mary Deubler to call her lawyer," the Countess said, standing up to walk to the phone. "Maybe he can help you."

"A lawyer can't do me any good. Tom told me to stay as far away from the courts as I could. He said there wasn't a judge in New Orleans that would take my word over Lawrence's. And you know as well as I do, Lawrence will tell the law I'm an escaped convict."

The Countess stood still, staring down at Jane. "Well, the only thing I can tell you, and I know it is not much," she finally said, "is give Lawrence enough room to ruin himself. You will see, justice will catch up with him."

"Justice! There's no such thing as justice for women in Louisiana and you know it. Was there any justice when they put me in prison for nothing and forgot about me? Where was the justice when that City Councilman Peter Baulfield came to Angola and we had to wait on him hand and foot because Emma Browne knew him and put him up like he was a house guest? You didn't see the courts forgetting about him, did you? No! He's a man and he only served six months of his sentence. And as for Lawrence taking my boys, I could kill him!" She was angry and getting angrier and angrier by the minute.

"I guess you are right," the Countess calmly said. "There's no justice for women, and it doesn't matter where you live or what a man does to you. Everything about the justice system is a farce. Trying to win a fight in it is like trying to catch smoke in a bottle."

Jane sat up straight, clutched the sides of her chair and pounded her fists upon them. "Damn it! Countess," she cried, "how do those Brownes get away with doing whatever they please to other people and never have a thing happen to them? I am sick of that man, sick of the way he is treating me. He's gone too far this time."

The Countess asked Nellie to mix up a tray of Gin Fizzes. When Jane finally stopped crying, she said, "Why don't you give Lawrence a few days? Maybe he'll cool off and bring the boys home. I don't think you have to worry about any harm coming to them. After all he is their father. I'll ask around and see if Deep Pockets knows their whereabouts. In the meantime," she said, motioning for Nellie to set the tray down on the table between them, "you stay put. If you go off half-cocked and try to find Lawrence on your own, you're liable to be picked up and put in jail. I know how you feel about your children but I don't see any immediate danger."

Jane sighed. She clutched to her chest the rag dolls Nellie had made the boys for their birthday.

"Lawrence must truly hate me to do this, and I've really tried to do right by him," she said. "I couldn't help it if I never loved him. Besides, if I'd had the misfortune to fall in love with him, it would have ruined me. He's a cold-hearted evil person, worse than Dennis Moody. He's prevented me from visiting Mildred Louise's grave, didn't give up on Georgia Ann until she had to leave New Orleans, and now he's kidnapped my boys. What is it about me, Countess, that brings out the worst in the men in my life?"

"Who knows about men?" the Countess said. "Name me a woman who can say she honestly knows her man, and I'll call her a fool. Oh, there may be a few good ones, but they aren't numerous. If what you tell me about your Charles Fisher is the truth, then he's the only good man I've ever heard of."

Jane sat on the edge of the chair and toyed with the dolls. "Yes, Charles loved me, that's for sure," she said, "but not enough. He married another woman, didn't he?"

"Come now, Cherie. You're not being fair. For all he knew you were dead or going to spend the rest of your life in prison. What did you expect him to do? Live his life alone in the hopes that someday you'd come back to him? Besides, you didn't hesitate to take up with Lawrence when it looked like that was your only option. You made the best of your situation at the time. Why shouldn't Charles have made the best of his?"

"You're right, of course," she said, standing up to kiss the Countess goodbye. "I'm being unfair and feeling sorry for myself. I think the best thing for me is to get to bed. Perhaps in the morning I can come up with something."

Jane crawled into her bed and hurt her knee on a lead soldier John Joseph had been playing with that morning. She picked it up and clutched it in her hand wondering about her destiny and whether she would ever see her sons again—wondering what she could do as she fell into a troubled sleep.

Twenty-Six

Beyond this place of wrath and tears
Looms but the Horror of the shade,
And yet the menace of the years
Finds and shall find me unafraid

—Henley

WHEN JANE WOKE the next morning her eyes were swollen from crying. She wished whoever was making that hammering noise would stop so she could go back to sleep.

She closed her eyes and flung her arm over her face. The pounding stopped when she heard the front door open then slam shut. Moments later a shrill screaming took its place. Nellie ran up the stairs like a wild horse and yelled, "Wake up, Miz Jane! Something terrible has happened to Ander."

She forced her eyes open, scrambled out of the bed and ran into the hall. Nellie was leaning on the railing, sobbing and wailing. Jane grabbed her by the shoulders and shook the hysterical girl. "What are you saying? Who was at the door? What's happened to Ander? Is he dead?"

"He's in trouble, Miz Jane. Been arrested for murder. The paper said he killed his wife."

"Oh dear, precious God. Please, don't let this be," Jane said. Her heart sank. She felt her face cover with perspiration as wave after wave of nausea swept over her body. "Mary Parthenia is dead?" she kept saying. "Murdered?"

"That's what the paper said, Miz Jane. That steamboat captain you knows from the north sent it over here. He said to tell you he didn't know much more except there's been two big fires in Pollock Town. People says it's arson. He also said something about the post office being robbed."

Jane shuddered as she glanced at her image in the full-length mirror. Her hair was a mess. She had slept in the dress she'd been wearing the day before. Turning her back on Nellie she flopped down in a chair beside her bed. "I feel sick—like someone reached in and ripped out my insides," she cried. She snatched the newspaper out of Nellie's hand.

"JUDGE BLACKMAN HOLDS INQUIRY INTO GRANT PARISH MURDER.

Judge Blackman, yesterday, in company with District Attorney Hunter, Deputy Sheriff Clinton of Grant Parish and court stenographer Murry Hetherwick, went to Nugents Station and held a court of inquiry in the home of Mary Moody, the murdered woman.

Over twenty-five witnesses, all residing in the neighborhood, were interrogated by the judge and the district attorney. It was difficult to find any motive for the perpetration of the crime by anyone, but after a thorough examination of the husband of the deceased woman, Judge Blackman last night ordered the arrest of Ander Moody, the husband.

Also charged with the killing are Ella Peck, Alfred Waits and Bud Waits. Steve LaCroix, charged with being an accessory to the crime, was brought in but was released under bond to appear for trial. The killing was a cold blooded and mysterious affair and its investigations will probably develop some very ugly and depraved features."

Jane could not believe what she read. She crumpled up the paper, threw it on the floor. She started crying from the deepest part of her heart.

"What can I do for you?" Nellie asked, pacing nervously in front of her.

"Would you please call the Countess," she replied.

She sat glued to the chair, listening to Nellie as she spoke with the Countess. "Yessum, our whole family is falling apart. Me and

Miz Jane gonna be all that's left of this family now," Nellie told the Countess.

There was only one thing Jane could do and she knew it. She'd have to take the chance and go to northern Louisiana to find out what had happened. She knew she had no choice; she'd have to try and help her son. "I know Ander wouldn't do anything like that. Mary adored him. He didn't kill her," she said.

"You really believes that, Miz Jane?"

"Of course I do," she said, but the quivering in the pit of her stomach left her uncertain. She rested her chin in her hands trying to comprehend everything she had read. *I don't know what I'm even thinking. I just don't know about anything.*

"Nellie, you run throw some clothes in your valise, then call the depot on Canal Street."

"No need to do that. The Countess said she gonna get us some train tickets. Says you're to sit still till she gets here."

"Well, run on and pack. Then come help me. We'd better hurry so we can catch the ten o'clock Southern. I want to get up there as soon as I can. No telling what those people will do to Ander."

When Nellie was out of sight, Jane quietly locked her door. Pushing the heavy chairs to the side, she rolled back the carpet and lifted up a short section of the mahogany floor board. She pulled out an iron strong box from her *hidey hole*. She took out all the money she had saved and carefully arranged it in a silk money belt to wear under her dress. *What good is this money to me if I don't use it to get Ander out of this mess he's in? If he hangs I wouldn't want to live anyway,* she thought. She began to pack her valise, leaving out a dark burgundy street dress to wear on the train. She went to fill her bath water. The memory of that awful day she left northern Louisiana flashed across her mind. *I left there in shackles, but I'll be damned if I'm going to go back there looking like some dowdy missionary sparrow.*

Jane finished her bath, drying off as fast as she could and patted lavender power over her body before she slid the burgundy street dress down over her head. She stood in front of the floor length mirror fussing with the big puff sleeves until they were both in place on her arms and glanced at her boots to see if they needed to be wiped. Picking up her little velvet hat, she placed it on top of her head, pulling the veil snugly over her face, wondering if anyone from northern Louisiana would be able to recognize her after all these years. Then she picked up her carpetbag and walked out of the high ceilinged bedroom. She knew that Nellie and the Countess were waiting for her downstairs in the parlor.

"Well, I must say, you look remarkably well for a woman whose children were kidnapped yesterday and who has had some rather disturbing news this morning," the Countess said.

Jane held on to the ebony bannister to steady herself. She paused for a moment on the bottom step and let the valise drop to the floor. "Disturbing is hardly the word for it, Countess. I think disaster and calamity would be more appropriate. Did Nellie show you the newspaper?"

"I read it."

"They're saying Ella Peck was arrested for killing Mary. I don't know how, but it seems that woman got Ander involved."

The Countess's eyes widened, but she did not comment.

Still feeling weak, Jane sat down on the settee and lit a cigarette. "I feel like killing her for getting Ander mixed up in all of this."

"Cherie. . . . "

"Well, it's all her fault. You know he's never had any sense when it came to that woman. How many times did I have to get him out of New Orleans and away from her? Ella Peck took advantage of Ander. Now she's trying to blame everything on him. I bet you that's what happened."

"Cherie," the Countess said, calmly. "I know you think I don't like Ander and the truth is, I just don't care for the grief he's caused you. Now, you may get upset with me for saying this. You know I don't care about anybody else's morals as long as they don't hurt people, but you know as well as I do, Ander doesn't care whom he hurts, especially you."

"Countess, I don't really feel like hearing your opinion about Ander's involvement with Mary's murder just now," Jane said, flipping the ashes of her cigarette into a spittoon.

"Well, you're going to hear it anyway. Were Ella Peck and those other people in the paper involved with the murder of Ander's wife? I have no doubt about it. Is Ander just as guilty as they are? I don't doubt that either, and neither should you. Cherie, there is going to come a time when you will have to let him go. Let him stand on his own two feet and take the consequences for what he does. But, I know he's your son, and you're going to try to get him out of it, but do try to be reasonable. Find out all the facts before you start spreading your money around. I know you think you have all the answers now, that if you have enough money you can buy anything. I want you to remember, you may have to spend some of it to get your little boys back. We may have to hire the Pinkerton Investigating Agency to find them."

Jane sighed. When she thought about what Lawrence had done it made her seethe with anger. "I think I've learned enough to handle this situation, Countess," she snapped.

"Maybe you have, Cherie. But sometimes you can pay off the politicians only so long. Sooner or later you get caught. And what if he is guilty? What if he did kill her? If you give them all your hard earned money and still lose, who will help you get your other children back? Think about it, Cherie. Now is the time for you to think about your other children. Think of a life for yourself. Think of what your life will be like if you don't have any money to fight Lawrence. Cherie, don't go up there and give away every cent you have."

The Countess asked her coachman to load the bags in her carriage. She had already sent someone to purchase train tickets and said they'd be waiting for them when they got to the depot.

Nellie emerged from the kitchen with a large wicker basket of food. "This is for the trip, Miz Jane. That train food will make us sick. No telling where it came from or who had their hands on it."

Jane smiled at her and Nellie hoisted the basket on to her shoulders. She went out the back door. Jane and the Countess walked out into the hallway. "Do you want me to send a telegram to let someone know you're coming?" the Countess asked.

"No, I don't think so," Jane answered. "I'll just get in touch with Georgia Ann when I get there."

She waved the Countess goodbye as the carriage made its way through the alley onto the street, and up Royal toward the Canal Street depot.

"YOU KNOW," Jane said to Nellie once they settled in their train seats, "this is the first time I've ever been on a train. When I think about it, it's only the third time I've really been anywhere that amounted to much. Moving with my children's papa and Charles Fisher around north Louisiana didn't amount to anything. The only real trips were to prison and to New Orleans."

Nellie got fidgety in her seat, nervously looking about while Jane admired the wood carved walls of the passenger car. "Miz Jane, ain't this the train Master Lawrence said Ander robbed?" Nellie asked.

Jane, tired of having to explain her son's actions to everyone, particularly to this girl, just said, "I believe it is, Nellie."

By the time the train began to make its way across the cypress-filled bayous, Nellie had unpacked the basket of food. Covering their dresses with large, white linen napkins, they ate in silence and looked at the changing scenery all afternoon until the sun set. The conductor came by with blankets and pillows at nightfall and as soon as they had washed up, Nellie pulled the blanket around her and fell asleep. Jane sat in the dark of the car, fascinated with the sounds of the train. She could smell the sweet tobacco of someone smoking in the seat behind her. Occasionally she saw the lighted windows of a distant farm house. The conductor was going from seat to seat, checking on the passengers comfort, and when he approached her she asked him why torches were glowing in the middle of the bayous. He told her it was the swamp men out gigging bull frogs and catching alligators with wire nooses.

The next morning when the train slowed down and pulled off onto a siding, she could see a giant wooden chute unfold from the water tower, filling the boilers of the steam engine. Black men, their faces dulled with the coal dust, shoveled heavy loads of fuel into the open tender behind the engine. It wasn't until the train neared Alexandria that Jane laid her head back against the seat and finally closed her eyes. She listened to the clickety click of the wheels on steel rails as her head wobbled back and forth from the motion of the swaying train. It seemed to her only a moment had passed when the conductor came back by and said they'd be pulling into Nugent's Station, the depot at Simms. She was tired and anxious to get off.

The train slowly slid into the small depot, jerking the cars as it came to a stop. Jane pulled her aching body up out of the wooden seat and headed toward the steps while Nellie carried their valises. The afternoon was very bright but slightly cool in northern Louisiana, and the sun blinded her as she stepped off the train onto a deserted wooden platform. When she turned around to take her valise from Nellie, she noticed the figure of a man walking through the escaping steam from the locomotive. Squinting her eyes against the sun, she looked back at Nellie and then at the man. He seemed to be swirling through clouds of steam, then suddenly a gust of wind blew from behind her and the haze slowly faded from his face.

"Afternoon, Jane," he said, as he stood face to face with her. "Since I didn't get a chance to say good-bye, I wanted to make damn sure I was the first to say hello."

"Charles," she murmured, unable to say anything more. The air in her lungs froze as they stood staring into each others eyes.

Then suddenly a familiar smile spread across his honey tanned face and he moved as close to her as the propriety of a married man in a small town would allow. He took his hand from behind his back and placed a single red rose into hers.

Tears came. She could not believe it, Charles Fisher standing right here in front of her. She wasn't prepared to see him this soon, and although she had known that at one point she'd most likely run into him during the days she would have to be here, she had had no idea it would be today. Her heart began to flutter so strongly that her knees were shaking and she had to fight the urge to fling herself into his arms and stay there until her yearning for his touch subsided.

"When . . . I thought I would never see you again," he said, breaking the deadly silence, "I went by the farm where we lived. I took a cutting from your rose bush and I want you to know, all these years, Liebchen, wherever I lived, I've had your roses near me."

She stood stock still. Her mouth was clamped tight. The engineer blew the whistle and her eye's wandered away from Charles, in a blank stare, over to the conductor. She watched him look at his pocket watch then jump on board the train as the huge wheels of the locomotive slipped and found their grip on the rails, pulling away from the station. The white steam turned to belching black smoke as the train melted into the thick pine forest.

Charles reached out and took both valises from Nellie's hands and without saying another word, turned his back to Jane and began to walk toward his buggy.

"Charles, please wait," Jane said, trailing in behind him, looking out over the small town toward the one hotel that sat between a wooden shack with U.S. Post Office written over the door, and a dusty stable yard that rested behind a rickety picket fence. "Where are you going? I have to find a place for Nellie and me to stay."

"I've taken care of that," he called back over his shoulder as she ran to catch up with him. "It's best if you stay at Ander's house. While he's in jail you can look after the children. It's been a terrible time for them. They haven't been the same since their mama died. It's a chore for Martha Ellen and Georgia Ann to take care of all those children. Those other two married daughters of Martha's don't do much of anything except mope around and shoot off their mouths."

Jane just stared at him as he loaded the valises in the buggy. He put his hands around her tiny waist and lifted her and then Nellie onto the seat. "I talked it over with Martha Ellen—she said she wouldn't think of you staying in a boarding house or a hotel. Besides, we're all sort of kinfolks now anyway," he chuckled.

"But, Charles, I don't know," Jane protested as he climbed upon the seat beside her, wiggling around until he settled comfortably with his leg touching hers.

"Don't worry. It's a big farm. Nobody will get in anybody else's way."

Charles pulled the buggy onto the road and glanced over at Jane. "Who would've thought when I first rode up to your door all those years ago that I'd end up related by marriage to two of your children?" Jane didn't reply. She sat glued to the seat, feeling his warm leg touching hers, sending shivers up her spine, and stared at this handsome man who had held her heart for so long.

He drove up the narrow main street of Simms. As they rode past rows of small wooden houses with white picket fences Jane thought how very much it looked like the little sawmill town she and Dennis had lived in when she first met Charles. The whine of saws echoed in her ears. When they approached the sawmill Jane noticed a fine mist of yellow sawdust hanging in the air. The streets were empty. She knew they would be until the night whistle blew.

The small town brought back many unhappy memories. Her mother's gentle face came back to her. Jane had always wondered how she had died; if they had buried her in a cemetery; or if the family had laid her to rest in the field beside her papa. It's true she had been spared, if you could call it that, the agony of her mother's death. Still, she wished she could have known when it had happened. Now she didn't know which was worse, living with the fact that her child had killed her papa, or that her brothers had been so heartless they had allowed her to go to prison and hadn't even sent word when her mother had died. But she had realized a long time ago if anyone of her family had cared about her, someone, at least one of them, could have tried to prevent her from going to prison. Didn't any of them understand how she had felt? How could they not understand her desperation to keep her child alive? *Oh Papa,* she silently cried, thinking back to the night of the fire, and a wave of fear engulfed her. *When Ander shot you, was it an accident?* She closed her eyes trying to squeeze out the memory of it.

They passed the murky green mill pond where a sea of logs floated. Charles turned the buggy down Claiborne Road toward his farm. Jane had a sudden urge to take his hand and feel his strong arm around her, but she knew behind every lace-curtained window curious eyes were looking, women wondering who was this strange woman in a fancy silk dress, riding down the road with Martha Ellen's husband?

Jane peered at Charles out of the corner of her eye. He smelled good, but then he always did. He looked just as handsome as the last day she'd seen him. The only difference was a touch of gray in his hair that made him look even more distinguished.

She loved him, still ached for his touch. His mere presence tugged at her heart strings. Closing her eyes she remembered the nights he'd held her in his arms and they had sung love songs together. She remembered the one he always sang when she was sad, and before she realized it she started humming the tune. It was as if all the years of separation faded away. He began to whistle Steven Foster's *Beautiful Dreamer* along with her.

They looked at each other. She knew he, too, was thinking of olden times. She remembered the two of them running across a field of clover with little Georgia Ann lagging behind, laughing and squealing out in delight when Charles would pick her up and swing her around in the air. She quickly turned her tear-filled eyes to the massive fields of brown stalks bearing white blooms where rows and rows of white and black men, women, and children stopped their cotton picking to look at the buggy rolling down the dusty road. *I'm a fool to think of these things,* she thought. *I'll only hurt myself. It's not right, not fair to me or him or his wife. My life isn't here anymore and this man's no more mine now than Lawrence is.*

"What are you thinking about, Liebchen?" Charles asked, and she jumped as the sound of his voice disturbed her daydream. "If it's the past don't feel guilty about it," he said. "We were very much in love and no one can ever take that away from us." He gently reached over to pat her hand.

She stiffened her arm when he touched her and her whole body felt like a stone statue. "I'm fine, really I am," she said. "I . . . I'm just tired. I didn't sleep the entire trip."

Charles made no further advances. When they arrived at Ander's farmhouse, he handed the reins to Nellie, jumped to the ground and lifted Jane out of the buggy. Then he removed the valises, set them on the ground and took the reins from Nellie and wrapped them around the porch rail.

"Ander's children are over at my house," he said as they walked up the steps onto the front porch. "So is Georgia Ann. She's been living on the farm since she married Martha's son, Gatlin." With both carpet bags in his hands, he opened the door of the small two story frame cottage, and when Jane walked into the front parlor, Charles dropped the valises and stood staring at her. She could see the wetness on his cheeks and she quickly turned away. She couldn't bear not to touch him. Her blood rushed to her head, pounding faster and faster trying to keep up with her heart.

He shut the door and stood quietly with his back to her, then slowly, turned and locked eyes with her. "Oh, Liebchen," he whispered and rushed over to her, pulling her into his arms, hungrily staring down into her face. "I thought I'd never see you again. The day they took you away from me I wanted to die in that water. I never wanted to come up. I let myself sink down and down and down until my lungs almost burst," he said, tears flowing down his face.

Jane put her arms around him and pressed her face against his chest, feeling his heart pounding against her cheek. "I thought you were dead, Charles," she cried softly. "All those years I thought you'd drowned and I never stopped blaming myself."

Charles put his hand under her chin. Gently he pulled her face toward his, touching her lips lightly with his finger. "Shh, Liebchen. Don't cry. None of it's your fault. I just couldn't bear to see you go. I was crazy with grief when I saw you on that boat. . . . It was an act of desperation that drove me into the river."

His voice started breaking. "Liebchen, what life has done to us! All these years I tried to find you. There were so many obstacles in the way . . . so many . . . I . . . I guess I didn't try hard enough. I'm a failure. I let you down."

Jane raised her finger to his trembling lips. "Hush," she whispered. "You're not a failure. There's no reason for you to go on like this. You owe me no explanations. Ander told me how you came looking for me. That was enough just to know you tried."

"Liebchen, I need to explain to you why I married Martha Ellen."

"There is no need to explain," she said, pulling away from him. "You were a man. You needed someone who could love you. Making a life for yourself was a normal thing to do. It would have broken my heart more if I thought you were alone. We both did what we had to do, Charles, don't . . . don't make this any harder for us than it already is."

"No, I have to tell you why," he said, stepping close, grasping her arm. "I can't live with it any longer. I don't want you to think I abandoned you, just let you stay in that awful prison."

She took a deep breath trying to brush his hand away. "What difference does it make now, Charles? It's over! Yesterday is gone forever. We can never get it back. Today is only what we can make of it. I don't want to talk about all those yesterdays. What would be the sense in it anyway?" She pulled away from his embrace. She knew if she stayed in his arms a moment longer she'd lose all sense of decency. She wanted to wrap herself around him tightly, so tightly they would melt into one, but if she gave in to her desire she would be lost in a world she'd never want to leave. "Charles it doesn't matter any longer. It can never be undone, don't you see that? As desperately as I want you, want you to take me in your arms and never stop saying the words I long to hear, it will never be, not now. Martha Ellen stands in our way. Regardless of how right or wrong it is, she's there."

She walked away from him and looked around the tidy cottage. Everything was in its place. Pictures hung in gilt frames on the brightly painted walls, a clean braided rug lay on the shiny pinewood floor, and small tables of various styles were neatly arranged around an overstuffed settee and two comfortable chairs. It was a cozy little cottage; she could see that Mary had taken great pride in making it a home for Ander, and she saw no visible signs that a tragic murder had occurred here. The only thing that seemed unusual was that the kitchen door was missing.

"What happened to the door?" she asked, nodding toward the open doorway.

"Georgia Ann's husband took it off. He laid Mary's body out on it."

Jane sighed. "How did it happen?"

"Liebchen, it's such a tragic story," he said, and she realized he was hesitant to talk about it. He looked so sad standing in front of the dead fireplace, his gaze fixed upon her as she sat upon the settee. She knew he wanted to talk about them, talk about all the pent up grief he had been carrying for so long. She could see it in his face. Tiny wrinkles began to form around his eyes and for a while he just stood still as if waiting for her to change her mind and rush back into his arms. She watched him silently as the cold began to creep into the small house. Then she asked if he would build a fire. She settled back on the settee and pulled her legs up, wrapping a knitted cover around her as he threw the logs into a pile, stuffing kindling tightly around the wood and striking match after match until the pieces of sticks flared up, catching the logs on fire. He sat beside her in silence until the fire began to crackle, blending the smell of oak wood and smoke. She too wanted to unleash all the years of frustration of being without him. Tell him how she really felt, tell him how she'd dreamed of seeing him again. But she knew it would not do either of them any good. So she asked him once again, firmly, "How in God's name did all of this happen, Charles? I realize how difficult it must be for you to talk about it, but I need to know. I need desperately to know if Ander had anything to do with it."

Charles reached into his pocket for a cigar and Jane instinctively took a sulphur match out of her handbag to light it. He cupped his hand around hers and inhaled until a bright red glow reflected in his eyes.

"When Ander and Mary Parthenia came back from New Orleans, I built this house for them," he said, leaning over with his elbows resting on his knees, staring into the fire. "Martha Ellen wanted Mary and the children close to her, and at the time it seemed like a good thing to do. I had built the rest of Martha's children a house. Willie O'Neal, Martha's son-in-law, works with me at Ball's Mill, and I tried to get Ander to go to work with us. But he came back here with a pocket full of money and less desire to work than before he left." He turned to face her, "You know how Ander is. If there's a gang of outlaws within ten miles of him, he's going to find them.

"Jane, Simms may look like a little country mill town, but it isn't. People from all over come here to work. It's a decent, God fearing community. Ander just didn't fit in. When Ella Peck's brother, Bud Waits, moved to town and they started hanging out with an outlaw called Steve LaCroix, people didn't take kindly to them. Ander set Ella up in a house near the railroad station in Pollock Town and it quickly got a reputation that a man could get anything he wanted there, day or night. It wasn't long before that house got nicknamed 'Little Dodge City' and every outlaw in north Louisiana went there. Well, a few months back, the Post Office was robbed and almost every wood building in Pollock Town burned to the ground. Most people around here believe the men who owned the buildings caused the fire to be set to collect the insurance money.

When Mary found the gray mail bag behind her bed, she knew Ander was involved."

Jane shuddered. "I'm a little chilly," she said. "I'd really like a brandy or whiskey. You think Ander has any around here?"

Charles stood up and walked out to the kitchen. She watched as he pulled a bottle out of the cupboard. He poured the Rye whiskey into small glasses, walked back into the parlor and without looking at her, he sat next to her again and handed her one. "The afternoon before her murder," he continued, "Mary came to the house and told me she'd found the mail bag from the Ball's Post Office. Said she was taking it to the sheriff and turning Ander in. She told her mama she was going to run him off, didn't want him living with her and the children anymore. She just plain had had enough of him."

Jane took a large gulp, swallowed hard, and said, "You think he killed her, Charles?"

"Jane, I don't know. The district attorney indicates Ander's involved."

"How does your wife feel about it?"

"Well, she's just like me. Doesn't want to believe it. She has a fondness for Ander in spite of the way he treated Mary. You know he has a way of making people like him, and Martha is the kind of woman who sees good in everybody."

"What about the rest of Mary's family?"

"Well, those sisters of hers believe Ander killed her. They're going to be the star witnesses for the prosecution. They want to see him hang."

Jane flung the cover from her lap and jumped up from the settee. She began to pace back and forth across the room. "What kind of an attitude is that, Charles? How do they know he had anything to do with it? From what the paper says there wasn't anybody in the house that night except Ander and the children. How can they be so sure he's guilty? How can people put another person's life in jeopardy like that? They probably just don't like Ander."

"No, they don't like him. Never did." After a pause he said, "I'm not making any judgments, Jane. I'm only trying to tell you how the family feels about it."

"I'm sorry, Charles. It's just that I'm so confused. I need to get to the jail and see Ander. I need to talk to him, find out what happened that night so I can help him."

"I'll take you over there tomorrow. They've got him in Colfax. That's where the trial's going to be. And don't worry, I'll stand by you. We'll hire the best lawyers in the state. If you need money, I have some and what I don't have, I'll borrow."

Jane pulled up her petticoat, took off the silk money belt and tossed it at Charles. "I have money. I can pay for Ander's lawyers. I don't want your help. I can take care of my son."

Charles bent over and picked the belt up off the floor and laid it on the table. He stared at her for a moment. "I see you haven't changed a bit when it comes to Ander, have you? You came here so you could take care of him, lick his wounds. You haven't even asked me about Georgia Ann or her children. All you care about is Ander, isn't it?" he said, his voice rising to a high pitch. "When are you ever going to allow anybody to help you? Do you still think you can take care of everything yourself, no matter what sacrifices you or anybody involved with you have to make?"

Jane's mouth flew open. Charles reached out and grabbed the money belt and thrust it toward her. "Why did you bring all this money? Are you foolish enough to believe you can buy him out of the trouble he's in?"

Jane put her hands to her face. "I don't know what I'm doing here. I only know I have to do something," she said, firmly. "If they find Ander guilty, they'll hang him, Charles. It's just that everything's happened so fast. . . . "

"Forgive me," he whispered, dropping the little bag on the table again. "I don't mean to sound so harsh. I know you're only trying to help your boy. I wouldn't expect anything less from you, and I'll do everything I can to help you get him off. Ander's hanging won't bring Mary back." He shook his head, "And I know what it will do to you."

Charles put on his jacket and then helped Jane with her shawl. They walked outside where Nellie was waiting patiently, and climbed up into the buggy. Charles drove the mare out of the yard.

Riding in silence the short distance to his farm, Jane noticed the lush and prosperous land spread out before her. She could see the results of Charles' engineering talents. He had laid out fence rows neatly; had left wild bushes and shrubs for the birds to build their nests, and lairs for the small animals so they might feed their young without danger; his barns were freshly white washed and the corn silos arranged in perfect order; his white-framed house sat off the main road and the narrow trail that led up to the porch was bordered with mature dogwood trees, as neat and straight as soldiers standing at attention.

Jane was envious of the woman who waited patiently inside for them. She wondered if Charles had told his wife about the great love they had once shared. "Are you certain this is wise, Charles?" she asked as he slowed the buggy and stopped. "After all, how could your wife welcome me in her home when there's a possibility my son murdered her daughter?"

Before Charles could answer, the front door of the house opened. Several women came out onto the porch and stood waiting for Jane and Charles to get out. Jane spotted Georgia Ann among them, holding her baby.

Charles lifted Jane down from the buggy. She got her first look at Martha Ellen—a small, dark haired woman limping toward her. She was wearing a plain cotton house dress and her hair was neatly arranged in buns on both sides of her face. The printed flour sack apron over her black dress was stained. There were smudges of flour on her hands and she had a peculiar look on her face.

Before Jane could speak, Martha Ellen took her in her arms. "I am so very sorry for both of us, Jane," she said in a soft, timid voice, kissing the air by Jane's face. "Please know how much I grieve for both of our children."

Jane fought to hold back her tears. She could feel the tension in Martha's touch, the resentment and anger. *This is all an act for Charles's benefit,* she thought as Martha Ellen took her by the arm and led her toward the house. When they got to the front porch, Jane stopped. She walked over and reached out for Georgia Ann. "It's so good to see you, Sugar," she said. Georgia Ann stepped slightly away, cowering behind a tall, sandy haired man as she pulled the infant to her chest. She never said a word to her mother.

Charles must have seen the hurt and stunned expression on Jane's face. Before they went inside, he pulled her back with him and Martha and whispered, "Don't be upset with her. Give her a little time. Everything's happened so quickly. We just buried Mary a few days ago. It was such tragic thing! None of us can think straight. Georgia Ann and Mary were like sisters. Ever since she's come to live with us, Georgia Ann has been one of the family, and when she and Martha's son had their first baby that just sealed the bond."

"I appreciate you taking her in," Jane said, as Charles released her arm and pulled open the screen door for her and Martha to go in. "She wouldn't come back to New Orleans when I sent word that my husband had left for New York. I guess I can understand why she's upset with me, but, I thought by now she'd have gotten over her resentment.

"This is not a time to worry about it," Martha said, as the three of them walked into the front parlor. "Like Charles said, give her a little time. She'll come around."

The house felt warm and comfortable. It smelled of pine wood, and the lingering smell of fat-back and onions brought back to Jane poignant memories of when she and Charles had lived in Castor Springs; those times when he would sneak green onions from the garden and put them in the cooking pots without her knowing it. She remembered how wonderful that life was. God, would she ever forget it? She shook her head wondering if Charles ever thought about it.

As they sat down at the linen covered table she noticed an effort had been made to get the dining room to look its Sunday best. The table was set with pretty Blue Willow china, and the rosewood sideboard was filled with platters of fried pork chops, boiled potatoes, blackeyed peas, home made pickles and freshly baked buttermilk biscuits.

Martha Ellen took her place at the far end of the table and insisted Jane sit on Charles' right at the other end. Georgia Ann sat between her husband Gatlin and Martha's two daughters, Balma and Leah. Their husbands faced them across the table.

The women were all neatly dressed in plain dark colors and Jane, who couldn't help but feel out of place, bowed her head when Martha Ellen began to ask the blessing.

"Ours is never to question You, not even when tragedy strikes at our door.

We can only pray that you will lead us to an understanding and an acceptance of both the good and the bad.

We pray that always You will help us to know and to understand that it is Thy will and not our will be done.

Bless our new friend and relative, Jane, as we pray for our beloved daughter, Mary Parthenia, for Ander Moody and their dear children, Harry, Dick, Denny and our precious Mary Agnes.

Forgive us our sins and help us to forgive those who have sinned against us.

Amen."

Jane tried to keep up a conversation despite the lack of response from anyone but Martha Ellen and Charles. The silence around the table was deadening. Even Georgia Ann didn't speak a word except to ask about the twins. Martha Ellen inquired about New Orleans and asked Jane to tell about the excitement of Mardi Gras; about the parades and revelers who crowded the streets and sang and danced until the clock struck midnight; and about the restaurants and all the wonderful food in New Orleans. When Jane finally exhausted all the tales she could think of, Martha Ellen forced a laugh. "Everything you say sounds so exciting, you're making a poor old country woman like me green with envy."

Before Jane could say any more Charles picked up the conversation and talked about the farm and how he studied books from Europe about crop rotation and how hard it was to convince local farmers to try that system. Georgia Ann fussed with her baby. Martha's daughters and their husbands asked to be excused from the table, although they had barely touched their food. Claiming she had to put her baby to bed, Georgia Ann and Gatlin also left the table.

Martha Ellen tried to make excuses for her family's rudeness. She asked Charles to drive Jane and her "little darky" back to Ander's cottage.

"I know you need to rest, so I'll keep the children here with me and bring them over to you tomorrow," she told Jane.

"That's very kind of you, but you have more than enough to do. I still know how to manage a buggy. Having the children with me will give me something to do other than think about my troubles. Now, if you don't mind, I'll just say good night to Georgia Ann."

Jane walked down the long hall and away from Martha Ellen's questioning eyes. Through a half open door she saw Georgia Ann seated on the bed, feeding her baby. She tapped on the door, waited for an answer, and walked into the room.

"Oh, Honey girl, it seems just like yesterday I was holding you in my arms nursing you," she said, sincerely, trying to reach out to Georgia Ann. "Now look at you taking care of a baby of your own."

Georgia Ann stood up and eased away from her. She walked to the other side of the room and lay the baby in its crib. "What are you doing here, Mama?" she said with a scowl on her face. "Why did you have to come back? It's been fine all these years without you, and now that I've found a family who really loves me, you have to come here and ruin it."

"But, Georgia Ann, I . . . "

"Don't say any more, Mama. I know you came back to take Uncle Charlie away from us, didn't you?"

"Georgia Ann, what's come over you?" She grabbed her daughter's arms firmly. "Do you really believe that's why I took the chance to come up here?"

"Well, that's what it looks like to me," she snapped, jerking her arms free, backing away from Jane. "You're here without your little boys. What did you do, finally get rid of Lawrence to make room for Uncle Charlie? Is that it?"

"No, that's not it!"

"Mama, you don't understand anything, do you? I have a good family now. I found a real mama who I can depend on, a mama with respectable friends who adore me and my family, not a mama whose only friends are murderers and gamblers and a prostitute who stands around a piano singing dirty songs with negra musicians. Martha Ellen takes care of her family. She doesn't stay up all night smoking cigarettes, afraid of who might walk into her house. This is a real family."

"Georgia Ann, if my coming here has upset you this much, please believe me that was not my intention."

"Didn't you see how Gatlin and his sisters were looking at you? They think the same thing I do."

"I don't care how those people were looking at me. I didn't come here to impress anyone, I came as a mother concerned about her children."

"Oh, really?" Georgia Ann said, as she raised an eyebrow skeptically.

"Yes," Jane replied, irritated at her daughter's strange behavior, "and I didn't come here to get your new family's approval of me. If that's the way they are, then I don't care what they think."

"No, I guess you don't, do you? Let's at least be truthful. You didn't come here for me—only Ander. You don't care about anyone but him. You never did. You'd do anything to save your precious son, wouldn't you?"

"Georgia Ann, don't talk to me like this. Seems to me this wonderful family you think so highly of has turned you against your own family. I suppose next you'll be saying you're going to be a witness against your brother."

"I might be," she answered sullenly.

"Georgia Ann, you're just mad at me because you had to leave New Orleans when you shot Lawrence."

"Yes I am, damn it, and it is Ander you came here to see, isn't it? Go ahead and admit it, Mama. He kills someone and you come running. I've lived here ever since I left your house and I only got one telegram from you. So you sent a few clothes once or twice. What's that? I can't put my arms around clothes. They can't tell me they love me."

While Georgia Ann vented her outrage, Jane did not try to defend herself. She had tried many times to make contact with Georgia Ann. It was Georgia Ann who had cut off communication with her. Georgia Ann was acting like a spoiled little girl, and Jane knew that all the years of turmoil in her daughter's life was the cause of the frustrated, confused young woman who stood before her. It hurt Jane to watch her child suffering this way. Once again she tried to embrace Georgia Ann. "Don't say these things, Sugar. Please, I know your life has been a mess. If I had it to do over again, if I thought it would have changed the course of our lives, I'd have never left your papa. I would have stayed with him until you were grown up."

Jane felt her child go limp and watched tears fill her deeply troubled gray eyes, eyes that held the hurt of many years of great sadness. They stood face to face, mother and daughter, and with much effort Georgia Ann said, "Mama, I wouldn't have wanted you to do that. All I've ever wanted from you was your love."

"My love? You've been rich in it. All I've ever tried to do is love my children."

"I wish I could believe you, Mama, but I don't. All you care about is Ander. It never mattered to you what he was or what he did. All my life it's been Ander, Ander, Ander! Well, let me tell you something you might not want to hear! Your precious Ander has gone too far this time. He killed a wonderful girl. What he did to her before that no human should ever have to go through. He and that damned sawmill whore need to hang for what they did to Mary!"

Her instinct was to reach out and slap Georgia Ann, but Jane couldn't. Somewhere in the deepest part of her soul, she knew her daughter spoke the truth. Her little girl stood before her trying to make her realize the wrong that Ander had done. Yet, in spite of herself, Jane could only think about Ander.

Before she turned to leave the room, she asked, "Georgia Ann, would you please come over to Ander's house tomorrow? Maybe we can talk some more then."

Georgia Ann did not answer her mother's plea. She only said, "Mama, I saw how you were looking at Uncle Charlie tonight. Don't try to deny it. I know you want him back, don't you?"

Jane stood frozen for a moment staring at her daughter. She took a deep breath, trying to retain her composure. "Of course I was looking at him. My feelings for him haven't changed. I still love

Charles, but I love him enough to see he has another wife and family and I love him enough to leave him alone."

"We'll see about that, Mama. We'll just see about that, won't we?"

Jane turned swiftly and as she closed the door, she heard Georgia Ann's angry voice in the hall, "So help me God, I'll never speak to you again if you take Uncle Charlie away from us!"

Twenty-Seven

OUT OF A TERRIBLE DREAM in which Jane was running frantically through a field toward Georgia Ann—Ander and her two boys being sucked in an undertow in the river—she was awakened by the clatter of pots and pans. With Nellie and the children asleep in the other bedrooms, she couldn't imagine who could be in the kitchen. Cautiously she got up and crept down the narrow stairs.

"Morning, Jane. Did you get a good night's sleep?" Charles asked. He was making a pot of coffee. Jane stood in the kitchen doorway staring at his handsome face, remembering how he had looked the last morning they spent in their small cottage on her papa's farm. It was an eternity almost, but it seemed like only yesterday and for a moment she thought she could hear the laughter of Georgia Ann and Ander as they frolicked about the house pulling a snow sled to the front yard where a steep slope was used for sledding. "Ohh . . . " she sighed, clutching at her chest, painfully aware of the memory of it. Slowly she walked into the kitchen. "What are you doing here so early?" she asked, leaning against the ice box observing his every move. "I thought someone was breaking in."

"I didn't mean to scare you," he answered, letting his eyes trail over her body. She noticed him take a deep breath before he said, "I remembered you like to get up early and I wanted to surprise you in bed with a cup of hot coffee."

"That's very thoughtful of you, Charles, but I don't think Martha Ellen would appreciate your bringing coffee to my bed."

"No, she probably wouldn't, but she knows I'm here. I told her I had to take you to see John Roberts this morning."

Jane brushed a fallen lock of her hair away from her face and moved over to the kitchen table. "Don't you think it's a little early to go into Pollock Town? I imagine those lawyers don't get into their office 'till around ten o'clock."

He sat the coffeepot down, and flung the dishcloth aside. He walked behind Jane and suddenly put his arms around her squeezing her to him. He was trembling all over as he lay his head against hers, nuzzling into her hair. "Please talk to me about us, Liebchen," he whispered in her ear.

She closed her eyes and for a moment allowed her body to melt against him. He still smelled of shaving soap and she imagined him standing in front of his mirror with his mug and brush in hand. She could almost feel the dampness of the towel touching his skin. She rubbed the back of her head gently across his chest, her whole body tingling as she inhaled his fresh bathed scent. She wanted him to hold her, kiss her, lead her back to bed and love her . . . but she thought about what she was doing. She stood stiff, concerned about the way he was holding her, his hands sliding up her waist to her breast, his breathing raspy. She shook herself loose and pulled away. She turned to face him. "Nooo. . . . " she said. "There is no us, Charles, not any longer. There's you and your wife, and there is me and my life in New Orleans."

He reached out and grabbed for her hands. She pulled back as he began to plead. "Don't do this to me. You know I love you," he said, "and I know you love me, too. Let's not stand here pretending it's not so."

"But love isn't a reason to think we can just do whatever we want, Charles. For us to love would ruin innocent lives. No, please, we can't talk about us," she said, reaching out for the table, grabbing hold of it to steady her legs. But she knew as soon as she pulled away from him it wouldn't work with Charles. He knew her too well, understood her like no one else. She could fight him until doomsday, kick him, bite him, slam doors in his face but her heart was his, and she ached with the need to touch him, to feel him a part of her again. They were alike, the two of them. They'd been two lonely souls from

the very beginning, in search of something. When they'd come together those many years ago they'd become one. She knew trying to
deny her feelings now would be even worse than acting upon them.

He ignored her turmoil as though he hadn't heard a word she'd
said. He caught her in his grip, crushed her to him, kissing her neck,
her throat, her eyes, her lips. Her heart was pounding, the blood
coursing through her veins and her mind screaming for him to stop,
but she couldn't say a word. She fell limp against him. He cried out
in anguish, "I love you. I want you. I need you. Tell me you love me,
Jane. . . . Say it! I'll gladly risk eternity in hell for you."

"There's a part of God in you, Charles, I know there is," she whispered. "I want you, too. I want to love you for the rest of our lives,
but if we do this there'll never be any turning back. Don't you understand that?"

He swept her into his arms and out of the kitchen he walked, carrying her up the narrow stairs into the bedroom, kicking the door
shut with his boot. "Say what you want," he whispered laying her
across the bed. "All I know is I love you. Right or wrong I'm going
to have you. Nobody is going to stop me. I've waited a long time for
this moment . . . begged and pleaded to God for it. I didn't give you
away. They took you away from me. Nothing is going to keep us
apart, Liebchen, not now, not ever again."

Pulling him down on her, she wrapped her arms around his neck.
All the memories of the years they had been apart faded into obliv-
ion as she trembled against the man she loved so desperately, clinging to him, calling out his name, over and over. She knew this was
right, regardless of how wrong it was. All the things that Georgia
Ann said to her were true. She did love Charles. She loved him with
all her heart. She'd never stopped.

"Something has to be done," he said in a serious tone, wrapping
his arms around her, cuddling her tiny body next to his, and looked
down into her eyes. Charles' face was drawn and there were dark,
unhealthy circles under his eyes. Jane could tell he hadn't slept much
the night before. He was shaking so much that his head wobbled.
"I didn't come here this morning with the intention of just having
you," he said as if he had to reassure her. "I came because I love you.
I'm a weak man when it comes to you. Always have been. I don't

want to go back home to Martha Ellen, not now that you've come back."

"I don't know . . . I don't know what to say, Charles," she stammered, and she wondered if this was really her saying these words to him. How could she not know what to say? Here he was confessing his undying love to her—willing to give up everything just to be with her again, and all she could do was babble about virtue. She thought for a moment and then she said, "But what will you do with her?"

"I intend to ask her to let me go. Legally we're not married anyway. I'm still married to you. I was only granted a divorce because I thought you were dead."

"Charles," she exclaimed, struggling to sit up. "You can't do that to Martha. For God's sake she just buried her child."

"Jane, prolonging the inevitable will not make this any easier for Martha. I thought about it all night. I've thought about it since I received that telegram saying you were on your way here. You can send me away if you want," he said, "but I won't stay away."

"Charles, I can't think right now. My mind is confused, and what about Martha Ellen? I can't get her out of my thoughts. I know how much she trusts you, trusts in your love. I'm sorry, but I just keep thinking. . . . "

"Jane, I know what you're thinking," he interrupted, placing his fingers over her mouth. "Of course I care for her, who wouldn't? She's probably one of the best, kindest, most caring women in the world, but I am not in love with her. If I'd have thought for one moment you were still alive, I would have never married her and she knows it. She knows you're the only woman I have ever loved completely. I've loved you from the first moment I saw you standing on that porch. You love me, too. I know you do." He threw his arms around her, pulling her back down beside him. "Come home to me, Jane. Come back to north Louisiana where we can be happy like we used to be. We don't need this farm. I'll give it to Martha and her children. We can go someplace else, someplace where we can start over again. Just you and I."

"No, Charles, it's not just you and I. I have small children, twins, two six year old boys."

"I know about your two little boys. When I say me and you, I mean anyone who comes with you," he said, and a broad grin spread across his face. "Where are they? Why didn't you bring them?"

"Oh, Charles," she said, "Lawrence stole my babies from me a few days ago because I told him I wasn't going to give him any more of my money."

"Why are you giving him money?"

"You don't understand. I've had to pay Lawrence every since the twins were born so he wouldn't turn me in to the law."

"Jane, why didn't you try to contact me as soon as Ander told you I was alive?"

"I was carrying the twins when I found out, another man's babies. How do you think I felt? And on top of that, you were already married and I didn't know if you loved her or not. I didn't know if you even thought about me anymore."

"Thought about you? I was married to Martha when I came to New Orleans looking for you. As soon as I found out Georgia Ann went down there, I knew you had somehow managed to live. I didn't realize how, until Lawrence made it clear to me how he felt about you. He made it clear no man would step in his shoes, and he suggested you felt the same about him."

"What difference would it have made anyway? You were still married to her and at the time I thought I was married to Lawrence."

"Maybe I could have done something about it then. You know I would not have cared about the baby. For the love of God, don't you know me at all?"

Jane knew Charles spoke the truth. She should have contacted him. But would it have made any difference? Once she met Martha Ellen she would feel the same as she did now. And she knew she couldn't be responsible for tearing apart this poor woman's world. *God, how Martha must love Charles if she married him knowing he loved another woman,* she thought. But then again, here they were, two people in love and had been since the first day they saw each other, all those years ago. It did seem foolish, as Charles said, for them to torture themselves at this stage in their lives. He didn't love Martha Ellen. *But the poor woman? How can I do this to her? How can I lie in your arms, Charles, when she must be at home this very moment thinking about it. In the midst of her terrifying grief for her murdered child, she has to worry about me—worry if I have the decency to stay out of your arms; to say no to you, to say to you the words she's praying I will say. No, I can't come between you and Martha Ellen. I just can't do it. I love you, but I just will not do it.* She sat up in the bed, pulling the quilt up to her chin, ashamed of her nakedness, ashamed she had given in to her desires. *Now I'm not any better than Lawrence,* she thought. *What a mess I've made of all our lives.* She made up her mind right then to set Charles straight.

"Charles," she said, "as wonderful as it is being with you . . . loving you . . . things have changed. There is nothing we can do about us now. Don't speak, please," she said, resisting his protest. "We've been leading different lives. We'd be living a fantasy if we thought that in one day things could be the way they were fourteen years ago."

"Jane, don't do this to us again," he pleaded. "You gave me up once for Ander. Don't do it for Martha. Remember what I told you when we first met, that there comes a time in everyone's life when they have to say to themselves, enough is enough. Sometimes we have to think about ourselves. Please don't make this decision without thinking about it. Think about all the years we lost because of your decision in that courtroom. Think about us this time. Please give us another chance."

Jane sat up and swung her legs over the smooth patchwork quilt, and let her feet dangle above the shiny hardwood floor. She felt around the bed covers and grabbed her white cotton nightgown, quickly pulling it down over her head. She did not want to think about Charles right now. She couldn't. She didn't know what the future held for her. She had no idea what her destiny would be. The only thing she could think of was getting to Ander, trying to find a way to get him out of trouble, and then get back to New Orleans and locate her children.

"I can't come back to you, Charles," she firmly said, standing up and slipping her feet into her warm slippers. "I love you, but I just can't come back. There are too many bridges left for me to cross. . . . I have my other children and besides, you're asking too much of me.

I don't want to come back and live in northern Louisiana. Why would I? It was living up here that took my life away from me in the first place. These so-called good Christians you speak of—remember the courtroom was full of them the day I was dragged in front of that judge. I wouldn't come back up here to live even if you and I were to be together again. I left north Louisiana chained to my young son and a Negro man and no one lifted a finger to stop it. If you think for one minute I'd come back, you're mistaken. Not the first one that I know cared if I rotted in Angola. I had to give myself to a man I detested, even risked being killed by his parents, to get out of there. I did what I had to do. No one from here could ever understand and certainly nobody from up here cared for my life. I could never live among these people again."

Charles sat up. He propped his back against the headboard. He stared intently at her as she wrapped her hair around the back of her head and stuck pin after pin into the thick bun to hold it in place. "Don't say that," he said. "I cared for your life. I did from the day I first saw you. I do now. I had no control over you going to prison and you're right, I can't imagine all you've been through. I've never been shackled and put in a God-forsaken prison that must have been worse than Hell. I love you for being strong enough to get your freedom, no matter what you had to do. But don't say that I didn't care!"

She was unable to speak and she breathed deeply to try to stop her teeth from chattering. Before she got too emotional, she decided to leave the room. She would go and relax for a while in a hot tub of water and then she could think more clearly. But, after an hour of soaking, the water failed to calm her nerves. She was still shaking when she went into the kitchen, and the thought of Charles begging her to return his love stayed with her, confusing her even more.

When Charles came out of the bedroom, Jane heard Nellie and the two boys playing outside by the old chinaberry tree in the front yard. Charles went straight to the kitchen counter and began breakfast as easily and naturally as he plowed the fields or laid track for the railroad. He poured the flour and buttermilk into the wooden bowl to make biscuits. She glanced up and down, looking anywhere except in his direction, trying to avoid any eye contact with him, and tears came to her eyes as she thought about him and Martha Ellen. Her heart was aching and without any warning she felt a sob rising, and before she could stop it, the sob forced its way out of her, and she thought she would die knowing he would never be hers again.

AS THEY silently ate breakfast with the children, she could not look Charles in the face, and when breakfast was finished, Jane hurried the children into their day clothes. "Charles, we need to hurry," she said, keeping her distance from him. "You go ahead and freshen up and I'll tell Nellie to hitch up the buggy for us. We need to catch the *Iron Mountain* by nine o'clock if we intend to see the lawyer about Ander."

"You're right, Liebchen. We'd better get going," he said, walking over to where she stood looking out the window, "but will you at least think about what we've talked about. Think about us?"

Jane turned around and stared at him, wanting so much to reach out and clasp his hand. She turned back to the window. She never answered his question.

Twenty-Eight

THE TRAIN RIDE into Pollock Town was so slow Jane thought they would never get there. Sitting next to Charles with things the way they were between them caused her tremendous stress, and the thought of seeing Ander again after so many years weighed heavily on her mind. She broke the silence when she asked, "You think he'll be glad to see me?"

"I think he'll be glad to see anyone besides the sheriff and his jailer," Charles answered. The tension was obvious between them and Charles shifted around in his seat, moving from one hip to the other until Jane thought she might scream.

"I'm the only one he's talked to besides the district attorney and Judge Blackman, and that's when they were interrogating him," Charles added.

"Why do you really think they arrested Ander?"

"For shooting his mouth off too much. They don't have any real evidence against him. All they're going by is what the neighbors and folks around here have told them about Ander, and none of it's any good."

Jane could see it was no use trying to talk to Charles right now. She sat silently until the train passed the Balls Sawmill and pulled into the train station. They got out at the busy Pollock Town depot and walked on the wooden sidewalk the short distance to J.B. Roberts' law office. Workmen were clearing away debris from the burned buildings and the smell of stale smoke still lingered in the air. It looked to her like half of what had been a bustling little sawmill town had been burned up. When they reached Roberts' office, two men were putting the final touches of paint on a new door and the window frames. From the smell of fresh cut pine, Jane could tell he hadn't been in this building very long. She assumed he had been burned out too. She wondered if the building across the muddy street was the Post Office that Ander supposedly had robbed.

Above her was a large photo hanging on the wall of the town prior to the fire. She thought about the mail bag and said to herself, *If he did rob the Post Office, how in the world did he get out of the fire so fast? From the looks of things outside it must have been a raging inferno that couldn't have taken very long to sweep through ten small wooden buildings.* She realized it had taken more than one person to set the buildings on fire. The Post Office was in the middle of the line of buildings and it wasn't even scorched. This had to be a carefully planned act of arson.

Sitting inside the little office, Jane and Charles waited for the lawyer. She felt guilty because she hadn't given Charles an answer before they left the house, and she looked up into his sad eyes knowing she'd have to do so sooner or later. She reached over and laid her hand upon his. "Charles, if you'll just help me through all of this, help me and this lawyer find a way to get Ander out of this mess he's in, I promise I will think about everything you've said. Right now I can't think about anything else. Ander comes first."

Charles' face darkened to a deep red. He tossed her hand aside and said, "He always has, hasn't he?"

Roberts came into the room at that moment, apparently oblivious to the tension. The thirty-nine year old attorney and his younger brother who shared the practice had the reputation of being the best criminal lawyers in Grant Parish. J.B. was highly respected in the community, a member of the Police Jury, and known to have never lost a case. He had a tendency to rattle on and on about everything in his stiff legal manner. However, when he walked in, he got straight to the point.

"Ma'am, there is no way out of this. Ander's going to stand trial for murdering his wife," he said, pulling a legal pad out of the top drawer of his desk.

"It doesn't look good, does it, Mr. Roberts?" she asked.

"Well, that's all in how you look at it. You see, there's no compelling evidence against your son—no gun, no fingerprints, nothing except the testimony of the dead woman's hysterical sisters and opinions of the neighbors. Purely circumstantial."

"How can they charge him with murder when there's no evidence?" she asked.

"It's my guess that Ella Peck and Steve LaCroix may have turned state's evidence, bought their way out."

Jane gazed out of the window for a moment, trying to understand Roberts. She didn't say anything, just reached out again for Charles's hand.

"Mr. Roberts," Charles finally spoke, "Ella Peck was involved in the burning of this town, wasn't she? Yet they're not about to let her stand trial. You and I both know that. She's got too much on the men who own these buildings for them to take a chance on her being put under oath and cross examined."

"I don't understand the indictment either, Mr. Roberts," Jane said. "The newspapers said the judge had conducted an investigation and interviewed I don't know how many people. Ella Peck and those brothers of hers were all arrested for Mary's murder. What in God's name happened if what Charles is saying is not the truth?"

"Whether what Mr. Fisher says about the reason for Ella Peck and the others not being charged is true or not, I don't know," Roberts in a calm steady voice said. "Knowing the politics of this parish, a reasonable man would have to assume there is more validity than not in what he says. However, the Grand Jury returned only one true bill, the one against your son. They concluded there was insufficient evidence to hold Ella Peck and the others. There's no use in fighting about it. Politics are politics, and it's going to be your son who stands trial."

"Charles, did you bring that money belt with you?" Jane snapped. Charles unbuttoned his vest and handed it over to her.

"Politics may be politics, Mr. Roberts," she said, throwing the money belt on his desk, "but I bet you can buy a whole lot of justice with this."

"That's a lot of money, Ma'am," he said, opening the pouch and running his finger over the edge of the bills. He took a steel tipped pen out of its holder and wrote a receipt. "Normally I'd advise you to put it in the bank, but I don't think that would be prudent. No use having people gossiping on top of everything else. I'll just keep it in my safe. If I need any money for expenses, I'll take it. When the trial's over, I'll give you a full accounting."

He handed Jane the receipt and opened the large Diebold safe that sat in the corner. He put the belt containing Jane's money into the safe and began rummaging among a pile of papers, finally producing a sealed, white envelope.

"I won't be needing this, Mr. Fisher," he said and handed the envelope to Charles. "Jane has more than sufficient funds to cover expenses and my fee as well."

"What is that, Charles?" she asked, wondering why this attorney would have anything that belonged to Charles.

"It's nothing of any importance, just a little business matter between Mr. Roberts and me."

"But you told me you didn't know this attorney," she said, questioning Charles with her eyes.

"It's more than just a little business matter, Ma'am," Roberts interrupted. "Right after they arrested Ander, Mr. Fisher came and asked me to represent your son. When I told him I would require a retainer, as I do in all my criminal cases, he gave me the mortgage on his farm."

Jane's questioning look melted into a warm smile. She shook her head at Charles, "Don't you realize that was a risky thing to do?" she said. "You could have lost everything you have." Then she said to the attorney, "I guess we should be going now, Mr. Roberts. I want to get over to the jail and see Ander." She shook Roberts' hand as Charles opened the door. "I'll tell Ander you'll be coming in to talk with him, that he needs to tell you the truth about everything that happened the night Mary was killed."

"Ma'am, that's the only way I can help him."

"MAMA, I THOUGHT you'd never get here," Ander said, when they arrived. He had been lying on the dirty cot in his cell in the

Colfax jail, playing solitaire with a deck of worn-out cards. When the jailer opened the wooden cell door, the musty smell nearly knocked her over. It smelled like his slop jar hadn't been emptied all day as it sat out in the bare room like a piece of furniture. He stood up, embraced his mother and began to cry. Images of the Columbia jail flooded her mind. She went weak in the knees. She could just see him twisting and grimacing at the end of a hangman's rope.

As she looked into Ander's face she tried to remain calm. This was no time for tears. They had a good chance of winning this case. Here there were no crooked judges and evil family members who wished to see him hang, only a district attorney who was prosecuting him on his wild reputation alone. He just assumed Ander murdered Mary.

"I need to know what happened that night. Now hush your whimpering and tell me about it," she said, brushing a lock of hair from his face.

Ander's upper lip began to quiver. Tears rolled down his cheeks as he told his mother his account of the murder. "Mama, the best I can remember, me and Mary had gone to bed that night and we were all sleeping when I heard a noise. I thought lightning struck a tree and when I got up and lit the lantern, I saw Mary'd been shot. Blood was everywhere, even on the children. I got scared as hell and took off running all the way to Charles' house. I woke them up and Charles and Gatlin took off on their horses back to my house. Then me and Georgia Ann hitched up a wagon and went back as fast as we could. And when we got there. . . . Oh Mama, the worst thing you can imagine happened while I was gone. Somebody came in the house and stuck a knife in Mary's throat. They tried to cut her head off."

Charles had to reach over to keep Jane from swaying when Ander told her what happened. Ander's body was shaking with each sob. "My wife is dead. My babies will never see their mama again. If it wasn't for my babies, I swear I'd kill myself. I loved Mary. I can't live without her."

"Ander, look at Mama," Jane finally said, firmly, staring into his eyes. "Did you kill Mary?"

"No, Mama, I didn't and I don't have any idea who did. I loved her just like everybody else. She was a sweet, God-fearing Christian girl who never said a bad word about anybody."

"Don't talk about it right now, Baby," she said, taking him into her arms. *He's distraught,* she thought. *I knew he couldn't do anything like that.*

"Mama, will you tell Dick I'm so sorry? Bring him to see me when you come back, will you?"

"He'd love to see his papa, I'm sure," Jane said, when the sheriff came to the cell and she got up to leave.

ALL THE WAY HOME from the jail, Jane sat in the train seat quietly beside Charles, wondering how much Dick remembered about his mother's murder. Looking out the window as the open fields rolled by, one after the other, she couldn't help but think how strange it was that Ander had asked only about Dick and not his other children. Even stranger, that he wanted her to bring the six year old boy to the jail. *Whatever happened that night,* she thought, *Dick played a part in it, and I intend to find out what it is.*

Later that night after the other children were asleep in the room with Nellie, Jane went in to talk to Dick. She woke him up and they sat in front of the fire talking and eating the sweet rolls that Charles had picked up for them in Pollock Town. Dick wasn't opening up and Jane didn't want to frighten the boy, but when she told him what his papa had said, he began to whimper and seemed unusually frightened. His hands began to shake. Jane took the roll, lay it on the table, and pulled him into her lap.

"Dick," she whispered, "will you tell Granny what happened the night your mama was killed?"

The child fidgeted from one side of the chair to the other and big tears rolled down his cheeks. Jane pulled her handkerchief from the cuff of her sleeve and wiped his face.

"If you don't want to talk about it, we don't have to," she said, changing her mind. "I just thought if I knew more about what happened, I could help the lawyer get your papa out of jail."

Dick snuggled his head against her chest for a moment sobbing as though his little heart was broken. Then he slowly sat up and looked at her. "We . . . we was laying in the bed, Denny and me, with mama that night. I . . . I . . . remember the rain when we went to bed and I. . . . "

"You said you were in bed with your mama. Where was your papa?"

"He . . . he . . . he wasn't home when we went to bed. He came in when Mama was feeding the baby." His voice was quivering and he began to wiggle around.

"Were you asleep when your mama died?"

"No. I was sitting up beside her."

"And your papa? Where was he?"

"Up there," he said, pointing to the stairs and tugging on her hand he pulled her up the steps into the bedroom. "That chair by the window, and Mama was here." He walked over to the side of the bed, patted his hand where Mary had been sitting up nursing her baby that night.

"Somebody shot at papa's head and killed my mama. See that hole in the window?" He pointed at the broken pane right above a cane-backed chair between the window and the bed. "Papa ran out then. Left us here."

"What did you do when your papa left?"

"I was scared . . . I pulled Denny down on the floor and pushed him under the bed."

"Where was baby Mary?"

"She was bloody and Mama was still holding her. And . . . and . . . I tried to pick her up but she kept slipping out my hands and . . . and . . . I was gitting under the bed and I heard somebody on the stairs. I thought Papa come back home and I ran to the door and I saw that old woman Ella Peck and a man in a black hat coming after me." He pointed to the window side of the bed, and kept talking. "That old woman had a knife in her hand. She went over there and stuck it in Mama's throat. She kept sticking it—sticking it—sticking it—then she saw me and raised it at me . . . and . . . the man took his hat off and . . . and . . . told her to leave the kid alone and . . . they put a lantern on the floor and she said to blow it up and blow us all to hell . . . even Papa . . . and then they left."

Jane couldn't believe it. *Ella Peck! Damn it! Ander lied to me!*, she thought, cuddling the crying child, holding him close to her heart.

Jane tossed and turned the entire night. She couldn't go to sleep—she lay smoking one cigarette after the other, getting up, time and time again to check on Nellie and the children. She was lying on the settee downstairs when she heard the rooster crowing. She watched through the window by the chimney as the sun came up. She heard the heavy crunch of a man's work boots. It frightened her. All kinds of things ran through her mind. *It could be the murderers,* she thought. The front door swung open.

"Charles," she screamed when he walked in carrying a bucket of fresh milk. "You nearly scared me to death. Why didn't you tell me you were coming over here this early in the morning?"

"Calm down, will you?" he said. Dick came flying down the stairs in a fright.

"Why didn't you tell me what happened here that night?" she asked.

He went into the kitchen and set the bucket of milk on the table then walked back into the parlor and wrapped his arms around her, trying to calm her down. She was near hysterics.

He took one look at Dick, then back at her. "Jane, if I'd told you what that child said he saw here that night, you'd have held it against me. Called me a liar, and you know it. I wanted it to be someone else who told you."

"Who? The district attorney? Were you going to wait until we all went to court and then say something? What were you afraid of? Maybe that I'd get up and tell the court I killed her. Is that it?"

"Shh," he whispered cradling her like a baby. Then he sat her on the settee and gently pushed her down, stuffed a pillow under her head, and covered her with the knitted quilt. "I want you to lie here quietly while I make you some coffee. The baby's awake. I need to take care of her," he said.

She watched Charles unpack a little basket he brought in from the front porch. There was part of a loaf of bread, fruit, some eggs and, he said, some stewed chicken. He built a fire and soon had the kettle singing. She watched as he fixed the baby a sugar tit. He handed it to Dick and told him to scoot on up the stairs with it for Nellie who was at the top holding the screaming baby.

Jane could smell the coffee. She began to relax. Her stomach wasn't shaking as hard as it was when he walked in. He brought two cups and set them on a table in front of the settee, then pulled her up, tucking the quilt around her body and put the cup in her hand. She took a sip out of the steaming mug. "Georgia Ann was right? He did kill her, didn't he?" she asked.

"I don't know, Jane. The child is the only one who could really tell us. I don't know if he can even remember everything that happened. He was hysterical when I got here that night and by the time I found out what he'd said, it had already passed through several mouths. What a terrible mess that night was," he said, setting his mug on the table, running his fingers through his hair. "A terrible, terrible night. A big storm had come through earlier in the evening and all the roads were washed out. Ander came running up to the yard in his undershorts about midnight, hollering that somebody had shot Mary. I got up out of the bed and woke up Gatlin. We rode our horses right on over here. Georgia Ann and Leah hitched up the wagon and brought Ander back home. There was mud everywhere and when they came into the house, Gatlin hollered for me to keep the women out of the bedroom. Leah took off up those stairs and when she saw the hole in Mary's throat, she started screaming and none of us could make her stop. She flew down the stairs and out the front door to get to Ander. It took me and Georgia Ann both, to pull her off. I couldn't reason with any of them, Jane, and by the time I finally did get everybody calmed down, the sheriff came in. I went on home to see about Martha Ellen. I didn't see the boy until the next day. That was when the sheriff and the district attorney came to my house to question him."

"Oh, Charles, what are we going to do?"

"We're not going to do anything. We've already done what we can. We got Ander a good lawyer and the rest is up to him and the court. If he can persuade the jury to believe him, there won't be any prison or lynchings. There's no evidence. They didn't even do a proper autopsy. All they know is she's dead."

"Then, what Dick told me, he obviously told the sheriff."

"Yes, he's told that story so many times the child probably doesn't know who shot whom. He's confused, Liebchen."

"But he said his papa was in the room when they shot Mary, and Ander had run out the house before they cut her throat. I wonder why Ander told me. . . . "

"Jane, if I had to take a guess," he said, interrupting her, "Ander knows who shot Mary. He robbed that post office as sure as I'm sitting here, and with whom I don't know. But I think Ander told those folks Mary was going to turn him in, and that's why they killed her."

"Well, Charles, at least he didn't pull the trigger."

"No, he didn't," Charles said, picking up their cups. He went into the kitchen, poured the milk into a glass jar and put it into the icebox. "Now let's get these children fed," he said. "Today is going to be another long day and I need to get out into the fields before I go over to the mill."

As tired as she was from lack of sleep, Jane, and Nellie, got the children dressed and sent them out to play. All day she spent cleaning and cooking until she was exhausted. She couldn't get the events of Mary's murder out of her mind. Every time she sat down to rest she kept thinking of Ander. She asked herself over and over throughout the days and nights that followed, *Did I bear an evil child because I am evil? Was I not a good enough woman to be the kind of mother that could have raised Ander differently? Is it my fault he does the things he does?*

Twenty-Nine

THE FIRST TWO DAYS of the trial were grueling. They had taken a toll on Jane. The state had called witness after witness and, it seemed to her, the state had a strong case. But in spite of all the witnesses, including Mary's two sisters, Roberts had said for Jane not to worry about it. Then it had rained all day Saturday soaking the streets to a muddy mess and Jane thanked God it had dried out by the time she walked into the courtroom Monday morning, the third day of the trial.

The Colfax Courthouse bore no resemblance to the Caldwell Parish Courthouse, but just being inside this stuffy old room made her ill. Even with the new fans hanging from the ceiling, stirring the humid air, she still felt as if she were suffocating. She followed Charles as he led her into the first row behind the defense table. The rest of the family weren't speaking to them. They sat on the other side of the aisle, except for Martha Ellen. She hadn't shown up for the trial at all.

Jane could see Ander sitting beside J.B. Roberts, wiggling around in his chair. Memories of the last trial flashed in her mind. *Good God in heaven,* she thought. *I hope Ander's not stupid enough to plead guilty again. Surely he learned his lesson from the first one.*

Roberts' brother had been excused from the case to sit in on another trial for Judge Blackman and this worried Jane, but when Roberts walked back to where she and Charles sat, he didn't seem to be worried about it. He told them he was ready to open his case for the defense.

"No sense in dragging this out, Ma'am," he said. "We might as well have Dick tell his account of the murder and get it over with. This may be the only break we get."

Although she had been prepared for this, Jane still had a hard time accepting the fact her small grandson had to testify. "He's even younger than Ander that first time in court," she said to Charles. "This could ruin his life."

Jane's eyes skimmed the courtroom. Sitting across the aisle, bouncing a young boy on her knee, sat Ella Peck, a smug expression on her face. The boy, who resembled Dick and Denny, was obviously Ander's son. "Put him with Dick and Denny and you'd have three little Moody peas in a pod," she whispered to Charles.

To Ella's left were two smug-looking men whom Jane assumed were Ella's brothers.

The bailiff called the court to order. Everyone stood up as the judge walked into the chamber from a door behind the jury box, sat down and rapped the gavel.

J.B. Roberts stood behind Ander. "Your Honor," he said, as he approached the bench. "This is a case that has caused much controversy and I ask your indulgence, as well as the indulgence of my friend and colleague, Mr. Hunter, the District Attorney. As both of you gentlemen know, there were no witnesses to this horrible crime except the defendant and his young child, Dick Moody. Since they are the only two people who really know what occurred that night, I ask the court to suspend precedent and allow me to call Dick Moody to the stand."

Immediately, the district attorney, John Hunter, a rather short stocky man who looked to be in his early thirties, jumped to his feet. "I object, Your Honor. May I remind the court that this child is only six years old. I suggest the request of the defense is not only out of order, but illegal. The court cannot allow it."

Jane held her breath while she waited for the judge to make a decision.

"Overruled," he said. "In the interest of all that is fair, Mr. Roberts, I will allow you to call the child. But I would remind you that in doing so, Mr. Hunter has not given up his right to cross examine."

John Roberts turned away from the jury of local merchants and farmers. He walked down the aisle of the courtroom until he stood beside Dick Moody. He led the frightened child back to the front of the jury. The child was sworn in. He was asked if he knew the difference between right and wrong. When Dick nodded and said that he did, Roberts said to the jury, "Ander Moody cannot tell you who shot and killed his wife because he did not see the perpetrator, but this little boy did." Turning to Dick he asked, "Who was it? Is the one you saw kill your mama in this courtroom?"

The child nodded and nervously whispered, "Yes."

"I want you to show this court who it was you saw in the bedroom that night. I want you to go and put your hands on the person who stuck the knife in your mama."

Dick slowly tugged on Roberts' hand pulling him down the narrow aisle of the high ceiling room when the district attorney began to shout, "Objection, Your Honor. This is improper procedure."

Jane jumped in her seat. The loud tone in Hunter's voice was frightening. She knew he was the one who had investigated Mary's murder and interrogated Dick for weeks after that terrible night. He looked to her as if he were about to pounce upon the small boy. She felt like charging up to the district attorney and slapping Hunter across his face for deliberately trying to scare Dick.

Judge Blackman half rose from his chair, pounding the bench with his gavel. "You will stop this right now, counselor," he said as the jurors leaned forward to see what the little boy planned to do. "You're out of order—I can hold you in contempt of court."

Roberts didn't look at Judge Blackman. He followed Dick down the aisle. Other than the sound of the child's hard-soled shoes against the oiled and worn planks in the floor, dead silence ruled the courtroom.

Placing his hand on the arm of Ella Peck as she tried without success to get out of his reach, Dick said, "That's her. She's the one who killed my mama."

What began as a trickle of whispers turned into a roaring flood of shouts when Ella Peck stood up. She pushed her son down in her seat. "That's a lie and you know it!" she yelled. "Somebody put him up to saying that." The room fell silent.

Pushing Dick aside, she rushed up the aisle toward Judge Blackman. "Can Roberts do this to me, judge? You had me arrested one time and you let me go. There's not one shred of evidence to connect me and my brothers to this crime and you know it!"

Before anyone could speak, Judge Blackman banged his gavel and sent the jury out of the courtroom. He immediately ordered Ella and her brothers to leave the courthouse, then he cleared the room of all spectators. Jane and Charles went over and asked Georgia Ann and Gatlin if they would like to walk across the street to Aunt Mat's Dining Room and get a bite to eat, but they declined. They fled with other spectators from the building to get to the stone benches that were spread out under the branches of oaks in the courthouse square. Jane and Charles waited outside the front door of the red brick building. Charles leaned against the big white door frame while Jane paced around in circles. It was almost noon before Roberts came out and told them the closing arguments had concluded and the judge had charged the jury and sent them off to reach a verdict.

Jane and Charles walked across the street to Aunt Mat's Boarding House, sat in the dining room and ordered lunch. Jane just picked at her food, wondering how it would all come out—wondering if it was right to have had Roberts let little Dick testify. She stared into her plate, pushing the steamed carrots away from her porkchop. *Was it the right thing to do? Or was I just thinking of what's best for Ander as always? Could he really be guilty this time?* she dared to think.

Less than an hour later a reporter with the *Colfax Chronicle* burst into the dining room. He hurried up to the table where Jane and Charles sat. He said the jury had announced their verdict to a closed court. They found Ander not guilty by reason of insufficient evidence.

Jane stared unbelievingly at Charles. She breathed a sigh of relief. She gulped her coffee while Charles paid Aunt Mat for their food. Then they hurried back toward the courthouse square just as Ander and Roberts came rushing out. She could see Georgia Ann and Gatlin sitting with little Dick on a stone bench under a large cottonwood tree and before Jane and Charles could cross the street a horseless carriage came to a screeching halt, nearly running over a buggy with a woman in it. Jane looked up at the woman. It was Ella Peck. Ella began waving frantically at Ander and did not notice Jane and Charles as they passed.

Terror struck Jane's heart. Nobody seemed to notice what was going on, not even Roberts who walked up to her and handed her the money belt wrapped in a brown paper package. What was Ella Peck doing? Was she here to pick up Ander as though this had all been planned? Jane looked from Ella to Ander and from the hand signals they passed to each other, and the kisses Ella was throwing into the air, in her heart, Jane knew. She finally realized what was going on. She felt sure that Ella had killed Mary with his approval. She walked toward her son in dead silence.

"Mama," Ander cried, as she approached him.

Her body trembled as Charles held her steady, but Jane stood stiff as a board looking at her son who began to cry like a broken man. The look on her face must have told him of her suspicions. Standing silently, face to face with Ander while a group of spectators passed by, covering their mouths and whispering, she finally said. "Ander, what have you done?"

Ander was speechless as he stared into her face. Jane clutched his hands wanting him to say something, anything that would put her heart at ease. And when he said nothing, she flung his hands aside despairingly, and said, "I'm glad I don't have to watch you hang. You're my son and I have loved you with all my heart, the kind of love I don't think you really ever understood. If they'd found you guilty and sentenced you to die, I believe I would have killed myself before I had to watch it happen."

"Oh, Mama, I'm so sorry," he sobbed, as he tried to embrace her.

"Sorry for what, Son?" she said. She pulled away from him and pushed his hands off her arms. "All these years, Ander, I've done nothing but clean up your messes. Even up to the day I went to see you in jail I believed you when you told me you loved Mary and didn't have anything to do with her murder. I believed you because I wanted to, just like I believed you all those times when you did things to hurt people, things that a mother can't believe her child is capable of doing.

"You may not have been the one that pulled the trigger, Son, but you killed Mary as sure as I'm standing here, and you know I know it. You're nothing but a cheat and a barefaced liar with no truth in you, and you always have been." Before he could get in a word she added, "I don't want to be involved in any mess like this again. I'm tired of always having to get you out of trouble. I'm going back to New Orleans today, and if I never have to hear another lie come out of your mouth it won't hurt me."

She turned and walked away from him.

"But, Mama, wait," he called out, and she could hear his footsteps on the wooden planks running after her. "What's going to happen to me?"

Jane turned around and looked at her son one last time. "I'm through with you," she snapped. "I'm not going to let you torture me any more."

She lowered her eyes and turned away once again. She was emotionally drained, but found the strength to walk with Charles across the street where they rented a livery buggy to take them the twelve or so blocks to the Colfax depot.

AFTER THEY HAD ARRIVED back at Ander's house in Simms, Jane tried with all her might to push her emotions aside. She hurried upstairs telling Nellie to pack her bag. She stuffed her own clothes into her valise as tightly and as quickly as she could. Then she looked down on the neatly made bed where she and Charles had spent that wonderful morning together those many weeks ago. She wondered if her life would ever be the same again. But thinking about that would not do her any good and she knew it. She had to continue her life. Charles had told her how to contact the Pinkerton Agency to help locate her twins. She had already decided to close the house, take what money she had left, and move some place where no one knew her, some place so far away that none of this grief could ever touch her again.

Picking up the small cloth case, she walked down the stairs and out of the little house without looking back. Nellie was sitting up in the buggy waiting for her, eager to leave. Earlier Jane had asked Charles to take her to the Springhill cemetery before she caught the train so she could put roses on Mary's grave. He was doing something in the back of the buggy when she approached the barn. When he lifted her up inside, she noticed his humpback trunk and his valise resting snugly behind the seat.

"I don't know what you think you're doing, Charles," she said, as he climbed up beside her. "I don't intend to be a party to this," she protested.

"I'm going with you," he said, shaking the reins to prod the horse forward.

"I never asked you to come. I've never given you the impression you could just walk out on Martha Ellen and come with me. I told you I'd think about it."

"You don't have to think about it anymore. I told Martha before I left for the courthouse this morning that I was leaving, that I was in love with you and that I was going to get the marriage annulled and remarry you."

Jane was too tired to think straight, let alone resist any more. She loved Charles and in one way it made her feel good that he was finally taking control of their destiny.

They rode silently down the single track dirt road, and Jane stared out at the dark green of the pine trees framed against the skeletal branches of cottonwood and other hardwood trees. The scent of pine and this rut filled road reminded her so much of the dark days when she had lived among her people, she wanted to cry. People hadn't changed very much in northern Louisiana. Their days were still dark. Their ways were not her ways. She could never come back to this desolation.

She was so choked up she couldn't talk. She wanted to ask Charles what he thought would happen to Ander. Then she decided against it. She knew how he felt about her son and the things Ander had done, but she also knew how much he loved her, and she knew he would not want to say anything to hurt her. Besides, it wasn't Charles's nature to criticize. Then she thought about Ander's children: *I wonder what will happen to them? And Georgia Ann—will I ever see her again?*

When they reached the top of a small hill overlooking the cemetery, Jane saw a buggy sitting on the side of the road and a woman, dressed in black, kneeling over a grave.

"Don't go, Jane," Charles said. "That's Martha Ellen. There's nothing to be gained by you going down there."

Without answering him, Jane climbed out of the buggy and walked down the hill toward the cemetery nestled in a grove of thick pine trees. The graves, most of them family plots, looked well cared for—some bore Mason jars filled with colorful flowers on the tombstones. The tall pines stood deathly still, and Jane was apprehensive as she cautiously approached Martha Ellen.

"Martha," she said, kneeling beside Martha who sat on the ground, crying and caressing the red clay that covered her daughter's coffin. "I hope you don't mind me coming here. I wanted to pay my respects before I left."

Slowly Martha turned her head to Jane and looked up, staring into her face. At first she didn't say anything but then, lowering her eyes, she said, "Somehow I knew you'd come. Somehow I just knew you had to."

Jane lit a cigarette while Martha Ellen stared at Mary's grave. "It's awfully hard, I know," Jane said. "My little girl died when she was six months old and I thought it would kill me. I can't even begin to imagine what it's like to bury a grown child."

"Yes, it's hard. The worse thing that's ever happened to me." Then she said. "I guess it was hard for you too, sitting in that courtroom, hearing strangers say terrible things against your son, wasn't it?" She hesitated a moment, "They let him go, didn't they?"

Jane nodded and crushed out her cigarette.

"I expected they would," Martha said, coldly. "There was a lot of hot talk, even from my own gals, but never any evidence that Ander was more than an unfaithful husband. And we both know that unfaithful husbands don't go to jail, don't we, Jane?"

Jane didn't answer, but she couldn't help but notice the accusatory tone in Martha's voice when she said, "I know your son has his ways, but I like to think he didn't have anything to do with it, especially for the sake of the children."

Jane could not see any sense in telling Martha what she'd figured out about Mary's murder. No sense in it at all. Martha would have to live with Ander in her life because of the grandchildren, and to tell Martha of her suspicion would only add to Martha's grief. Besides, the tension was so obvious between them, Jane didn't know what to say. But then Martha blurted out, "Jane, this has been so hard for me. In the last month I've had to find a way to cope with Mary's brutal death. I've had to bury my own daughter while I wiped the tears from the eyes of your daughter. You come up here with your money and spread it around and everybody knows it. Now you take my husband away from me."

"But . . . Martha Ellen, you don't understand. . . . I just found out myself Charles is leaving you."

"Jane, I don't believe you. Sure, he admitted you didn't know anything about it, but you don't expect me to believe either one of you, do you? I should have listened to my neighbors. Ever since you came people have been telling me you were everything from the Devil Incarnate to someone who'd take my husband away from me. They remembered when you went to prison for trying to kill that sharecropper on your papa's farm; how you admitted to it in court without any remorse. I just told them I didn't want to hear any of their foolish talk. But now I'm sorry. I should have listened to them!"

Jane didn't say anything, just lowered her head as tears dripped down her cheeks. She let Martha say what she needed to.

"All my lady friends thought I was a fool for marrying him, knowing how he felt about you, and I can see why he'd want you over me, anyone would, but I also know you're not good enough for him. You're not even a good mother. You gave up your own daughter for that man you were living with in New Orleans."

Jane's mouth flew open to defend herself but Martha would not be stopped.

"I never thought you'd come back; it never occurred to me that even someone as low as you could do such a wicked thing. Now the children and I will be paupers, thanks to you."

Jane's fingers were crushed tightly across her mouth as she stared in disbelief at what Martha was saying. She couldn't believe such terrible words were coming from her and without a word, she backed away from Martha and ran all the way back up the hill. She could feel Martha's eyes glaring at her as she reached the buggy. Martha's words kept echoing in her mind as Charles lifted her up on the seat beside him.

Unable to say anything, she sat, silent, as Charles maneuvered the buggy down the dusty road into Simms. Chills went through her body and in her mind's eye all she could see was Martha leaning over the grave, crying for her dead child, crying because Jane was taking her life away from her, too. *I shouldn't have gone,* she thought, agonizing over the scene in the graveyard. *Charles was right, I should have listened to him. I never should have gone to that grave. Oh God if I could just go back to the day I was arrested, I'd never have taken the blame. What good did it do me? Not one of them cared about me, not even Ander. I should have let him go to prison for killing Papa. If I had, maybe Mary Parthenia would never have met him, maybe she'd be alive today. Charles and I never would have been separated, so he'd never have married Martha Ellen, and the babies I had would have been Charles'. Oh God, if only I had it to do over again, I would do it so differently.*

Her thoughts were interrupted as she saw the depot from a distance. It was a cool day. The air was dry and stung her face. The isolated town of Simms was so quiet it seemed to Jane not even sawdust was stirring as they passed the sawmill, approaching Nugent's Station.

Charles pulled off the road. He stopped under a towering Sycamore whose limbs were bare. An old black man, obviously stooped from years of pulling cottonsacks on his back, waddled up to them. Charles unloaded his trunk onto the loading dock along with the carry-on valises. He paid the Negro man to return the horse and buggy to the livery.

As she stood quietly waiting to get on board the train, the station master came out of the little wooden depot calling out to her, waving a piece of paper in his hand. "Ma'am, this telegram came in for you this morning. I didn't bring it out to the house. I knew you would be in court today."

Jane thanked him and took the slip of paper. It was from the Countess. She read that Lawrence had abandoned her children to the Sisters of Charity. He had told the Countess to get word to her that he would be back in a few months at the end of the east coast racing season. He was coming for the money she owed him.

Jane sighed a great sigh of relief. Her boys would be waiting for her when she got home. *And Lawrence? He will never give up.* She shook her head as she watched Charles struggling to get his trunk aboard the train. *How very different Lawrence and Charles are,* she thought, and she wondered if Martha had stood watching as Charles packed up his belongings to walk out of her life. She knew from her own agony how it felt to be snatched away from someone you loved. As she stood watching him, she realized she could not live with herself if she took Charles away from Martha Ellen. But how was she going to tell him? They'd endured so much just to be together again. They were entitled to some happiness.

She walked over and stopped Charles from putting his trunk in the baggage car. A few passengers who were traveling south brushed past them and stepped up on the train. A small boy stood on the wooden platform clutching a woman's hand, staring up at her. Jane looked into Charles's sad face and the memory of all those years she had had to live without him came back to her, but knew she had to do what was right.

"Charles," she said, "you know you can't come with me." And as much as she hated to say it, her voice was almost a whisper when she finally told him, "Go back home to Martha Ellen. She's your wife. You have to stay with her. You made that decision when you married her."

He reached out for Jane's hand. She drew back.

"Goodbye, Charles."

"Don't do this," he said, shaking his head desperately as she backed away from him. "You destroyed me once, Jane. You took away everything that I ever lived for when you stood in that court-room taking the blame for all those scoundrels. Now you come back to taunt me with it, deny me once again our life together. Kick me in the teeth, torture me with words of hatred, tell me I'm not worthy of your love, but don't try to tell me how virtuous we should be for the sake of decency. Don't say you're destroying us again for what may or may not be right or wrong."

Without saying a word, Jane turned. She pushed Nellie ahead of her, and stepped up on the train. Cold wind came blaring from the other side. She pulled her shawl tightly against her shoulders and turned back to face Charles. The train jerked and she swayed, nearly losing her balance.

"Please, don't do this to us again," he pleaded. "Without you, Liebchen, my life is not worth living."

"Charles, don't say that. I know you. You'll only hate yourself one day if you do this to Martha Ellen."

His eyes widen and his lips parted. He stared at her and looked as if she had struck him in the face. He stepped back as the train began to move away from the platform. He seemed to realize what Jane was saying, realized that he must grow up, fling fairy tales aside, and accept responsibility for his commitment to Martha Ellen. She turned quickly and followed Nellie into the car before she could change her mind. She was throwing away the love of the man she'd longed for, for so many years. In her heart she felt she was doing the right thing, yet her act of sacrifice gave her very little comfort. She could feel her strength draining from her. The conflict within her was an emptiness so familiar it was hard to bear. She knew she would love Charles the rest of her life.

Gaining distance, the train passed into the piney woods near the cemetery. She clutched the back of a seat as the train rounded the bend. Through the window she could see Martha Ellen climbing up into her buggy. She saw her turn to see the train pass, and very slowly Jane sank down into a seat, watching Martha until she was out of sight. *Martha will go home and find her husband,* she thought. *I know this is the best thing. If I'd let him leave that poor grieving woman, a woman he admires and respects, one day he would come to hate himself and, eventually, me. I've got my dreams. I will always have my dreams of Charles.*

Fighting to control her emotions, she settled back against the cold seat and stared out the window unseeingly. The clickety click of the rolling wheels and the sound of the train whistle emphasized her loneliness. The locomotive gained speed carrying her farther and farther away from Charles. She didn't know how she would survive without him, but she knew she would. Just like her mama's roses, she had been burned badly but she would live through it.

Her mind began to grapple with the problem of how to get out of Lawrence's clutches and make a life for herself and the two little boys waiting in New Orleans for her.